THE CRYING CAVE KILLINGS

WES MARKIN

Boldwood

ALSO BY WES MARKIN

DCI Michael Yorke thrillers

One Last Prayer

The Repenting Serpent

The Silence of Severance

Rise of the Rays

Dance with the Reaper

Christmas with the Conduit

Better the Devil

Jake Pettman Thrillers

The Killing Pit

Fire in Bone

Blue Falls

The Rotten Core

Rock and a Hard Place

The Yorkshire Murders

The Viaduct Killings

The Lonely Lake Killings

The Crying Cave Killings

First published in Great Britain in 2023 by Boldwood Books Ltd.

Cover Design by Head Design Ltd

Cover Photography: Shutterstock

A CIP catalogue record for this book is available from the British Library.

Paperback ISBN 978-1-80483-768-9

Large Print ISBN 978-1-80483-769-6

Hardback ISBN 978-1-80483-770-2

Ebook ISBN 978-1-80483-766-5

Kindle ISBN 978-1-80483-767-2

Audio CD ISBN 978-1-80483-775-7

MP3 CD ISBN 978-1-80483-774-0

Digital audio download ISBN 978-1-80483-771-9

Boldwood Books Ltd
23 Bowerdean Street
London SW6 3TN
www.boldwoodbooks.com

To Peter and Janet

PROLOGUE
2003

PC Paul Riddick stared at Knaresborough over the River Nidd, wondering what loss on an unspeakable scale felt like. From behind him came the incessant buzzing of colleagues searching out the truth.

Truth!

A mere consolation prize to those over the river about to experience the unspeakable.

Riddick burned his nostrils with a deep winter's breath and, with his back still to the Petrifying Well at Mother Shipton's Cave, he closed his eyes, exhaling as he revisited his memories.

Eight years old and on his first visit to Mother Shipton's with his father. He'd been wowed by the Petrifying Well. In profile, it looked like a giant's skull and Riddick's eyes had been wide and innocent. There'd also been another boy beside him, a little older maybe, but equally fascinated.

Riddick remembered some of the boy's words as he pointed at the stone objects hanging from the lip of the well.

'Everything is frozen solid. Fixed. Still. Why call it the Petrifying Well when everything looks so peaceful?'

After that day, eight-year-old Paul Riddick had asked to come again.

Begged, in fact.

But his old man didn't possess those same wide, innocent eyes. 'It's not worth the money, son.'

At fourteen, Riddick had been given another chance. A school geography trip with Mr Thomas. Little had changed in the Petrifying Well. Hanging from the lip of the cave, bathing in the mineral-rich dripping water, remained the same array of 'petrified' items: the road bike, the bowler hat, the china teapot and the cricket bat. Frozen solid. Peaceful.

Mr Thomas' voice, laced with excitement, had broken his reverie. 'It doesn't take long for the sulphate and carbonate in the water to give these objects their stone-like appearance.'

Riddick opened his eyes to the present and took another deep burning breath. He was grateful to have memories because he wouldn't be able to come to this wondrous place again. How could he ever unsee what was behind him?

Again, he closed his eyes, and returned to that school trip. To the moment he'd bought the small carbon-encrusted bear from the shop. A bear that had first become lost in his mother's belongings in the loft, and then, following her passing, lost completely.

'Three months, Paul!' enthusiastic Mr Thomas had said on seeing his student's chosen souvenir. 'It took only three months to petrify that bear!'

Riddick had smiled at his teacher. 'He doesn't look petrified, sir. He looks... I don't know... peaceful?'

Opening his eyes, Riddick realised that he'd been distracted for too long. He'd a job to do. He looked at the logbook. Recording the visitors who came and left the crime scene wasn't the most glamorous of jobs, but it was a start. The first step on the path to the truth.

He turned from the River Nidd.

Graham Lock, fifteen years old, sat on the ground beneath the Petrifying Well, dead centre, legs crossed. Head hanging forward as the drips fell. Wet hair and clothes plastered to him.

Three months, Paul! Only three months to petrify that bear!

Riddick sighed and wondered, with no small amount of shame, how long it would take to petrify a dead boy.

He watched the forensic team chew through the scene. He tried to capture insightful words that floated over on the light breeze but caught only groans. Beside the dead boy, mineral-rich water pattered against the white suit of the pathologist.

It seemed busier than Riddick had expected. Almost chaotic. He'd expected it to be more controlled.

There was a cough beside him.

He turned to see DCI Derek Rice and DI Anders Smith.

Riddick had never spoken to these senior officers before but had seen them about. DCI Derek Rice was a squat hothead, who liked to shout a lot. DI Anders Smith was a tall athletic man, who often had people laughing in his company.

Derek growled as he logged himself in with Riddick, who hoped he wasn't the cause of the DCI's discontent. 'I'm the SIO, and DI Anders Smith here, is my deputy.'

'All right, son?' Anders said.

Riddick nodded. 'Yes, sir.'

Anders raised an eyebrow. A ghost of a smile. 'Your first?'

Riddick nodded again. 'Sir.'

'Not pretty, eh? I remember standing where you were, and I can tell you've got this in hand.' Anders offered him a wink. 'Keep at it while we sort this chuffin' rabble out, PC Riddick.'

Riddick smiled. He felt a warmth rushing through him. He felt as if he'd been communicated with properly for the first time since he'd got this gig.

Riddick watched Anders and Derek slip on white over-suits and his eyes weren't the only ones fixed firmly on the two leads. The sudden quiet that descended over the crime scene suggested that the leaders had been noticed by their colleagues, too.

After suiting up, Derek made a point of surveying the scene with his face screwed up. He wasn't happy about something. Maybe, like Riddick, he considered it too crowded?

Riddick had heard that Derek had a tendency to lose it with his colleagues, and he wondered if he was about to witness it first-hand.

Anders placed his hand on Derek's arm and the two men exchanged a glance. The SIO gave a swift nod to his deputy, then quickly, efficiently and politely, Anders reduced the number of SOCOs and officers, while leaving the pathologist to examine the body.

After logging out those asked to take a backstep for the time being, Riddick noticed how organised and *controlled* the place now looked.

Anders then knelt in front of the sitting boy identified as Graham Lock, shaking his head and staring. Eventually, he said, 'Poor lad.' He turned and looked behind him at some of the officers. 'Graham was a good lad, eh? Good little footballer. Is Cassandra here?'

'She left just after she saw the boy,' an older officer replied.

'Chuffin' hell,' Anders said.

'Chuffin' hell indeed!' Derek mimicked. 'Why? Does she not realise what we're dealing with here?'

Anders stared at Derek for a moment. He looked unruffled, but the length of his stare spoke volumes. 'Sir. Cassandra's kid is Graham's best friend. They played on the local football team together.'

Derek looked away, shaking his head.

'Cassandra will have been shocked and upset, understandably so. I doubt very much she'll have approached the father; however, let's be prepared for any eventuality.' He pointed to an officer. 'DS Sykes, can you see if we have eyes on Graham's father, yet? If not, can you get over there yourself? We don't want him driving here.'

'Of course, sir.'

'And on your way out, Detective Sergeant, check we have a strong presence at the cave entrance.'

'Will do, sir.'

'Unbelievable,' Derek said, looking at Anders.

Anders gave him a brief shake of his head and Derek looked away again. 'We have a volatile, trying situation here, for many. Let's all keep that in mind.'

When it came to the emotional fallout, Anders had his finger on the pulse, and Rice clearly relied on that. As a result, you'd be forgiven for thinking Anders was the SIO here. That warm feeling from before swelled in Riddick. Here was a man to watch... a man to emulate...

As the team worked the crime scene, Riddick, who was already suited, edged as close as he could without being too obvious. He eventually ended up with a reasonably good view of the body, which both excited and repulsed him in equal measure.

The pathologist put one hand to Graham's chin, and the other on the back of his head, so he could tilt and reveal the face. One evening was not enough to encrust the boy's skin with carbonate. Riddick saw only young flesh, wet and grey. Sad and lifeless.

'Fifteen years old,' Anders said, hovering above the pathologist, shaking his head. 'How?'

'Nothing obvious, I'm afraid.'

'Well, he didn't come here alone in the middle of the night,' Derek said. 'Someone killed this boy. Why the hell choose here?'

The pathologist looked up at the mineral water raining down.

'Locals used to drink and shower here,' the pathologist said. 'They believed it had healing powers.'

Derek grunted. 'What're you getting at exactly?'

The pathologist shook his head. 'Nothing. I'm just telling you what I know. Maybe someone thought they could heal him?'

'Well, it didn't bloody work. Listen, it's a bit early to be sieving through local folktale and other horse shit,' Derek said, turning to walk away. 'Get me a cause of death and a time, please – let's start in reality.'

Anders followed him. Derek stopped and turned. 'Don't start, Anders, for crying out loud! Let's just establish facts first.'

'I agree,' Anders said, keeping his voice low. 'But just go easy. Everyone is going to be wound up by this one, not just us. Let them speak, or they may just end up clamming up. Welcome anything, sir.'

'Whatever you say,' Derek said, sardonically. 'I can't wait to hear that Mother Shipton used to predict the future, and we should really consider trawling through her prophecies.'

He turned and continued walking away.

Anders caught Riddick looking at him and rolled his eyes.

The warmth that Riddick was feeling before started to boil. That eye roll! Anders had just trusted him with his reproach of Derek's over-the-top sarcasm.

As the night wore on, the crime scene was processed. Plastic bags were taped up. Camera flashes tore through the cave's blackness like lightning. Numbered markers peppered the damp stones.

All the while, the dripping on Graham Lock's head continued.

Drip, drip, drip.

How long did it take to petrify a dead boy?

The dripping from the well may have been slow and steady, but the thrashing of Riddick's heart was anything but. He'd always wondered what it would feel like to be at the centre of something so different.

He felt excited... alive...

And disappointed when Anders logged himself out of the crime scene. 'I'm going to catch up with the person that found our boy. The security guard.' He shook his head. 'Aye, I know. Not deserving of that title is he, eh?' Mother Shipton's Cave was privately owned. Trespassers were an expected hazard – either via the Nidd or from the fields above. 'Seventy thousand visitors a year, Paul; I think they should splurge on tighter security.'

Riddick clocked the use of his first name and his adrenaline surged again.

A short while after Anders had left, Riddick tried to blank out the investigators, and imagined the Petrifying Well in the early hours of the morning: dark, quiet and empty. The security guard doing his rounds... whistling, perhaps... master of his domain, in love with a job that took him away from the rat race...

Until...

The moment when he looked down on that dead boy.

Never had the well's name seemed so fitting.

Growing tired now from the excessive adrenaline, Riddick turned back to the river again and the glowing lights of Knaresborough. Before long, he was lost in his memories again.

That rapt boy: 'Everything is frozen solid. Why call it the Petrifying Well? Everything looks so peaceful.'

His overly enthusiastic Geography teacher: 'Tufa and travertine rock. That's what forms around the objects.'

And his ever-miserly father: 'Take a gander at that stone lobster, my boy. Cost a bleeding fortune. Bleeding waste if you ask me.'

Riddick turned and wandered closer to the well to see if the stone lobster still hung there.

He sighted its pincers, forever poised, ready to grab.

Over to his right, Riddick heard the mutterings of a confident SOCO. 'Over there, in that smaller enclosure, that's where Mother Shipton was born to a local prostitute. Her mother fraternised with the devil. They used to say the Petrifying Well was cursed by the devil...'

Derek, who'd, unfortunately for the SOCOs, overheard, growled, 'She also predicted the end of the world in 1881. Was she right?'

No reply.

'Was she right?'

It was the first time Riddick had heard him use his infamous loud voice. On any other day, it would've unnerved Riddick, but today, in the presence of *this*... it felt trivial – at least to him.

'No sir,' the once-confident SOCO murmured.

'Anyone mentions witchcraft in this crime scene again so bloody help me...'

Riddick forced back a smile, and thought again of Mr Thomas, his geography teacher. 'Mother Shipton predicted the Great Fire of London in 1666.'

Closely followed by his father, who had moved away from the lobster and onto the next object. 'That sock. Looks in better nick than yours, Paul!' And the next one... 'Look at the state of that thing! Looks more like a bloody gargoyle than a teddy bear.'

And then Riddick noticed something.

In the here and now. In, maybe, the most consequential moment of his thus-far inconsequential life.

The teddy bear was gone.

And this was a memorable teddy bear. Not just one of those little stone bears that the shop had flogged to him as a souvenir. It'd been unique. Larger than most. Fat, maybe? Or was it just swollen? It was most definitely ugly.

Repulsive.

His father had called it then. 'It looks reyt evil that bear. Imagine having that in ye bed. Kid that originally owned it was better shot of the beggar.'

As a confident fourteen-year-old, Riddick had moved closer to the bear, wondering if it hung low enough for him to jump up and grab it. Of course, he hadn't, but it allowed him a clearer look. The stone had either concealed one of its ears completely, or it'd never had one to begin with. One beady eye poked out through the crust, but where the other eye was set, there was nothing. The stone on its forehead was creased and folded, making the bear look angry and intimidating, or evil as his father had suggested.

It was something he'd not given a thought to for a decade, yet, in this moment, at this crime scene, he saw the monstrous little toy clear as day.

'The bear is missing,' Riddick said, only realising on the final word that he'd delivered it as an announcement rather than an intended murmur under his breath.

'Come again?' Derek said.

Shit! Riddick felt his stomach turn. He looked at the DCI, whose screwed-up face suddenly appeared more malevolent than any cursed stone bear.

Nothing for it now, I guess. 'I noticed something. I thought it might be important.'

'Something important, new recruit?' Derek said, edging closer. 'Spill the beans then.'

'There's a bear missing.'

'A bear?' Derek looked around to see if anyone else was paying attention. Of course, they all were, but very few had the guts to look in his direction as they did so. 'A grizzly bear?'

He was taking the piss. 'A teddy bear, sir.'

Derek nodded as if giving it careful thought. Riddick's cheeks burned. He wondered if his embarrassment was noticeable. He hoped that people would just assume the bitter wind had reddened his cheeks.

Derek nodded. 'I see. And that's important, how?'

'Well, it's *gone*. And it was definitely there. At least when I was younger. It was ugly. I guess that's what made me interested in it. It was bigger than your average teddy bear, and it looked angry. Aggressive, even. It really sticks with me. I saw it when I was four-teen. Maybe, eight, too, but I'm not sure...' He realised he was waffling, so he broke off.

'So, we're missing a pissed-off bear?' Derek asked, breaking his scrunched-up expression with a raised eyebrow. 'That you haven't seen in ten years?'

Riddick bit his bottom lip and gave a swift nod. He wanted the ground to open up and swallow him whole. Saying that, in about ten seconds, DCI Derek Rice would save him the wait and simply bury him headfirst in it.

Derek put his hands to his face and rubbed it for a moment. 'Give me strength. I've a dead child, a pathologist contemplating the spiritual elements of the case and a new recruit babbling about a stone monkey.'

'Bear,' came a deep, recognisable voice from behind him. 'Not a monkey.'

'Sarcasm, Anders.'

'Aye, sir, I got that. Humour is welcome. It's nice to keep the tone lighter, but I think the kid may have something.'

'Something?'

'Well, sir, we know, from our years of dancing this jig, that everything at a crime scene matters. *Everything.* Maybe we should set the standard, here.' Despite the seriousness of what he said, he applied a gentle tone as if he were advising rather than telling.

Derek nodded. 'I see your point.' The scowl on his face suggested otherwise.

'We owe it to Graham over yonder to cross every t,' Anders said. 'Not that we ever don't, sir.'

'I'll leave you to dot the i's then Anders with...' He eyed Riddick and flicked his head to request his name.

'PC Paul Riddick, sir. I'm not a new recruit... and I may have been babbling but that wasn't my intention... I just... you know...'

'Felt nervous?'

'Yes.'

'Around DCI Rice?' Anders asked, unable to resist a little chuckle. 'I don't believe it.'

Derek creased his brow and regarded Anders over his shoulder with a wry grin. 'You cheeky bugger.'

Anders snorted. 'Come on... I like him. Throwing his ideas out to a grumpy old goat like you. He's got balls.'

'A real lion tamer,' Rice said, rolling his eyes. 'Have him then. All yours.' He turned and walked away.

Riddick could barely breathe.

Anders Smith had his back.

Anders bloody Smith!

He turned and looked up at the DI looming over him. A large hand fell onto his right shoulder. 'He's all bark. I've seen him cry, you know?' Anders winked. He put a finger to his lips. 'Between you and me that is.'

'Thanks sir,' Riddick said.

'For what? You can handle yourself, I bet. Plus, he knows the deal. He needs people like you and me. People who *see* things. That old codger can't see beyond the end of his bloody nose. Anyway... tell me what you noticed, son. Something about a bear?'

'Yes sir,' Riddick said, enjoying the man's solid grip on his right shoulder, feeling as if he could recount his tale concisely now. No nervous blabbering here. 'I was on a school trip when I was younger...'

* * *

My dear bear!

My large and misshapen, dear bear!

With your one eye and one ear. A freak of nature? Like me? Or beautiful? Like me?

I know, more than most, that perception is fallible. So, I will try to give you the truth: your skin is stone now. Unbreakable. Frozen. Solidified.

Not preserved...

No.

How can anything be truly preserved? Fire could destroy a taxidermist's best efforts. Let's be careful in our classifications and diligent with the truth, my dear bear.

So... I have a place for you, dear bear, where you can last forever. And it's a place that no one will ever find you or touch you again.

Finally, you have what you wanted... what you needed...

In you go then...

I know it's dark.

I know it's cold.

But it's safe!

Don't you see?

My unbreakable, frozen, solidified and most dear bear. Let me lock you away forever.

1

His dead wife stroked his upper arm.

Riddick opened his eyes, the words, 'You in the mood, are you?' on the tip of his tongue. He stopped himself just in time.

His heart sinking, as it did every time he woke, he looked up at the woman leaning over him, rubbing his arm.

Claire Hornsby. Grief counsellor.

'Oh shit, I'm sorry,' Riddick said, straightening up in his plastic chair and looking around. The last thing he remembered was sitting in a circle with fourteen other people. Now, their plastic chairs were all empty.

He sighed, immensely relieved that he'd not just accidently propositioned this woman he barely knew. 'I've never done that before.'

'Fallen asleep in a meeting?'

'Yes.' He rubbed at his face and leaned forward.

'So just my meeting then?'

Riddick looked up at Claire – she appeared pissed off. 'I didn't mean it like that. It was fine. I...'

She smiled. 'Relax... just messing, although you *genuinely* are the only person who's ever drifted off in one of my sessions. Most people tend to stay awake when others are pouring their hearts out. Kiera was—'

'Kiera! Bloody hell. She lost her husband in a fire.' He rubbed his face again. 'Christ, I feel bloody awful. Did she notice?'

'I'm not sure. You didn't snore, so maybe not. But everyone *did* notice when they got up to leave and you stayed put.' She pointed at his damp shoulder. 'Dribbling. I did consider leaving you for the cleaner in the morning. You look exhausted.'

He stood. 'Bad time at work.'

'You're a detective. Crime doesn't always choose the daytime, I guess?'

'Something like that.'

'But you're going to come again?' Claire asked.

Riddick looked away.

'I guess that means no.' She sounded disappointed.

It did.

'After only two sessions.'

'I tried.'

'You slept through most of it. And you still haven't spoken to the group.'

Riddick struggled to look her in the eyes. This was awkward. 'I just don't have a great deal to say. I mean, I don't know anyone here for a start.'

'Yes... that's kind of the point.'

'But they've their own grief. I respect them for doing it, but I, you know, just can't. Never been all "woe is me". Not my style.'

'Traditional man, are you?' She folded her arms and gave a wry smile.

'No. I'd feel this way if I was a woman.'

She shook her head. 'Why'd you even come in the first place?'

'A friend... She thought it'd do me good.'

'You were never actually serious?' She now sounded irritated.

Riddick bit his bottom lip and offered her an apologetic look. 'Sorry...'

'Do you always do what your friends tell you to?' Claire asked.

'Just this one. I owe her.'

'What's her name?'

'Emma.'

'Why do you owe her?'

'She pulled me out of a few scrapes. Some pretty significant ones to be fair.'

'You're lucky to have a friend like that.'

Riddick nodded. 'I'm stupid in many ways, Claire. Many *bloody* ways. But that's one thing I do get. Crystal clear on that one.'

'Let's hope she asks you to come again.'

'I think she probably will do.' *And I'll probably do as I'm told*, he thought, sighing. *Like a good little boy, because, if it wasn't for her, I'd be still lost at the bottom of a bottle of tequila, and nowhere near salvation. In fact, I'd probably be dead.*

'I hope so,' Claire said. 'I think unloading your grief here will make you feel—' She broke off when Riddick rolled his eyes.

'Shit... sorry. You saw that?'

'Yes,' Claire said, grinning. 'So, now I'm begging you: get it off your chest.'

He sighed. 'Everybody around here knows who I am. Including you, by the way. You *all* already know what happened to Rachel and my children. You also know that I wasn't everyone's favourite copper around here for a very long time...'

'Straight off the bat, Paul, you know that not everyone reads the newspapers. Try living without all these assumptions,' Claire said.

'So, you don't know?'

'I know, but my point still stands. And listen, this place is exactly what you need. This is the safest place you can find to confront loss without judgement. No one here will judge you. That's not why they're here.'

'Maybe.'

'Maybe? You sound unconvinced.'

'I always wondered if things like this were... you know... just a spectator's sport,' he said, gesturing at the circle of chairs.

'What do you mean?' She cocked her head.

'Using other people's problems to feel better about their own. I mean, after all, there's always someone worse off. Hear their story, feel marginally better about your own. You see my point?'

'No. I think you have a very narrow-minded view of people. Everyone who comes here wants to live with their grief, accept it, see it as a natural part of life. People aren't looking for quick wins. A shrug.' She made a gruff voice. 'A "pull yourself together, man, some have it a lot worse".'

Riddick smiled. Her impression reminded him of his father. 'You really have me down as a chest-beating neanderthal, don't you?'

'No...' She grinned. 'Not chest-beating anyway...'

'Look, I appreciate it Claire, I really do, but it wouldn't work for me anyway. Most people here have only lost one person. I lost all of them. I'm not sure I can find the perspective here you're promising.'

He looked at her. She had a sympathetic expression on her face.

'And don't do that.' He pointed at her face. 'Shit, I'm over sympathy.'

'How about this?' she said, giving a large fake grin.

'Better.'

He hadn't really noticed how attractive Claire looked before now. About his age, mid-forties, and height. Slight build. Long dark hair. Not too heavily made up. Similar cheekbones to Rachel. Green eyes, too.

She also listened, and seemed, at least up until now, good humoured.

And no wedding ring.

'Do you want to go out for a drink sometime?' he asked.

The fake grin plummeted.

Riddick flushed. 'Shit... sorry. Did I just say that? No idea where that just came from.'

'I do,' Claire said. 'It came from you wanting to open up, Paul. And you realise you can open up to me. And that's why you really should keep coming here.' She put a hand on his upper arm. 'Don't confuse those feelings with attraction. And don't be embarrassed. Please. In another life, in another situation, I'd be flattered. Come back. Eventually, you can share with me, and everyone else here.' She raised an eyebrow.

He found himself nodding without even thinking about it.

'Have you got your phone?' she asked.

'Of course,' Riddick said, taking it out.

'Take my number,' she said, removing her hand from his arm.

She told him her number and he punched it in.

'Now, if that friend of yours, Emma, doesn't get through to you, and you decide to abandon my lovely little group, please call. We can meet for coffee... to talk.'

Riddick nodded and laughed. 'Thanks. You're good! Most therapists I've ever spoken to have just irritated me. You're a natural.' He wanted to continue with the compliments but managed to stop himself, to avoid coming across as a complete flirt.

She smiled. 'I've not actually been doing it that long. It was a rather late career change.'

He nodded. 'What drew you to it?'

'A life-changing experience.' She kept her eyes on Riddick's.

'My husband took his own life and...' She opened her mouth to say something else, but then seemed to change her mind and closed it. A moment later, she spoke again. 'So, I decided I could use my experiences to help others.'

Riddick stared at her. She barely flinched. She wasn't stony-faced, but the sadness in her expression wasn't clear like the sadness that radiated from his own. 'I'm sorry.'

'It helps, Paul. All of this helps. I wouldn't do it if it didn't.'

'I think I'm a prick. Sorry.'

She smiled. 'Forgiven. Although, I don't really think you're a prick. Chest-beating neanderthal, but not a prick.'

Riddick smiled. He looked at his watch. 'I best get off. That job I was telling you about. I may not be the nicest person in the world, but I need to go and check on someone who is a lot worse.'

'Don't get burned out.'

'I'll try not to.'

A lie.

She looked at him for a moment. 'Come back, Paul, please. Give it another shot.'

If it means spending more time with you, Claire, then yes, I'll give it careful consideration...

Riddick gestured at the phone he still had in his hand. 'I'll let you know. I promise.'

* * *

Although it hadn't snowed all day, and the council had fulfilled their gritting duties, the low temperatures ensured the roads carried some threat. Riddick drove slowly.

At his destination, he reversed in between the same two cars he'd parked between the previous night. His car skidded slightly on some sludge, but not enough for him to clip the bumper of the black Renault.

Christ, Paul, that wouldn't have been the most subtle way to start an evening's surveillance. Exchanging details with one of the bastard's neighbours!

He slumped down in his seat and killed the engine. It would get very cold in this car quickly, so he lifted the hood of his fur-lined ski jacket. He'd survived the poor temperatures for a number of hours last night. He'd survive them again. He felt a twinge of excitement over the fact that this could be the last night, having been assured the warrant would be ready tomorrow. The backlog had really dragged this one out. Their system, as was the case with most systems in this sodding country these days, was a bloody mess.

He looked up at the glowing window on the second floor of the red-bricked terraced house opposite him. The room was nearly always lit when Riddick came to visit, even during the middle of the gloomy winter days.

Morgan Lark. Fifty-two. Unemployed, depressed and living alone. Reported, many times, by anxious locals who had taken offence at him hanging around the local parks looking at their children. From benches; from his car; leaning on a rusted fence. Morgan had covered all bases. However, he hadn't approached any of the children. Yet. He was a disaster waiting to happen.

Hence, the reason a warrant, albeit *frustratingly* delayed, was on its way. Riddick knew, as many of his colleagues knew, that there'd be evidence of his moral decline in that house. Most likely in the form of child pornography on his computer.

He stared at the glowing window.

In that room, I bet. Where you spend most of your days and nights – when you aren't outside, learning to prey. Refining your skills.

For the past few days, Riddick had followed Morgan to those

parks; Knaresborough market for groceries; a few charity shops; the White Bull, twice, for a couple of pints early afternoon; the job centre; and one of the local schools, where he had parked up to watch the children finish school for the day.

Riddick couldn't watch him twenty-four hours a day, but he tried his best in between his other duties, a couple of hours' sleep a night in a warm home, and, of course, a visit to a grief session at the Methodist church. He ensured he stayed here until at least II p.m. in case Morgan should *evolve* to the next level and decide to hunt those children not under the protective gaze of their parents, wandering streets and parks at ungodly times.

It was seven o'clock. Riddick had four cold hours ahead of him. He wouldn't even use his phone in case the light in his vehicle betrayed his cover.

Bored, but committed, he hunkered down and stared at the glowing window once more.

* * *

Riddick was seized by sudden cramp in his leg.

He bounced it up and down, rotating his ankle. *Shit!*

He looked down and focused on massaging it back into action.

It was slow, painful going. What he needed to do was jump from the car, walk it off, but, of course, it wasn't an option.

Someone knocked on the driver's window. He almost jumped out of his skin. He flicked his eyes away from his leg to the window, only to be blinded by a torch shining in.

'Is everything all right, sir?'

No... no... piss off!

Riddick made a futile hushing sound as if the torch-wielding maniac could somehow hear him through the door.

What he really wanted to do was shout, 'Shut up man! You'll

bring Morgan bloody Lark to his window!' But shouting would be the final nail in this coffin.

So, he cracked his door open and a rush of winter air iced his skin. He brushed the torch aside and out of his eyes, and looked up at a young, suited-and-booted police officer.

Riddick slipped free of his vehicle with a finger pinned to his mouth, life coming back into his leg, although he paid it little heed right now. He closed the door gently behind him to kill the interior car lights. 'Please, lower your voice lad.'

Riddick saw a nervousness ticking away behind the inexperienced officer's eyes. It was familiar. He remembered that ticking well.

The officer took a step back into the road. Fortunately, no cars were coming, or that would've ended Riddick's unauthorised surveillance with a real set of fireworks. 'Sir, we've had reports that—'

'Shh... I'm police too. Keep your voice down,' Riddick hissed, gesturing he lower the volume with the palms of his hands, and taking a step towards him.

The young officer swung his torch up, blinding Riddick, who staggered back towards his vehicle, covering his eyes.

'I need to see some identification.'

You stupid, keen as mustard, witless fool.

He fumbled around in his coat pocket for his ID and held it up. 'DI Paul Riddick,' he whispered. 'Now, get your bloody torch out of my eyes and listen.'

The officer directed it onto the ID and badge. 'Keep it there, sir, please, so I can see the photograph...'

'You need to listen...' *You bloody fool. You absolute bloody fool. If Morgan Lark looks out of his window, then he'll know! He'll sodding well know...*

'Thanks, sir. I'm sorry.' He pointed at the house beside where

Riddick was parked. 'They were concerned that someone was watching them.'

'I wasn't watching them. I'm watching this house.' He gestured up at Morgan's window.

For the first time in three long days, the light was off.

'Christ almighty,' Riddick said, willing himself not to start screaming obscenities. 'You bloody buggered it!'

'Sir, what? Why? I only responded to an emergency—'

'Shut up, let me think.' He hit his forehead with the palm of his hand. 'It's buggered.'

'What's buggered, sir?'

'My surveillance, you pillock. And stop calling me sir. Please just go back to your car.'

As he watched the officer climb into his vehicle, he half expected the idiot to hit his lights or siren. The officer didn't leave immediately. In fairness, he was doing the right thing. Phoning in Riddick's ID number just to confirm this was police business.

He wondered about the response. It certainly wouldn't be confirmation of this surveillance, as it didn't exist. None of this was police business. Hopefully, the ID would be enough to send the tyke on his way. Something along the lines of... yes, that's DI Paul Riddick. He's often out on his own, raising merry hell. I'd run along, young man. The MIT works in mysterious ways. You're best staying the hell out of it...

Riddick slipped back into his vehicle, his heart hammering and the nerve endings around his eyes twitching.

He looked up at the dark window. 'Shit.'

The officer started his car and drove away.

At last! Although it's too late.

His fault, of course, not the wet-behind-the-ears officer.

He took a deep breath and considered.

Had Morgan slipped out? Taken the back door because he'd seen Riddick's badge in the light of the kid's torch?

Jesus... had that been enough to push Morgan over the edge? Knowing his window of opportunity was closing, had he bolted out to make his first grab?

Riddick looked up at the window again and narrowed his eyes.

No... you're still there, aren't you? Watching me from the darkness, you paranoid, scared little shit.

He hunkered back down, praying, and then praying some more, for that bloody light to go back on.

I'll stay here all night if I have to.

* * *

Time passed. The light didn't go back on, nor did Riddick's nerves settle.

His mind circled around his limited options: sit here all night, go home or break into the house.

And risk everything that could come with that?

Damaged evidence... a suspension... and, worst of all, a power shift to the criminal?

Or, would his lottery numbers come up? Confirmation that Morgan had left to nab a child? His war cry to his colleagues, and then a glorious sense of relief as the fledgling predator was swooped up, caught in the act...

Riddick was distracted by two boys, who couldn't be more than ten, coming up the pavement on the other side of the road. At quarter past ten! What was up with these bloody parents?

One of the kids was vaping. The other one was kicking a deflated football across the street. Both were spitting and shouting obscenities.

Another day, another time, Riddick would've hopped from the

car, given them a stern talking to and found an excuse to drive them home and admonish the parents.

Because if they'd been his daughters, Molly and Lucy, that would have been what he'd have wanted to happen. Them to be brought back to him. So he could ensure they were safe. Always safe. With him. With him and Rachel.

But the boys would have to be saved from themselves another day. If his cover hadn't already been blown, you could bet your house that a torrent of verbal abuse from pre-pubescent boys would do the trick.

The child with the bust football suddenly launched himself over a garden wall and disappeared up a dark path towards what must have been his home.

'In a bit,' the other boy shouted after him, before turning and crossing the road directly in front of Riddick's vehicle. He leaned over and spat on the bonnet of the car.

Little shit! I've a good mind to come out of these shadows and scare the living piss out of you.

When he reached the other side of the road, the kid took a deep lungful from his vape pen and blew a large cloud into the air before slamming the pen in his pocket and pulling his hood up over his head. He drew a mobile phone out of his pocket, stopped and then perched on – of all the bloody places – Morgan's wall.

Riddick shook his head. *Move on, kid. Christ almighty, move on.* He raised his eyes up to the second-floor window, which was still dark. *You in there, Morgan? You watching?* He took his eyes back down to the boy. He couldn't see his face because it was swamped by the hood of his top, but the tyke was engaged by whatever he was looking at on his phone. Very engaged. Unfortunately.

Okay, enough is enough now; toddle on back home, stop teasing the monster in the closet...

His phone vibrated in his pocket.

Had one of the big dogs already heard? He was setting up a PR shitstorm, after all.

He carefully took the phone from the inside pocket of his ski jacket and tried to look at it with the coat shielding most of the light.

Emma.

His DCI, one of his closest friends, and the reason he was still in this job in the first place. Had she already been alerted?

Her desperation to rein him in would emerge in a foul-mouthed rant. He sighed. Maybe it was just her twenty-four-hour check-up on his sobriety?

He let the call end, slipped the phone back in his pocket and again looked out through his car window—

He felt the whip of adrenaline in his gut.

The light in the room was on again. And the boy was still on the garden wall, fiddling with his device.

The upstairs window darkened, and now he felt the whipping adrenaline in his chest too. Someone was so obviously standing there.

Morgan?

I see you. Do you see me? Do you think I'm using this lad on your wall as bait? Good. Stay cautious. Stay inside. Away from him. We'll be back to put an end to you tomorrow. No need for any fuss.

The boy stood.

You move along now.

Before the boy had cleared the garden wall, his phone rang. He stopped, answered it and started to talk. Loudly.

Okay, fine, swear at your parents, whatever, but keep walking...

The boy took a step, as if he'd heard Riddick's thoughts, but then seemed to change his mind, and turned.

Shit the bed... is someone doing this to me on purpose? He looked up. *Give me a break.*

The window had brightened; Morgan was no longer watching. The boy continued yapping down the phone, swearing as loudly as he could as if it was a new football skill he'd discovered and he was showing it off to all who'd watch. He took a few steps before turning and stepping the other way.

Pacing. I do that on the phone too, kid, but it's really not the time.

The front door opened.

Definitely not the time.

Riddick bolted up in his seat and clutched the steering wheel.

You really couldn't help yourself, could you?

The light was on downstairs, so Morgan's large silhouette filled the door frame.

Riddick's hand closed around the car door handle.

The boy had yet to notice and remained engrossed on his phone as he paced.

Behind you. Look, behind you. Run... as fast as you can. Please. Before the curtains are raised on an avoidable shit show.

The boy turned and saw Morgan in the doorway.

Riddick held his breath. The boy looked in both directions.

Doesn't matter which way... just pissing well get on with it...

Morgan stepped out onto his garden path. The boy continued to meander. Riddick exhaled.

Last chance, boy. Go... run... or I'm coming.

Morgan was holding something in the air. As yet, he hadn't used the binoculars, but Riddick reached for them now. He used them to identify what Morgan was holding.

A photograph, perhaps? Hard to tell in this light.

Whatever Morgan was doing, worked.

The boy didn't opt for left or right, he opted for the bloody path.

Riddick threw the binoculars onto the chair and opened the car door. The interior car lights flared into life. No point in caring about that now. After all, it would be better if Morgan saw and slammed the front door before this went any further.

The boy was already standing close to Morgan, staring at whatever he was holding in his hand.

Riddick burst from the car and charged across the street.

'Piss off! That's not me,' the boy said, loudly.

Riddick reached the garden wall; unbelievably, neither of them had noticed him yet.

'Come in. I have more,' Morgan said, putting a large hand onto the boy's shoulder.

'Get off me!'

The adrenaline had been whipping at Riddick for some time, but now he was filled with it. 'Police! Stop!'

He scaled the waist-high garden wall, catching Morgan's wide eyes as he did so.

Full of panic and fear.

'Stop!'

The bastard didn't. He was backing into his house.

The boy, however, had broken away and was sprinting up the path past Riddick.

Riddick could've turned, left the monster. No one was in danger and Morgan was in the crosshairs anyway.

However, when it came to adrenaline and impulse, Riddick had never exercised the best control.

Finish it now. The bastard is spooked. He might wipe his hard drive.

Morgan tried to close his door, but Riddick got his foot to it first. 'Police, stop! You tried to abduct that child. I saw it happen. You're under arrest.'

A reason. All he had. Would it wash? Would they buy it? He thought of the fact that he'd been seen watching the home by that young officer. What would be made of all that?

Morgan was scurrying up his stairs like a rat. Riddick wanted to squash him before he could destroy any evidence. Several steps up, Riddick reached out for Morgan's bare foot. His hand brushed against skin, but he was unable to take hold. Morgan stumbled slightly, but regained his footing just in time, so he was able to reach the landing and turn.

When Riddick turned onto the small landing, Morgan was already at the end of it, beside the grubby little room that faced the street.

The rat threw himself inside, and the light that had kept Riddick's attention for the previous three of days burst free, filling the landing.

As he neared the door, Riddick looked around for something to use as a weapon, but there was nothing.

Hold fire, don't go in there blind, call back up...

Realising that this voice in his head was Gardner's and not his own, he forced it back, replacing it instead with an image of Morgan smashing his computer to pieces.

Riddick burst into the lit room.

2

Her sleeping daughter's hand was cold to the touch, so DCI Emma Gardner eased it beneath the duvet. After kissing Anabelle on the forehead, not for the first time this evening, Gardner reached over to the bedside table to stop the CD player and welcomed the sudden silence. Bedtime rhymes may have been soothing for Anabelle, but they bloody irritated her. She also dimmed the night light globe.

Outside the room, Gardner turned back and gazed in at her seven-year-old daughter.

See you at three in the morning!

Gardner didn't mind. Carrying Anabelle back to bed at three to tuck her in wasn't the worst thing in the world. When Gardner had first been seconded up here to Knaresborough, she'd been forced to live without her daughter for three months. It didn't get worse than that. So now she saw Anabelle's early morning interruptions as rather refreshing, a reminder that they were back together again. In the past, she'd always questioned whether her motherly instincts were strong enough. Realising they were felt pleasant. She appreciated being needed and being that source of comfort.

Emma shuffled along to the adjacent door, which was also ajar, and went in to her niece Rose, who was also sleeping. After kissing her on the forehead, she regarded her little face. Anabelle was almost a whole year younger than Rose, but, right now, you'd be forgiven for thinking them identical twins.

Rose's father, and Gardner's brother, Jack Moss, was presently serving prison time after breaking the conditions of his parole. While Rose's mother was currently being rehabilitated following prolonged drug addiction.

Gardner had stepped in to foster this little gem, and their time together, so far, had felt nothing short of special.

A horrendous snoring sound kicked up from downstairs.

Gardner sighed.

She looked at her watch. It was *bloody* early. Guess there'd be no television now that the snoring pig had commandeered the sofa.

Gutted, she headed for the spare room.

Fostering Rose and restoring Anabelle into her life had come with the heavy price of having to relocate her dying marriage up to Knaresborough too. Despite the fact that the plan had always been for Barry and Anabelle to join her one day, the re-emergence of Emma's brother had put the brakes on their relocation. Having Anabelle anywhere near Jack wasn't an option.

It had still hurt like hell though. However, there had been an upside – the space had given Gardner time to accept the truth that her marriage to Barry was well and truly over.

Jack's incarceration had paved the way for her daughter to be with her again, but Barry wanted to be part of the family package. Even if she'd had the appetite for a prolonged court battle, it wasn't an option. She could only foster Rose with a settled family home.

She sighed again.

Living with a man who showed her no attention, and that she'd long lost any affection for, was a high price to pay.

But one she was *willing* to pay to be with these two wonderful little girls.

For now, at least. Until this secondment ran its course and she could go back down south, where she had a strong family network.

She closed the door of the spare room behind her, shutting out the horrendous sound of her husband. She sat on the edge of the bed she'd slept in the night before, and the night before that. They hadn't argued about it. In fact, they rarely argued at all now. He didn't seem to care about anything apart from Anabelle and his job – *which he could do from home, lucky bastard!* No, the heated exchanges were rare. She could've sat at the other side of the room and thrown darts at him, and he probably wouldn't even have noticed.

She eyed up the paperback on the bedside table, and thought, longingly, of that bottle of red downstairs.

But she was going to hold back. She'd put a bit of weight on over Christmas and getting up and running at the crack of dawn was also bloody harder with alcohol in her system. And she needed those runs. It cut through the stress like a hot knife through—

Her phone rang, and her heart sank when she saw the name on it.

Chief Constable Rebecca Marsh.

This late that could mean one of two things: a crime scene or...

She answered the phone.

'Ma'am?'

Marsh sighed. 'It's not a crime scene, Emma.'

Bollocks. 'What's he done now?'

* * *

Riddick's door opened.

They stared at one another, neither speaking.

Eventually, she delivered a brief shake of her head.

Riddick rolled his eyes, turned, leaving the door open, and walked away. She followed him in and closed it behind her.

'Paul—'

'Not now boss,' Riddick said, heading through the door off to the right.

Gardner paused, looked down at the floor, sighed and then followed the pain-in-the-arse DI into his kitchen.

He sat at the head of the table and put his hands around a steaming mug. 'Don't worry, just coffee. Not Irish either.'

'It's a bit late for coffee.'

'Bloody hell, you just can't win; should've chucked the whisky in. Throw a pod in the machine if you want to join the wild party.'

'Such the host, but no, I'm okay. I value the three hours of sleep I get a night. I'll sit for a minute, though.'

Riddick smirked. 'I bet you will.'

She sat, surveyed him for a moment, working out how best to bollock him without him spitting out the dummy. There were very few options available where Riddick was concerned. So, she just went with her default – something she'd learned from her good friend, DCI Michael Yorke. *Begin with a compliment.* 'Your passion is commendable, Paul. Your heart is in—'

'Piss off!'

Well, Yorke, it seems your strategy finally just met its match...

'I'll save you time,' Riddick continued. 'Your prized rottweiler just got off its leash again and you've been sent round to put its muzzle back on. Are we done?' He looked at his watch. 'If you head back now you may be able to build on those three hours of sleep you had.'

Gardner nodded, accepting the brush off, before delivering her reflection. 'Rottweilers are obedient.'

Riddick snorted. 'Brutal! Maybe you've got more in common with Marsh than I first thought...'

Chief Constable Rebecca Marsh knew nothing about her nickname 'Harsh Marsh'. Her usual 'harsh' behaviour would be akin to a romantic date in a cocktail bar compared to what would happen to the unfortunate soul who let the nickname slip.

'Anyway, you're more like a cat, Paul. How many bloody lives you got?' Gardner sighed. The truth was, there was only so much more of Riddick's reckless behaviour she could stomach. Since she'd arrived in Knaresborough, she'd spent more of her time saving Riddick's career than anything else, doomed by the fact that she was extremely fond of him. He was a natural detective who was instinctual, passionate and courageous. However, Gardner knew that there was a fine line between courage and just being a loose cannon. Throw recovering alcoholic into the mix and you had a lot of volatility on your plate.

'So,' Gardner said, 'not even a hint of remorse?'

Riddick took a mouthful of coffee and then sighed. 'Okay, I see how it looks.'

'Like a dog's dinner?'

'Aye.' He shrugged. 'But someone had to keep an eye on Morgan Lark. I didn't see any other volunteers.' He pointed at his eye. 'And my eye was available.'

'Your *unauthorised* eye.'

'Look, if it takes my unauthorised eye to keep children safe, then, well...' He sighed. 'What's the point? You know me well enough.'

'Don't I just! And now here we are. Because, as it turns out, Lark wasn't a danger to anyone, after all.'

'How was I to bloody know that?' Riddick asked before taking a mouthful of coffee.

'You weren't,' Gardner said. 'Hence the reason you follow the process.'

'Hindsight is a wonderful thing.' Riddick grunted. 'But if they're going to drag their heels over a warrant, I'm not taking that risk. I just can't.'

'Marsh is talking about suspending you.'

'Fair play. But if she'd seen what I'd seen, she'd have reacted the same way! Lark was trying to coerce a kid into his house for pity's sake! Imagine if he *had* been bad news!'

'Maybe, but Marsh wouldn't have been there in the first place.'

'Not the point I'm making.'

'Besides, Lark *isn't* bad news so it's irr—'

'We don't know that for absolute sure yet...'

'We're fairly certain.'

'Fairly, precisely... not good enough! If he had been bad news then they'd have thanked me for sparing their blushes over taking too chuffin' long with the warrant, not threatening me with suspension.'

'A moot point, Paul. It hasn't played out that way. In fact, it's playing out in a completely unexpected way, and you'd be better off distancing yourself now. Be contrite.'

Riddick shook his head. 'I dunno. Something's *still* off.'

Such a pain in the arse! 'You need to let it go, man!'

'The oddball had pictures of children on his wall...'

'Missing children. Children who've disappeared from Yorkshire over the past couple of years. Children he was *actively* looking for. Yes, he was mad as a hatter but—'

'Mad is an understatement.' Riddick widened his eyes. 'He's been hanging around parks looking for young children who went missing in other areas? It's a first for me!'

'I get that, but *mad* isn't *bad.*'

Riddick tensed up; he wasn't letting this go without a fight. 'How do we know he didn't disappear them?'

'For a start, Rob Ellis, the ten-year-old Lark tried to coerce into his house, backs up his story. Lark thought Rob was Harry Michaels, a boy who disappeared a year back in Leeds. When Rob denied being Harry, he was invited in to look at some pictures to see if he recognised any of the other missing children.'

'Proves nothing. Lark could've been about to turn Rob Ellis into another missing person – a photo for his collection – a handy addition to his good Samaritan disguise.'

'There're reports of someone fitting Lark's description wandering around Leeds city centre, showing these same photographs,' Gardner continued. 'The man's made a career out of searching for these kids. Not sure he'd attach himself this blatantly to his victims.'

'Man's a concern whatever way you look at it. He needs to be under constant observation.'

She laughed – she couldn't help herself. *Insufferable!* 'Okay. He needs help. It's clear. It just may not be a jail cell, or DI Paul Riddick tearing his fragile little world to pieces.'

'You make *me* sound like the monster in all this,' Riddick said, raising his eyebrows.

Gardner shook her head again. 'Imagine if the press gets a hold of this?'

'Might be a good thing – expose Lark—'

'Really! Depends how they portray him! After all, the press love a local Samaritan, while they don't have much time for... well...'

'Me?'

Gardner shrugged. 'You said it.'

'DI Riddick. Knaresborough's wolf in sheep's clothing?'

'Something like that. Anyway, let's try our best to control the damage now and I'm sure we'll keep it out of the press.'

She could tell from his twitching eyes that he couldn't let it go. *Exasperating! As usual.*

'I mean what's Lark's motive for being this good Samaritan anyway?' Riddick asked.

Gardner sighed. 'Turns out his own brother went missing when he was a kid and was never found. He started there and just grew...'

'Hmm, likely story.'

'It's a great story for sympathy, and we know plenty of journalists who'd eat that up.' *Anyway, this had been going on for far too long now.* 'Let it go, Paul. It's *still* going to be looked into – just not by us. I give you my word. You think if he's been bumping off children for the past ten years, they won't find anything? Behave. Just be contrite, nod and accept you got this wrong and let's move on. Keep a tight lid on this.'

'I—'

Gardner hit the table. 'No, Paul! Put it to bed!'

His eyes narrowed.

They eyed each other for a short while, frustration creasing both their brows.

Eventually, Gardner softened her expression, and said, 'Please. For me. *I'm* asking you now. Not Marsh, or the department. *Me.*'

Your friend.

This in turn softened Riddick's expression. He looked down, thought for a moment and then shrugged. 'You're right. I got it wrong... *Probably.*'

'Probably?'

He looked back up and raised an eyebrow. 'Maybe?'

She raised her eyebrow back at him.

'Okay.' He sighed. 'I'll let it go. Contrite as can be.'

'Thank the lord. Now, please, listen to me, without causing more seismic ripples. You're going on sick leave for a few days while we tie this up.'

'Great!'

'You haven't really given Marsh much choice.'

He sighed. 'No. I suppose not.'

'Work with her and hopefully you can avoid investigation.'

'Be a difficult one! I was seen by a kid officer conducting unauthorised surveillance – I wasn't just driving past...'

'Trust Marsh. She's good at this. Persuasive. One of her strengths.'

Riddick disappeared off onto his own train of thought for a moment and then sat up straight. 'Hang on, did I just slip through a crack in the space-time continuum and fall into another dimension?'

'Come again?'

'Is this really the morally perfect DCI Emma Gardner saying I should let Marsh help me dodge a bullet rather than bite it?'

Gardner shook her head, sat back and crossed her arms. 'Do you ever bloody stop?'

'What about *accountability*?' He snorted. 'Remember when you pushed and pushed for Marsh to look into your conduct? You were desperate to be hanged, drawn and quartered—'

'This is different.'

'How so? You bent the rules doing what you thought was right, and I did too.'

He was right. Despite their protestations at HQ, she'd pushed and pushed for them to hold her to account for her conduct in the Operation Bright Day case. Eventually, they had done, by sweeping it under the carpet with a paltry warning.

She rose from the chair.

'You know I'm right. So, you'll hold yourself to account, but not me? That doesn't make sense, boss. It's like double standards but the wrong way round.'

She stared long and hard at her smug colleague, who seemed to love nothing more than to debate these bloody things to death. 'I got a second chance so, you know, I—'

'Really? How many chances do you think I'm on?'

Good question. She'd rather not know. However, if Riddick was thoroughly held to account for shadowing Morgan Lark, then she may be bidding him farewell – and that option just didn't figure.

Being accountable was important but losing Riddick in the ongoing fight for truth and justice because he cared so much, just seemed ludicrous. But he was right, if it'd been the other way round, she'd have hung herself out.

'I'm going,' Gardner said. 'Phone in sick tomorrow… *please*?'

Riddick looked down and gave a swift nod.

'And lay off the coffee.' Gardner turned and headed towards the front door.

'No point if I don't have to be up for work.'

She went through to the hallway, wondering if he'd keep his promise. She considered turning and drilling home her point again but dismissed the idea. She'd infuriate him.

When she placed her hand on the door handle, she heard him jumping up in the kitchen.

She'd time to press the handle, open the door and potentially leave before Riddick reached her. But she didn't.

Instead, she just froze.

When Riddick's hand touched her shoulder, she felt her heart rate increase.

'Thanks, Emma.'

His voice sounded gentle, and far more genuine than usual. He also used her name. She felt her skin flush.

'You've always got my back.'

'You're a good detective and we're better off with you than without you.'

'Is that the only reason?'

Damn you, Paul. Why ask me that?

His hand seemed to increase the pressure on her shoulder. *No.* It was just in her mind. Her entire attention was on it, after all, intensifying the sensation. She tried to focus on the door handle instead.

'Are you sure you don't want to stay? Have a *decaf* coffee?'

Yes. I'd like that very much.

She could feel her pulsating heart in every part of her body now.

She closed her eyes, recalling the last time she'd felt like this. Many months ago, when he'd been drunk and had come to her house for support. He'd fallen asleep on her sofa, and she'd fallen asleep on another. When she woke in the middle of the night, he was alongside her, and that was when she'd felt as she did now.

The flushing. The increase in her heart rate.

He'd wanted to confess something to her. But she'd stopped him. She didn't want to hear it. Because if it was what she'd suspected – that he'd developed feelings for her – that might be enough to make her crumble. Succumb.

And a relationship with Paul Riddick was not good for her. Or him. Or anyone on God's green earth for that matter!

She managed to find it in her to open the door, and slipped away from the hand on her shoulder.

'I'll speak to you tomorrow, Paul,' she said, forcing herself not to look back.

* * *

The journey home was a short one, allowing Gardner no time to settle back down.

She hoped Barry was still asleep on the sofa. The last thing she wanted was an interrogation over her flustered expression.

Of course, she was being irrational. Having Paul Riddick on her mind wouldn't endanger her marriage. How could you endanger something that was already extinct? Also, as if Barry would notice. He hadn't taken a blind bit of notice of her in a long time.

However, she'd like to be calm, just for herself. Otherwise, she'd end up scrubbing her mind clean under a shower of red wine, and dry January would be no more.

As she neared her housing estate, the heavy snow started again. She cranked up the windscreen wipers and turned into her estate. She negotiated the roads slowly and slowed further still when she noticed that someone had parked on her driveway. Easy to notice as they had their headlights on.

Gardner pulled up on the road, killed her own lights and regarded the Mini Countryman.

Now what do we have here? she thought as she watched snow sparkle in the beams from the vehicle. She exited her own car, locking it behind her. Shielding her eyes from the snow, which was intensifying even now, she hopped over the slush and wandered over to the Mini. She could make out the shadowy figures of two people in the front of the vehicle, and then looked up at the front door, which stood ajar.

Her heart, which had already put in one shift after Riddick had touched her, was given another jolt. This time, it was more of a cold feeling than a warm one, and she reached into her pocket for her mobile.

Maybe she was being paranoid, but having her brother

commit ABH on her lawn in front of her months before had dosed her with anxiety.

Shielding the screen from the snow, she dialled the emergency services but kept her finger off the call button just yet. Then, she marched forward and banged hard on the rear window, before stepping quickly back, in case the *visitors* decided to reverse over her.

She kept the phone ready in her hand, knowing it was all she had.

The passenger door opened.

Gardner squinted at the man stepping out. 'Barry? For God's sake. You scared me; the front door is open – what the hell is going on?'

'Emma,' he said. 'I'm sorry.'

'Who's in the car with you?'

The other door opened. A woman stepped out. She was tall, striking, although rather heavily made up. She certainly wasn't dressed for the snow, and if she stood there for too long, she could kiss that excessive mascara goodbye.

'Me,' the woman said. She put her hands on her hips and stared hard at Gardner as if she was here to right some kind of wrong.

Her pompous attitude infuriated Gardner.

'Well, *Me*,' Gardner said, 'I was about to wake the neighbours with the emergency services, so if you could tell me what you're doing on *my* driveway, before I—'

'Emma, if you go inside, I'll explain,' Barry said, his voice laced with panic.

'Shut up, Barry,' *Me* hissed over the car. 'You've had your chance.'

It quickly dawned on Gardner. *You've got to be kidding me...* 'Sandra?'

'Yes,' Sandra said. Her hands slipped from her side. 'Yes... so, you do know?' Gardner could hear from her tone that she'd been destabilised.

'Yes... well, no, not really,' Gardner said, sighing. 'I knew of someone called Sandra that went to Alton Towers with my daughter. A work colleague struggling with a divorce. How's that struggle going?'

Sandra glared over the car at Barry, and then looked back at Gardner.

'But since then, nothing,' Gardner continued. 'He hasn't mentioned you. Sorry to be the bearer of bad news.'

'He's a liar.'

'Did he promise he'd tell me about you?' Gardner asked, slipping her mobile back into her pocket, now that she realised there was no immediate danger.

'Yes.'

'I wouldn't take it too personally,' Gardner said. 'He's self-absorbed, you see. Very self-absorbed. Have you driven up from Wiltshire?'

'Unfortunately.'

'That's some journey. You must be shattered.'

'And irritated.'

'I bet. Are you in love with my husband?' Gardner asked.

It was hard to tell in the heavy snowfall and the lack of light whether Sandra's face reddened, but her voice certainly suggested embarrassment. 'I... I... sorry.'

'It's okay. You're forgiven,' Gardner said.

'Shit,' Barry said. 'I told you not to come here, Sandra.'

Gardner started to walk down the path. As she passed Sandra, she offered her a genuine smile. This wasn't down to her. Not really. Barry had targeted her vulnerability. This was on him. 'Look, there's not going to be a scene out here. The neighbours are already struggling to warm to me, and I'm too shattered anyway. Weirdly, I feel the urge to ask you in because it's cold and you're probably tired, but that wouldn't be appropriate, not with my children in the house.' She looked up at Barry. 'I think you should both go and find somewhere for tonight.'

'I'm sorry, Emma,' Barry said. 'This was over. I promise.'

Sandra shook her head. Gardner was close enough to see tears in her eyes.

'Not here, Barry,' Gardner said, not wanting to look at him in case she lost her cool. 'Not with the children in the house.'

'Okay,' Barry said.

Sandra touched Gardner's arm. 'I'm sorry.'

Gardner looked at her hand, up at her face and then pulled away.

When Gardner reached her open door, she heard Barry call out behind her, 'Emma, I'm so sorry.'

She went into her house and closed the door behind her. She leaned back against it for a few moments.

She didn't feel sad, or angry. If anything, she felt empowered. In control.

The wine could stay in the rack.

Dry January and all that.

Knowing that Barry would be away for the night, she opted for her bedroom now. She lay back, enjoying the comfort. It didn't take her mind long to drift away from her spineless husband...

And back onto Riddick.

3

Pete Wilson talked far too much.

Still, Milo Hardy was fine with that.

Milo preferred just to listen – always had. Conversation, itself, wasn't one of his strong points.

Not that he had many strong points.

Crap at football, crap at running, crap at all sports in fact, crap at computer games and, of course, crap at socialising. Suffice to say, he didn't have any friends – apart from Pete – and girls gave him a wide berth.

Walking back and forth along the knee-high brick wall running alongside the Co-op service station on Boroughbridge Road – just as he had done as a small child when walking with his mother – Milo waited for Pete to finish up.

Pete had gone in to buy a couple of bags of crisps and had given a cheeky wink when using the word 'buy'.

Pete, his new, his *only*, friend, was everything Milo was not.

Pete was good at football, good at running, good with computer games and, of course, good with girls – or so he said. Milo did trump Pete in their classes at school to be fair, although you could argue that it was because Pete was rarely in. And who wanted to be the class champion anyway? Especially when you were fifteen, and in your final year at school.

Milo pirouetted on the wall and headed back the other way, feeling the snow on the end of his nose. He pulled his hood up.

He couldn't believe it was only two weeks ago that their English teacher Mr 'Jonno' Johnson had moved Pete to sit next to him in class. They'd never spoken before, which was probably the rationale behind Jonno's decision. In fact, they didn't talk that lesson – Pete was only one warning away from being excluded. Not that this usually stopped him. But at that stage, Pete simply didn't have any interest in talking to Milo.

Milo had been unconcerned.

He had no friends, and he was used to people showing no interest. To be fair, he'd have been far more uncomfortable if Pete had tried to initiate conversation. So, that English lesson passed without incident. It had been Pete's actions the following day that had come as a surprise.

Milo was reading a Batman comic in the school playground with his back to the wire fence that surrounded the tennis court. He looked up to see Pete, who was on a record-breaking consecutive day in school, looking down at him.

At first, Pete didn't say anything, and Milo wondered if he'd strayed from the football crowd to give him a beating for no real reason. It wouldn't have been his first beating... and it certainly wouldn't have been his last.

Pete spat on the floor, then he screwed up his face and pointed down. 'Batman?'

'Yes,' Milo said. 'You want to look?' He offered the comic.

'Nah.' He grunted. 'Do I look like I'm eight years old, kid?'

Milo nodded. He considered pleading the case for this issue of Batman. Explaining that this comic was for mature readers. That it was violent and shocking. But Milo didn't do conversation, never mind persuasion. Besides, he was stuck on Pete's reference to him as 'kid' – they were the same bloody age!

Pete sat down next to him and held his hand out. 'Give it 'ere then, kid.'

Milo did.

Pete flicked through it, pausing over some of the more graphic images with a hint of a smile on his face.

His smile broadened and he nodded with approval when he reached an image of the Joker wielding a razor-sharp playing card which had been used on someone and dripped with blood. He also read aloud a couple of the many profanities which caused him to chuckle.

'You can borrow it if you want?' Milo said.

Pete looked up and around, a concerned expression on his face. Was he worried about his reputation? He handed the comic back to Milo, stood up and left without another word.

Yes, Milo thought, he's worried about his reputation.

Milo watched Pete return to the football crowd. It'd been one of the most peculiar interactions of his life, and he dwelled on it for the rest of the day.

The out of the ordinary had not finished with Milo and, that evening, Pete knocked on his front door. Milo's mother was already in bed. Thankfully. Pete was rather infamous around here. Milo's mother wouldn't have been best pleased.

'Coming out, kid?' Pete asked.

'Where?'

Pete shrugged. 'I know some places.'

Milo felt uncomfortable. He'd never been in this situation before. The evening was for comic books. He'd never had any reason to deviate from this.

'Okay,' Milo said. 'Maybe I should just tell my mam.'

Pete swore and laughed. 'You're almost sixteen, kid.'

Milo nodded. Did he really look that pathetic? 'Okay... she's asleep anyway.'

'Whatever you decide to do,' Pete said, glancing both ways, probably to check no one was close enough to hear on the street, 'grab some of those comics, would you?'

Milo nodded. 'Okay.'

'Stick 'em in a bag though.'

Milo nodded.

He did check on his mother but she was still sleeping off another rough day. He kissed her thinning face as he always did when he left the house, and went into his room to bundle comics into a backpack.

Pete took Milo to a country lane. Some older teenagers with dirt bikes were smoking marijuana. Pete seemed to know many of the lads and nodded at them. Sometimes, a car passed, the horn would blare and Pete would hold the palm of his hand in the air in greeting.

It soon became clear that although Pete was well known, he didn't seem to be close with anyone. Milo wondered if it was just in this spot, or whether this was also the case elsewhere.

Was the persona he presented at school a lie? Was Pete a loner, not unlike himself?

Together, that first night, they found a quiet spot, away from any wandering eyes, and there, the bag was opened, and Gotham City unleashed. On many occasions, by the torches of their mobile phones, Pete would ask Milo what some of the more complex words meant.

Milo was more than happy to tell him.

More than happy?

He was ecstatic!

That night, Milo arrived home past eleven, and his mum was still sleeping.

He kissed her lukewarm cheek and then he sat in his bedroom, unable to sleep, knowing, but not quite understanding how, his life had changed.

* * *

Pete threw him the pink packet.

Milo didn't like prawn cocktail. 'Thank you.'

'Why're you saying thank you, kid?' Pete spat on the floor. 'I didn't pay.' He grinned.

They were standing under a streetlamp, so Milo could see how yellow Pete's teeth were. Maybe he should tell his friend to lay off the smoking? The smoking hadn't done his mother any good. And wasn't that what friends did? Offer advice?

Milo decided against it. If he started with the Pete's teeth, he may feel obliged to mention his pale skin and suggest more sunlight. Then, he might comment on his waif-like appearance, and suggest more nutritious food. Before he knew it, a friendly suggestion may have dragged him into a minefield.

He'd turn a blind eye to the yellow teeth. For now, at least.

Despite being repulsed by them, he opened the crisps. The smell was putrid. Forcing himself not to gag, he threw one in his mouth, bit down and smiled.

'Good, huh?' Pete opened his, ate a few and then looked at his watch. 'Shit! Thirty minutes until we meet KG.'

At the mere mention of the name KG, Milo's stomach gurgled.

'You okay?' Pete said.

'Yeah,' Milo said, 'just not hungry really.' Milo closed the packet in his fist and then jumped down from the wall onto the pavement.

Pete, wolfing down his own crisps, climbed over the wall and stood alongside him. He yanked on Milo's rucksack which he wore with both straps.

'You got those Judge Death ones you told me about?' Pete asked.

'Judge *Dredd*.'

'That one, yes. He executes people, yeah?'

'Criminals. He's allowed to. It's his job.'

Pete sucked in his bottom lip, nodding. 'There's a bench over there. We got some time to burn, kid.' He snatched the crisps from Milo's hand. 'And I'm not wasting them.'

Milo was relieved.

* * *

It'd been five days since that first night together on the country lane with the weed smokers and joy riders, and Milo hadn't seen Pete again.

He was absent from school. Nothing unusual there, so it wasn't a worry. It was just disappointing. How stupid he'd been to believe he'd found a friend!

With each passing day, his stomach sank further, until he eventually faced up to the reality that he was alone again.

But the evening of the fifth day brought an unexpected surprise. Pete at his door again. 'You still on for tonight, kid?'

Milo couldn't recall agreeing to anything, but this didn't stop him being over the moon. 'Yes.'

'Batman?'

'I have one called "the Batman who laughs".'

'Violent?'

'Yeah. Brutal. Batman and Joker work together.'

'Okay, grab it and let's go.'

'I'll just say goodbye to my mum.'

'A right Mummy's boy, aren't you, kid?'

Milo felt his cheeks flush.

'Chill. I'm winding you up.'

After filling his bag with comics, and kissing his sleeping mother goodbye, Milo walked alongside Pete.

Just like last time, Pete smoked marijuana the entire journey to the country lane and spoke the entire time. 'Shit just gets busy, you know? One minute I got to go Donny. Next minute, Wakey. Non-bloody-stop! Nice to get some money, like. I'm not complaining.'

Pete offered him his joint, but Milo shook his head. He wasn't scared of what it would do to him; he was just worried about his mother finding out. 'Best not. My mam. You know.'

'Get some mints, kid,' Pete said.

Milo shook his head again. His mother would know. Especially if his eyes went as red as Pete's.

'I like that you love your mam,' Pete said as they turned onto the first of several country lanes.

Milo didn't know how to respond to that, so he just nodded.

'Nothing wrong with it at all. Stop getting all embarrassed and shit! My dad is a wanker. The only thing that keeps him off my back is the cash that I give him. Cheap rent, you know. Also, I kind of feel sorry for him. He was better before my mum died. Actually tried sometimes.'

Milo looked at his friend. He often gave so much thought to what he was about to say but what Milo said next came out without any thought whatsoever. 'My dad's already dead, and my mam is dying.'

Pete stopped and looked at him. 'Shit. Sorry, kid.'

Milo was surprised by his impulsive outburst. Consequently, he thought long and hard about what to say next. And, on this occasion, he didn't get there before Pete spoke again. 'Life sucks. Let's go and read a comic.'

* * *

The walk to the Co-op, and the subsequent pacing up and down the wall had kept Milo's body temperature up. Now, sitting on the bench, immobile, the bitterness of the weather hit home. He kept his teeth clenched, trying not to reveal to Pete that he was starting to shiver.

The snow was continuing to fall, but at least the tree beside the bench was sheltering his beloved comics.

Milo had seen a lot more of Pete over the previous week. His new friend had only been called away on business once and had even made three rare appearances at school. They'd also spent several evenings together, wandering the streets of Knaresborough. Despite this, Milo struggled to hold Pete's undivided attention. He seemed very preoccupied with his phone, sending and receiving messages regularly.

Milo had also noticed that Pete kept changing phones. He never really recognised any of the brands, but they all had that same plastic, cheap feel.

Tonight, Milo hadn't explained away a single complex word to Pete. His vocabulary was growing rapidly. It was remarkable. Pete was being educated by Milo's extensive collection of DC comics.

Several people had already passed Milo and Pete on the bench, but no one had halted or spoken to them. So when the boy in the red puffer jacket stopped and leaned into the tree that was sheltering them, it drew Milo's attention. He looked damp, and the Fortnite bag on his back had a thin white layer of snow on the top. Milo couldn't see who it was because the boy was staring away from the bench at the road.

Milo looked at Pete to see if the hesitant boy had caught his attention too.

He hadn't.

There'd been a time when Pete had been concerned about his reputation and had admitted on more than one occasion that he didn't want to be seen reading kids' comics. But so strong was his new-found addiction to the world of DC that he'd ceased to care about someone else's views on the matter in much the same way he smoked joints openly on the streets, unconcerned about reaction.

And right now, he appeared completely engrossed.

Milo looked back at the boy, who was still leaning against the trunk.

Pete laughed beside him. 'Shit! This is bare savage! Look at this, kid. This Judge completely dusted him.'

The young lad against the tree turned, and Milo recognised him immediately.

Stephen Best was in the same year as them at school, but they'd never spoken with one another. There were, after all, about three hundred plus students in Year II. However, Milo was keenly aware of who Stephen was, because he was a loner, too. Stephen retreated to the library during breaktime and lunch at school, and was quiet, avoiding eye contact with most, and spending the bulk of his time reading; although, for him, it was books instead of comics.

Milo suspected Stephen was as introverted as he was. So, unless a reason for them to communicate ever cropped up, it was unlikely to ever happen.

Until now that was.

Stephen looked emotional. His eyes were red and were darting from side to side. He looked as if he was experiencing panic. He mumbled something. A car went past at the same time, so Milo was uncertain as to what he'd said.

'What do *you* want?' Pete was no longer oblivious to the lingering boy.

Stephen shook his head erratically. He mumbled something else. This time, there was no car, but he was still incoherent.

'Piss off!' Pete said.

Pete's aggression made Milo flinch. It was hard to see a change in Stephen's demeanour though. His red eyes continued to dart about.

Pete dropped the comic into Milo's lap and stood.

If Milo had been in Stephen's shoes right now, he'd be running. He certainly wouldn't be standing there, staring at one of the toughest lads in school, anxious and mumbling.

Milo sympathised with Stephen, while he could tell that Pete was growing more and more frustrated. Pete was an edgy character, who considered it essential to watch his back. He'd want this lad out of his space.

'I warned you...' Pete said, walking towards Stephen.

Whatever was keeping Stephen rooted to the spot and causing those tears to continue to spring up in the corner of his eyes was obviously of far greater significance than the beating he might be about to receive. What was wrong with him?

Pete stopped a metre from him and pointed at the Fortnite bag. 'What's in there?'

Stephen shook his head.

'Open it,' Pete said.

Stephen continued shaking his head, more erratically now.

'Okay then, I will.'

The situation was spiralling, and it was no time for Milo's usual hesitance. He forced himself to his feet. 'Pete, let's go, leave it—'

Pete looked around at Milo. His eyes were bright red, not unlike Stephen's.

'Kid,' Pete said. 'Let's just find out what's in his bag. Look at the state of him. It could be booze.'

Milo didn't like this. This was the side of Pete that had earned him his reputation. A side he'd never really seen before tonight.

But, although he didn't fear Pete himself, he was unable to summon up the right words to defuse this situation. 'He's upset about something.'

'Yes,' Pete said, looking back at Stephen. 'And he could be pissed...' He glanced at Milo again. 'Everyone handles it in different ways. I told you about my dad, didn't I?'

Yes, he had. His dad drank a lot. He tended to get emotional and cry when he was drunk. That was tolerable. The lashing out that followed, less so.

Pete looked back. 'So, have you got booze in your bag or what?'

Stephen was still shaking his head. His face was rigid. He looked as if he was staring at some kind of monster, rather than Pete.

'No?' Pete said.

Pete glanced back at Milo and shrugged.

Milo looked at his watch. 'Have you seen the time? We should go—'

Pete turned back and grabbed hold of Stephen's backpack.

It was only at this point that Stephen seemed to briefly snap out of his mute terror. 'No!' He yanked away from Pete.

Pete did not yet have a good grip on the backpack, and Stephen retrieved it too easily. He stumbled backwards, caught his foot on a tree root and fell onto his backside. Momentarily in charge of his senses again, he scurried backwards, his backpack on his stomach.

Milo saw the anger on Pete's face and, despite it going against every grain of his personality, he acted impulsively, and charged forward so as to get between Pete and his downed victim.

'We've got to go,' Milo said.

At first, the rage remained on Pete's face, but then his expression softened. 'You're right. And be careful with that, kid.' He pointed at the comic Milo was crushing against his chest. 'I haven't finished it yet.'

Milo turned and, thankfully, saw Stephen Best sprinting off down the street.

* * *

After finishing The Killing Joke *Pete was happy to declare that it was the best one yet.*

Milo was over the moon with this.

Almost two weeks ago, the prospect of having a close friend had seemed unlikely, while the prospect of having a close friend with similar *interests had just been completely ludicrous.*

Yet, here it was, happening.

Feeling more comfortable around Pete, Milo was able to come out of his comfort zone to ask, 'Why does everyone think you're bad news?'

Pete laughed. 'Oh, they do, do they?'

He reached into his jacket pocket, pulled out a cigarette packet and slipped out a joint. He held it up. 'Well, there's this...' He lit it and took a long drag. He blew out a plume of smoke. 'Then, there's the fact I sacked off school. Add to the fact that my father is an alcoholic ex-criminal. You need more?'

He knew there'd be more, but he didn't want to push him. He shrugged.

Pete whispered, 'Oh, and there's KG.'

Milo creased his brow. 'Who?'

Pete smiled and whispered again, 'KG. My boss.'

'Is that who you're always texting?'

'Yes... among others.' Pete laughed. 'Why the interest, bro? You want to earn some money?'

Money?

The answer to that was obvious, but he forced it back. 'What do you do, Pete?'

'A little bit of this and that. Do you want a drag?' He offered the joint.

Milo declined as he always did.

'But you want money?' Pete asked and took another hit himself.

Milo looked up at the sky. The air was bitter and sharp tonight. He took a lungful of it and watched the stars. I'm just glad to have you as a friend, Pete. Even if you are bad news, even if you do intimidate everyone apart from me. I'm glad. 'It's probably not a good idea,' Milo said.

Pete shook the comic. 'You'd be able to buy more of these.'

It'd been a long time since he'd bought one of them. In fact, since his dad had died two years ago, he'd probably only managed to buy three or four.

Pete looked at him with one eyebrow raised. 'You'd be able to take better care of your mum.'

Milo looked at the stars again. He thought about her sleeping in bed. With every passing day, there seemed to be less and less of her there. They'd some benefits to live on, but it was nothing special. He didn't know how long she had left. Wouldn't it be nice to take her on holiday one last time?

Just ask her where she wanted to go and just, you know, take her there?

'It's probably not a good idea,' Milo repeated.

'That's a shame, kid... KG expressed an interest in meeting you.'

Milo imagined himself lying back on a sun lounger watching his mother in the water.

Swimming for the last time.

4

Riddick stared at his empty kitchen cupboard.

Empty for a very good reason.

Old habits die hard, and the alcohol that used to reside within that cupboard had exerted too much, if not total, control over his life.

It wasn't the events of tonight that had him reminiscing over a time in which he'd medicated his sorrows. If anything, he was relieved that Morgan Lark was unlikely to be a threat and that children were not in imminent danger. Nor was he concerned about his career because that had been up and down for as long as he could remember, and he was used to the volatility.

Neither was he staring at the disused cupboard because of the empty seats around the table. Yes, not a day, not a *second* went by that he didn't miss his family... *pine* for them... but this wasn't the source of his anxiety right now.

He was staring at that cupboard because of a phone call he'd made months earlier while pissed. A brief phone call, but one rich in consequence.

A two-minute phone call, a transferred payment from the

insurance pot collected following the loss of his wife, and then Ronnie Haller, his family's killer, was no more.

Fatally stabbed in prison.

He placed his hands on the table and stared down at it, slowing his breathing. Long deep breaths. His doctor's answer to panic attacks. That, and 20 mg of a substance he couldn't recall the name of.

Ending Haller's life should have healed his wounds. At least, that's what his drunken mind had concluded. If he'd been sober, he may have realised that it was destined to inflame his wounds further.

Long deep breaths.

It barely helped.

He was no better than any of those bastards he'd put away.

He was a liar. A con artist. Pedalling truth and justice.

A bloody hypocrite.

When his mind skipped to Anders, the man he'd admired above everyone, he lost control of his breathing, and he closed his eyes, knowing that a wave of dizziness was impending.

He felt Anders' large hand on his right shoulder as it had been that night at the cave decades earlier.

Tell me what you noticed, son. Something about a bear?

He recalled the blossoming warmth he'd felt in that moment.

In his mind's eye, he saw Anders again, many years later after he'd nurtured Riddick's career to DI. It was Anders' retirement party, and also the night Anders told Riddick he loved him like the son he'd never had.

Then, a truly gut-wrenching moment. Anders in his own home, on that fateful day earlier last year. The truth spilling out of him like oil from a ruptured pipe in the ocean.

Anders Smith was *also* a liar. A con artist. Pedalling truth and justice.

A bloody hypocrite.

He saw Anders again, broken, hunched over in a chair, his back ruined, looking up at Riddick with bloodshot eyes. *What do you want me to do, Paul?*

And then, it wasn't Anders in that chair any more. It was him.

But the question was the same. *What do you want me to do, Paul?*

Riddick waited until the panic attack passed and straightened up.

He'd been so close to telling Gardner that night on her sofa. So close to admitting that he, like Anders, was a murderer. But she'd pushed him back at that moment. Why? Had she sensed what was coming? Had she been desperate to avoid the truth, so she could preserve her version of DCI Paul Riddick as a moral person, driven by truth and justice, plagued by tragedy, but desperate still to fight the good fight?

The *inaccurate* version.

But that morning, when they'd woken up together on the sofa, the alcohol had been retreating from his system, leaving him frayed and nervous.

And he'd bottled it.

If he'd told her the truth, she'd have turned her back on him.

Then, he'd have had no one.

Is that what'd happened with Anders? Had he kept the truth from Riddick so he wouldn't turn his back on him? Had Riddick left that man *alone* when he most needed help?

He pulled his eyes from the empty cupboard and took his phone from his pocket. He scrolled through to Gardner's number. His finger hovered there for a moment.

For Christ's sake, man, have you not put her through enough?

He looked through his other contacts, realising how many

bridges he'd burned over many years. Then, he saw Claire Hornsby's number.

Again, his finger hovered momentarily.

Had it really come to this?

Was he *this* pitiable?

Leave her be.

His anti-depressants weren't working, neither was the deep breathing. Drinking alcohol was out of the question, as was bothering someone who had their own shitty messes to deal with.

Only one option available really.

It was tried and tested.

He grabbed his coat.

A walk in the fresh, yet often bracing, Yorkshire air.

Riddick opted for a thin waterproof. Nothing cleared the cobwebs like the Yorkshire chill. He wasn't totally mad, so he did wear a hat, but he struggled to locate his gloves, so he kept his hands in his pockets.

He shivered at first, but a rapid pace soon brought his body temperature in line with the demands of the weather. He managed a fair distance and eventually found himself walking down the Wetherby Road hill. It was late now, so the roads were quiet, but the occasional car came uphill, unwittingly blinding him with their headlights.

Eventually, he reached the turn off onto Abbey Road, eager to take on the long stretch by the Nidd. He'd put his boots on as it got notoriously icy around here – he recalled a particularly painful experience in his twenties when he'd twisted his ankle rather badly and spent most of Christmas limping.

Listening to the moving waters of the Nidd mixing with the

hiss of the winter wind in the surrounding treetops made him feel rather small and inconsequential.

It made the pain he felt, and the damage he'd done, seem less significant.

Who needed anti-depressants and alcohol? Look where he lived! He had nature. And if you had nature, you had perspective.

Coming the other way was a dog walker, who gave him an 'ey up' and a swift nod of his head, while his springer spaniel eyed Riddick up suspiciously. The walker was followed by a car, which Riddick allowed plenty of space. The driver responded in kind by dimming his beam, sparing Riddick's eyes.

It was a dark stretch, but he could see movement up ahead on his left. As he continued his careful stroll in the centre of Abbey Road to avoid the snow piled up at the sides, he kept his eye on the source of movement, expecting another dog walker to suddenly stroll out of the gloom towards him.

Nothing.

Another car came out of the murk, momentarily illuminating the person up ahead on Riddick's left.

Someone in a red, puffer jacket, leaning against the gate to St Robert's Cave.

Again, Riddick gave the driver space by moving in between some mounds of snow.

After the car had passed, Riddick continued his journey to the solitary figure. When he was close enough to realise that the person was young, mid-teens perhaps, he called out, 'Are you all right, son?'

Even in the limited light, Riddick could see the panic in the teen's eyes when he swung them in the DI's direction.

'I'm police... there's no need to worry.' He was about to reach into his pocket when he realised his badge was in his suit at home. *Shit.*

The young man continued to stare in Riddick's direction, yet to respond. He did not look comfortable at all and, although he was still some distance away and the light was poor, there was something very off about his facial expression.

Some of his colleagues would've raised their guard at this point, but Riddick being Riddick, lowered his, and increased his pace.

As he drew closer, Riddick realised that the young man, who looked to be around fifteen or sixteen, was trembling. He was pale, and the muscles on his face were twitching all over the place. He looked terrified.

Riddick stopped a metre away. 'Is everything okay?'

The teenager hadn't taken his eyes off Riddick, but the DI was convinced he wasn't staring at him. There was a faraway look in those eyes as if he'd disappeared somewhere else.

Riddick, now gravely concerned, reached out to offer him a reassuring pat on his arm.

The boy's eyes widened, and he recoiled. He was lucky not to go over the fence and crashing down the stone steps.

Riddick snapped his hand back. 'Sorry... listen... I'm a police officer. I haven't got my badge, but you can trust me. It's okay. What's your name?'

The boy mumbled something. Riddick couldn't understand what he was saying. He was slurring his words.

'Have you been drinking, son?' Riddick asked.

The boy mumbled again, and this time Riddick thought he caught the words. 'It *won't* end.'

'What won't?' Riddick asked.

The boy's eyes widened even further and then seemed to focus for the first time – although not on Riddick, but rather on something *behind* Riddick.

Riddick turned and almost jumped out of his skin when he

saw a Tesla in the centre of the road with its lights off. He squinted, trying to identify the driver, a dark silhouette behind the front window screen, but failing. There was hardly any light out here.

The electric car barely made a sound.

What're you doing?

Riddick made a gesture with his hands to indicate that the driver needed to turn their lights on.

The lights stayed off.

Riddick then attempted to wave the driver onwards and stepped to one side to allow space.

The car remained still.

Riddick looked again at the boy, who appeared even more terrified than he had before. His eyes were darting back and forth, and his lips were now drawn back in a grimace, exposing his teeth.

'Do you know who this is?' Riddick asked.

The lad didn't look like he could comprehend anything right now.

Adrenaline pumping, and heart racing, Riddick turned his narrow eyes back on the black, electric motor. *Sod this.* He started to approach.

'It won't end,' the boy said again. His words were disconcertingly clear this time, considering the state of him. 'It won't end.'

Keeping his eyes on the car, Riddick muttered, 'What won't bloody end?'

The lights on the vehicle came on. Full beam.

'Jesus!' Riddick hissed, shielding his eyes. 'Turn off those lights, you dickhead!'

The silhouette behind the wheel remained still.

Shit. Enough is enough.

He moved closer to the vehicle, but keeping to the side, in case whoever was playing tit-of-the-year decided to surge forward.

The car reversed backwards at roughly the same speed Riddick was approaching at. *I'm dealing with a first-class clown here.*

Blocking his eyes as best he could from the glare, Riddick made a mental note of the registration number.

The gate behind him banged shut.

He turned, seeing the back of the young man disappearing down towards St Robert's Cave, a yellow rucksack bouncing off his back.

'Wait! Not down there – it's dangerous!' Riddick shouted. 'You'll slip on those bloody steps for a start!'

He turned back to the vehicle, shielding his eyes again, and checked the number plate a second time. 'To be continued.'

He turned, bolted towards the gate, yanked it open and started down the steps.

He considered making a phone call on his descent, to rally support. He could only imagine the groans. *Does this man ever stop causing trouble?* Something was going on here, no doubt, but it was better to maybe see *what* before raising the alarm bells.

'Wait... my name's DI Paul Riddick! I only want to see if you're safe.'

Where the hell will he go when he gets down there? Into the River Nidd?

In these temperatures, they'd be fishing him out in the morning.

Bollocks.

Riddick upped his speed. A ridiculous decision, albeit one that felt right after his imagination had shown him what may come to pass.

Halfway down, Riddick caught a patch of ice, and slid. For a moment, he couldn't sense his heartbeat, which was terrifying as he'd been keenly aware of it seconds before. As he skidded, he looked down at the multitude of stone steps which would shatter his bones and surely knock the life out of him.

When his palms hit the limestone walls, indicating that he'd skated *across* the step, but not off it, he became aware of his palpitations again, and he heard Gardner's voice in his head. *How many bloody lives you got?*

Too many, he thought. *And I can't cope with the stress of them all...*

After a deep breath, he continued his journey, and realising that he was effectively heading down into darkness, he plucked out his phone, opened it and hit the torch.

His phone's torch wasn't the most impressive, but it kept enough of the stone steps illuminated to prevent him from tripping.

'Where are you, son?' he said as he reached the bottom step, swinging the torch over the Nidd gorge and onto the wall of the cave in which Robert Flower, son of the mayor of York, had decided to live over eight hundred years ago.

'Where're you? I want to help you!'

He shone the torch over the ruins of the chapel just beside the steps, hoping the boy was crouching there. He sighed when he saw that he wasn't. He cast limited light over the leafless trees lining the gorge, desperate to catch sight of the terrified youngster. When he didn't, the image of the boy floating off down the freezing cold river momentarily revisited him and he shuddered.

He stepped around Robert's grave, long since exhumed, and approached the rock-cut bench, sheltered by the cliffs above. 'I'm DI Paul Riddick. If you let me help you... I can get you home. Get you warm.'

He shone the torch over to the entrance to St Robert's Cave. The water from the Nidd that sat at the bottom of the cave shimmered in his torch light. If this young man was in the cave, he'd be very cold and wet. Sometimes, it got treacherously deep in there.

He moved slowly towards the cave entrance, still calling out for the child, recalling the story of Daniel Clark, a murdered man discovered here, way back in in 1759.

At this distance, it was still pitch-black inside and, besides that shimmer of the water, his torch wasn't focused enough to illuminate the interior. He'd need to get closer still. He edged forward until his pinprick of light speared the darkness.

The shimmering water now appeared more like a thick oil lapping against the cave walls.

His breath caught in his throat. There were *things* floating in it. Large shapes – any of which could be a body...

He took back control of his breathing. Get a grip, Paul. It could just be large rocks breaking the surface of the crested water.

He heard footfall behind him. He turned, swinging his phone torch with him.

He felt pain in his head but nothing after that.

* * *

Oh my dear bear!

It does pain me to see you this way, it really does. Twisted up. Inside out. Warped and contorted. Broken.

Yes, no one is immune to suffering. I, more than anyone, know that. But your suffering is different. Like mine was. All-consuming.

Who better to hear you, dear bear? Who better to know you? Who better than me?

See my compassion.

Do they have compassion?

I see only bloody knuckles and bloody faces.

Bang. Bang.

They punch us, dear bear, believing they're compassionate.

But if they were, if they truly were, would it hurt so much?

We know. People like me and you, dear bear, we know.

It is too late for all of them now. They had their chance.

Don't run, don't be scared... come with me. There will be no bloody knuckles here. No bloody faces.

Only compassion.

Let me take away your true suffering.

Then let's see them try to break you again!

That's it! Come with me, dear bear. You're doing the right thing.

True suffering comes to an end with true compassion, I promise.

And after tonight, you will be locked away in the darkness... in the cold...

But you will be unbreakable...

5

Before heading through the gate that led into Jacob Smith Park, Pete had a good look up and down Scriven Road and then Park Way opposite it. He looked bewildered.

Despite his own anxiety, Milo didn't question this. He was silent at the best of times and, right now, being a fish *completely* out of water, he was not about to buck any trends.

'No sign. KG drives a new Tesla.' Pete shook his head and looked at his watch. 'We're on time. Still, the boss is *allowed* to be late I guess.'

Milo nodded. He felt like he was in a daze. It'd started the moment Stephen Best had hit the ground beneath the tree alongside the Co-op. Doubt and fear had infiltrated his every thought. Being with Pete suddenly felt too dangerous.

This morning, when Milo had first woken, he'd been excited, rather than terrified, about meeting the infamous KG. Why wouldn't he? Pete had delivered one hell of a sales pitch, and the prospect of good money had been tantalising.

One last good holiday for his mother. And she deserved it after everything she'd been through – *was still going through.*

Yet, seeing that look in Pete's eyes when he'd pushed Stephen had shaken Milo's mind and the second thoughts had come tumbling out. Pete was unhinged. And, as much as he liked him and relished his new-found friendship, this just wasn't safe.

And what if everything went badly wrong? Then what? A holiday would be the least of his concerns, because his mother may have to vacate this world in pain and turmoil, her final thoughts revolving around her failure in raising her son properly.

'You ready?' Pete said, squeezing Milo's shoulder.

No. I've changed my mind.

Pete squeezed harder. 'Are you okay, kid?'

'Yes,' Milo said and nodded.

They entered the park through the gate.

Jacob Smith Park, gifted by Winifred Jacob Smith to the community of Knaresborough, had been one of Milo's mother's favourite spots back when she was well, and Lottie, their golden retriever, had still been with them. Not many of his memories glowed, but this one was positively a beacon. Both of his parents, alive and well, and Lottie's searing runs over the hilly fields and through the woodland.

He heard Pete make a show of taking a long deep breath beside him. 'Smell that.' He pointed at the overflowing bins beside Milo. 'Dog shit!'

Milo smiled, politely acknowledging his new friend's attempt at comedy, but distracted now by the weight of both nostalgia and terror.

It was late, and there were no dog walkers about. The fields were snow-topped, so rather than walk over them, they entered the woodland that framed the park. The icy ground crunched under foot, and Milo didn't have the footwear for it. Still, his shoes held, and his socks remained dry.

'You're being quiet, kid,' Pete said, looking at him. 'If you've had second thoughts?'

Milo shook his head, and completed his lie with a grunted, 'No.'

'It'll be all good. I got your back, kid. And KG, you know, he has this way about him... it can be unnerving... but he's always been fair to me.'

Milo flinched when he heard scurrying.

'Squirrels!' Pete laughed and pointed at one darting up a tree. 'Relax.'

They took a right and headed uphill. They walked for about five minutes, and then sat down on a fallen tree.

Milo surveyed the trees, and recalled Lottie weaving around them, burying her face beneath the bases of the trunks, lapping at water.

'Let's get back on with Judge D,' Pete said. 'Who knows how long KG will be.'

* * *

Unable to focus on a comic, Milo kept his eyes on the direction they'd come. When he saw the tall man approaching uphill, he tapped his engrossed friend on the leg.

Pete looked up at the approaching man too, and then handed the comic over to Milo. 'Put it away and stand up.'

Milo thrust the comic directly into his rucksack with trembling hands, not bothering, as he always did, to sheath it in a plastic wallet.

They stood.

KG was yet to look up, his attention focused on the icy ground. He'd a three-quarter grey coat on, which hung loosely around him because it was unbuttoned. As he drew closer still, Milo saw that he'd a beige suit on beneath the coat.

He stopped a metre or so from them, and Milo had to suppress a gasp. There was a splatter of blood on his buttoned white shirt exposed by the open coat and beige jacket.

KG lifted his head and smiled at both of them in turn. Perfect teeth glowed white. 'How do? I hope I haven't kept you waiting. Cold out, isn't it?'

'Yes,' Pete said. 'But we're fine.'

'Held up by unforeseen circumstances,' KG said. His smile fell away, and he sighed.

Milo realised his eyes had darted down to the blood again, so he moved them up, and caught KG looking directly at him. The smart dresser then peeled off his leather gloves and buttoned up his jacket, hiding the stain. After slipping back on his gloves, he extended a hand to Milo.

Milo took his hand. KG's grip was strong, and the leather felt cold.

'Milo... Pete speaks highly of you. You've got a good head on your shoulders.'

Pete patted Milo on the shoulder. 'He'd be loyal, KG.'

KG grinned and looked at Pete. 'Loyal... good.'

Milo considered pulling his hand back, but KG still had it, and he didn't want to appear rude.

'You know how this works, Milo?' KG asked, looking back at him and finally releasing his hand. 'Pete filled you in?'

'I told him it involved making deliveries, KG. I didn't go into any more detail.'

KG nodded. 'Good. We need to be sure... to be certain. Are you a trustworthy lad, Milo?'

'Yes, sir.'

'KG, please.' He laughed and looked at Pete. 'In my experience, everyone tries to do over the boss at some point – better to keep this as a family. Right, Pete?'

Pete nodded. 'Yes, KG.'

KG winked at him and then looked back at Milo. 'Pete tells me you're a family man. Is that right?'

Milo thought of his mother lying in bed. He thought of his desperation to offer her some happiness in these last months. 'Yes...' He stopped himself from saying 'sir' just in time. 'KG.'

'Good,' KG said. 'Because doing over your family is very different from doing over your boss.' He put a hand to his chest, roughly where the concealed blood was. 'It's a bridge too far for a man like me.'

Milo was no dummy. He sensed the threat and fought back against his fear. *You've nothing to worry about. You'd never betray a man like this.* He knew he didn't have it in him.

KG regarded Milo for a moment longer and then put a hand on his shoulder. 'You're a good kid – go on Pete's next run with him.' He then drew his hand back and turned back to Pete. 'You came up a little short last week, Pete.'

Milo glanced at his friend. Pete's confident expression had disintegrated.

'I thought we'd discussed this already...' Pete's voice shook.

KG sighed. 'Yes, we did. You showed me your bruises. The recipient didn't appreciate how short it was.'

'I didn't pack it, KG. Whoever packed it must've lightened it.'

'Yes. That was our conclusion, wasn't it?' He nodded. 'But, you know, the packer of that bag was adamant it wasn't him. And... well... I was rather insistent.' This time, KG placed a hand on Pete's shoulder and stared for a while into Pete's eyes. Pete maintained eye contact with him, although you could clearly sense that he was uncomfortable doing so.

'The packer is no longer part of our family,' KG said. 'Keep the ship tight, Pete.'

'I will KG.'

KG took his hand back and smiled at Milo. 'I see great promise here. Show him the ropes.'

'Yes, KG.'

KG looked between the lads. 'The bag is wedged beneath the dog shite in the bin at the entrance to the park.' He then gave them an address in York. 'Say it back to me, Pete.'

Pete said it back.

'Again,' KG said.

Pete did.

'Okay.' He looked long and hard at Milo. His face was serious. Milo forced himself to keep eye contact, despite wanting to crawl behind the trunk he was standing in front of. 'The number one rule, Milo. You never met me. You'll never meet me. In fact, I don't exist.'

Milo nodded.

'You break that rule, not only are you out of this family, but I'll visit your mother. Do you understand?'

Milo thought about his mother lying there, weak, close to the end, this sharp dresser with perfect teeth standing over her, telling her that her only child wasn't the child she'd believed him to be.

'Yes,' he said.

'I feel good about tonight,' KG said, pointing at Milo. 'I feel good about you, Milo.'

He turned and walked away.

* * *

'Not the most glamourous part of the job,' Pete said with his arm in the dog waste bin by the entrance.

Milo was standing by the gate, looking out onto the road for any dogwalkers that fancied the cold at this hour. Having someone stumble on Pete, shoulder deep in dog shite, was a situation best avoided. Especially with a boss that claimed to value anonymity above anyone's life.

Pete gagged.

Unsurprising.

Milo could smell the shit from several metres away.

'KG has a sick sense of humour. Why not just choose a normal bin out there? I'm sure one of these bags of dog shite is split... my hand is wet...' He gagged again.

Milo felt his own stomach turn.

'Thank God,' KG finally said, lifting a dark blue Slazenger holdall from the bin.

He threw the bag over at Milo's feet, then stepped back, looking at his hands. 'I need a bloody shower.'

Milo looked down at the bag in disgust.

'I got it out,' Pete said. 'You're carrying it.'

Milo picked it up. It was quite heavy. He lifted it to his face, sniffed it and winced.

'I'll give it a wipe when I'm home,' Pete said. 'Let's shoot.'

'Do you think we should check what's in it?'

Pete laughed and shook his head. 'Not if you value your life, kid! You never open it. We deliver. That's all we do.'

'But your bruises?'

Pete shrugged. 'Every job has its risks, doesn't it?'

6

2003

On the day that the Mother Shipton's Cave investigation came to its heart-rending conclusion, PC Paul Riddick was sitting alone in the canteen, feeling as he'd felt the previous two weeks at HQ.

Like a spare part.

In all honesty, he really shouldn't have been here. A lowly PC like him should have been pounding the pebbles.

But DI Anders Smith was anything but passive, and when a large Yorkshireman with Scandinavian Viking blood coursing through his veins requested something, he rarely came up short.

So, his peculiar demand that PC Paul Riddick be present on, potentially, North Yorkshire's most significant investigation in over ten years, was fulfilled.

Despite this, Riddick's role had been limited, and most of the duties had been farmed out to the most experienced. Yet, Anders was forever checking in with Riddick to remind him that he'd 'got the ball rolling'.

If anything, this was a curse. It made Riddick feel like he was walking on eggshells around the colleagues who'd earned their stripes with hard graft. Still, despite being subjected to long, lingering stares, he was never confronted. To do so would risk the wrath of Anders. The only person who would dare to take Anders on was DCI Derek Rice, but he was completely oblivious to Riddick's existence, in the same way that he was oblivious to most people's existence, even that of his own son, DC Phil Rice.

Riddick was finishing his coffee in the canteen when he heard commotion in the corridor outside. He went to investigate discreetly. But Graham Lock's suspected murderer was shouting obscenities so loudly, no one would've noticed Riddick rubbernecking.

Russell Lock was being led away in handcuffs. Or rather, *forced away* in handcuffs. Riddick's mind flicked to that first moment he'd seen Russell's son, Graham, in the Petrifying Well at Mother Shipton's Cave. Sitting up in death, his head slumped forward, while his wet, black hair was hanging limply like a shroud over his face.

Russell, bereaved father and suspected murderer, was raging against the officers, screaming his innocence.

For the briefest of moments, Riddick wondered if his superiors were wrong.

He shook his head, admonishing himself for responding to the emotion in Russell's pleas. He was too inexperienced to make judgements like that! If Anders was the *deputy SIO* on this case, who was he to question it?

The two lead detectives watched the broken father being led away, their postures stiff and their faces serious.

They waited for Lock's exit before the tension fell from them, but the demeanours of the two men were in stark contrast to how they usually were.

Derek Rice, often the curmudgeon leader, now had a spring in his step, and started to slap backs left, right and centre. Some officers were overjoyed by this, if not a little bemused, and looked like startled children who'd just been told their stern father was proud of them for the first time.

However, despite smiling and also participating in the back slapping, there was something decidedly off about Anders. It was subtle, but there was something missing from that confident, imposing presence. His eyes regularly darted up and over the colleagues he was celebrating with to gaze off in the direction that Lock had exited. Then, his body seemed to shrink slightly, almost as if his back was giving him some trouble and stooping released the discomfort.

After watching the celebration for a couple of minutes, Riddick turned to head back into the canteen.

'And where do you think you're going?' Anders asked.

Riddick turned. 'Sorry, sir... Congratulations, by the way. But, I... I—'

'Have decided to not share in the celebrations?'

Riddick, who failed to see what there was to celebrate in such a tragic event, nodded. 'I don't really belong here.'

Anders guffawed. He lifted his eyes up to the heavens as if to quiz God over the reason for the existence of the imbecile before him, shook his head and then clapped both of his big hands onto Riddick's upper arms. He shook him very gently, which must have taken some effort in restraint considering the size of the man. 'Don't *belong* here. Christ above.' He leaned in and lowered his voice. 'You've more right being here than most of the sorry sacks of shite around here.'

Riddick wondered briefly if he was including Derek in this elite grouping.

'It was you, Paul.' His voice was booming again now. 'You got the ball rolling...'

There it was again. It was wearing thin on Riddick, who was now feeling more of a fraud than ever, but it certainly wasn't running out of steam with Anders. He delivered it with even more umph than usual.

'You notice things. That bear,' Anders said. 'That *bloody* bear. Or rather, you noticed the *absence* of the bear.'

'It would have been noticed without me there,' Riddick said, unable to hold back his true feelings any longer. 'You'd have seen it in a photograph. Failing that, the people who worked there would've spotted it too! I didn't do anything out of the ordinary, sir, I really didn't.'

'Bollocks,' Anders said, gripping the sides of his arms more tightly. 'You accelerated the process. And this game is all about acceleration, Paul. No one can afford delays when a killer is out there. No one. You made us hunt for a bear and look what we found...'

It began with a transaction made by Russell Lock in the shop at Mother Shipton's Cave for a book on the calcification process that occurs in the Petrifying Well. In this book, recovered in Russell Lock's house, there were lots of notes and words underlined.

There were also circled pictures.

One of those circled pictures had been of the stone bear that was missing.

Although the bear was still to be recovered, it was damning evidence. It'd been the bedrock of the investigation. *Why the obsession with the stone bear? Why the fascination with calcification?*

Why'd you kill your son?

Unfortunately, none of these questions were ever answered by Russell Lock, but Anders and Derek had persevered undeterred. Lock was bipolar and had a history of erratic behaviour. It soon came to light that the excessive amount of sleeping pills in his son's blood stream – enough to kill him – had been his. A witness came forward to say that he'd seen Russell and his son walking near the path that led down into Mother Shipton's on the night Graham had died.

'Did he confess?' Riddick asked.

'He confessed to hitting his son. Those bruises we found on his back. The bastard did that to his own kid.' Anders pulled his hands away and looked off in the distance in disgust. 'Enough is enough. The CPS is satisfied.'

'That's good, sir...'

Anders nodded, but he continued to stare into the distance, and Riddick remembered his earlier demeanour, as if he'd been weighed down by something.

Are you satisfied though, Anders?

'To do that to your own kid, eh?' Anders said, shaking his head. 'Your own flesh and blood.'

Is this what's weighing you down?

'What was his motive, sir?'

'Motive?' He fixed Riddick in a stare. 'Everyone always wants an explanation, don't they? And you know, those in the court will demand it. But Russell Lock was a very sick man. And when he saw the life ahead of his son as being plagued with pain and desperation, like his own, he looked for a solution. He felt duty bound to spare him the trauma that had eaten his own life.'

'He said that?'

Anders sighed. 'Not exactly... but you could see it, in his eyes. Clear as day.'

Riddick stopped himself from asking why he went to all that effort to take his son to a cave before overdosing him but stopped himself. Anders had concluded. Did he look happy with his conclusion? Not really. Was it Riddick's place to question that? Certainly not.

'And now, son. We move on. As we *always* move on.'

Riddick nodded.

Colour returned to Anders' face, and he beamed down at Riddick. 'So, let's start with this lovely wife of yours. Rachel, is it?'

'What would you like to know, sir?'

'I don't want to know anything from you!' He laughed. 'I'm sure she can tell me all about herself! Sally is cooking on Saturday, and we expect you both there at seven.'

Inside, Riddick glowed, just as he'd done that night at the Petrifying Well when Anders had clutched his shoulder and the bond had been formed.

Then, he was hit with a wave of guilt. In the space of two weeks, his life had changed radically because of a poor dead boy. Was something positive allowed to come out of something so heinous? Instinctively, he opened his mouth to refuse the invitation, but Anders got there first.

'And maybe after dinner, we can talk about your ambitions? There's a detective in there, son, and the sooner we get him out and put him to work, the better.'

7

Riddick opened his eyes to darkness. 'Bloody hell...' His temple felt as if it'd taken a blow from a sledgehammer. Had it blinded him?

He identified the cold of the wet ground on his left cheek.

Think...

He lifted his head, groaning. The pain was unbelievable. He worked his way onto his elbow. The ground wanted him back, the pull of gravity immense.

Stay awake...

Stay the hell awake...

Shapes began to form. Not blind then. Thank God.

The physical world around him reformed, while memories ploughed him.

The boy's wild eyes... the blinding headlights... the steps... the bouncing Fortnite backpack... the River Nidd... shimmering oily water lapping at the cave walls... Robert Flower...

Robert Flower?

St Robert's Cave.

He sat up, assaulted by the memory of the young lad fleeing down the steps.

He tried to take in his surroundings, but his vision was still a mess.

What the hell happened?

'Who's here?' he moaned. 'Is *someone* here with me?'

He recalled the phone and its feeble torchlight. He moved his hands over the ground, desperately trying to locate it.

Suddenly overwhelmed by the dizziness, he stopped and closed his eyes.

You need medical assistance, Paul.

The kid... where'd he go?

He took deep breaths and opened his eyes again. His surroundings were clearer this time. He looked at the cave entrance.

Are you in there? Drowning in knee-high oily water?

He tried to get to his feet. Almost made it up. But the dizziness struck him back down to his knees again. *Goddamn it!*

Behind him, he could hear the hiss of the wind over the Nidd.

The Nidd.

More water.

More danger.

He managed to swivel slowly onto his knees. As he did so, he could feel a growing sense of control over his body returning, but his mind felt lost. Memories blurred: *Graham Lock... on the ground beneath the Petrifying Well... dead centre... legs crossed... head hanging forward as the drips fell... wet hair and clothes plastered to him...*

No. Wrong time. Get a grip, Paul!

He completed his turn and his eyes fell to the boy lying face up in front of him.

No... no...

Was this now? This moment? Or another treacherous memory in his cluttered mind?

His body was weak, but Riddick demanded more. He crawled towards the kid. 'Wake up...'

The boy didn't.

Out of breath, pain raging in his forehead, nausea desperately trying to make him puke, Riddick reached the young man and looked at his bloody forehead. *You were hit too? Did you see who did this to us?*

'Wake up... please...'

Riddick hovered over his face and the reality of what he was seeing started to pummel him.

Graham Lock... young flesh... wet and grey... sad and lifeless...

'No. Stop it,' he said out loud, addressing his swamp-like brain. *This is a different time. A different place. This isn't Graham Lock!*

'I'm here to help.' He put his hand on the red puffer jacket just above the boy's chest. 'Please wake up.'

Still no response.

Riddick touched the boy's cheek.

It felt *so* cold.

Listen, Paul, you dickhead: this isn't Graham Lock! It's not that poor, dead boy. Help this one. Wake him up.

Riddick put his fingers to the boy's neck.

No pulse.

He patted the boy's chest. 'Wake up, kid. I'm telling you to *just* wake up. You're *not* him.'

He's dead, Paul. He's dead.

Riddick noticed the yellow Fortnite backpack from a swirling memory. Struggling to stay in touch with reality, he reached over and dragged it towards him.

The zip was partly open. Riddick glanced something poking free from it. He pinched something soft.

No... it can't be...

He didn't bother with the zipper, he just tugged at the sides of the bag to unzip it further.

Pinching the soft material again, he worked the object out.

His breath caught in his throat.

He held the object in front of himself by its ear.

Tell me what you noticed, son.

Riddick dropped it.

Something about a bear?

He noticed a glow beneath the dead boy's legs.

A torch.

His phone.

He worked it free and dialled the emergency services.

8

Gardner recalled her first investigation in North Yorkshire; standing behind the castle keep looking at the viaduct, striking over the Nidd, while Riddick, her new deputy at the time, pointed out the famous cave, tucked away on the left. There and then, she'd vowed to visit it one day.

Tonight, however, she was standing beside St Robert's, a neighbouring cave, and no closer to getting Mother Shipton's Cave ticked off her bucket list, but that didn't keep Knaresborough's most famous tourist attraction from her mind. When she'd arrived twenty minutes ago, Riddick had been lying in the back of an ambulance, rambling on. 'Listen to me, boss... *listen to me...* Graham Lock. He was *supposedly* killed by his father at Mother Shipton's Cave in 2003. And there was a missing teddy bear. A missing *petrified* teddy bear.' At that point, the paramedic had decided enough was enough, and taken him to the hospital.

With her back to a crime scene that now glowed courtesy of several Samalite portable area lighting units, she looked over the Nidd, which didn't seem its usual peaceful self when flowing to the soundtrack of buzzing SOCOs.

A missing petrified teddy bear.

Of all the things, Paul...

Still, it was Riddick, and his track record of finding the truth – despite some of the questionable methods by which he did so – earned him the right to be heard. So, she gave some consideration to the toy in the victim's backpack.

But, firstly, this teddy bear wasn't petrified.

Petrified, she'd been reliably informed, meant calcified by mineralised water.

Secondly, this wasn't Mother Shipton's Cave, and there was no Petrifying Well for a start. Additionally, this bear had been found in the child's backpack; whereas, the previous bear had been removed from the scene and never found at all!

So, was this other teddy bear really something to stand up and take notice of?

Riddick seemed to think so. But Riddick had taken one hell of a blow to the temple. Rational thought was going to be hard to come by.

She sighed.

There never was a dull moment with Riddick. Drama positively glued itself to him.

Someone moved beside her. 'Are you not cold, Emma?'

Marsh.

Gardner, who was standing in only her business wear and a paper-thin white suit, said, 'Yes, ma'am. Bought myself a snazzy new Jack Wolfskin last week to combat your Northern tempests too. But, when I heard about Paul, I panicked and forgot it.'

Gardner looked at Marsh, who wore a hat beneath the white hood of her over-suit. She also had on a very capable looking ski jacket. Marsh, herself, didn't entertain panic.

'Wouldn't worry. There're few tougher bastards,' Marsh said. 'And very few thicker skulls.'

'He mentioned this petrified bear.'

Marsh guffawed. 'Mentioned? Everyone's ears are bleeding, Emma. Just the rantings of a madman who has concussion.' She sighed. 'At least the concussion side of things will pass; the madman, well...'

'So, there's *definitely* nothing in this bear?' Gardner raised an eyebrow.

Marsh smiled, took a deep breath and blew out a plume of white air. 'Oh, there's plenty in that bloody petrified bear... you can be sure of that! A story with real legs that one! One of a kind. Surprised you haven't heard it.'

'No. Maybe it is relevant, ma'am.'

'Not today. Listen, it had a lot of relevance to him, yes...' Marsh eyed Gardner. 'Once upon a time. Once upon a *happier* time. I guess it makes sense he hasn't told you. It's connected to that turncoat, Anders. He probably sees it as something to forget, rather than celebrate.'

'Until tonight?'

'Until someone brained him...'

Gardner felt her frustration growing. 'This isn't making a great deal of sense, ma'am. Maybe if you just tell me the story then—'

'Emma, believe me, it'll be a waste of time. Paul has taken a knock. In twenty-four hours, he'll see things differently. Not that he'll be anywhere near this case. He was personally involved. He'd chased the boy down to the place he was murdered. He woke up beside the corpse. This has nothing to do with the Mother Shipton's Cave murder in 2003. The killer of Graham Lock, the father, Russell Lock, was arrested, and then, fortunately for the world in general, carked it in jail. It's going to take more than a teddy bear to throw his guilt into doubt and lead us to believe that the real killer has lain dormant for twenty years before coming out of retirement. As for Riddick's bloody petrified bear story, even if I wasn't sick to death of it, I still wouldn't tell it to you.'

'He's a suspect,' Gardner said, out loud, as if realising it for the first time. 'So, we'll be hearing *everything* he's got to say.'

'True, but...' Marsh looked at her very seriously. 'Your first port of call is to put that suspicion to rest. He's a madman, but he's *my* madman. I'm the only one allowed to shut him down, and life is far more interesting with him in it. Besides, Riddick harming a child... come on...'

Gardner agreed. The thought of Riddick harming a child was ludicrous to say the least.

She took a deep breath as another realisation dawned on her.

Who was to be her deputy SIO?

Ray Barnett, surely? He was the most capable senior among the rest.

'Ma'am?' A familiar voice.

Gardner and Marsh turned to watch DS Phil Rice walk towards them.

She inwardly sighed. You never knew what you were going to get with Rice. Every conversation with him either ended in complete infuriation, or a quiet acknowledgement that he was rather competent.

His white over-suit flattered him. The hood hid his premature balding, and the baggy fit hid the fact that he was overweight. 'A teddy bear at his age! Shit! My old man found me in bed with one at nine and he knocked ten tonnes of shite out of me.'

She couldn't tell if he was expressing pride over the way he was brought up, or if it was a sneering, condemnation of his dad. That was the thing with Rice. You could never really tell. He was a complicated fellow.

Gardner forced back a smile when she considered Riddick's

most likely retort. 'Ten tonnes of shite along with all your sensitivity?'

'You wanted to speak to me, Phil?' Marsh said.

'Yes, ma'am. We know who it is. Written on the label of a white sports shirt beneath his jumper. *Stephen Best. Year 11.*'

'Potentially making him fifteen or sixteen,' Marsh said. 'If it's not an old shirt, I guess.'

'If he's a kid, it's another bloody magnet for the press,' Rice said.

'A sodding speeding fine around here's a magnet for the press when we're involved... still, if he's a schoolboy, the temperature will rise, yes.' She sighed. 'Good work, Phil,' Marsh said.

Good work! Gardner stopped herself from rolling her eyes. One of the SOCOs had probably read the label on his shirt out loud – how did that constitute 'work'?

Gardner recalled Riddick's claim that Marsh and Rice must have been shagging. Why else would he be so in favour? Some of Rice's attitudes would've been dismissed as archaic even by the least forward-thinking workers in a seventies coal mine in Doncaster.

She recalled Marsh's earlier comment about Riddick being her madman. Maybe, she saw it the same way with Rice. Her bigot?

'Oh,' Rice said, looking at Gardner. 'About the petrified bear. It's bollocks.'

'I see,' Gardner said. 'I've never heard such a well-thought out, sophisticated dismissal of a lead from a witness. Thanks, Phil.'

His face reddened and he narrowed his eyes. 'It's not a lead, boss. It's bollocks.'

This stunned her – where had this new-found belligerence sprung up from? She'd have to knock that out of him.

Rice continued, 'It's a totally different kind of bear. This one is smaller. Cuter—'

'Regular bear connoisseur, aren't you?'

Gardner caught Marsh staring at her. Her eyes suggested she hear him out. An argument between three seniors wasn't a great idea. 'Go on then.'

He nodded, smiling. 'The original bear from the investigation. It was an ugly looking thing. Totally different.'

'Okay, Phil, thank you,' Gardner said, not wanting to irritate Marsh. 'Let's just see what we have here and now then first—'

'My father closed that case,' Rice said.

Gardner looked at Rice, expressing confusion.

'Phil's father was DCI Derek Rice. He led the team that caught Russell Lock.'

'I see.' Gardner looked back at Rice. 'You must be very proud of your father and his team.'

Rice nodded. 'The team, yeah. Not my father.'

She hadn't expected that.

Rice continued, 'He was a right old—'

Marsh coughed. 'Okay, Phil, enough.'

'Hated him. But he got the right man,' Rice said. 'He always got the right man.'

So, Rice was unhappy to have his family's legacy called into doubt by Riddick – someone he'd never had the time for anyway. 'Thank you, DS.'

'*DI*, ma'am,' Rice said, looking at Gardner. His frustration was quickly replaced by a ghost of a smile. 'You forget.'

She hadn't forgotten. Two weeks ago, he'd made DI. It'd been a slip of the tongue.

'You don't have much time for him, do you?' Marsh said as Rice re-joined the SOCOs.

Gardner shrugged.

'He has his uses,' Marsh said. Gardner nodded, conceding the truth in this statement. Some of his contributions to the last two cases had been excellent. 'Liability, though.'

Marsh said, 'He's cannier than he looks. He's only passing narrow-minded comments to wind people up. Not a people person, granted, but he's not as unreliable as Paul.'

'He doesn't have Paul's instincts, though.'

'Not many do.'

Where was this going?

'His father, Derek, was a bastard,' Marsh said. 'A right vicious bastard. Those who think I have my moments – well, trust me, they've no idea! When I was starting out, there were many stories about that shitbag, and I never heard a pleasant one. When his heart gave out, there weren't that many tears. When Phil talks about having ten tonnes of shit beaten out of him, he's playing it down. It was probably more like thirteen or fourteen.'

Gardner's eyes remained fixed on Marsh. *You're not shagging him, are you? You just care. Behind that harsh veneer, there's compassion. I've had you all wrong.*

'Make him feel comfortable while he's your deputy SIO, Emma.'

You absolute bitch.

'Ma'am—'

'Excuse me, Emma,' Marsh said, patting the pocket of her ski jacket through the white suit. 'My phone. It'll be the powers that be. Don't want to keep them waiting.'

'Of course, ma'am.'

She shook her head as she watched Marsh walk away, then turned and observed Rice talking to a SOCO. She sighed. This was going to be a trial.

En route to look at the body, she passed Fiona Lane, the manager of the SOCOs, getting her own hands dirty rather than simply barking orders at everyone – something Gardner respected. She was kneeling on a protective plate, casting a footprint.

Gardner greeted her and continued towards Dr Hugo Sands, the pathologist, who was down on his haunches near the victim.

He looked deep in thought. He either hadn't noticed her, or he was being deliberately oblivious.

She suspected it was the latter as Sands noticed everything.

She coughed.

'DCI Gardner,' he said, without looking up from the boy's face.

Deliberately oblivious it was then.

Of course, Gardner was uncomfortable with this, but it would probably pale into insignificance when compared to how Sands was feeling. Months ago, he'd made advances towards her. She'd agreed to go to an Ed Sheeran concert with him, only to pull out when he came around to collect her.

The reason: Paul Riddick had been drunk in her lounge.

Gardner and Sands hadn't spoken since. If not for their jobs, it would've remained that way.

Not that Sands had ever been a conversationalist. Most of his responses were monosyllabic and he seemed intent on only revealing facts. Problem was, facts often took time. Sometimes, conjecture was essential.

'Dr Sands. Any ideas?' Gardner asked, knowing immediately that it was the wrong choice of words. He'd never give her an idea.

He held his finger up but still avoided eye contact. 'One moment please. I'm thinking.'

She rolled her eyes and glanced down at the body again. Under the glare of a portable light, it looked as if it was floating in a yellow pool.

The first time she'd seen the victim, she'd taken a moment. The pain and trauma of seeing someone so young cut from the world was something you never got used to. Of course, the fact that Riddick had woken up beside this body was no small part of her shock. It'd taken some deep breaths and a quiet moment by the Nidd to recover.

Looking again now, she felt more resilient, but she was still forced to take a deep breath and steady herself. The victim was no more than a child.

How she longed for him to move. A rising chest as he breathed? A moving Adam's apple as he gulped? A smile as he thought about being home with his family?

There was a messy wound on his forehead not dissimilar to the one she'd seen on Riddick. The victim's eyes were closed, and she wondered here, as she always wondered in this instance, if the killer had closed them with their fingers – perhaps, not wanting them staring in their direction, judging them, inspiring guilt.

Up ahead at the entrance to the cave, a bright dagger of light cut through the black. A SOCO emerged and looked in Gardner's direction. The headtorch they were wearing stung her eyes. She blinked several times, and when she turned her focus back on them, she could see the SOCO shaking their head at a colleague.

A sudden, sharp wind stung her through her feeble winter gear, but it seemed to flare her into life and took her, momentarily, from this well of melancholy. 'Dr Sands, *please*, whatever you can give me.'

Sands looked up at her for the first time. He appeared irritated at having his focus interrupted, but she suspected that this was just bitterness over her rejection. She held his eyes until his stern expression melted. *This isn't about us, you ridiculous man. Do your job.*

'I'm willing to say that the head wound *could* have killed him. As yet, I cannot find any more visible injuries.'

Gardner nodded.

Sands pointed at a large rock near the boy's head. 'There's

blood on this one. He could've just slipped over and hit it. Likewise, he could've been pushed over, or...' He shrugged. 'Someone could've picked it up and used it on him. Of course, this rock could've been used on your partner too. There're many variables. We have a lot of testing to do.'

Partner! You know his name, Hugo...

But in the world according to Dr Hugo Sands, he'd crashed and burned on the final hurdle to Gardner's heart, due to Paul Riddick.

She thought about giving him the reality. That Sands had never been anywhere near Gardner's heart. That she'd been too busy with a sociopathic brother, a disintegrating marriage and a colleague well and truly off the rails to have a heart that was in any way available.

But it wasn't really the time.

At that point, exhibits officer Tony Reid came up alongside Gardner holding a plastic bag with gloved hands. The rock inside looked heavy.

'Another rock,' Tony said. 'Traces of blood.'

Gardner looked between the two rocks. One for Riddick, and one for the young boy. This was no accident. The chances of them both slipping over and banging their heads simultaneously?

Her new deputy SIO, Rice, did his best to demonstrate his belief that both subtlety and patience were a waste of time by raising his voice from over five metres away. 'Boss. I just spoke to Ray. Stephen Best was reported missing by his father over an hour ago. He's still in Year 11 and is fifteen years old.'

Everyone had stopped working to stare, leaving Gardner to inwardly sigh and wonder why the foghorn couldn't just walk five metres to tell her.

She knelt beside Stephen, ignoring Sands on the other side of him.

Everything feels messy right now, Stephen. Cluttered and messy. But I'll put things in order. I promise. For you and your family.

She fought the urge to take his hand.

* * *

Dear bear, I see them now.

Hovering over you. Poring over you. Thinking you're broken.
They can't see the smile on my face, nor hear my sighs of relief.
But if they could, would they understand?
Of course not, dear bear!
When have they ever understood?
Don't be fooled by sadness, the sympathy, their self-righteousness.
They will hunt me as if that will somehow change things. But it won't.
And they know that. Hunters hunt simply because they enjoy the chase.
But now, you're frozen, and you'll never thaw.
Look at their tears, their complaints, their cries for judgement!
Look at how they leave no bloody stone unturned.
They act as if everything is fluid.
That everything can be changed.
No, my child, they are wrong.

9

Rice knocked on Gardner's passenger window as she started her vehicle. She only wound the window down a touch, forcing him to angle his head awkwardly to speak through the gap.

'Shall we go there in the same car? Prep how we're going to approach our chat with Ron Best?'

Professional and keen. Are you trying too hard now, Phil?

'No. Meet me there. I've a personal call to make,' she lied, hitting the controls.

He opened his mouth to respond, but the window closed him off.

She drove away.

Phil Rice... Deputy bloody SIO!

Her life was always so full of bloody surprises. She scowled. Was a good one every now and again too much to ask for?

She indicated left off Abbey Road onto Wetherby Road. A late-night jogger was coming down full pelt, kitted out in full Gore-Tex, looking warmer than she ever seemed to feel in the north of England. His headlight bobbed to his gait. She waved him across.

A runner herself, she appreciated how irritating it was to stop to allow cars out, and then have to start up again.

She watched him, both envying his stress-busting run, and admiring his ability to weave around the slush piles.

She moved out onto Wetherby Road, trying to keep her mind focused on Stephen Best, and how best to break the news to his father, Ron, who would inevitably become a person of interest.

She ran through the words in her head as she always did when tasking herself with the worst moment in the job.

Her mind wandered. The pull of her fracturing personal life was too much.

It'd been a shameful situation to have to contact Barry to bring him back home from his hotel room to look after Rose and Anabelle after she'd been called to the crime scene. It was like an admission that she desperately needed him – that she couldn't handle the pressure alone. She sighed. The fact of the matter was that she probably couldn't.

Still... she'd need to work out how to. After all, change was coming.

Barry and Sandra.

Perhaps they would start a life together?

Gardner would be fine with this if Sandra didn't want to take on the responsibility of Anabelle. Avoiding a custody battle would make their split more than amicable – it would make it a relief. Still, there was the situation with Rose. Would she be allowed to continue to foster her niece if Barry left?

A wave of guilt washed over her.

What the hell are you doing, Emma? You've just left a fifteen-year-old boy who's had the life knocked out of him. Get a grip on yourself. You and Barry are done. This contemplation is dead weight.

Time to start focusing.

Her hands-free rang. She was surprised by the name on her screen.

'Paul?'

'Boss, we need to speak.'

'Yes... I know... but are you okay?'

'Fine. Painkillers. The X-ray was fine. Got lucky. Some stitches and a mild concussion. They *still* want to keep me overnight.'

Gardner felt relieved. 'So, you'll do as they say.'

'Was that a question?'

'No. If you come out of there tonight, I'll put you straight back in with a second head wound.'

'You need my statement.'

'Which we'll get from the hospital bed. I'll send Lucy and Ray.' She stopped short of telling him that she was going to see the father of the victim with her new deputy SIO – Phil Rice.

'Do you know who the boy was?'

'Nothing confirmed.'

'Who do you think it is?'

Was now the time to tell Riddick he wasn't privy to the information? That he was, and never would be, involved in this case? Surely, he knew that already? Although, who'd be thinking rationally after his experiences tonight?

However, she didn't want him winding himself up. His health was important to her. 'As soon as I know anything worth telling you, I'll call.' It was a lie.

'You need to listen to me regarding the Graham Lock case... I mean, you really need to listen to me.'

The petrified bear again.

She forced back a sigh. *Sorry, Paul, that didn't really stick. Phil said it was a completely different bear. Oh, and it wasn't petrified either. And just in case that isn't enough to settle your mind, can I also add that*

Marsh speared the suggestion like a fish and then fed on it like a ravenous hunter...

'Okay, I will.' She considered prompting him over this infamous story regarding the bear and his former DCI, Anders Smith, but decided against it. That could be a can of worms and she was only five minutes away from destroying someone's life with some terrible news. 'Did you tell me everything about what happened tonight, Paul?'

'I'm not sure... I don't remember a great deal about what I told you. Things were still very hazy at that point.'

Gardner listened to Riddick's story as she followed her satnav through a mazy batch of residential streets. The snowfall was on a break, so the roads weren't completely treacherous.

Something changed in the story. 'Hold up,' Gardner said. 'You didn't mention a vehicle when I was with you in the ambulance.'

'Are you sure? Why wouldn't I? That was why the lad ran down the steps...'

'I'm positive. You just said the lad got spooked when you approached.'

'Really? I must've been out of it. That's not what happened, boss. I did spook him, yes, but he didn't run until I was preoccupied with this car that pulled up... I think I approached it... I also think it blinded me with its headlights.'

'Think? What car was it?'

Another pause. 'Bloody hell, boss, it's weird, but I can't see it properly. I can tell it's black, but I'm struggling to get a distinguishable shape. Maybe, it was because of the beam... no, but I *shielded* my eyes... I'd have known the car. I *know* cars.'

Gardner was gripping the steering wheel tightly.

'Shit... sorry...'

'Don't be a cretin, Paul,' Gardner said, pretending not to be frustrated. 'You've taken a knock. It'll come. Don't force it.'

'I would've taken the registration. Yes, I'm positive... *yes, I did.* I made a mental note of it before chasing the boy. I *remember* making a mental note of it but I can't bloody remember it.'

Gardner took a deep breath and held it. She didn't want the sounds of her breathing interrupting him as he desperately tried to recall the number plate.

He swore angrily. 'I just can't find it! It doesn't make sense. I've never *forgotten* a plate. Not once. But it's not there!'

'It'll be the concussion, Paul. When you recover, it'll come back.'

'And if it doesn't? Then what? What if someone else gets killed and I'm sitting here with the bloody person who did it in my head?'

Gardner could hear him pacing round. He was out of his bed. Frustrated.

'Get back in your bed and speak to the doctor. It'll be temporary. Winding yourself up isn't going to help.'

She waited until he'd confirmed he was back in his bed.

'Now finish telling me what happened.'

Riddick obliged, but his voice was slow and laboured as if he was doubting himself at every word. She ached to be sitting with him, holding his hand, reassuring him that this was just part of the healing process. That he'd get his head back together again in no time.

'I don't understand how I was clocked though. I didn't hear anyone else coming down those steps after me. I mean, sure, they could've crept down, but I was swinging that torch all over the place, and I'd have noticed... I would've done. Unless, maybe, I did see the killer? Do you think they meant to kill me?'

'I don't know, Paul. If they did, though, wouldn't they have hit you again to make sure?'

Silence.

'Paul?'

'I'm lucky to be alive, aren't I?'

Seems that way. 'Let's consider the possibility that the killer was already down there, waiting for the boy.'

'No, the car up on Abbey Road. I'm adamant there was a car.'

'The killer had an accomplice? Or the car belonged to a concerned citizen wondering what was happening? You said yourself that the boy was spooked when he saw you – how might that have looked to a passer-by?'

Riddick sighed. 'Maybe, but no. I get my memory is soup right now, but it seemed to be connected. The car seemed to be the reason the boy ran. Plus, if the killer was already down there, I'd have seen him. I looked every—'

'But you didn't see the boy either?'

'No, but—'

'Because it's dark down there, and there're places to hide.'

Riddick was silent for a time as he processed Gardner's suggestions. Meanwhile, Gardner stopped her vehicle outside the home of Ron Best. She looked up at the chimney. Judging by the plumes of smoke billowing from it, Ron had quite the fire burning tonight. She looked around the street. No other smoking chimney compared. It must be toasty in there.

For now, she thought, sadly. *Soon this house will be the coldest on the road.*

'Boss, I need to tell you the story about the Graham Lock investigation.'

'And I want to hear it, but I haven't got the time right now.'

'It involved Anders Smith,' Riddick said, deliberately trying to provoke curiosity, but of course, she knew this already.

Rice's vehicle pulled up behind her. She shook her head. Last thing she wanted was him pounding on the window and calling for her while Riddick was on the phone still unaware that his job had been temporarily nabbed.

'I have to go, Paul... I'm sorry. I'll call back.'

She looked in the rear-view mirror. Rice was out of his car now.

'Emma, *listen*, please. You must let me tell you.'

'Lucy and Ray will be with you shortly; talk to them about it.'

'I will, but I'll see you in the briefing tomorrow.'

Like hell... Rice was walking alongside her car. 'See you then.'

Despite expecting it, Rice's loud knock on her window made her jump out of her skin.

Fortunately, the deluded, emotional, yet forever enigmatic DI Paul Riddick, had ended the call.

* * *

She could sense that Rice was eager. The last thing she wanted was him going in guns blazing.

'Remember,' Gardner said. 'This man contacted the police at 9 p.m. concerned about the whereabouts of his son. It's now 3 a.m. This is a concerned parent. Soon to be a bereaved parent. We respect that first and foremost.'

'Do you really think I'm a monster?' Rice said.

She looked at him. 'We've been told that Ron Best wasn't squeaky clean when he was younger. I worry about your tendency to be judgemental...'

'If he's been paying his taxes, and keeping his nose clean, he's nothing to fear from me.'

'Does he have to go to church as well?' Gardner asked.

'It helps.'

'Let me talk, Phil. If you cause any problems, this will be the shortest audition for Deputy SIO in the force's history.'

After knocking gently on the door, Gardner caught the reflection of herself in the lounge window to her left and adjusted the collar on her business suit. She took a swift glance at Phil who was on her right. 'Tuck your shirt in.'

He complied.

After knocking on the door a second time, she glanced down and reached into her suit pocket for her badge. As she was bringing it out, she looked up and caught someone watching her from around the side of the curtain in the lounge window and jumped out of her skin.

Rice, who had clearly not been taken by surprise, was pointing at the man and gesturing the front door with his thumb.

The man she assumed to be Ron Best didn't move. His eyes were wide, and his mouth hung open slightly. Most of his hair was gone apart from two thick patches above his ears.

He knows.

He'd reported his son missing. Now, there were two police officers standing at his door in the middle of the night. It wouldn't be hard to read a dire conclusion.

She nodded at him and raised her identification to the window. She tried to keep her expression neutral; a sympathetic one might send him spiralling further.

Rice was muttering behind her. 'For Christ's sake man, open the door. It's freezing.'

Gardner's identification didn't bring Ron from his stupor.

Gardner could feel herself dissolving inside as she witnessed the bereaved father's moment of realisation. She couldn't hold back on the sympathy any longer. She proffered a gentle, kind smile.

His eyes seemed to start trembling, but it was soon apparent that they were filling with tears.

A hard knock on the door made her jump out of her skin

again. She glared at Rice. 'Hush, man!'

'It's the middle of the night, boss, and freezing,' Rice said.

'I don't care,' Gardner hissed. She turned back to the window to see that Ron was gone. 'The poor man.'

'Overly dramatic. It just makes me more suspicious,' Rice said.

Gardner looked at him. 'Jesus wept, Phil. Have you ever lost someone?'

Phil looked at her, his eyes narrowed slightly. 'Of course. My father.'

Who treated you like shit? And was disliked by all? But she sensed something stir within Rice so she bit back any retort.

The door opened.

'Mr Best,' Gardner said, still holding up her identification.

Ron nodded. His cheeks glistened from the tears. He opened his mouth to speak, but his lips trembled too much. He closed his mouth again.

Gardner introduced herself and Rice. 'Please can we come in?'

Ron succeeded in speaking on this second attempt, although his words quivered as they left his mouth. 'How? How'd it happen?'

Rice exhaled audibly. 'How'd what happen, sir?'

Gardner reached out and gently gripped Rice's arm. Rice looked at her, wide eyed. Once she'd ensured he'd understood this cue to shut it, she swung back to Ron. 'Can we come in please, Mr Best?'

He nodded and then turned to lead the way.

She turned to Rice, who was still looking down at her hand gripping his lower arm. To some, his curiosity may have seemed appropriate, but on her watch, it wasn't.

Listen, you unsympathetic bastard. Go in with that cold attitude again, and you'll be a passenger. Not just in this investigation, but in every investigation I run in North Yorkshire from this day forth.

She didn't say this for fear of Ron hearing, but Rice would hear her thoughts loud and clear.

She withdrew her hand and followed Ron into his home.

* * *

Gardner hadn't needed to ask for a photograph of Stephen Best.

Ron had photographs of his only child strewn all over the coffee table.

Immediately, the father reverted to the mode he must have been in before he'd heard the fateful knock at the door – he perched on the edge of his sofa, hunched over the coffee table, and continued revering each photo, one by one. He must have been hoping – *praying* – that he'd see his son walk through the door, alive. As if the steady worship of these frozen, cold images could somehow restore the living, breathing version.

Gardner and Rice exchanged a glance.

She wondered what the cynical detective was thinking.

Was it: *So, the stage production continues unabated?*

Or was it the same as she was thinking: *The man is destroyed by the loss of his son, despite the fact that we're yet to tell him?*

Rice's doubt itself wasn't an issue. You'd be a poor investigator if you didn't waver between different options. And innocence should never be sold by a reaction alone. Many solid, yet guilty, performers over the years could be offered up as evidence to this.

The issue she had was Rice's regular displays of coldness. As if he was exempt from the responsibility of displaying emotional intelligence in this work.

Gardner and Rice sat opposite Ron Best, who was now moving around the photographs on the table as if playing a game of Patience.

The fire crackled beside Gardner. As she'd suspected earlier, the place was indeed hot. She took off her suit jacket and laid it on her legs. She went through the lines she'd rehearsed in the car. 'We've reason to believe, Mr Best, that the body of a young boy discovered only hours earlier outside St Robert's Cave—'

She was interrupted by a piece of wood splitting loudly on the fire, a burst of sparks and the sound of sap sizzling like an aggressive snake.

'—may belong to Steph—'

'My son?' Ron said, looking up, his hands suddenly frozen on the photographs.

'I'm sorry, Mr Best. There will need to be an identification, but having seen the photographs—'

'It's him.' Ron looked down and carried on moving the pictures.

Gardner and Rice looked at each other.

'Can you confirm what Stephen was wearing, Mr Best?'

'He'd his school PE kit on and a red puffer jacket. His name would be on the label.' He continued to move the photographs around. 'He also had his horrible yellow backpack with him with that computer game on it.'

'Fortnite?' Rice said.

Ron nodded.

Any doubt over his identity was quickly eroding.

'Once again, I'm so sorry, Mr Best,' Gardner said. 'When you feel up to it, we can arrange a formal identification... unless you have other family?'

'How'd it happen?' It was an obvious question. Gardner was surprised at how long it'd taken Ron to get to it.

'We don't know at this stage, I'm afraid. He seemed to have a head wound, but that'll need investigating. How'd he seem in himself, earlier?' Gardner said.

Ron shrugged, dismissing the question. He stroked one of the photos. 'Did he suffer?'

Gardner didn't know. 'I don't think so.'

'Where'd you find him?'

Gardner didn't want to divulge everything at this stage, but this was his son, and refusing to tell him would shatter any trust she was building. She considered it best to just tell him. So, she did. She felt Rice squirming in the seat beside her.

He looked up with a raised eyebrow. 'At that time? Why? My boy must've been freezing. Could it have been an accident? A fall?'

'It's possible. We'll look into everything – you have my word.'

Ron held up a photograph of himself with a middle-aged woman. They were standing behind Stephen who looked to be about ten years old. 'We've already had enough suffering in this family, you know? Lynda died of breast cancer three years ago.'

Widower... bereaved father...

'There's just me now.'

Gardner couldn't help but think of Riddick. Another wanderer in that unenviable realm of extreme loss.

'I know this is the worst possible time, Mr Best,' Gardner said, leaning forward. 'But, if we're able to ask some questions?'

Ron put down the photograph, sat up and leaned back. 'Of course. I want to talk about him. I *really* want to talk about him right now.'

Trying to hold onto him just a little longer. Just like with all these photographs. Because what comes next? Acceptance of emptiness? Yearning hollowness? Nothing?

'Could you take us through what happened with Stephen yesterday?' Gardner asked.

'Nothing unusual,' Ron said. 'Until it was, I guess. Until he didn't come home before seven. He always goes walking after dinner, but he always comes home.' He nodded. 'Television with me... reading on his own if I'm tired... homework, perhaps. When he didn't come home tonight, I knew something was wrong...' He closed his eyes and was silent for a moment.

Gardner didn't prompt him, but she could feel Rice moving about, and gritted her teeth.

'By nine or so,' Ron continued, 'I phoned the police, but they didn't seem in any hurry – I guess a fifteen-year-old boy late home by a few hours doesn't raise a great many red flags these days. However, I, I started to think the worst... he has never been late... not once...' He pressed his thumb and forefinger to his temple and squeezed his eyes closed. He took another moment, but kept his eyes closed when he eventually spoke. 'I'm no stranger to life's worst cards – so it's hard not to be continually paranoid about being dealt another one!'

Gardner smiled, nodded and reached into her pocket. 'Do you mind if I make notes?'

Ron shook his head, still pinching his forehead with his eyes closed.

'Please talk me through the day.'

She scribbled as he spoke.

Packs lunch in morning... sets off early to walk to school... returns home at four unless he has after-school chess or Warhammer club... not today... makes dinner... today, macaroni cheese... leaves to walk at six... returns before seven... not today...

'Does he ever walk with anyone?'

'Kyle.'

'Surname?'

'Alexander. His best friend. Both of them love Warhammer. But I know he didn't walk with him today as Kyle's laid up with flu. I saw Luke, his old man, on a market stand today in the town square. Selling his fresh chutneys. He chucked me one for free.'

'Okay, that helps,' Gardner said. 'Other friends?'

'If there is, I don't know any of them. It's just Kyle, really. Kyle this... Kyle that... Thick as bloody thieves.'

Gardner circled Kyle Alexander.

'Did Stephen tell you where he was walking tonight?' Gardner asked.

'No. Like I said, he never does. He just sees where it takes him. Like his mother. She always liked a bloody ramble. They used to get on at me for spending too much time on the sofa. But rest is as important as exercise in my opinion.' He looked up and smiled briefly. It quickly fell away.

Gardner glanced at the fire; the flame was dying, although this room was in no danger of growing cold any time soon.

She'd so many more questions she'd like to get through, but she was mindful of his needs, and would have to prioritise. He needed a short period to process. The family liaison officer would be through that door as soon as she and Rice exited – as long as Ron consented. If he had a good FLO, the process of acceptance could start then.

'Had Stephen been worried about anything recently?' Gardner continued.

Ron thought about it. 'Stephen was a worrier. He also got that from his mother. The pair of 'em would worry about anything.'

'But is there anything that sticks out this last week... anything in particular?'

'He had some mock exams he moaned about. He *always* worried about the quality of his Warhammer paintings. He even got wound up over the bloody gas prices!'

Gardner paused making notes and raised an eyebrow. *A fifteen-year-old?*

'It was kind of my fault, that one. I'd been ranting about them. He also got onto me about my drinking.'

Rice questioned this. It was the first time he'd been brave enough to speak, so Gardner allowed him. It was a fair question, and he didn't push aggressively.

'He thinks I drink too much beer.' He patted his stomach. 'But as I kept telling him, there's no weight on me and my blood pressure's fine.'

Gardner persevered, but after another sequence of questions, she remained frustrated in her search for anomalies or shifts in Stephen's life circumstances.

Still, she began to build up important details. There were the regular visits to the Warhammer shop in Harrogate; tournaments he attended for chess; and the fact that he sometimes did odd jobs for Kyle's father, Luke Alexander, delivering jars of chutney around town on a Saturday.

She saw that Rice was making notes and was glad of it. She'd often had to hound Riddick to get his notebook out of his pocket.

'Such a clever bloody lad,' Ron said. 'All I ever wanted for Stephen was to avoid the mistakes I made. I'm sure you both know I used to steal cars and sell them. I mean, every pillock who's interviewed me for a job since my prison sentence certainly did! But Lynda saved me. If I hadn't have met her I'd never have pulled my socks up. Spent most of the last twenty years as a manual labourer. Sometimes the money can be good, other times not. If it wasn't for Lynda's money before, and after, she passed... we wouldn't be in this house. Bloody hell, we wouldn't even be in Knaresborough! But we are. And I'm happy about that because it's safe and he stays out of bother. And every time I think about how lucky I am to have got my son into a safe life, I come down hard on him. Sounds ridiculous, eh? But I do it because I want him to enjoy everything I never had... including going for an interview without having to look at that sodding expression on a pillock's face.' He leaned forward and picked up the same photograph of his wife and child again, and shook it in front of him. 'And now this. Can you believe it? This happens.'

'Mr Best,' Gardner said. 'Stephen had a teddy bear in his rucksack. Does this mean anything to you?'

At first, Ron looked bewildered, but then his eyes widened slightly as something dawned on him. 'He had a bear we gave him as a child. Used to sleep with it until he was seven or eight.'

'And where's that bear?'

'Well, when Lynda was sick... near the end this was... Stephen dug it out from his old things and put it in bed with her. She kept it until... you know... the end. After that, well I don't know? Maybe he took it back, but I never saw it.'

Gardner made notes.

The fire had died away to a glowing mass of embers. They were moving towards the part of the interview that Gardner knew would sting. The part that would have Rice's heart fluttering in his chest no doubt. 'Ron, could you talk me through what you did yesterday please?'

He flinched at the request, but if he was angry about being a person of interest, he kept it out of his tone of voice. 'I'm out stacking shelves at six thirty at Lidl, before Stephen even gets up. He gets himself ready. The next time I saw him was at five. I warmed us up two pizzas. Both vegetarian. He doesn't like meat – he doesn't like me eating it either. Don't mind a few sacrifices. As long as he understands the beer stays. I'm not budging on that. I'm not an alcoholic or anything, but I need a couple of beers on an evening...' He nodded over at Rice. 'You know how it is.'

Rice nodded.

Just because I'm female, doesn't mean I don't like a few beers on an evening, Gardner thought, trying to fend off any irritation.

'Then, he went walking.' He picked up a picture and stared at it. 'Like he always does. Back for seven. Except... except...'

Not tonight, Gardner thought, feeling her heart sink. *Or ever again for that matter.*

'And what were you doing, Mr Best?' Rice prompted.

'I'm a creature of habit.' He nodded over at the sofa Gardner and Rice were on. 'I nap on there until Stephen comes back and wakes me. As I said, that's usually seven. Tonight, I woke up at past eight, and then I phoned his mobile until I was blue in the face, but his phone was off.'

Gardner made a note. She would be able to check those calls.

'Apart from going out my mind, and calling you up, there's not really much else I can give you.'

'What time did you call emergency services?'

'Nine-ish.'

He died around midnight if Riddick's narrative was accurate.

'I was told someone would be in touch. I left the phone next to me, had a few drinks, as you do when out of your mind with worry, and, well...' He looked away in shame. 'I fell asleep again and didn't wake up until just before you arrived.'

Gardner knew that the heat would build on him over the next few days, because without an alibi, or another traceable phone call to put him in his home at the time of the murder, he'd be fair game.

'Why'd no one phone me back?'

Because your son is fifteen, and had only gone walkabout for a few hours. You would've been low on someone's priority list. 'I don't know. I'll find out,' Gardner said.

Eventually, Gardner asked if they could have a look in Stephen's bedroom. Ron showed them upstairs, and both officers extracted latex gloves from their pockets and fitted them over their hands.

Having seen the state of many a teenager's bedroom during her years of investigations, Gardner was impressed with Stephen's. His bed was made, and all the shelves were organised and uncluttered.

She noticed a row of trophies that suggested he'd a talent for chess. Above his bed was a poster of a battlefield from Warhammer 40,000.

Forensics would take a much closer look, but Gardner worked through a checklist in her head comprised of hidey holes that had yielded success in cases gone by.

She checked beneath his mattress, and beneath his bed. Not even a dust bunny.

She pulled out the drawers from the chest of drawers and looked behind them. Nothing. She hopped up on a chair and ran her hand over the top of the wardrobe, dirtying her hand.

After recalling the yellow Fortnite bag, she scanned the room for any more backpacks, but came up short yet again.

'The most organised kid in the history of kids,' Rice said.

'Yes,' Gardner said. 'It happens, I guess. But it does make you wonder. Everyone hides something... somewhere. And when something's *this* immaculate, it screams *disguise* at you.'

She went over to his desktop and moved the mouse. The monitor's screen flared up. Stephen had three messages in Outlook. All from the Warhammer mailing list. Nothing personal. She tried the other folders: draft, sent and deleted.

All empty.

'Now that's organised. Do you delete your already deleted mail before it's run its course?'

Rice shrugged. 'I did it once because I got a warning that I'd bashed through all my email space, but not as a habit, no.'

All word documents were school homework documents.

She had a quick look through his favourites and history on the internet and, apart from Warhammer, chess and some sites on Nazi Germany, which connected with some recent essays he'd written for history, Gardner was coming up with blanks.

As tidy in the digital world as in the real one...

Who are you, Stephen?

Downstairs, Gardner asked Ron, 'Did you tidy his room?'

Ron shook his head. 'Why would I tidy a fifteen-year-old boy's room? Also, have you seen it? It's always that way! I often try to get him to do the rest of the house.'

'We obviously have Stephen's mobile phone. Do you know if there's another?' Gardner asked.

Ron creased his brow. 'Why would he need two?'

Gardner nodded. 'How about a journal?'

'A diary?'

'Yes.'

He shook his head. 'Not that I know of.'

'How close would you say you are?' Gardner asked.

Ron had sailed through the questions relating to his whereabouts, but this one had him stony-faced and silent.

She felt a wave of guilt but waited for an answer, which came in the form of a grunt. 'He's my son.'

'So, your relationship was fine?' Gardner pressed. 'No recent arguments?'

'A few disagreements. I harp on at him sometimes. But like I said, I want the best for him. Is that not what fathers should be like?' He looked at Rice.

Rice didn't have children, which probably explained why his next question was delivered with no subtlety. 'Harp on about what?'

Ron looked indignant. 'Like I said before, I want him to stay away from trouble, you know? I don't want him going down any roads I went down.' He looked away as he said this. He looked very heavy all of a sudden. He backed up against the wall to steady himself.

'Are you all right, Mr Best?'

'Yeah, I think so... I need to sit.' He staggered back into the lounge.

Gardner located his kitchen, and a glass, and poured him a glass of water. Back in the lounge, she found him with his head in his hands. 'The family liaison officer will be with you soon.' She placed the glass on the table beside the photographs. 'There's some water here.'

'Thank you,' he said, from behind his hands.

'I'll be in touch as soon as I know something,' Gardner said. *Or I need to speak to you again.* As Gardner headed to the front door, she turned back. 'Oh, one more thing.'

'Yes.'

'Did Stephen say anything to you when he left?'

Ron looked up from his hands. 'Yes... he asked me if I still missed his mother.'

'Why do you think he asked that?'

Ron wiped his eyes with the back of his hand. 'I don't know. He's brought her up a few times recently. I didn't mind. It's healthy really, isn't it?' He paused to consider it.

'And what'd you say?'

'I said yes, of course,' Ron said. 'I loved her and I love him. Both of them. More than anything else in the world.'

Gardner smiled and turned, willing herself not to choke up.

* * *

Gardner scheduled the briefing for 8 a.m. and, after toying with the idea of heading to HQ now at five in the morning, she played it safe instead and drove home, knowing that by the afternoon, she'd be grateful of this decision to catch a few hours.

At home, she poked her head around Anabelle's door, and then Rose's. Both sound asleep, oblivious to the world's trials.

'Never be in a rush to grow up,' she often told her daughter. *And never be a copper*, she'd add in her head. She'd wait until Anabelle was much older before vocalising this – the reasons why were just too much for a young mind.

Her bedroom door was open, so she assumed the adulterer had opted for the spare room for once. She was glad there was no sign of Barry. Their next conversation was going to be awkward, and it could happily sit on the backburner.

She kicked off her shoes and threw herself fully clothed onto the bed. After slipping her phone from her suit pocket and chucking it on the bedside table, she closed her eyes.

She tried her best to keep her mind still, but the image of Stephen's pale face and his father's broken, tearful expression at the lounge window tugged at her.

I loved her and I love him.

She wondered how long it would take Ron to accept that Stephen was gone too.

Her mind shifted back and forth between the events of the day, both in her professional and personal life, before sleep finally came to her aid.

Then, she dreamed, unpredictably, about the night she'd slept beside Riddick on the sofa.

She woke, barely an hour later, and felt a sudden bolt of disappointment that Riddick was not actually there beside her.

She grabbed her phone off the bedside table and set to work researching Graham Lock's murder at Mother Shipton's Cave in 2003.

10

Gardner's New Year's resolution had been to knock Costa Coffee on the head. The battlelines had been drawn, and she'd been winning for most of the month. The war with her willpower had been bloody. She'd been throwing back even more tic tacs than usual, and that was saying something.

Last night's experience had breached her defences. She picked up a Massimo latte with a caramel shot and relished the spike in her focus as she marched into Incident Room 2.

'How do, boss?' DC Lucy O'Brien put another cup of coffee down on the desk in front of her.

'Better now! Lucy, you're a gem.' This was particularly nice of Lucy for two reasons. Firstly, she must have been knackered after pulling an all-nighter with DS John Ross to get the incident room ready and gather all the necessary facts together for the operation's launch. Secondly, during the summer, Gardner had asked Lucy to mind Rose. Unfortunately, Gardner's sociopathic brother, Jack, had decided he wanted to see Rose, leaving Lucy badly injured in the process. Roles-reversed, Gardner hoped she would have been as forgiving as Lucy.

Realising she was going to smell like the inside of a coffee machine after this second drink, Gardner patted her suit pocket.

She was reassured to feel the tic-tac container.

Then she put her hand up, ten pairs of eyes turned in her direction and silence fell. Most of those eyes were surrounded by the lines of middle-age and poked out of male heads, so to have their attention was a rather impressive feat. It'd been hard fought for.

'Okay, I know you lot get cranky on little sleep,' Gardner said. 'So, the canteen has pie and peas in for lunch.'

There were a few nods of approval.

'No need to thank me all at once.'

She paused, waited and then cupped her hand to her ear.

'Thank you, boss,' everyone said in chorus.

'Don't bother saving me one,' Gardner said. 'I value my stomach lining.'

'What's the southerner going for?' John called out.

'Stargazy pie,' Gardner said with a raised eyebrow.

'Is that the one with fish heads poking out of it?' John said. 'Jesus.'

'Too complex for a Yorkshire palate,' Gardner said with a wink. 'Anyway, back to the matter at hand... I'm sure he's already let you know, but Phil will second on this investigation.'

Rice was usually slumped in his chair, but today he was sitting up straighter than she'd ever seen him. It was rather disconcerting, but she couldn't exactly bollock him for being positive when she'd spent the best part of the previous investigations challenging him over a poor attitude.

She turned to the board and read out the randomly generated operation name.

'Operation Lost Light.'

Her eyes fell to the picture of Stephen Best. He'd had no social media profile, so it was a copy of a recent school photograph.

Lost Light.

Too much of it.

She wondered how Stephen had dealt with losing his mother at twelve. Had he coped?

She turned, half-expecting to see Riddick sitting just before her, arms crossed, looking up with quiet eagerness on his face. Her heart fell.

She glanced over at her HOLMES 2 operative, Matthew Blanks, to check he was ready. She did a double take when she saw that he'd cut his hair. He even looked like he'd dry-cleaned and pressed his suit, or potentially purchased a new one. 'Ready, Matthew?'

He nodded, and Gardner recognised something in him she'd never seen before because of his mountain of hair. Presence. Strong, sharp cheekbones, and a focused, determined expression.

'Stephen Best was fifteen. A good lad by all accounts. No records, and an initial glowing comment from his headteacher, who was contacted by Lucy early doors. Thanks again, Lucy. The father, Ron Best, is beside himself, but he accepted the FLO.' She briefly went over her discussion with Ron, highlighting the fact that he claimed to have applied pressure to his son to stay out of trouble. 'Stephen also seemed preoccupied by the loss of his mother to breast cancer three years previous. His final words to his father were to ask if he still missed her.'

'Chess club and Warhammer. He's not a delinquent,' Rice said, turning his head to address his colleagues. 'We won't be trawling through the local gangs on this one.'

'I remember the panic in the eighties over Dungeons and Dragons,' Ian Riley, one of Gardner's oldest detectives, added. 'Getting the kids into devil worshipping and the like.'

'Wasn't that American bullshit?' Rice asked.

Riley shrugged. 'Just saying. Cults and all that. Might be worth considering.'

Rice turned and looked at Gardner, rolling his eyes. Fortunately, he kept his mouth shut. If he wasn't second on this, he might've been a lot more vocal with his opinion.

Gardner coughed. 'Thanks Ian. Like I said before, Ron has been very receptive to the FLO Lyndsey Mort, so we will be taking regular updates from her. To be honest, I detected little else but adoration in the father, but we all must appreciate that the time of death is eleven onwards, and he claims to have been asleep—'

'So, he's not out of the woods yet,' Rice said.

Gardner didn't appreciate Rice's interruption, but she nodded anyway.

Barnett's hand went up. 'Murder or accident? Which way we leaning?'

'We're not leaning yet,' Gardner said. 'Hopefully, Dr Sands will be more forthcoming with his findings this morning.'

Gardner pointed at the picture of Stephen Best. His smile looked awkward and was clearly one he'd been instructed to perform for the photograph.

Below it, was written: St Robert's Cave. Phoned in by DI Paul Riddick. 11.23 a.m.

She read this out.

'Do we need a picture of DI Riddick up there, ma'am?' Rice asked.

Gardner glared at him. She wanted to say something but was too angry over his question, which had been loaded and spiteful regardless of what he'd argue.

His face reddened.

'We know what he looks like,' O'Brien said.

Gardner nodded, glad at O'Brien's quick attempt to defuse the situation. 'Lucy, could you talk us over Paul's version of events please?'

Rice said, 'I don't mind.' He held up his notes, emphasising that it was his job.

Gardner was too incensed with him to even respond. She stared at Lucy, trying to appear professional. 'Lucy and Ray, thank you for going to the hospital to interview him. I appreciate that it must've been awkward.'

O'Brien informed the team about the details of the discovery of Stephen's body, including the mysterious car which Riddick was struggling to recall in detail.

'We're looking into this,' O'Brien said, who glanced at Barnett, nodding beside her. 'We're working through a list of vehicles that continued along the Waterside, but so far we've drawn a blank. The other option is that the vehicle turned and headed back down Abbey Road onto Wetherby Road – the direction Paul walked from. The nearest ANPR is up by St John's retail park, but there're a lot of cars passing there and it's an exhaustive list. If the driver went left up Wetherby Road, it gets even more difficult, especially if they went into the residential area around Aspin, because CCTV is scarce. Still, with our specific time frame, and CCTV dotted about, we have a strong reason to pursue the angle. As soon as the briefing is finished, ma'am, we will carry on trying to triangulate, and start knocking on any relevant doors.'

'Thanks Lucy... and Ray.'

Rice was looking up at Gardner. She was still sore with him, but he needed his turn in the spotlight. If he didn't, he'd march straight in to see Marsh, and make a frosty cold situation frostier.

She nodded at him.

He cleared his throat. 'DI Paul Riddick *claims* to have seen no one when he first followed Stephen down there. He was operating with an iPhone torch so his claim seems valid, and there're rocks and undergrowth in which someone could skulk in the shadows.'

Gardner nodded. So far, so good. Not accusatory...

'Despite his memory loss regarding the car, Paul is adamant that he was struck and his head wound was not the result of a fall. The obvious assumption is that Stephen's killer struck Paul; however, that raises questions. Like why not finish him off?'

Gardner flinched over the choice of words.

'And if it was the killer, how'd he ambush Paul? He must've already been down there. Hiding in those shadows and undergrowth. I guess whoever was in that vehicle could've followed him down, but wouldn't Riddick have noticed?'

'It's possible he didn't,' Gardner interjected. 'It was dark.' Although, she did concede it was strange – Riddick would've been swinging that torch all over the place.

'It seems plausible to me that Stephen was going down to meet the person who killed him?' Ross asked.

'Nothing is off the table,' Gardner said. 'Phil and I will start working through everyone that Stephen associated with straight after this briefing.'

'I have another question,' Barnett said. 'If the killer was already down there, and Stephen had run down *before* Paul arrived on the scene, then where was Stephen at that point? Paul didn't see a body before he was struck?'

'No, he didn't,' Gardner said. 'So, we work on the idea that Stephen was hunkered down, hiding, fearing for his life *or* he'd already been struck and killed out of sight. And it was only after Riddick had been knocked unconscious that the body was displayed.' Gardner looked around. Everyone was nodding. Deep in thought. Good. There were so many angles to consider – she wanted no stone unturned.

'Forensics will hopefully start to make the picture clearer,'

Gardner said. 'Dragging? Footprints? The scene has been well processed – we should start to hear back soon.'

Matthew Blanks tapped away. She looked over at him, taken aback again not to see his black hair waving back and forth as if he was headbanging to distorted electric guitar. She turned back to her crowd.

'Assignments are at the front. An important one is to find out what the bloody hell Stephen was up to last night. What took him to St Robert's Cave? His best friend, Kyle Alexander, although laid up with flu, might be able to shed some light on that. I know we've spoken to the headteacher, but we also need to get into the school.

'Look, I accept it may turn out to be an accident, but I don't want anyone being too focused on that conclusion yet. I want us driving forward assuming someone took this boy's life. We're not taking any risks and we all know the importance of the first forty-eight hours. If someone killed Stephen, there's motive. I accept he may not be a delinquent, but there's more to any boy than chess trophies and Warhammer. And we all know, from past experience, that those children who fall below the radar often make the easiest targets for more insidious folk. We have his mobile and we're acquiring call logs. Social media appears a no-go, but we're not ruling it out. I remember more than one investigation where victims had more than one identity online. We will reconvene at six, unless something crops up; in that case, you'll all be notified.'

She drank back the cold cup of coffee that Lucy had placed in front of her earlier.

Disgusting. Not a patch on Costa.

It was at this moment that she realised how hard her New Year's resolution was going to be to keep.

She took out the tic-tac container from her suit pocket.

One left.

Shit.

* * *

Riddick was sitting in Gardner's office behind her desk.

'Shit,' she said, closing the door behind her.

Riddick snorted. 'Quite the welcome, boss.'

'Where do I start?' Gardner said and pointed to the large blood-stained dressing on his forehead. 'To begin with, *that* needs changing.'

'They were planning on doing it sometime this morning.'

'So, why'd you leave before they got to it?'

'Because I spoke to Ray, and he told me about the briefing. He obviously didn't realise that I hadn't received my invite.'

Annoyed, Gardner stepped towards her desk and thrust her finger down on it. 'Park it, Paul. You know how it is.'

'Rice as my replacement?'

Shit. The real reason he's pissed off.

'It's not my choice.'

Riddick snorted. 'Told you they were shagging.'

'I don't think they are. I think she feels sorry for him.'

'Hmm... well, she's getting soft then. You didn't think to challenge it?'

'Like I can.'

'Doesn't sound like you...' Riddick said with a raised eyebrow. 'You don't think making him deputy SIO is taking the right royal piss? Unless you're warming to him?'

Gardner sighed and looked away. She really didn't want to get into this now. She took a deep breath and looked back. 'Aren't you concussed?'

'Feeling better.'

'So, you *drove* here?'

'Taxi.'

'Good.' Gardner raised an eyebrow. 'Paul, you need to go. You're not being fair.'

'It's me who's supposed to be pissed off here, not you!'

Gardner crossed her arms and sighed. Silence descended on the room. She'd nothing more to say. Hopefully, he'd used the thinking time to see sense. Eventually, he smiled. 'You always have this way of making it about you.'

'That better be your attempt at humour, dickhead.'

'I need to work on it if it is – you didn't laugh.'

'I want an apology.'

'Sorry, okay? I know your prime suspect can't be deputy SIO, but Rice, Jesus, can't you see how that could hurt?'

'Yes... now, again, piss off! Everyone thinks you're in the hospital. And you're not the prime suspect, or you wouldn't have got out of the hospital unnoticed.'

Riddick held up his hands. 'Okay, I'll just take a quiet back seat, and when you need—'

'No, Paul,' Gardner said, shaking her head. 'No, no, no.'

'Are you going to let me finish?'

'No.'

Riddick folded his arms. 'Well, I am. When you need to speak about Graham Lock, I'll be available.'

'I read about it online earlier.'

'And?'

'It's been twenty years and there're a lot of differences there. I'm sorry, Paul, but it feels like a distraction.'

'How many people get killed in caves around Knaresborough?'

'Be that as it may, Paul, it looked like an open and shut case. The father did it. And now the father's dead. Well done on the petrified bear by the way. It seems your superiors at the time wanted you to take credit for that—'

'Superior. One. Singular. Anders. No one else could give two hoots about my ego! Do you know who the SIO was on that case?'

'Rice's daddy, yeah.' Gardner shook her head incredulously. 'He doesn't get the best write up.'

Riddick shrugged. 'In fairness, Derek Rice had little to do with me. Think he saw me as an irritating little ant that he didn't even have the motivation to squash.'

'Sounds like he saw most people that way.'

'Anyway, you've only read about the version of the case that sells newspapers.'

Gardner shook her head. 'Paul, I'm sorry. Two different caves. Two different types of bears. One of which wasn't petrified and wasn't taken by the killer. The boy carried the bear around because his mum gave it to him, and his mum died of cancer. There's nothing in this. I assure you. It's possible that this lad wasn't even murdered. I think the trauma of being hit has made you connect the two moments together. Fused them in your head. This is exactly why you should get some rest.'

Riddick's entire expression froze, and the colour drained from his face.

Shit, Gardner thought, *here we go.*

'That's it then?' Riddick said. His voice had dropped in volume. It was a quiet rage, unless this was the calm before the storm.

'I looked, Paul. I listened. I think we can put this case to bed very quickly if we don't get distracted.'

Riddick nodded and looked away. He kept on nodding. He was a bubbling kettle. 'So, my suggestions mean shit.'

Well, technically, yes... You're not on the case after all. She held back on the rationale.

'Did you give it any thought, eh?'

'Actually, I did Paul. For you, I did. Hours of it. But there's a twenty-year gap between deaths, and few similarities – I can't make it a focus in the briefing.'

He was taking deep breaths. Credit to him, he was trying to hold back. Eventually, he seemed to reach a compromise in his own head. 'Okay, okay, just one thing then...'

'What Paul?'

'The police report – at least read the police report from the Graham Lock case.'

'I'll see what I can do.'

'You're lying.'

'No, I'm not,' she lied.

'You need to, boss. Something really doesn't add up here.'

'Like what? Be specific.'

'Anders wasn't happy at the time. The outcome just didn't sit right with him.'

'Did he say that?'

'Not as such... no... I could just tell.'

'Could you? How? Hadn't you only just met?'

'We always had a connection. I sensed it...'

'Okay,' Gardner said. 'Here's my deal; you go back to the hospital, apologise for walking away and have your bandage changed. Then, you go home, hit the sofa and watch *Homes Under the Hammer*. If you do those things, then, I'll look. But only then.'

Riddick rose from his chair. 'Thanks, boss.'

Don't thank me, yet. I'm only reading these reports if I get a spare minute, and that is unlikely.

'Please don't get in touch until we get in touch, Paul.'

'It won't be long before Rice slips me in those crosshairs. Unless he has already?' Riddick said.

'Don't be paranoid. We have your DNA... are we going to find a motive?'

'No!' Riddick said. 'I didn't know the kid. You still haven't told me his name.'

And I'm not going to. 'Then you'll be exonerated in due course – rest easy.'

As Riddick drew level with Gardner on the other side of the desk, he said, 'I can't remember the last time I rested easy.'

Gardner nodded at him. She was close enough to see now how truly bloodshot and tired his eyes were. 'Remember your side of the bargain, Paul. I'm not asking.'

'You're telling me?' he said with a grin.

She leaned in, so their faces were close. 'Would there be any point? You struggle with orders. No, Paul, I'm *begging* you.'

Riddick scrunched his brow, flinched as if something had offended him and then jolted away.

However, he turned back to smile at her as he was exiting. 'Run out of tic tacs, boss?'

'Piss off,' she said.

After he'd left, she held her palm in front of her face, checked her breath and winced over the smell of stale coffee.

11

Milo went to knock, but the door swung open before his knuckles made contact. Pete stood there with the Slazenger holdall that they'd dragged out of a bin full of dog shit.

'Smell that,' Pete said, thrusting the bag under Milo's nose.

The thought repulsed him, so he held his breath instead. 'Can't smell anything.'

'Precisely. Scrubbed it down.' Pete stepped out. The daylight revealed a fresh black eye.

A deep male voice shouted profanities at Pete from inside the house.

Pete ignored him and closed the door. Then, he gave Milo a squeeze on the shoulder. 'You good, kid?'

Milo nodded.

As they walked the garden path, Pete turned and stuck his middle finger up at his house. 'Laters, bellend.'

Milo regarded his friend out of the corner of his eye, wondering whether he should ask him if he was all right. He opted against it.

Pete pointed at Milo's backpack. 'You got *Birds of Prey* comics?'

Milo nodded.

Pete patted Milo's stomach. 'My man.'

Milo smiled, but he couldn't keep his attention off Pete's black eye – it looked painful. It seemed to be bothering him more than it bothered Pete and he continued to hold back on questioning him over it.

They headed in the direction of the main road.

'You know, it's okay to be nervous, kid... Everyone gets nervous on the first run.'

'I'm okay,' Milo lied. 'I'm quite excited.'

'Ha,' Pete said. 'Knew you had it in you! Me and you belong in Gotham City, know what I mean?'

They turned the corner onto the main road. Pete continued, 'I like that you're getting to use your dough on your mam too. Family first. I envy that.'

Milo nodded.

'I did consider spending my money on my old man. Rat poison is on sale... But nah. He ain't even worth that. My dough goes on me and you. I'm thinking, women. You game? My shout.'

Women? With him?

It sounded ridiculous, and highly unlikely, but it filled his stomach with butterflies regardless.

When they arrived at the train station, Milo watched Pete head off to pay at the machine. He noticed a swagger in his step that hadn't been there last night. He'd also seemed chattier than usual – which was saying something! It all seemed strange considering the injury.

Pete came back over and shoved tickets into his hand. 'I got time... just taking a piss.'

It was then that Milo saw past the black eye and noticed Pete's eyes looked different somehow. The pupils, in particular, looked dilated.

Milo watched Pete sprinting to the station toilet door, gripping the holdall as if his life depended on it. Which, Milo guessed, it did.

When Pete returned, he had white powder on his nose.

Milo felt his heart sink. Surely, he wouldn't? KG had warned them to not even look in the bag – so to actually use what was in there seemed suicidal.

Milo considered asking, but, as usual, his considerations led him to silence.

'You all right, kid?' Pete said, sniffing and wiping off the remaining white powder.

'Yes...' He looked away from Pete.

Pete must have detected his suspicion because he nodded down at the bag. 'I wouldn't...' He patted his pocket. 'Don't worry, I have my own supply.'

Milo felt relieved.

'Like to get myself charged up for these drops, you know? You want a sniff?'

Milo shook his head. 'I'm good.'

'Are you still pissed off with me?'

Pissed off? Why would he think that? He shook his head.

'For going for your mate last night, outside the Co-op.' He grinned.

'He's not my mate,' Milo said, confused.

Pete punched him gently on the arm. 'Just messin' with you. I know he ain't. But you didn't like it, did you?'

Milo shook his head. 'He looked... I don't know... desperate? I just thought it best to leave him alone.'

'Me and you are *so* different, eh kid?' Pete said.

Milo felt his face redden. 'He looked in trouble,' Milo protested. 'That's all. I just didn't want you to get into trouble too.'

'Hey, kid, don't sweat it. I like that we're different. It solves nothing lashing out. I was in the wrong last night. I like your control.'

Milo could see the train rumbling along the tracks in their direction, but Pete didn't turn to look – he kept his dilated eyes firmly on Milo. 'That boy was sad; I see it now. I'm so glad you were there to hold me back. You're the sidekick that keeps the reckless hero in check.'

The train pulled up.

Milo felt Pete's arm around his shoulder. 'I think you're the best mate I've ever had, Milo.'

Pete turned Milo towards the train, and they boarded together once the doors had opened.

Best mate.

Milo felt on top of the world.

12

After having his bandage changed, Riddick was subjected to another impromptu police interview. The frustration of not being able to remember the make of the vehicle was irritating him, but the interviewing officers' obvious confusion over this drove him completely nuts. 'Why would I bother telling you about the vehicle if I was lying?'

Later, during the taxi ride to his house, Riddick considered his promise to sit on the sofa and watch *Homes Under the Hammer*. But he was far too frustrated and irritable for that nonsense. Acknowledging that Gardner probably wouldn't keep her own promise to read over the old case files on Graham Lock from 2003 anyway, he instructed the driver to change direction with a clear conscience.

If nobody else considered the Graham Lock investigation relevant, then it would just have to be down to him.

And where better to get the truth than right from the horse's mouth?

He made the necessary calls to organise the visit to his former mentor.

* * *

Putting criminals behind bars often gave those in law enforcement a sense of closure.

The dickheads are in the bin! Let's get to the bar. Whose round is it, anyway?

As the prison guard led him towards the visitor's room, Riddick felt envious of those lucky colleagues.

For him, closure had always been so elusive.

Regarding Ronnie Haller, he'd tried paying for closure. Not just with money, but with his morality too. It hadn't worked. If anything, he felt more tormented than ever.

The guard opened the door for Riddick and nodded him into a small room. Into more torment.

On the other side of the solitary table was the seed from which the roots of his career had flourished.

Anders Smith.

It hadn't even been a year since he'd seen him, but he looked different somehow.

It wasn't his face; Anders had been wearing that sad expression the day that Riddick had arrested him, and the day he'd looked over at him in court. And just like those last times, Riddick had no idea if it was real, or just more of the old man's manipulative bullshit.

Neither was it his physical presence; Anders remained tall and imposing, despite the stoop in his back that had worsened over the previous couple of years, and had forced him into using a cane, although that was nowhere to be seen right now.

Riddick stood there, regarding him, trying to figure out what it was, and then it hit him – it wasn't so much a difference in appearance, but rather the *absence* of what had always made Anders who he was.

A striking and commanding aura. An encouraging and reassuring essence.

Anders was yet to speak a word, but Paul could tell from the cold empty feel of the room that the man's warm and confident control was gone.

But why was Riddick surprised?

He'd taken down the king.

He'd broken the unbreakable.

Power was fragile, and Riddick had proven that.

'You came, son,' Anders said, and smiled, but it did little to shift the sadness from his face. 'You *came.*'

Riddick felt a tightening in his stomach, and an immediate sense of regret. He looked at the guard and nodded.

The guard left them alone. Riddick's rank had allowed him privacy, and Anders had been a model prisoner to date, and was not considered high risk.

Riddick looked back at Anders. There were too many emotions running through him now to accurately identify a single one. Yes, there was clearly anger, but there was most certainly some sympathy, as well as that sense of awe he'd always felt in his presence, but what caused Riddick the most discomfort was the sense of longing he still felt for this man.

'It's okay, son... I understand—'

Riddick rose a finger but didn't use it to point. 'Don't, Anders. Just don't. Call me son again, and I...' He paused, wondering what to threaten. He wouldn't walk away – he'd come to see him for a reason. A very important reason.

'I won't, Paul. If that's what you want... then I promise that I won't.'

Riddick was relieved; his mind was racing too hard for him to think up a decent threat.

'What happened to your head?' Anders asked. His expression was sympathetic.

Don't pretend to care. 'I don't have long, Anders.' A lie. He could have as long as he wanted. But in some ways, it was the truth, wasn't it? How long could he really cope being in a room with the man who'd betrayed him?

'Did you get my letters then?' Anders asked.

'Yes,' Riddick said. *Twenty of them. But I never opened a single one.* 'That's not why I'm here.'

Anders nodded. 'I'm glad you've got them though. You can read them in your own time. Please sit down, son. Sorry...' He held up the palms of his hands. 'Force of habit.'

Anders looked frailer than he'd looked in the courtroom at the back end of last year.

Riddick sat opposite him and pulled his notebook from his pocket.

Anders nodded at the notebook and creased his brow.

'I need to ask you some questions.' Riddick looked down at the blank page and scribbled with the pen to get the ink flowing.

'Things have changed then,' Anders said. 'Used to have to beg you to make notes. Remember what you used to say to me?'

Got the memory of a dolphin, boss. A dolphin can learn and remember the unique whistle of every other dolphin they encounter for twenty years!

'Let's stick to why I'm here, okay?' He wanted to make notes because he didn't trust his memory right now. Forgetting the details of that vehicle had knocked his confidence for six.

'How's Marsh? How's the old crew?'

Even though the ink had started to flow already, Riddick scribbled some more as he ignored the question. 'Something happened, Anders. A boy died. I want to know if you can help.'

'A child.'

I think so. Although I don't know his actual age or name yet. 'Yes.'

'Of course. I'll help however I can.'

Riddick told Anders the story of his eleven o'clock jaunt the previous evening.

Anders turned his head from side to side as Riddick reached the tragic conclusion. Riddick hoped the horrified expression on his face was genuine. Until his legacy had been destroyed, DCI Anders Smith had been well known as a passionate policeman, driven to find justice. Riddick often lay awake at night wondering, hoping perhaps, that some of that fight for good had been sincere.

'Did the kid die from the head wound?' Anders asked.

'I've told you everything I know.' Although he was still to mention the bear.

'Yes. I assume you're not on the case. Still, someone in there could keep you fed, no?'

Riddick sneered. 'Things have moved on since the glory days, Anders. People tend to value integrity, and their careers. No one is feeding me.'

'Not even your pretty new DCI?' He raised an eyebrow.

'Especially not her. It's not the Wild West any more.'

Anders smiled and said, 'And there're no more cowboys?'

Riddick could tell from his expression that he was insinuating something. 'Can you help me or not?'

'Wouldn't you be the one breaking the rules then?'

'A boy, *a child*, is dead. A killer may be on the loose. I'll worry about it later.'

Anders nodded.

You smug bastard, Riddick thought.

'How can I help?' Anders said.

'There was a bear... a bear in the boy's backpack.'

Anders looked confused. 'A bear? What do you mean?'

'A teddy bear, Anders. A chuffin' teddy bear.'

Anders sat back in his chair. He was silent for a moment as he processed this information. Then, his face paled. He stared at Riddick for a long time but didn't speak.

'I thought that'd get your attention. The cave. The bear—'

'Was it petrified?'

'No,' Riddick said, worried that Anders was now going to be the next in a long line of people dismissing it.

Anders placed his index finger against his lips. 'Have you tried to tell the team?'

'I shouted it from the *bloody* rooftops.'

'And?'

'And... nothing. Different cave. Different bear. No one's interested.'

Anders nodded. 'There's a twenty-year gap, too, Paul. This boy wouldn't have even been alive when Graham Lock was killed. Still, why a teddy bear in a teenager's backpack?'

'My boss let it slip that it was a gift from his deceased mum – which is why he kept it on him.'

'Strange... but not the strangest I've heard.'

'Something just doesn't feel right.'

Anders tapped his lips with his index finger and thought. 'Nothing will ever feel right about a dead child in a cave, Paul, but I can understand the scepticism.'

'Jesus! Why'd I bother? Any second now, you're going to ask me about bloody concussion. Listen, if you're not interested, fine... sorry I wasted your time.'

Anders pulled his index finger from his mouth and used it to point at Riddick. 'Hold on, I didn't say that.' He stood, wincing. His face was pale. He regarded Riddick again and then shook his head. 'Give me a moment. My back is worse than ever.' He turned around and walked over to the wall. He placed the palms of his hands against it and arched his back to try and stretch it.

Riddick stood. He'd allowed the bastard enough thinking time. 'So?'

Anders groaned. Riddick winced when he heard his old mentor's back cracking.

'Anders. That day you sent Russell Lock down for the murder of his son... you weren't happy, were you?'

Anders didn't turn. 'What makes you think that?'

'I could tell. Something wasn't sitting right with you.'

Anders stretched out again.

'You had doubts,' Riddick said.

Anders turned. 'Doubts? Of course. Who doesn't? And enough of the you! I wasn't the only person involved in sending down Russell Lock, there were other people involved too...'

'Like DCI Derek Rice?'

'Among others. Yourself included, remember?'

'I spotted an anomaly at the crime scene – that's all I bloody did!'

'And got the ball rolling.' Anders winked. 'And launched a career from it.'

'Piss off, Anders,' Riddick said. 'If I'd had an inkling you were using me, I'd have walked away there and then.'

Anders hobbled back over to the table. 'Used? What do you think it is I used you for?'

'As a pet project to show your altruism... to present yourself as not only the best detective, but someone willing to guide others, make them as successful as you. You just wanted to be everyone's damned hero.'

'No,' Anders said. 'You have it all wrong. Why do you think I *chose* you? I had hundreds, *thousands*, of officers I could've built from the bottom up. If I was so preoccupied with myself, as you claim, then how would I have noticed you?'

'Because of the bear.'

Anders guffawed. 'You spotted a missing bloody bear! So what?'

Riddick couldn't believe it. His eyes widened. He sat up straight.

Anders shook his head. 'Don't look so stunned. Yes, I was complimentary about it at the time—'

'Complimentary for about twenty bloody years!'

'Yes. And in a way, I was grateful you'd spotted it, but you know, we did take an inventory of the scene after. We'd have found it ourselves. I think even you pointed that out to me at the time.'

'Great... so if not for the bloody bear, why the hell did you go on and ruin my life?'

'Hardly ruined your life. Your career is staggering. Your tragedies are just that, tragedies. They could've happened to anyone... anywhere.'

'But they didn't, did they?' Riddick said, thumbing his chest. 'They happened to me. Why *did* you choose me, you bastard?'

'Why do you think? For the very reason you're standing across the table from me right now. Your passion. Your relentless nature. Your desire for the truth. You want me to go on?'

'And these things remind me of you?' Riddick said, sneering and raising an eyebrow.

'Goddamned right they do, son!' Anders said, raising his voice as he slammed his fist on the table.

The door flew open.

'Is everything all right?' the guard asked.

Riddick turned and nodded. 'It's fine. He's just stretching out.'

The guard regarded them curiously for a time before nodding and exiting.

Riddick turned back. 'Well, if you're anything like me, then you'll already know I'm not letting this go. If you ever gave two hoots about me Anders, really, then tell me what the hell happened back in 2003.'

Anders closed his eyes and massaged his temple with his thumb and forefinger. 'One of the worst bloody things I've ever done, that's what.'

Riddick felt his heart accelerating. 'Come on then – what?'

Anders dropped his hand from his temple and fixed Riddick with a stare. 'Something I rarely did. Usually, for very good reason...'

'Spit it out, man, for God's sake! What did you do?'

Anders sighed and pushed his hand through his hair. 'Very well. I did as I was told.'

13

While she waited downstairs in the lounge with Rice, Gardner winced over the sound of Stephen Best's closest friend, Kyle Alexander, coughing his guts up in his bedroom.

His mother, Collette, was already upstairs prepping him for the impending questions. She'd said she planned to avoid the word *interview* so as not to sound intimidating to a fifteen-year-old boy diagnosed with autism and ADHD, who was currently suffering from both the flu and the hell of losing his best friend.

While they were alone in the lounge, Gardner turned to Rice. 'No point in us both getting the lurgy; you can wait outside if you like.'

Gardner expected something along the lines of 'Just trying to get rid of me boss?' but instead, Rice nodded. 'Yes, history of pneumonia. Probably best?'

Spineless! However, she was never averse to a break from Rice. She smiled. 'Best be safe.'

Collette came and led Gardner upstairs. She felt the heat coming out of the small bedroom before she entered it. The germs would be having a field day in there.

Best put Operation Lost Light to bed quick smart before I go down with it.

While Stephen's room had been immaculate, Kyle's was cluttered and messy. There were clusters of Warhammer models everywhere. On the chest of drawers, some peculiar creatures straight from a Tolkien novel were engaged in warfare, while on the windowsill some futuristic soldiers were taking out some spiny-looking aliens. 'Hello Kyle. Thank you for seeing me.'

He didn't look up at her. She wondered if this was part of his autism, or the grief he was experiencing. He coughed twice.

'Your figures look fantastic, Kyle,' Gardner said. 'Did you paint them all?'

'Most of them. Some of them belong to Stephen.'

Gardner nodded. 'I wish I could paint like this.'

'I've some new Dreadblade Harrows to paint.' He screwed up his face. 'Can't paint with this chest.' He coughed again and pointed at his phone on the bed. 'I could show you a YouTube channel. It shows you how to paint perfectly.'

Collette jumped in from the doorway. 'Some people change up the colours; Kyle doesn't like to do that.'

'Obviously,' Kyle said, who glared at his mother. 'You have to get them perfect.'

'Sounds fair enough,' Gardner said, winking at Collette.

Kyle leaned forward and broke into a coughing fit. Eventually, he reached for a tissue and spat into it before throwing it into a bin by his bed.

'Sorry about that,' Collette said.

'Don't be,' Gardner said. 'We've all been there.'

'And sorry about the mess.'

Gardner shook her head.

'Mum blames my ADHD,' Kyle said and coughed again. 'I keep telling her that if I know where everything is it's not a mess.'

Gardner caught Collette rolling her eyes.

Gardner pointed at the very end of the bed. 'Can I sit there please?' Not because she wanted to be as far away from the mucus factory as possible, but because she didn't want to get too close and intimidate this sensitive young man.

'Yes,' Collette said.

'Kyle?' Gardner asked. It was his bed after all.

'Uh-huh.'

She sat.

'You know there's going to be a Warhammer movie and TV show?' Kyle said.

'No, I didn't know that...' Gardner said.

'Stephen told me. I hope it's a twelve.' He looked up at his mum. 'Not a fifteen. I'm not allowed to watch fifteens yet. Even though I *am* fifteen and everyone else is allowed. But if Warhammer is a fifteen, can I watch it? Mum?'

'We'll see. You need to talk to Mrs Gardner now, Kyle.'

'Okay.' He reached over to his bedside table and picked up a stretchy stick man.

'Just call me, Emma, Kyle.'

'Okay,' Kyle said, pulling the two arms on the man to ridiculous lengths.

'I'm sorry about Stephen,' Gardner said.

Kyle pulled harder at his toy. Gardner wondered if its limbs would break. 'It's the Warhammer club on Sunday,' Kyle said, looking up at his mum. 'Who am I going to go with?'

'We'll work that out, honey.' Gardner could see the tears in his mother's eyes.

Gardner looked back at Kyle, acknowledging how difficult this interview was going to be. She was so glad Rice had run screaming from the lurgy – he'd have had no patience for chit-chat and would already be chipping away at the poor boy.

She opted to leave her notebook in her pocket too. Whacking that out would probably send Kyle further into retreat. Not quite sure where to begin, Gardner tried the familiar. 'Do you like school, Kyle?'

He grinned but still didn't look up. 'School sucks!'

'I hear that a lot. Must be something you like though?'

'Break times. Lunches. Art is okay.'

'What do you do at break and lunch?'

'Hang out with Stephen. Once a week, they let us use the art rooms to paint our figures. Most days we head to the library though. We're *always* allowed our figures and dice in there.'

Gardner looked at Collette.

'It's actually on his personal passport,' Collette said. 'That time helps keep him focused during lesson time.'

Gardner nodded. 'Personal passport?'

'If you're on the SEN register,' Collette said, 'you get a personal passport. Suggestions of things that can help the student. Teachers use it to support the students in lessons.'

'Mr Phillips doesn't!' Kyle said.

Collette looked at Gardner. 'Mr Phillips teaches PE. Kyle doesn't like PE and thinks he shouldn't have to do it. It's a long-running issue.'

'I see,' Gardner said. She continued to question Kyle on his school life and then moved on to his social life. He seemed happier during this stage of the interview – especially in the parts that involved Stephen and, of course, Warhammer.

'Do you and Stephen have other interests?'

Kyle looked at Collette. 'Marvel and DC! When I'm allowed to watch them.'

Collette looked at Gardner. 'Kyle has a very active imagination. Haven't you honey? Talented imagination. He can write good stories, can't you?'

Kyle nodded. 'I'm the best in my class.'

'And modest too,' Collette said and smiled. 'Sometimes violence in movies can be a little much. I tend to watch them first.'

'I love violence!' Kyle said, grinned and then coughed.

Come and do my job, Gardner thought. *It'll soon put you off.*

'I'm more inclined to let him watch them if he's taking his ADHD medicine,' Collette said. 'Unfortunately, that isn't always the case.'

Gardner looked at Kyle. 'Why's that?'

'Don't like them. They make me feel odd.'

'They calm you down, Kyle,' Collette said.

Kyle scowled and shook his head.

'We've been having real problems with it,' Collette said to Gardner. 'He took last month's supply to school and chucked them in the bin. Now, we're having to take them into school ourselves, directly.'

Kyle shook his head. 'I don't want to take them.'

'When you've done your GCSEs, you can make these decisions yourself, Kyle.'

He coughed and glared down at his stretchy man.

Gardner took the conversation back to Marvel for a while to try and lighten him up, and then discovered that Black Panther was Kyle's favourite character. Kyle looked at Gardner for the first time. 'You know that the actor died?'

Gardner shook her head. 'No.'

Kyle gave her the details. He didn't sound sad as he spoke, just enthusiastic. He was a curious young man but they had yet to discuss Stephen's death.

'Have you noticed anything out of the ordinary with Stephen recently?' Gardner asked, feeling guilty for such a strong question, but knowing it was long overdue.

Kyle didn't respond. He stretched the man to breaking point.

'Has he been behaving differently?'

'I don't understand,' Kyle said, throwing his stretchy figure down and reaching over to his bedside table for a squeezy ball.

'Stephen had been coming over a bit less,' Collette said.

Kyle squeezed his ball. He looked irritated. 'Yes, but he still played with me at lunch.'

'Do you know why he was coming over less?' Gardner said.

'He had a new friend.'

'Who?'

Kyle shook his head. 'I don't know.'

Gardner felt a spike in her heart rate and gave Collette a puzzled look.

Kyle continued, 'He was still my *best* friend, though. I asked him.'

'I'm sure that's true. Did you know if the friend was a boy or a girl?'

Or a man, perhaps?

'A boy.'

'Did you ever see this boy, Kyle?'

'No.'

'How'd you know about him?'

'Stephen told me.'

'His name?'

'No. I told him I didn't want to talk about him. Why would I?'

Collette interjected, 'Kyle did mention this to me. It didn't bother him too much, because like Stephen assured him, he was still his best friend. But over the last two months, he wasn't coming here as much at the weekends.'

Kyle looked up at Collette. 'He was still going to the Warhammer club. *With me.*'

Collette nodded. 'Yes, honey, he was.'

'I know it's hard, Kyle, but is there anything you can tell me about this other friend?' Gardner asked. 'Anything at all?'

Kyle carried on squeezing the ball. He didn't look like he was giving it much thought. Eventually, he said, 'No.'

Collette said, 'You did tell me something though, Kyle, didn't you? Remember? Last week?'

Kyle glared at his mother.

Gardner said, 'We want to find whoever did this to Kyle. And I'm sure you do, too.'

Kyle squeezed his ball harder.

Gardner looked at Collette and nodded.

'He's older and doesn't go to school,' Collette said. 'He loved Warhammer too. Apparently, he'd an army you'd like to have seen, isn't that right Kyle?'

Kyle looked away. He clearly didn't want to talk about this.

Collette continued, 'Stephen said he couldn't see it, that this was his friend and Kyle had to find his own. Kyle got upset about it.'

Kyle looked saddened by this.

Gardner wondered if Stephen's father knew that his son had a 'special friend'? When he went out for these walks, is this where he was going? Also, if he wasn't coming to Kyle's any more at the weekends, did his father know where he was going?

At this point, it pained Gardner not to have her notebook out on her lap. The possibility of missing a detail filled her with dread. As soon as she was back in the car, she'd pepper those lined pages – Rice would have to wait with his questions.

She continued probing Kyle, but was only met with continued frustrated expressions, vicious ball squeezing and then back to the yanking of the stretchy man, concluding with a painful-sounding coughing fit. Further attempts to find anything out of the ordinary in Stephen's life yielded nothing, and questions regarding

Stephen's enjoyment of evening walks also came to little, because Kyle claimed a complete lack of interest in them.

Gardner glanced at Collette. She seemed happy with this lack of interest. What mother wouldn't be? Their child out walking in the dark? Especially a vulnerable child who may not be as alert to danger as some of his peers.

Gardner realised she was becoming frustrated in this interview, and although she was professional and compassionate enough to not let it show, she was fully aware that the young man in bed would be feeling ten times worse than her. Knowing that there was little more to take here, at least for the moment, she paused and smiled. 'I'll look out for that Warhammer movie.'

Kyle nodded. His eyes darted up to her face, before darting away again.

'And let's hope it's a twelve,' Gardner said, smiling again.

'It will be,' Kyle said. 'Stephen saw it on the internet. He's never wrong about these things. We're going to see it together.'

She waited for Kyle to correct himself. *We were.* It didn't happen. Gardner felt a wave of sadness. *We'll find out what happened to your best friend, Kyle.*

Downstairs, Gardner asked Collette some more questions, using her notebook this time.

'I guess you know Ron Best well?'

'Not as well as you'd think considering our children were close. I used to get on much better with his wife, Lynda, before...' Collette broke off. 'That was awful... such a tragedy, and out of the blue too. Ron is a quiet man... very private... and he just retreated further into himself after that. We have little in common with him and, to be honest, our children are quite different too. We have a lot more challenges with Kyle. He tends to get overwhelmed more often, as you've probably just seen, and some of his meltdowns are quite challenging – especially now he's getting bigger.'

'You said upstairs that Stephen wasn't coming over as often, potentially to go and meet this mysterious friend. Was his father aware of this?'

'I'm sorry... I really wouldn't know. Stephen just used to turn up here at the weekends. Like I said, Kyle is more of a homebird, so Stephen was happy to come here.'

At the door, Gardner turned to Collette. 'If you think of anything else...'

'I'll call in a heartbeat.' Her eyes filled with tears. 'This is awful. I almost can't believe it's happening – it feels like a dream, you know?'

Gardner nodded, feeling that wave of sadness again.

'I can't even imagine how Ron must be feeling. I couldn't... you know... it would destroy me.' She wiped at her eyes. 'And my son, oh God, how will he recover from this?'

Don't worry. He has you, Collette. And his father. Together, you'll help him.

Gardner handed her card over. 'If you need anything.'

'Thanks. Is my son in danger?'

Gardner opened her mouth to reply *no*, but she forced it back at the last moment. She didn't know that, did she? It would be foolish to offer her unsubstantiated reassurances which may then lead to Collette letting her guard down. She answered carefully. 'I've seen nothing to suggest that, but it would be best to remain vigilant. Just until we clear this up. And we will clear this up. Like you said, he doesn't really go out on his own, and he *is* sick, so this should help ease your mind somewhat.'

Back in her car, she scribbled down as many notes as she could remember, waving Rice away when he came to the window. He hovered there while she circled a couple of key takeaways: mysterious friend; Warhammer club; Ron – distant, uncommunicative. She racked her brains for more – certain she'd missed something –

but came up short. The perils of not making notes. As she so often told the stubborn Riddick, who'd once argued back by comparing himself to a dolphin. She smiled. *Ridiculous man.*

Rice was getting impatient and looked cold.

She wound down her window. 'Wait in the car, I need to make a phone call.'

'Boss?'

She wound up her window. He looked pissed off.

She phoned Barnett for an update, made a few notes and then gave him a task. 'Contact the FLO, Lyndsey Mort, and ask her to speak to Ron. Did he know about this special friend? Did he know that Stephen was spending less time with Kyle?'

'Will do, boss.'

'Thanks, Ray.'

Rather than get Rice back out of the car into the cold, she contacted him by phone and told him all that she had learned.

14

_____

Kyle Alexander spat into the tissue, examined it, wondering how something so disgusting could exist inside your lungs, and then dropped his waste into the bin.

His bedroom window overlooked the car. He watched DCI Gardner talking on her phone.

Nice lady. Likes Warhammer. She's going to watch the movie.

It'd been a shame to lie to her. He hated lying. Especially to the ones who liked Warhammer. It made his insides feel like they were on fire.

He reached under his pillow and took out his mobile phone.

He went through his messages to the image he'd been sent earlier from his new friend to cheer him up.

The Slaves to Darkness army all lined up. Fully painted. He reached out and zoomed in on the Daemon Prince, tall and hulking in the centre, with obscenely large red wings.

Stephen had told him what an incredible painter his friend was. Better even than Eugene, the manager of the Harrogate Warhammer shop. Better *even* than Lewis Coombs, the YouTube Warhammer painter that clocked up thousands of views a day.

And Stephen hadn't been exaggerating.

How Kyle longed for that army – or at *least* to see it. To touch it. To hold the figures.

He read the message that accompanied it.

The centrepiece of my Grand Alliance of Chaos army.

And the next message:

Stephen loved them.

Then, the next:

You'll love them too.

And then, the final message, received seconds before DCI Emma Gardner had come into his room.

Want to meet?

Kyle coughed and thought. His mum was out shopping in the late afternoon. His dad away on business.

He glanced out of the window again. Gardner was driving away.

It looked cold outside.

However, his temperature had dropped over the last hour and he felt marginally better. He glanced at the Beechams Cold and Flu remedy packet on his bedside table. His secret weapon.

He texted back.

Where?

15

'Graham Lock's murder at Mother Shipton's Cave rocked Knaresborough, Paul,' Anders continued from the other side of the table. 'I'm sure you remember?'

Paul nodded.

'I won't insult your intelligence by telling you folk used to leave their doors unlocked at night, but I'll say this, they *used* to let their children play out past six o'clock, and no one ever freaked out when they momentarily lost their kid down the wrong aisle in a supermarket. Knaresborough was a safe place. No one expected Graham Lock to happen.' Anders stretched out in his chair, wincing over the pain in his back and then continued, 'So, a shed load of money was thrown at the investigation to make Knaresborough safe again. The powers that be wanted a line drawn firmly under this one asap. There weren't many stones unturned I can tell you... We're talking unprecedented levels of overtime; press conferences taking over daytime television; forensics experts called in from all corners of the country – I think at one point, we rounded up all the ducks on the Nidd beside the cave on the off chance one may have evolved enough to communicate what they'd seen.' He smiled, but Riddick wasn't interested in this man's humour these days. 'But then, as you well know, all the evidence started to point towards the father, Russell Lock. The book on petrification in the shop with the circled bear; Russell's sleeping pills in Graham's system; the admission of child abuse. Russell properly laid bruises on his own kid – did you know that?'

'Yes, of course,' Riddick said. 'I saw the photographs.'

'So, do remember in all of this, Paul, that Russell Lock was a mean bastard.'

'But was he a killer?'

Anders sighed. 'I'll get to that. I know it's common when you get a breakthrough for a lot of evidence to start tumbling in. But it was different with this investigation. Tumbling was an understatement; it literally started to pour.'

Riddick nodded. 'Seems like a pretty good clue that it was all bollocks.'

Anders nodded. 'And to begin with, I was the only one in Russell's corner *despite* what he did to his son... but, as I previously mentioned, there was a ravenous hunger to get this one closed. My defence of the old bastard became an irrelevance.'

'So, you stood by while evidence was planted?'

'Stood by?' Anders chortled. 'You know me well enough! I don't do standing by, son.'

'Stop calling me that.'

'Okay, *Paul*. I kicked up a stink. In fact, I went one better – I had someone else for the murder... I made that crystal clear to top brass.'

'Who?'

'George Jacoby. About your age at the time. Early twenties. He hired out rowing boats on the Nidd down at the Waterside. Directly opposite Mother Shipton's. You may remember him?'

Riddick had a vague recollection of a short, vocal man trying to entice customers to his Waterside boat hire shop.

Anders' eyes narrowed. 'Squat man, but broad on account of all the rowing he did. He was often seen taking out his own boats outside of business hours. Reminded me of a car salesman – choosing the right words to spike your interest and smiling at all the right times to put you at ease. The man was peculiar though.'

'How so?'

'Well, he may have come across as the most extroverted man that ever lived while touting his wares, but the man was a complete loner off the clock, and despite my digging, I could find no hint of a social life. You know how I feel about bloody actors.'

Yes, you'd call them trained liars, Riddick thought. *Told me often, in fact. And I listened. God, I always listened! Before I discovered that it was you who was the actor... the ultimate actor... a goddamned Oscar winner.*

'Yes...' Anders said. 'The greatest showman during office hours; a bloody anxiety-ridden recluse in his own time. I saw his medical records – he struggled. He was a blatant wrong 'un, Paul. I knew that then and...' Anders closed his eyes and sighed. 'I know that now.'

'What made you notice George Jacoby in the first place?' Riddick asked.

'Several eyewitnesses reported seeing him deep in conversation with Graham Lock on the week leading up to that grim night at the cave.'

'Jesus...'

'Yes, precisely, yet the locals were more suspicious of Jacoby than my bloody colleagues.'

Riddick took a deep breath in through his nose and shook his head. He clenched and unclenched his fists. 'You at least interviewed him?'

'Aye. Of course. What do you take me for? I interviewed the living shit out of him. But, as I said before, he was a skilled actor. He claimed Graham was just chucking coins in the well near where he was stationed and kept coming over to chat to him about boats and whatnot. Said he kept telling the kid to leave him be, but it kept falling on deaf ears.'

'Did you buy any of it?'

'From that show pony?'

'You're persuasive, Anders. I don't believe for a second you couldn't raise some alarms at HQ.'

'Well, believe it Paul. I started off trying to pull Derek round. It was a mistake.'

'He hung off your every word! You were pulling the strings. Always were.'

'And before that day I spoke to Derek, you'd have been right. But something changed in that moment. He went behind my back. Despite me carrying his career for bloody God knows how long, he chose this moment to stab me in the back. So, when Derek told them I was looking elsewhere, I was marginalised, while that miserable apeth, who would've been a desk sergeant at that point if not for me, continued to toe the line, and told me to keep my head down! Never in my life! I was lost for bloody words.' He looked off into the distance. 'I should've known better, and after that case, I *did* know better.' He smiled. 'But that's a different story.'

Riddick sighed. 'Why would top brass risk leaving a real killer out there though?'

Anders shrugged. 'Those above us didn't want us looking anywhere else but Russell Lock – they were convinced it was him and wanted it shut down and the media frenzy silenced. At the time, I tried to convince myself that maybe they were right, but then more evidence came to light. One hour before we charged Russell Lock, an eyewitness came forward. Donna Morfett. One of my schoolteachers growing up.' He nodded. 'Yeah. Great woman. Gone now of course. Well... an hour before Graham was murdered, she was walking her dog and saw a boat gliding over the Nidd towards Mother Shipton's Cave. It was dark, but she was certain there were two people in the boat of roughly equal size... I checked... Graham Lock and George Jacoby were about the same size.'

'But... it can't be... Graham and Russell came down the back way to the cave before the killing. They were seen near the entrance to that path by another eyewitness.'

'Aye,' Anders said, leaning against the wall. 'The battle of the eyewitnesses, eh? Well, actually, not that much of a battle. No one wanted to know about the ravings of a senile old woman.'

'Ravings?'

'Yes... I think that was the word Derek used when I tried to mount one last protest.'

'Someone must've listened in HQ. *Someone.*'

'Why? Those who were so desperate to close it already had that eyewitness report on Graham being led to his death by his father – why question it? One eyewitness was a forty-year-old Conservative politician from the south on his holidays... and the other was Donna – a retired schoolteacher with dementia.'

'I'd have gone for the schoolteacher,' Riddick said.

'Me and you both.'

'So, you were pissed off,' Riddick said. 'I just *knew* there was something up with you that day.'

'And I thought I did a pretty good job of hiding it, eh? Seems not. Spotting I was upset is even more impressive than spotting the missing bear.'

'Because you're a good actor too.'

Anders shrugged. 'Which is why I can spot them a mile off... and George was one of the best I ever came across.'

Riddick looked down and reflected on these revelations. Then, he looked back up at the man he'd tried to emulate for nearly his whole career, until the truth behind his corrupt nature was exposed. 'But how, Anders? How could you live with that? You let an innocent man go to jail for the murder of his son. He *died* in jail.'

'Let's not forget he did *beat* his son.'

Riddick shook his head. 'Even so... you knew the real killer could still be out there. What if they killed again? In fact, they *may* have killed again!'

Anders shook his head. 'No... listen to me, Paul, and listen good. I was *always* planning to do something... I really was. I was going to let the dust settle first so as not to jeopardise careers around me. It's not as simple as marching into a room of those above you with your balls swinging. Not only would they crush you, but they'd crush everyone else you worked with.' Anders nodded in Riddick's direction, implying that he was one of those people.

'Don't bring me into it. You should've done the right thing!'

'I was going to. I had plans. But then two things happened over the next three months. Russell Lock died of a heart attack, and then, George Jacoby had a stroke. A big one too. Ended up with that locked-in syndrome. You heard of it?'

Riddick nodded.

'Completely paralysed, apart from the eyes,' Anders said. 'That's all he could move. A fate worse than death.'

'So, your strategic plan to expose the truth, to bring about justice? What happened to that?'

Anders narrowed his eyes. 'For what purpose?'

'Clear the father's name for a start?'

'It's romantic, Paul. And it's how we all want to see the world, but can't you see how it was better left alone? There was only one thing that was significant here, and it wasn't the truth. Whoever killed Graham was finished, and there's nothing more significant than that.'

'Maybe George healed...'

'George Jacoby is bedbound, the living dead. I never took my eye off that. We cannot find any more justice here, no matter what you believe. The world moved on. New battles to be fought...'

Riddick stood and slammed his palms down on the table. He leaned in. 'I woke up next to a dead boy last night. A dead boy! And there was a bear in his goddamned bag.'

'Paul, it can't be connected. Did you not hear what I said? It *cannot* be connected. Even if the father was innocent, which he may not have been, then that only leaves George... and he's not capable.'

'Someone else then.'

'It's been twenty years!'

'Still... whoever it was could've moved away. Done this in other places. Maybe they've only just come back.'

Anders shook his head. 'No... don't you think we would've heard about any crimes similar to the Lock murder? It would make national news, potentially international.'

Riddick felt frustrated and had the urge to lash out. 'Still, even if it's not connected, you've still potentially let a guilty man go free.'

Anders guffawed. 'George Jacoby is suffering far worse than anyone in this prison with me. I can assure you of that!'

Riddick put his hands to his face and rubbed at it.

Anders' argument was compelling.

He shook his head, still not freeing his face from his hands.

Compelling, yes.

Wasn't it always? Wily old bastard.

He freed his face. 'It must've felt good to get that off your chest.'

Anders looked away, lowering his face slightly.

'Let me ask you, is this real? Is the guilt and regret really gnawing away?'

Anders sighed.

'Or are you just as fake as all those actors you claim to despise so much?'

Anders looked back. 'I've acted, Paul. I won't deny it. I've been on that stage large parts of my life. Did I hate it? Yes. Do I regret it? Most of it, yes. But some of it was necessary. The world is different now... and you're not always allowed to do what's necessary. Who do you think suffers for that? Not us, Paul. No. The people we're paid to protect—'

Riddick looked up at the ceiling. 'Spare me. Jesus, please, not this sanctimonious bullshit again. You're a relic. Crime on *their* side, or *our* side, it doesn't matter. It's still crime. Someone has to draw a goddamned line!'

'Like you, Paul?'

Riddick raised an eyebrow. *What's he referring to? Does he know about Ronnie Haller? Surely not...* 'I'm not perfect, no. I think you saw to that, Anders. But I'm going to make an effort... and I'm going to start with what really happened to Graham Lock, and hopefully to this other boy. Because something isn't right here. And I've got what I need – George Jacoby. I'm going to try and put right the things that *you* got wrong.'

Anders sighed and looked down. 'Be careful, Paul. I know you hate me. Can hardly blame you—'

'Don't you think it's deserved?'

'Yes, and I'll wallow in pain until my final breath. But you know I'm not acting when I say that I love you.'

'Enough.' Riddick stood. 'You don't need to worry about me, old man.'

Anders opened his mouth to speak but hesitated. He raised an eyebrow instead.

'What's on your mind?' Riddick asked. His chest went cold.

'Nothing,' Anders said. 'Should there be?'

Ronnie Haller? Do you know? Shit, Anders, do you know?

'I'm fine.'

'Good. I hope so,' Anders said. 'It's all I ask for before I go to sleep in the evening.'

'Whether I get in touch with you again will depend on what I find out,' Riddick said, staring at the man, recalling the hand on his shoulder all those years ago, that feeling of awe and that booming voice: *He needs people like me. People like you. People who see things.*

You made me feel special, you bastard. You made me feel like I could do anything.

'Did you read any of my letters, Paul?'

'I think you know the answer to that.'

'Read the last one when you get home.'

'And why would I do that?'

'Humour an old man.'

Riddick sighed.

'Please?' Anders said.

'Okay. The last one. Then, we're done.'

'Thank you, Paul.'

Riddick stood and knocked on the door. The guard opened it.

'Paul?'

Riddick turned.

'How do I know you're telling the truth – that you'll read the letter?'

'Because, unlike you, I could never bloody act.'

16

Milo loved York. Back before his mother's illness, they'd visit regularly. She particularly enjoyed wandering around York Minster, the large gothic cathedral. Milo had never been as inspired as his mother by the multitude of stained-glass windows and the impressively high ceilings. If anything, he'd found it unbearably overstocked with noisy tourists.

However, even he had to admit there was something magical about the Central Tower at the Minster. Almost three hundred steps would take you to panoramic views of the city – and it was here that he'd learned and studied the geography of this impressive, medieval city, including the two-mile wall incorporating some of the city's original Roman structures. Not forgetting Clifford's Tower, which was originally built out of wood by the Normans in 1068, before being replaced in the thirteenth century by a stone fortress to now become the oldest remaining part of York Castle.

But nothing, *absolutely* nothing, beat a ramble through the Shambles. Narrow fourteenth-century streets with timber-framed buildings. As a younger child, Milo had been fascinated with spot-

ting the meat hooks hanging outside these old stores, as the place
was, and remained, a hotspot for butcher shops.

Milo had never ventured far away from the major attractions,
so after disembarking the train at Tang Hall, to the east of the city,
he initially felt disorientated. Pete had been making deliveries to
this area for a while now, and so took them to a greasy spoon he
was fond of. Pete vanished to the toilet twice, claiming with a grin
that he was off to 'powder his nose' and Milo hoped to God that
his friend knew what he was doing.

Milo recalled Pete's claim that he was dabbling in his own
supply and tried to find some reassurance in this, but his mind
kept flicking back to the bloodstain on KG's shirt, and his heart
would start to race again.

As they ate, whatever Pete had powdered his nose with made
him talk quickly and without many breaks. There wasn't much
need for Milo to speak, but occasionally Pete would pause to ask
questions that Milo enjoyed answering. Questions such as 'What
was Batman's son called?' and 'How old was Batman in *The Dark
Night Returns*?'

Pete ate very little of his bacon roll and offered the remainder
to Milo.

As Milo ate, he struggled, like earlier, to keep his gaze from
Pete's darkening eye.

'Is it that bad?' Pete asked.

Milo shook his head.

'Don't worry, kid. Dad will get what's coming to him soon
enough – he's a dipshit.'

Milo thought about what he'd do if he was in Pete's situation.
'Maybe you should tell someone?'

'Tell someone? Are you thick?' Pete snorted. 'You do realise
what we're involved in, don't you?'

Milo's face reddened.

As they were leaving the café, Milo's head was down. Pete clapped him on the back. 'Don't get all sensitive on me, kid. Just a reminder of how high the stakes are.'

Milo nodded and forced his head back up. He still felt sore at the comment though – he'd only tried to help.

At one point, he felt a cold blow to the back of his head. He touched it and felt the icy wetness of snow. Smiling, he turned to see that Pete had deliberately lagged a few paces behind so he could launch a snowball at him.

'Bastard,' Milo said, scooping one up and launching it back.

They traded snowballs for a few minutes, until they were laughing hard enough to melt the sour atmosphere that had threatened their adventure.

As they continued onwards to their destination, Pete slipped his available arm – the one not clutching the holdall – around Milo's shoulders. 'Seriously, though, I'm glad to have you with me, kid.'

Milo nodded. The feeling was mutual. He couldn't recall anybody ever expressing this much interest in him – apart from maybe his mum or dad.

Milo followed Pete on a short walk through a run-down residential area.

'Can I tell you something?' Pete asked.

Milo nodded.

'How you feel about your mum, kid... I get that. I can relate.'

Milo smiled.

'When I was about eight,' Pete explained, 'I was obsessed with Nike trainers. And they cost a fortune. We never had any money, and my mum used to clean and iron for the local rich barmpots, but she still got me a new pair every time an old pair wore out, or I grew out of them. I never took the bloody things off! Still got them all you know. Bottom of my wardrobe. Fifteen pairs.'

Milo looked to his side and watched Pete's expression glaze as he journeyed off into his own world. Occasionally, a smile flickered across Pete's face, but a minute or so later, Milo was sure he caught tears forming in his eyes.

Had Pete's mother died?

Did they both have this in common?

Was this the reason Pete had sought him out as a friend?

Maybe it hadn't been the comics, after all, but rather the fact that Milo was about to lose his mother in a similar fashion to how Pete had lost his?

'What happened to your mum?' Milo asked, and then gulped, surprised at himself for asking the question.

'She didn't die,' Pete said, 'if that's what you're thinking.'

Milo reddened.

'We're almost there,' Pete said. 'You follow my lead.'

What lead? Milo thought. *Don't we just swap this holdall for a bag of money?*

Pete led them into a small industrial estate.

There were four units alongside each other, all with their shutters down. The first bore the sign: 'Mike's Motorbikes', which seemed incredibly imaginative when compared to the second unit which was simply headed 'Refurbished Refrigerators'.

The third unit didn't have a sign; it did have a couple of tacky ornate fountains outside though, which you'd never see in an ordinary home. The fountains were discoloured, and full of ice. Milo assumed there wasn't much call for tacky ornate fountains in Tang Hall, and he couldn't imagine the wealthy from further afield travelling into this neck of the woods. Seemed a doomed business idea, which probably explained why the products had been left to the elements.

The final unit, also without a sign, sat alongside a patch of shrubbery which marked the end of the small estate. The plant life was so overgrown that even the recent extreme temperatures had done little to reduce its widening grasp on the area.

There were two white BMWs parked outside. Both sparkled. An unusual sight in the winter months when white cars suffered more than most with grime.

'Come on,' Pete said, increasing his pace towards the shutters of the fourth unit. He'd a grin on his face.

Milo struggled to return the grin in so eerie a place.

As irritating as York Minster could be with its hordes of tourists pounding those stone floors, he'd welcome it with open arms right now.

Milo stayed some distance behind Pete as he pounded his fists on the shutter.

He recalled the reasons he was doing this. One last good holiday for his mother. His friendship with Pete. He gulped and then marched over and stood alongside Pete.

The shutter rolled up. A large man stood there in greasy over-alls; behind him, junk was scattered everywhere in the gloom. The man interlocked his heavily tattooed hands and cracked his knuckles, swiftly and aggressively. 'Name?'

'Obi-Wan.'

The man stepped to one side and waved the two boys in. After they'd crossed the threshold, he lowered the shutters behind them.

There were no windows in the unit, and the old strip lights were on their last legs. It was also colder inside than out. Milo felt his reasons for doing this were being severely tested again.

'Two of yer?' Knuckle-cracker said, still to turn and face his guests.

Pete looked at Milo and smiled.

Milo forced a smile out, but really, he wanted to vomit.

'I'm training him,' Pete said.

Their host turned; he had three lines shaved into an eyebrow he raised in their direction. 'To do what? Get on a bloody train and drop a bag off?'

Milo hoped to God that Pete wouldn't give this hulking maniac any lip.

'It's normal practice,' Pete said.

Knuckle-cracker took a step towards them. He looked at Pete. 'Well, Obi-Wan, no one told me! Who the hell is this?'

'He hasn't been given a name yet,' Pete said.

'And you expect me to believe that?'

'Phone KG if you want,' Pete said. He dropped the holdall on the floor. 'Or you could just take your delivery.'

Milo slipped his hands in his pockets, glancing longingly at the steel shutter separating him from the outside world.

'Hands where I can see them, you nameless fu—'

'It's fine. Leave them,' another man said from elsewhere in the unit.

Pulling his hands from his pockets, Milo turned. The second person, thinner, but just as tall and intimidating, was weaving himself towards them through scattered car parts.

He wasn't dressed in overalls like the other one. Instead, he wore army pants and a fleece. He stepped to within a metre of the boys and grinned over their heads in the other's direction. 'KG confirmed there would be two.' He looked down at Milo and winked. 'Also, really? Look at him? Poor lad. First run out and you bite his head off! Does he look armed to you?'

Knuckle-cracker didn't respond.

The thinner man leaned in, craning his neck, and Milo couldn't help but think of a giraffe. 'Well, lad, you armed?'

Milo shook his head and lowered his face. He managed to open his mouth to respond. The word 'no' fluttered out on a whisper.

'Look at me, lad,' Giraffe-neck said.

Milo looked up. Giraffe-neck's face was young, but his eyes seemed much older, and twitched from side to side as if reading and assessing Milo. Milo tried to keep his gaze steady, despite the overwhelming anxiety.

Eventually, Giraffe-neck turned his focus onto Pete. 'Here's a soldier no stranger to the run. Well, Obi-Wan, all good I hope?'

Pete nodded.

Giraffe-neck clicked his fingers. 'Product?'

Pete reached down to pick up the holdall he'd dropped before, and then handed it over.

Milo swept his eyes over the interior of the unit, wondering how he'd managed to get himself in so dangerous a situation. He also wondered if there was any chance of escape if the situation deteriorated. The place was scattered with the husks of old cars. One was raised up on a ramp. Off to the left of the unit was an office. It looked more like a tiny portacabin that had been dragged in.

'Wait here,' Giraffe-neck said, turning.

Milo tracked him as he made his way to the office and then shut himself inside. He glanced over his shoulder at the shutter. Knuckle-cracker resembled a tall goalkeeper protecting his net. Taking a penalty against him would be scary enough, never mind trying to manoeuvre around him.

He looked at Pete who gave him a grin, followed by a swift nod. 'Easy, kid. No worries. We're just going through the motions.'

'Could we at least wait outside?' Milo asked.

'No,' Knuckle-cracker said. 'And shut it, too; I've got a headache.'

Milo, feeling a rush of anxiety, tried to steady his breathing. He glanced at Pete, whose expression offered him some reassurance. He mouthed, 'It's fine. Trust me, kid.'

They all stood in silence for several minutes, until the office door opened again.

Giraffe-neck marched out, smiling. He weaved himself around the multitude of car parts with more energy than he'd had before. As he did so, he whistled. When he was close enough, he stood in front of the two boys, and placed a hand on Pete's left shoulder and then one on Milo's right.

'You delivered.'

Milo wanted to breathe a sigh of relief. Was that it? Were they done? Could they go?

Pete scrunched his brow. He looked confused. Milo didn't like it. It was like fearing flying in a plane and then seeing concern on a flight attendant's face when hitting turbulence.

'Yeah...' Pete said. 'I always do?'

Giraffe-neck laughed and then looked over the boys' heads to Knuckle-cracker. 'Kids today, eh?' He dropped his eyes back to Pete. 'Obi-Wan... I like you...' He took his hands from the boys' shoulders, clenched his fists and joined them together lengthways. 'You got balls.'

'So, can we go?' Pete asked.

He laughed again. 'Wouldn't you prefer the money first?'

'Yes,' Pete said, creasing his brow again. 'Of course.'

'Then one of you come to the office with me.'

Pete shook his head. 'It didn't work this way last time.'

'This time isn't last time!' Giraffe-neck laughed. 'I like you Obi-big-balls-Wan, but don't make me ask again.' He pointed at Pete's face, then he moved his finger to Milo's. 'One of you.' He moved the finger back and forth.

'I'll go,' Pete said.

Giraffe-neck froze his pointed finger at Pete. 'As I expected. Looking after your padawan, Obi.'

'So, can he wait outside?' Pete asked.

'Why?' the man asked. 'He has perfectly good company, and it's windy outside. What kind of host do you think I am?'

Milo's heart dropped as he heard the man guarding the shutters cracking his knuckles again. If there was any truth to the claim from his mother that it caused arthritis, then this man was destined for a world of pain.

'Follow me,' Giraffe-neck said, heading back towards the office. 'Watch you don't trip on anything. Wouldn't want you to be sending lawyers after me.'

'Of course not,' Pete said.

Giraffe-neck put a hand on the handle to the office, laughed out loud and looked back at Pete. 'You crack me up.'

Pete looked back at Milo and nodded towards him with a stern expression. He was trying to reassure him, but Milo could tell he was unsettled.

He turned and disappeared through the door, and Giraffe-neck followed him in. The door clicked shut behind them.

The next ten minutes were slow and awkward.

Milo had no intention of turning to look at Knuckle-cracker, never mind talk to him. He feared that he'd lose control of his breathing and be hit with a panic attack if he did so; instead, he kept his eyes firmly on the office. Their voices were muffled. Occasionally, the bright window light dimmed as somebody passed in front of it, partially blocking the light.

At some point in that awkward ten minutes, Knuckle-cracker attempted to engage him. 'You'd do well to get yoursen away from that tyke.'

Milo didn't respond, not because he disagreed, which he did, but because he was terrified.

Knuckle-cracker did try one more time in that ten-minute spell. 'Seen many a kid come unstuck because of tykes like that. Seen many of them *bled dry*.'

Milo nodded this time to show that he was listening. He didn't want to risk offending the large, unhinged man.

Come on, Pete, please hurry, he thought after those ten minutes. *What's taking you so long?*

He thought of Giraffe-neck putting his fists together in a crude attempt to signal two balls. Of course, Milo didn't possess these same balls. If he'd have had balls, he'd have questioned Knuckle-cracker over what was causing the delay.

Time passed relentlessly slowly.

Milo fought to keep his breathing steady.

Everything would work out.

He'd give his mother what she needed in her last few months.

What she needed and *then* some.

He suddenly felt calmer than he'd been since the shutter closed.

The muffled voices in the office grew louder. It sounded as if an argument had broken out.

He turned to look at Knuckle-cracker who had his arms crossed.

'What's happening?' Milo said.

Knuckle-cracker unfolded his arms.

Pete started to scream from the office.

Knuckle-cracker stepped towards Milo.

17

Gardner paced the cleaning area outside the mortuary.

She looked at her watch, and then up at Rice who was leaning against a set of stainless-steel sinks. 'How long is Sands going to keep us waiting?'

Rice shrugged. 'You know him better than most.'

'And what's that supposed to mean?'

How the hell did he know about the 'almost date' with Sands?

Rice raised his eyebrows. 'Nothing, boss. Just meant that you had a lot of dealings with him on the previous investigations. Back then, you wouldn't have let me anywhere near forensics, if you recall...'

'Give over,' she said, feeling relieved.

Dr Hugo Sands came out through the door, chewing. He had a brown McDonald's bag screwed up in his gloved left hand.

You've got to be kidding! While you're examining a body?

She shook her head. It was a softer touch than Riddick would've given. He'd have asked straight out: *What the hell is wrong with you man?*

Sands swallowed his food, gave a swift nod to Gardner and then offered a verbal 'afternoon mate' to Rice.

Immature dickhead, practically blanking her.

'Afternoon fella,' Rice said.

Gardner fixed Rice with a stare. He flinched. 'All lads together' was not taking root on her watch.

Hugo pinned his foot to a lever on the bin and threw the empty wrapper in. Then, he yanked off his gloves with a snap and threw them in too. He was deliberately stalling.

'So, what do we know?' Gardner said.

Sands went to wash his hands.

She suddenly missed Riddick's impatience, and went for his jugular herself instead. 'Sorry to interrupt your working lunch, Dr Sands, but we haven't got much time.'

He deliberately cleared his throat while drying his hands. 'Cause of death, heart attack,' he said, turning to face Gardner. 'I've left him open on the table if you want a look.'

Normally, she'd agree, preferring to see everything first-hand, but the thought of Sands chewing on a Big Mac as he peered into Stephen Best's chest cavity was still nauseating her. And she wanted to spend as little time with this massive prick as possible. 'A heart attack? Not blunt force trauma?'

'The head wound was severe,' Sands said. 'There was *some* swelling.'

'But that didn't kill him?'

'No. The heart attack killed him. It was a massive one too. But the head wound *could* have brought it on.'

'Could you explain in more detail please?'

'As you wish,' he said, picking at the meat between his teeth. She couldn't believe she'd ever even considered going on a date with this man. 'Internal organs are controlled by our autonomic nervous system.' He pointed at his head with the finger he'd just been working his teeth with. 'That's in the brain. Breathing, digestion and heartbeat. Evidence shows that concussion leads to the ANS taking tighter control over the variability of heart contractions per minute to ensure that the brain is getting the correct amount of blood and pressure to heal. Not too much, not too little. It's a protective mechanism, but it does put a strain on the heart. Stephen may have had a weakness there already which could be what caused the cardiac arrest.'

'How likely do you think that is?'

Sands shrugged. 'We'll conduct tests on the heart. We may find a weakness, we may not. Like anything in life, sometimes these things just happen.'

Sands was deliberately trying to sound lazy and disinterested; he'd not behaved like this on their previous two investigations.

'So, how'd he get the head wound? Was he struck, or did he fall?' Rice asked.

Sands shook his head. 'Hard to say.'

Gardner could feel the frustration bubbling away inside her. 'Would the head wound have killed him if the heart attack hadn't?'

'Potentially not,' Sands said. 'The skull was fractured, but there was no bone in the brain, and no rupturing or bleeding. Some slight swelling, but people have survived much worse.' He looked away as if that was it, and Gardner felt her blood boiling. She was about to open her mouth to demand more when the irritant lifted his head and said, 'Two other things of note.'

Gardner nodded. *I'm all ears.*

'We found semen in Stephen's anus.'

Gardner felt her back stiffen. She took a deep breath. *Of note! Understatement of the year.* 'He was raped?'

'It could've been consensual,' Rice said.

Gardner looked at him. 'He was fifteen, Phil. He was raped.'

'There was lubrication,' Sands said. 'There isn't much bruising. I'm not suggesting it wasn't forced, but it seems unlikely. It happened pre-mortem.'

Gardner lowered her head, which was spinning. Collette had mentioned that Stephen's visits to Kyle had become less frequent these last two months due to a new, mysterious friend that was older and didn't go to school.

'The semen has been submitted for DNA testing,' Sands said.

'And the second thing *of note*?' Gardner said, wondering if she'd managed to keep the sarcasm from her voice.

'Traces of something in his stomach which had inflamed the lining. A medication perhaps. Toxicology will hopefully tell you more over the next twenty-four hours.'

Gardner recalled the Graham Lock case from twenty years ago, and the sleeping pills he'd been drugged with. His father's sleeping pills. She shook it off. It was twenty years ago.

Still... 'Was he drugged?'

'It's best you wait for toxicology.'

Walking from the hospital, Rice turned to Gardner. 'So, do you think Stephen was groomed?'

Gardner looked at him. 'We've scoured his social media already. Nothing on there. Nothing apart from Warhammer blogs, forums and discussions. His mobile phone hasn't thrown up anything of interest either.'

'So, where next then?'

'How's your knowledge of Warhammer, Phil?'

He creased his brow. 'Do I look like someone who paints toys?'

'What does a person who paints toys look like?' Gardner said, turning and reaching for the handle of the car.

He didn't respond.

'I'll meet you outside the Warhammer shop in Harrogate and,

please, Phil, whatever you do, don't march in there and offend anyone with preconceived ideas about what toy painters look like.'

Again, he didn't respond, and when she was behind the wheel of the car, she watched him marching off to his own car, head down.

18

Right now, Riddick was less welcome at HQ than a dermatologist in a sunbed salon, but he still carried some clout. So, he made the necessary phone calls to get George Jacoby's address and other relevant information.

Riddick parked and looked up at George's large home on the Waterside. These days, the cost of buying a place in this location was eye-watering. However, this was the Jacoby family home. George had been born here, and the mortgage had not outlasted his parents.

Riddick looked off down the Waterside to where people *still* hired boats to float up and down the Nidd between the sandstone cliff faces on one side, and Mother Shipton's Cave on the other.

You lived very close to work in 2003, George, didn't you?

Riddick recalled an image of the squat, muscular man, standing by his carefully lined up boats.

Riddick had never hired a boat on the Waterside, so he closed his eyes, and tried to remember a moment when he may have communicated with George in the past.

Nothing.

All he had was Anders' memory of his persona. The salesman. The actor. The show pony.

Riddick imagined George addressing the crowds with a booming voice. 'The sun is shining, and the Petrifying Well over at Mother Shipton's Cave is crying her heart out! Why not slide over and take a look... half price for an hour... go and see the crying cave.'

Riddick opened his eyes and glanced at the wishing well opposite the boats. Eyewitnesses had seen Graham throwing coins into the well on several occasions *before* heading over to chat to George.

'Said he kept telling the kid to leave him be, but it kept falling on deaf ears,' Anders had told Riddick earlier.

Riddick remembered the late schoolteacher Donna Morfett well – she'd been a local legend and had taught several generations of Knaresborians. Yet, the eyewitness testimony that she'd seen two people out on the Nidd in a boat around the time that Graham was killed had been disregarded. Ridiculous.

Following George's stroke, the boating business was sold. On paper, the new owners bore no relation to the Jacoby family, but Riddick had already made a mental note to talk to them regardless, see if they could remember anything themselves from back then.

Those he called on at HQ had also come good with medical confirmation that George Jacoby was indeed a sufferer of locked-in syndrome and had been reduced to simple eye movements for the previous twenty years. It was possible to experience partial to complete recovery, but there were no existing reports of him having such good fortune.

The salesman. The actor. The show pony.

How much could you get away with if the world believed you couldn't move?

Riddick exited his vehicle, headed to the front door and rang the doorbell.

A young woman in blue scrubs answered the door. Riddick showed his identification and introduced himself. 'I assume you care for George Jacoby?'

She nodded, her eyes immediately gravitating up to the bandage on his head.

'I was involved in an accident. Can I see your identification?'

She pulled at the lanyard at her neck and slipped the card out from beneath her scrubs.

'Thank you, Ms Hartley. I'm sorry to bother you, but I could do with having a conversation with George.'

She creased her brow. 'You do know what's wrong with him, don't you?'

'I do, Ms Hartley, yes.'

'Then you know he can't talk?'

'He can communicate with his eyes, is that correct?'

'Not in my experience, Detective Inspector.'

'And you've been here for...?'

'Five years.'

Riddick felt the heavy weight of disappointment but wasn't about to give up just yet. 'Okay, I see... Is it just you, Ms Hartley?'

'There's three of us – we work in shifts.'

'Round-the-clock care. It must cost a fortune,' Riddick said.

'It's a private company and yes, it's expensive. Unfortunately, it doesn't seem to translate into a decent salary.'

'It's chilly out here,' Riddick said. 'Can we chat inside?'

She nodded and let him past.

Riddick went into a lounge that look dated. The wallpaper was covered in an image of the same five pink roses. It meant to create tranquillity he supposed, but the dramatic presence of thorns, due to the repetition of the image, was aggressive.

'How often does he leave his room?'

'He's taken along the Waterside every morning. In the evening, he's given a bath – which takes two of us. That's it.'

The salesman. The actor. The show pony.

'Are there times when he's alone?'

'Yes... when he's sleeping – which is most of the time. We do check on him regularly though. And if he's awake, we ensure the television is on for him.'

'And you've never seen him move?'

She raised an eyebrow. 'He can't. I can *assure* you of that. Sorry, DI, what's this concerning?'

Riddick took a deep breath and looked at her standing by the wall, framed by pink blooms and deadly thorns. 'I'd like to try and speak to George.'

'I was in there a moment ago – he was asleep. Without some kind of medical approval, I can't let you wake him. Can I help?'

'It's about a suspicious death.'

She opened her mouth to speak, but then closed it.

'Could you tell me who was with George Jacoby yesterday evening around 11 p.m.?'

She shook her head. Riddick could tell from her expression that she thought this was ridiculous.

'Just me... Who died?'

'I can't confirm that just now. Did you see him at that time?'

She thought about it. 'I can't say for sure without checking the log. I do see him regularly, but he sleeps most of the time these days.'

'Could you check for me, please?'

'Of course.'

She left the room and returned less than a minute later looking through a leather book.

'I administered meds at 9.30 p.m. and went in the room at

10.15 p.m. to check the temperature; he was asleep both times. Then, a visit at 12.30 a.m.'

'So, you didn't see him for over two hours between quarter past ten and half twelve?'

She flushed. 'Yes, but that is acceptable.'

'I'm not questioning your conduct, Ms Hartley – I'm just trying to establish what he was doing at that time.'

She regarded him for a second. 'He can't move, Detective Inspector! He's barely ever awake. Is there something you're not telling me?'

He looked away, chewed his lip and thought. He considered the car he'd seen just before chasing the boy down to St Robert's Cave. The one he'd forgotten. He looked at her again. 'Does he own a car?'

She shook her head, suddenly looking very concerned. 'Is it possible I could call someone at the office? I think it's maybe best if—'

'Does he own a car?'

'Please, DI, he can't move.'

'But he could still own a car?'

'Not that I know of.'

Riddick was aware that he was becoming intimidating 'I'm sorry. It's just part of my job. Routine. I hear everything you're saying.'

She regarded him for a moment, and then started to nod. 'Routine, yes. Bane of my life too. What made you think of George though?'

Riddick sighed. 'Someone gave us a description matching George... I have to rule him out. The way it is.'

'A description,' she said. 'What kind of description? He's pushed along the Waterside in a wheelchair.'

Riddick stared at her. 'I know. Ridiculous, eh? Can I just take a look at him? Put my mind at rest? I won't disturb him, I promise. I'll be quiet as a mouse.'

'I'll have to make a call first.'

He let her make the call, knowing already what the response would be.

Sure enough. 'Sorry, Detective Inspector, not without some kind of appointment... there are medical considerations... channels to go through.'

Frustrated, he excused himself, considering how best to get the permission he needed when he was supposed to be lying low...

* * *

Outside the house, frustrated, Riddick ran his eyes over the windows on the second and third floors.

Which room is yours George?

As he walked towards his car, he considered Gardner. Could he share what he'd discovered? Get her to buy in and get the necessary permissions to confront this actor?

He'd have more chance of getting pigs to fly him into the show pony's bedroom.

'Piss off, Anders,' he said as he climbed into his car. He closed the door. *What've you started here? You saw the way she was looking at me! She thinks I'm a madman. Which I am. As if the prick has resumed killing after twenty years of lying dormant? Literally lying dormant. Why didn't you just grab the bastard when you'd the chance, Anders? Instead of leaving it hanging out there. A loose thread. Blowing in the wind. Waiting for this moment. This moment of doubt.*

The urge to drink, which was ever-present, worked its way from the back of his mind to the front. He banged the wheel. 'Shit!'

An elderly man regarded him through his car window. Riddick held his hand up in apology.

He started the car.

He'd head home and read that letter Anders was on about. Maybe, just maybe, he'd elaborate on this bloody narrative he'd started.

And he knew for a fact, there was no alcohol in his home.

* * *

I see how lost you are.

They don't understand how to fix you, do they? They never understand. A crying shame.

They claim to know us... to be able to identify us... to see our problems.

But fix us?

Ha.

Not the foggiest.

But don't worry, my bear, I can fix you. In the same way, I always fix. You won't be my first bear, and you won't be my last.

Yes, they hunt me. Like ferocious predators with saliva dripping from their teeth!

But in all their fury, in all their relentlessness, they do not see me.

I hide in plain sight, my bear. Plain sight. You know me.

They know me.

Yet, they don't see me.

And tonight, my bear, my broken, but ever-so-fixable bear, you will come to me.

And not only will I show you. But I will give to you. Everything you deserve.

To be broken is to be fluid... changeable...

We all need shape, dear bear.

So, tonight you will be frozen.

Tonight, you will be solidified.

19

Knuckle-cracker guided Milo forcefully to the office door. 'Open it.'

Milo gulped and reached towards the key poking out of the lock, but he struggled to close his trembling fingers around it.

'It's not locked,' the large man behind him said.

There was another anguished cry from inside the office. Louder than last time.

Milo winced.

'Open it now,' Knuckle-cracker ordered again.

Milo, who'd stopped focusing on his breathing since the first scream, and was feeling light-headed and weak, managed to press down on the handle.

He leaned in on it and the door glided open. A blast of warm air hit him.

Milo stumbled into the office, swinging his eyes around. Filing cabinets strewn with coffee cups lined the sides of the narrow unit; a glowing halogen heater sat ominously next to a microwave on a fridge. The holdall lay unzipped on the floor beside Pete, who was sitting in an office chair with his back to Milo. There was a mound of white powder on the desk beside a computer screen. Giraffe-neck was currently standing over his friend gripping tightly to his hair.

'Not again...' Pete said, pausing to cough. 'I can't... *no more.*'

Giraffe-neck forced Pete's face down into the white mound.

'Hoover it up,' Giraffe-neck said. 'All of it.'

Milo winced over the different sounds coming from his friend. Gagging. Choking. Spluttering.

'Stop it!' Milo cried. 'Leave him alone.'

He felt Knuckle-cracker's hand tight on his shoulder. Then, he heard the large man hissing in his ear and smelled his stale breath. 'Shut it. You want to be next or summin'?'

Giraffe-neck raised his voice. 'It's going everywhere, you piss ant!' He yanked Pete back from the drugs by his hair.

The tortured boy was coughing again. Attempting to catch his breath as he tried to plead. 'My... my... eyes... burning...'

'My heart bleeds,' a familiar voice said from the computer screen.

Milo's breath caught in his throat.

KG.

What was happening? It suddenly felt like a trap.

Milo took a step back, but the way was blocked by Knuckle-cracker – he may as well have been a brick wall.

Pete squealed, 'I can't see. My head's splitting open...'

'If you like it so much,' KG continued, 'then you'll not waste a single grain.'

Giraffe-neck forced Pete's head down again.

'Not a single grain!' KG shouted and the sound distorted through the speakers.

Milo resisted the urge to shout out as he still had Knuckle-cracker gripping tightly to his shoulder, and his warning – *you want to be next?* – still reverberating around his head.

The noises coming from Pete were turning his stomach.

'You want your bones broken, soldier?' Giraffe-neck shouted. 'Where're those balls now? Take it like a man... I want to hear every breath as you suck it up... good soldier... *now*... harder... *suck it up!*'

Milo's eyes filled with tears. He couldn't help himself. 'Pete—'

He was cut off by Knuckle-cracker's hand over his mouth. 'Think about yourself, dipshit. It's too late for this leech.'

Milo wondered if Knuckle-cracker could feel his tears stream onto his massive, tattooed hands.

Giraffe-neck pulled Pete back again and this time released his hair. His head then lolled forward. The occasional cough, moan and splutter confirmed that he was still conscious.

'Whose fault is this, Pete?' KG said. 'You have the audacity to lie to me? To claim that the personal supply in your pocket isn't skimmed from my product? Did you think we wouldn't test it? That we wouldn't match it to ours? How *bloody* stupid are you?'

'I'm sorry, KG... I'm sorry... it was a little bit...' It was difficult to tell if Pete was speaking through tears, or if he was just struggling to speak full stop.

'Bollocks! You bit off way more than you could chew.'

Pete slipped from the chair, landing with a thump on his knees.

'How much is left?' KG asked.

Giraffe-neck leaned over the table. 'Shed loads.'

'Well, we can't sell it now, can we?'

'No,' Giraffe-neck said. 'It's covered in shite. Blood and snot...'

KG tutted. 'You really did, didn't you, Pete? Bite off more than you could chew?'

Giraffe-neck yanked Pete's head back by his hair again. 'Answer.'

'Yes... yes...' Pete said. His voice was sounding weaker with every moment that passed.

Milo bit his lip. It was awful watching his friend being tortured, but if they didn't ride it out, then what? Knuckle-cracker's warning rang true. He'd be next up for some punishment.

'I don't want any waste,' KG said. 'None. You bit it off – *now* you can chew it all.'

'There's a lot here,' Giraffe-neck said. 'And he's starting to look like shit.'

'*No* waste.' KG's voice rose. The speakers distorted again.

'Okay,' Giraffe-neck said.

Giraffe-neck wandered over to the closest filing cabinet and threw a stare at Milo. He slipped a teaspoon from a cup, dried it on his sleeve and headed back over.

He scooped up a teaspoon of the soiled drug. Then, he pushed the office chair away, so he could kneel behind Pete, and reach around him to grab his chin.

'No... no...' Pete said, suddenly finding his voice again. 'My head... it'll explode.'

'You *chew* it all down,' KG said. 'Prove you're not a snivelling slug, and all is forgiven. Don't prove it... well, then, what use are you?'

'Do it, soldier,' Giraffe-neck said, holding the teaspoon under Pete's nose.

Pete snorted. He gasped and shook his head.

'Good lad. Again,' KG said.

Giraffe-neck reached up to the table from where he was kneeling to refill the teaspoon. Then, he yanked Pete's head back by his chin to give him another dose.

Pete snorted.

'Now turn,' KG said. 'Your trainee is here.'

Pete's head was hanging again, and he didn't look capable of turning; so, Giraffe-neck lowered himself down to give assistance.

Milo gasped when he saw his friend's face, streaked with white powder and blood. His eyes were swimming, and his lips, and other muscles in his face, were twitching aggressively.

'Milo?' Pete said. 'Kid...' He was slurring his words. 'Sorry...'

'No,' Milo said, 'it's not your fault—'

Knuckle-cracker tightened his grip on his shoulder, cutting him off.

'Tell him, Pete,' KG said.

'It's my fault...' Pete said. 'I stole from him.'

KG said, 'So, we carry on. Every grain.'

Giraffe-neck forced him to snort from the teaspoon again. Pete's head hung forward, blood, snot and tears forming strings that reached down to the floor.

'How's your mother, Milo?' KG asked.

Milo felt his entire body freezing over.

'She's in a bad way. It can't be easy,' the monster continued.

Milo nodded. It was all he could think to do. He'd no idea of what KG wanted to hear.

'You've done nothing wrong here, Milo, have you?' KG asked.

'He hasn't...' Pete murmured. He was barely audible.

'This could still end all right for you, and for your mother, Milo,' KG continued.

'He's done nothing wrong...' Pete murmured.

Milo looked at his friend, forcing back tears.

Pete retched.

Milo felt his heart rate intensify. He felt the urge to throw himself forward and help Pete before he started vomiting. Knuckle-cracker's hand on his shoulder, coupled with KG's veiled threats over his sick mother, steadied him.

'He needs more medicine,' KG said.

'No,' Milo said. 'He's had enough... please... he's sorry.' This time he ignored Knuckle-cracker's tightening grip.

'Well, if he doesn't finish it, then *you* finish it, Milo. No one is wasting a grain.'

'Okay,' Milo said. '*Okay.* That's fine. Just leave him alone.'

'No,' Pete said. 'No... Milo... no.'

KG laughed. 'Think he's bailing you out, Pete... I'd take him up on it if I were—'

'Piss off,' Pete forced out. He gasped for air.

'Did you really just say that?' KG asked.

Pete sucked down more air. 'Yes, dickhead. Piss... off...'

'No,' Milo said, realising what Pete was doing. 'He doesn't know what he's saying. He's had too much! It's fine. I'll do it.'

Pete looked at Milo. 'I'm okay, kid...'

'Okay, then,' KG said. 'There we have it. Pete is confident he can do it all by himself. Let's get on with it.'

Milo lurched forward. 'No—'

Knuckle-cracker pulled him back, further from the scene.

Giraffe-neck knelt with another spoonful of white powder, looked at Pete's haggard face, turned to the screen and then said, 'Sir... I'm not sure—'

'Give him his medicine... *now.*'

Giraffe-neck turned, yanked Pete's head back again and thrust the powder beneath his nose.

'Milo,' KG said. 'Did Pete tell you about his *own* mother?'

'No,' Pete said. 'You're a—'

'Take it,' Giraffe-neck interrupted. 'Or I'll put your friend next to you and feed him the rest.'

Pete snorted.

KG said, 'Anyway, did Pete tell you his mum was a prostitute?'

Pete was gasping. 'Piss... off...'

'He *needs* more,' KG said.

Giraffe-neck forced more into him.

'Stabbed one of her customers,' KG continued. 'Can you believe it?'

Pete retched, clutching his forehead. 'Raped... she was... raped.'

'Murderous whore,' KG said and laughed. 'Two sides to every story. Give him more!'

Giraffe-neck refilled the spoon. 'There isn't much...'

'More!'

Pete was muttering and twitching. His words were so slurred that they were incomprehensible.

'His mummy, the whore, in jail, and I was there for him, and this is how little Pete repays me?' KG said.

Pete's response was nonsensical.

Giraffe-neck forced his chin up again and wedged the spoon underneath his nose.

'Breathe deep, my boy. Every last grain,' KG said. 'In a way, Milo, you're lucky to have this lesson. If only Pete had had this same lesson, then maybe, just maybe, he—'

Pete retched again, but Giraffe-neck held firm to Pete's chin. It was a mistake. He vomited. 'Jesus... that's disgusting.'

Pete fell to all fours, still vomiting again – this time all over the Slazenger holdall.

Giraffe-neck was shaking the puke off his hand. 'It's soaking into my sleeve.'

'The bloody product,' Knuckle-cracker said, barging past Milo. Milo thumped into a filing cabinet.

Knuckle-cracker kicked the holdall away from the pool of sick. It spun away beneath the office table. Pete continued to vomit and covered Knuckle-cracker's foot.

'You pig.' Knuckle-cracker kicked Pete in the face.

The force of the blow sent Pete's head upwards, so it cracked against the edge of the office table. Then, Pete fell forward again, landing in a pool of his own sick.

Keenly aware that there was now an unblocked escape route behind him, Milo couldn't resist looking between the open office door and his best friend lying face down in his own vomit. Could he somehow escape? Get help?

Then he thought of the closed shutter, and his courage drained away.

Knuckle-cracker was shaking his foot and Giraffe-neck was shaking his hand. In the background, KG was trying to speak, but his actual words were unclear over the effing and blinding.

Milo edged towards Pete, wanting to kneel and take his close friend into his arms, sick or no sick, stroke his head until he recovered from this forced overdose.

But then his friend started to fit.

The two thugs darted back from their convulsing victim.

'What the bloody hell is happening?' KG shouted.

'He's having some kind of sodding fit, face down in his own puke,' Giraffe-neck said.

'What? Get it sorted!' KG hissed.

The two men looked at each other. Knowing they'd no choice, they knelt in the mess and together, flipped Pete over. He continued to convulse on his back, making a gargling sound, his mouth frothing.

Milo, terrified for his friend, but at the same time, useless in this situation, had an idea. It wasn't the most ambitious, but it was all he had. He started to move backwards towards the open door.

The gargling stopped.

Milo felt a bolt of relief over the fact that the fit had ended. He reached the door to the office.

'Jesus,' Knuckle-cracker said. 'He's stopped breathing.'

Milo put a hand to his mouth, fearful that he might betray his retreat.

'Mouth to mouth!' KG said.

Milo was already through the door. *Hold on Pete. Please. I'll get help – I'll come back.*

'No pulse. There's no pulse,' Knuckle-cracker said.

'What?' KG said.

'He's dead.'

'Switch the computer off now!' KG was shouting. 'Disconnect it!'

'But what do *we* do? What do we do?' Giraffe-neck asked.

'Unplug it. Unplug it or I'll—'

The computer died. One of them must have complied.

'CPR... are you giving him CPR?' Giraffe-neck asked.

'Like I know how to do that?' Knuckle-cracker said. 'We stopped his goddamned heart.'

Milo had frozen at the doorway.

There's no pulse.

We stopped his goddamned heart.

Was this really happening?

It was as if the scene before him was an incomprehensible nightmare. The type that left you so disorientated upon waking that your brain was forced to rally a defence and vanquish all traces of it from memory.

Unfortunately, this wasn't a nightmare. This *was* happening. There was no defence mechanism in his brain to cut out the experience. And, if he lived to fight another day, the damage may just be irreparable.

He was too late. He couldn't save Pete.

Right now, he wanted to collapse to the ground in tears, but what purpose would that serve?

He'd be as dead as his best friend—

'Shit... the other kid!' Giraffe-neck said.

Shocked into action, Milo slammed the office door and turned the key. He tore it from the lock and threw it as hard as he could into the mess of car parts strewn about the place.

He turned and sprinted across the unit floor, weaving around the debris.

When he reached the shutter, he heard the door of the office being shaken violently. 'Kid... get the hell back here!'

Milo knelt and started to lift the shutter.

Behind him, he could hear one of the large men ploughing themselves into the door. It wouldn't last. He could already hear it splintering.

When the gap was large enough to let him free, Milo rolled beneath it and was back outside in the icy wind and natural light.

He jumped to his feet and ran as fast as he could. It was only when he reached the entrance to the industrial estate that he heard the shutter being completely rolled up behind him.

He ploughed down a side street onto a main road. Then, he took a random turn off onto a residential street.

He ran for thirty minutes, turning onto different roads whenever he could.

Eventually, he stopped to rest. Down on his haunches, sucking back breaths.

There's no pulse.

Pete was dead.

We stopped his goddamned heart.

At that point, Milo was unable to stop the tears.

20

Gardner waited for Rice outside the Games Workshop in Harrogate.

'Dark already,' Rice said, dusting snow off his jacket. 'I hate winter.'

'Vitamin D's the answer,' Gardner said, turning to the door.

'Is it in beer?'

Gardner put a hand on the door and looked back. 'If you don't offend anyone in this store, I'll order you some.'

'Offend? Why are you so down on me, boss?'

'You stereotype too much.'

'Do I 'eck as like! I just understand groups of people. It helps. I need to recognise a money-grabbing ex-wife, and a greedy banker with no morals, if I'm going to have any chance in this job.'

She couldn't deny that grouping people based on traits and interests could help with motive, but that wasn't her concern. What concerned her with Rice was his patronising and aggressive attitude towards groups he didn't like – of which there were many.

Rice continued, 'These guys are geeks; might be something in that...'

Case in point. 'Calling someone a geek is offensive, Phil.'

'It's not. There's a place for geeks. Computer and science breakthroughs and whatnot.'

She shook her head. 'Are you really from this century? What group do you belong to?'

He shrugged and grinned. 'The group of effective police officers?'

She guffawed. 'Really?'

He raised an eyebrow as if pleading. 'Thanks! Why? What group do you think I'm from?'

Oh, I don't know... the group of bigoted pricks? 'Let's just focus on your qualities.'

'Which are?'

She pushed open the door without answering.

It wasn't a large store. There was a counter off to the right, where a checkout stood empty. Besides that, a shelf full of expensive paints in tiny pots. At the centre of the room, between the shelves filled with colourful boxes, sat a large table covered in intricate terrain and painted miniatures. Gardner stepped forward, admiring the rising hillocks and ruined castles that held golden armoured figures and multitudes of snarling green creatures. It was impressive not just in the expanse, but also in how many hungry youngsters it'd drawn towards it. Gardner counted ten children in total, of varying ages from about thirteen to sixteen, huddled around this monolithic battle, rolling dice, crying out in despair and delight in equal measure. Most were boys, but Gardner was pleased to see there was a reasonable female contingent holding their own, too.

She imagined Stephen Best sitting there, among this small crowd of young enthusiasts, cheering and groaning as he launched his dice onto the bloody battlefield.

The store manager, wearing a T-shirt with a red goblin on the front, and baggy combat pants, was circling the table and the children. He was leaning in regularly to point his finger at a miniature and issue a suggestion. Gardner struggled to understand the guidance. It seemed the world of Warhammer came with its own niche vocabulary.

The manager was so engrossed in the game, he was yet to notice his visitors.

Rice came up close beside Gardner and spoke quietly. 'You see how many children are here? *Opportunity.* Watch... they're eating out the palm of his hand.'

Gardner didn't nod. He'd be DBS checked for sure, but that didn't mean the risk didn't exist. The risk *always* existed.

The special friend. Someone who'd also had a keen interest in Warhammer...

She looked at Rice. She could tell now from his eyes that he was thinking the same thing. Was the person who had hit Stephen with a rock at the cave and left him to die, here?

A shiver ran down her spine.

At that point, the manager, who was on the far side of the table, looked up and caught Gardner's eyes.

He stood ramrod straight.

She could have smiled, put him at ease, but the racing thoughts of an early life being cut tragically short had her mind in knots.

The manager leaned over and said something to one of the boys, then stood and circled around the table. He marched towards them, solemnly, clearly aware that Gardner and Rice were not paying customers.

'Hit!' one of the boys cried out.

When the manager was directly in front of them, they showed their IDs and introduced themselves. He squeezed his eyes shut and sighed.

Gardner and Rice exchanged a glance.

'Wound!' another child shouted.

He opened his eyes. Gardner noticed they were bloodshot – as if he may have been crying earlier.

'I'm Eugene Scarrow, the manager.' His eyes darted between the two detectives. 'Are you here about Stephen?'

Gardner's heart fluttered. The name had not been disclosed yet. 'What makes you mention Stephen, Mr Scarrow?'

Eugene turned to look at the energetic children, and then back at Gardner, 'Please... keep it down. They don't know.'

'Good. They shouldn't know.' Rice's voice was laced with aggression.

Eugene flinched.

'Mr Scarrow... how do *you* know?' Gardner prompted.

'Ron Best phoned me before today's session. About half past three. He told me his son wasn't coming in today. Please... let's move over here. I don't want them to hear.'

'Save!' one of the players shouted, sounding ecstatic.

Eugene led them over to the counter. On the counter was an array of overly priced paintbrushes and some collector cards, all displaying weapon-wielding maniacs.

'Our after-school sessions start at four and finish at five thirty. There're about thirteen in this little team, but not everyone shows up every week. Still, I never get a phone call from parents when they don't show. So, when Ron phoned, it took me aback.' He ran his hand over his stubbly cheek and stared off into space.

'Mr Scarrow?'

'Yes... well, I didn't know what to say, so I just thanked him for letting me know, and then asked him if everything was okay with Stephen. Like you do, you know... There's a lot of flu going about, isn't there? And he just came out with it! He said his son was gone, that he wasn't ever coming in again... that...' His eyes were filling up. 'That he'd been killed! Oh God, I shouldn't have asked him, should I?'

'I don't think you did anything wrong by asking that question, Mr Scarrow.'

Gardner made a note to check the store's phone records to verify the claim.

There was a loud cheer from over at the table, and another kid shouted, 'What a crap roll! I've not lost three to battleshock for years!'

Eugene looked over and nodded. 'Brad's finally fallen.'

Gardner looked over as the young boy who'd just shouted jolted away from the table with an angry expression on his face. He turned, kicked out at the air and then marched over to the back of the shop to look at some boxes on the shelves.

'He'll be okay,' Eugene said.

'You know these children well?' Gardner asked.

Eugene nodded. 'Yes. Like I said – I run this club three times a week for them. After school.'

'That's good of you,' Rice said. 'Is that part of the service?'

'Well, part of our role is to offer a weekend club, but the week-night ones are dependent on take up. I used to go to one when I was younger, you know? I want to give back. Loved it.' He sighed. 'Still do.'

'How long have you been working here, Mr Scarrow?'

He did a brief calculation in his head. 'Over four years.'

Gardner wrote this down. 'How long have you been the manager here?'

'About half that time.'

'What days do you work?' Gardner asked.

'Monday to Thursday, and Saturday. We have a mobile manager who covers days off in the region, which in my case is Sunday and Friday.'

'Can I get their name?'

'Yes. Alexia Reynolds.'

Gardner made a note of the name. 'Does she run this club in your absence?'

'It's *they*.'

'Sorry?' Gardner said.

'Alexia prefers the pronoun, *they*.'

'Ah, I see,' Gardner said. 'Good to know.'

She glanced at Rice, fearful he might voice his opinion on this matter. She could tell from his expression that he was desperate to, but fortunately, he held back. Maybe she was rubbing off on him?

'But no. It's only me who runs this club.'

She could sense Rice becoming restless beside her and hopping from one foot to the other. She valued the details that built the foundation of their complete understanding – he just wanted to get straight to the point.

'Look... I'm not under suspicion here, am I?'

'Establishing facts,' Gardner said. 'That's all we're doing, Mr Scarrow. Everyone is questioned.'

She looked over at the children. *Apart from them right now.* Guardians would be required for that. She made a note to get her team to make it happen. Any of these youngsters could know something about Stephen and his relationship with... well... his relationship with whoever was responsible. 'How'd you describe your relationship with Stephen?'

His eyes widened and he genuinely looked offended. 'Same as with all the other children!'

'Which is?' Rice asked.

'I detect a tone...'

'I apologise, Mr Scarrow. We've got to consider everything. There isn't a tone,' Gardner said.

'Yet,' Rice said.

Eugene scowled.

Gardner inwardly groaned and glared at Rice. She then looked back at Eugene. 'Sorry, Mr Scarrow. Please tell me how your relationship worked.'

Eugene swooped up a souvenir coin from his counter. Gardner could see an imprint of a futuristic looking soldier on it. Eugene fiddled with the coin. 'There's genuinely very little to say. They come after school. They talk Warhammer. *We* talk Warhammer – that's all we do. *Genuinely.* No one wants to talk about school, or anything else for that matter.'

Gardner looked over at the children again. *Makes sense. They're here for a complete break from reality by the looks of things.*

'I don't have personal relationships with these children,' Eugene said. 'Honestly. In fact, the only time anything personal happens is when it's a birthday, and I present them with a free figure. But that's it.'

Gardner made more notes. 'What was Stephen like?'

Eugene passed the coin from hand to hand, clearly agitated. 'Quiet when we weren't playing, and when we were, solely focused on the game. Stephen often came with his best friend, Kyle, and I didn't really see him socialise with any of the other children. Good kids both of them. They could certainly play too—'

The shop door opened. A man in blue overalls tilted a delivery trolley stacked with several boxes and worked his way backwards up and over a step into the shop.

Eugene looked back at Gardner and Rice. 'Sorry. Can I have a moment please?'

'It's okay, we can wait,' Gardner said.

'Thanks,' Eugene said, circling around the counter and then marching over to the deliveryman.

The deliveryman settled the trolley and then brushed snow off his blue beanie hat which sat over long black hair. He looked around the shop, taking in the children. 'Busy one, Eugene?'

'Always,' Eugene said.

The deliveryman glanced at Gardner and Rice, nodded a greeting, handed a clipboard to Eugene and then bent at the legs to unload the boxes.

Eugene read over the delivery details and then signed it.

The deliveryman looked up. 'The kid loved Hedonites of Slaanesh. You knocked it out the park with that one.'

Eugene nodded. 'No problem. Any other recommendations required?'

The deliveryman laughed as he finished unloading. 'On my salary? That'll do for this month.'

After the deliveryman had stood again, Eugene handed the clipboard back to him with the souvenir coin on top.

The deliveryman regarded it. 'Nice.'

Eugene knelt to inspect the boxes. He didn't bother opening four of them, but he pulled at the tape on the fifth.

The deliveryman rolled the coin over the back of his fingers on one hand – a nifty-looking trick that Gardner had seen before, but very few people could do.

Meanwhile, Eugene pulled out colourful packets of figures and proceeded to count them. 'Only four packs of Lumineth Realm-lords...' He looked up at the deliveryman. 'I ordered five?'

Lumineth Realm-lords! Gardner smiled. *Who thinks up these bloody names? Not just that, but who'd be able to remember all these odd names?*

The deliveryman shook his head and made a note on the clipboard. 'Not the first time this has happened today. They need to get their house in order! It's not me who packs them. I'll make sure that's expressed over to you tomorrow. Do you want to check the other boxes?'

'I will... later. Thanks.'

The deliveryman apologised again, and Eugene held the door open for him. The snow was coming down harder now, and Gardner watched the man's blue beanie hat quickly whiten as he pushed his delivery trolley past the shop window and away.

Eugene returned to the counter, sighing. 'If they get an order right before I'm sixty, I'll retire a happy man.'

Gardner smiled. 'I imagine dealing with stock comes with challenges.'

'Yes. Shouldn't do though.'

Gardner continued to interview Eugene, all the while feeling a dead end looming, getting larger and darker, until it blocked out all light, and hope.

She let Rice get the details of his alibi for the previous evening. Turns out he was on a date with Alexia Reynolds before spending the night with them. Gardner made a note to get Lucy O'Brien to confirm this – she was suitably young and considerate enough to get their pronoun choices right – she certainly wouldn't trust any of those middle-aged men in her team, having heard some of them express their views on this change in culture already.

On the way back to their vehicles, shielding their eyes from the snow, Rice said to Gardner, 'What'd you think?'

'Dead end, but we'll definitely speak to Alexia, and the children in that club,' Gardner said.

'No... I meant of the game?' He smiled. 'You keen to get involved?'

'I haven't even got the patience to set up a game of Monopoly.'

Rice laughed. 'I'll let you into a secret, boss.'

She looked at him.

'I tried painting one of those figures when I was young. Just one, like. They were made of lead back then. Still got it in my loft somewhere.'

She smiled. 'You're a dark horse! Phil Rice, the Warhammer aficionado!'

'Hardly. I'll dig it out one day. It didn't look like any of the figures in there, I can tell you. It looked as if it'd been left by the fire and melted!'

Gardner laughed.

21

When he arrived home, Milo sprinted to the toilet and threw up.

Surprising really, having thrown up three times already on his journey back from York; once on the train station platform, once in the train toilet and once in the doorway of a barbers on the high street.

When he went into the kitchen for water, he saw the back door was ajar.

Mum?

This wasn't the first time his mother had left it open when she ventured out into the back garden. He looked out of the kitchen window. No sign of her.

She must have left the door open when she'd returned to bed – that wouldn't be the first time either.

With still trembling hands, he closed the back door and latched it.

He went to the sink and turned the tap on. The sudden rush of water made him jump.

There's no pulse.

We stopped his goddamned heart.

Closing his eyes, he leaned on the sink, and saw, again, his best friend lying dead in his own vomit.

His stomach lurched again, but no more crap came up his throat. He turned, trying to slow his breathing.

Behind him, the rush of tap water seemed to intensify.

Pete...

Milo slipped down to the floor, hugged his knees to his chest and rocked.

Why'd you do it Pete?

Why'd you have to steal from them?

And what about me? What'll happen to me?

He clutched his head with both hands. *Think... Milo... think. What next?*

You witnessed a murder.

He shook his head from side to side.

No... no... no...

You witnessed a murder, and they will kill you.

That was the reality.

The pain of his great loss was going to be short-lived anyway. They would come for him, and then nothing would matter any more. At least not in this life.

His eyes flew to the kitchen door which he'd only just latched.

Had it been his mother... or had it been someone else?

Tears in eyes, overwhelmed by nausea, Milo surprised himself by getting to his feet.

Think... think... You need to get help...

He didn't have a mobile phone. Having no friends, it'd never really interested him. And he'd rather spend his allowance on comics than phone credit.

But his mother had one by her bed.

He killed the tap and listened. He could hear nothing in the silence of the house.

For good measure, he yanked a kitchen knife from the rack, and worked his way through the house to his mother's bedroom. The knife trembled in his hand, and he wondered if he possessed the coordination to use it if it became necessary.

Close to his mother's room, he heard her laboured breaths, and relaxed slightly. He didn't want to wake her. The door was open and as he drew closer, he could see her lying there, propped up into a sitting position by her pillow. Her face was gaunt and grey, and her bald head, which she usually kept covered even in bed, was exposed.

He sighed with relief that she was there. Safe and alive. At least for now.

As he entered the room, he held the knife behind his back, in case she woke.

Despite her rattling breaths, he felt alone. In fact, he'd never felt so alone.

Pete was gone.

Soon his mother too.

He saw the phone on the bedside table and continued.

His mother's arms were above the sheets, and they looked ever so thin. Veins stood out on the backs of her hands.

As he passed, he placed his own hand gently on top of hers and whispered, 'I'm sorry, Mum.'

She didn't wake, but it took an age for her to reach her next breath, which made Milo wonder if she'd heard.

He looked at her phone on her bedside table by a glass water. He placed the knife alongside it, and glanced back at his mother again, tears in his eyes.

I made a mistake, Mum.

I just wanted to give you one last holiday.

Looking at her now, in this state, the idea seemed ridiculous.

A cold sensation spread over his body.

Have I known this all along? Did I do all this for my own selfish reasons? Just to bring some excitement into my sad little life?

He wiped his eyes with the back of his hand and then reached down for the phone.

He picked it up and tapped in 999. *Let them save us, and then let them punish me.*

He pressed call.

The door closed behind him.

Breath trapped in his throat, he turned sharply to see KG standing in front of the closed door. He pushed the phone to his ear and with his other hand, reached behind himself for the knife.

'Don't,' KG said, stepping forward, finger in the air. 'Your mother is beautiful.'

Unable to feel the knife, Milo ran his hand vigorously over the table. There was a clunk and a swoosh. The glass of water. He yanked his hand back. No knife.

'She doesn't deserve this,' KG said, reaching the foot of his mother's bed.

The call connected. 'Emergency. Which service?'

KG was suddenly less than a metre from him with his hand out. He mouthed, 'Give me the phone.'

'Emergency. Which service please?'

Milo opened his mouth, but quickly closed it again when he realised that both he and his mother would be dead before anyone got here.

'Sorry. Is anyone there?'

Milo placed the phone in KG's hand and watched him end the call.

22

Feeling his painkillers kicking in, Riddick placed his phone down on the kitchen table and sighed with relief. Not just over the temporary easing of his headache, but over the fact that a close colleague at HQ had worked her magic.

Riddick had permission to visit George Jacoby in his home at eleven tomorrow with a doctor supervising.

While making a Pot Noodle, Riddick looked at the pile of letters that had been building up for months. Mainly bank statements and quarterly energy bills, but there were at least five letters from Anders in the pile that he hadn't bothered to read. The ones prior to that he'd thrown in a drawer in the lounge.

Riddick recalled Anders' request. *Read the last one when you get home.*

He really couldn't face it now. He'd had enough emotion for one day. Reading a letter that would surely consist of Anders pleading for forgiveness, yet again, may just push him right over the edge and into the off-licence around the corner that always seemed to tug at him like a magnet whenever he walked past...

His phone buzzed. Suspecting it was Gardner, he felt a burst of excitement. However, he was disappointed to see that it was just a special offer on spicy pizzas tonight at Papa John's. He returned to his steaming hot Pot Noodle. *Two minutes too late, Signor John.*

He blew on a forkful of noodles and stuck it into his mouth. Not a single update from Gardner.

Sidelined was an understatement.

Still, surely he was due another interview. He'd woken up next to a young man's body, after all, and still didn't even have his name. Shouldn't they be asking him more things?

Unless...

You have someone else, don't you, Emma?

He'd give anything to know which direction she was running in. Not towards George Jacoby that was for sure.

No one, including Gardner, had been in the slightest bit interested about a link to Graham Lock's murder.

Maybe they're right, after all?

Am I chasing delusions?

He threw his Pot Noodle away; his appetite was gone.

No.

Once upon a time, Anders had been good at his job.

George and Graham had been seen in conversation...

Donna Morfett had reported a suspicious late-night boat journey...

Had someone shut down George Jacoby so he couldn't kill again? Was the stroke a ruse? Had they somehow given him brain damage? But why do that? Why protect George Jacoby's innocence only to render him one of the living dead? Unless...

Someone else was being protected... someone connected to George Jacoby...

He headed to his laptop and researched George's background. Both George's parents were dead now, but both had worked in government. Interesting. George's mother's occupation raised the biggest alarm bell. She had been the serving Conservative MP for Harrogate between 1997 and 2010. And between 2002 and 2010, she served as the minister for crime and policing.

RT HON CASSANDRA JACOBY

'Your mother had quite the job, George...' He drummed his fingers on the table. 'Wouldn't have done for her son to be the most infamous killer in the history of her constituency, would it?'

He took a deep breath, recalling Anders' words. *One eyewitness was a forty-year-old Conservative politician from the south on his holidays.*

Did one of your peers crawl out the woodwork to help you?

He sat back in his chair and sighed. Surely this couldn't be true? No one could have that kind of influence, could they? To let a child killer walk free and frame an innocent man for it?

He typed Cassandra Jacoby into the search bar.

Wikipedia gave him what he needed and sent the temperature of his blood plummeting.

He sat back in his chair and put a hand to his mouth.

Cassandra's maiden name.

He pulled up her family tree. Confirmed it.

'Bloody hell.'

Maybe he was suffering from delusions. In fact, strike that. Maybe he was in a coma, and this was a most peculiar dream conjured up by his dying brain.

He glanced at his watch. Gardner would probably be leading her briefing right now.

Would his career survive if he gate-crashed?

He heard Gardner in his head. *You're more like a cat, Paul. How many bloody lives you got?*

23

During Gardner's previous two cases up in the wilds of Yorkshire, results had come in thick and fast. She'd barely had time to breathe.

She looked around her predominantly male crowd, expecting hands left, right and centre. For revelations to strike at the heart of Operation Lost Light so they could tame the wilds once again.

But contributions were at a premium today.

Heads were low. Disappointment and fatigue were vicious animals at the best of times, but throw in the death of a child, and you had a truly dangerous one, gnawing deeper than it did in other murder investigations.

She'd already noted the absence of O'Brien right at the start.

Unusual. She was always here.

Despite the subdued atmosphere, she ensured everyone said their piece. There were a lot of findings to trawl through, and although nothing got Gardner's blood flowing, the information needed a meticulous scrubbing.

Phone records and social media were particularly disappointing. If Stephen had been in touch with a mystery friend, he wasn't using any of these media, which meant all communication must have been in person, or the mystery friend had provided Stephen with an as-yet unrecovered phone. Again, they went through the time frame, some findings on CCTV cameras and door-to-door reports, but it didn't expand horizons.

For her conclusion to the briefing, Gardner returned to Dr Sands' report which she'd been through earlier, because this offered some glimmer of hope. 'And we have toxicology first thing. Find out what inflamed the stomach. DNA too, hopefully.'

Out of the blue, a question regarding Ron Best's current state of mind fluttered over from the back.

Rice answered it. 'I keep checking in with the FLO. He's barely moved or spoken.'

'We'll take another run at him first thing,' Gardner said.

'When the shock passes, he may give us more,' Rice said.

When the shock passes? I wouldn't count on that happening for a long time... But Gardner kept her thoughts to herself.

Gardner returned to the board and tapped *mystery friend.* Here, there were the beginnings of a bullet point list. Warhammer fanatic. Older. Unknown personally to Kyle. 'Someone knows who this is.' She turned back. 'And by this time tomorrow, we will know too, okay?'

Everyone murmured in agreement.

She was just about to say good evening when Rice said, 'We need to take another run at Paul.'

Rice wasn't saying this because he disliked him, even though he did, intensely. For once, Rice was calling this just right.

'I can do it?' Rice offered.

Over her dead body!

Gardner looked up. 'You're right, Phil. *I'll* speak to him first thing. *Alone.* Anyone have anything else—'

The door to the incident room opened. O'Brien stood there

with a brown folder in her hands. She was out of breath, but she was young and fit enough to get it under control quickly. 'Sorry... but I found something, and... well, I just got sucked in. Sorry, again.'

Gardner straightened her back. The room suddenly had some electricity in it. 'What you got, Lucy?'

O'Brien opened the folder and, starting with Gardner, handed out grainy photographs.

Gardner saw two boys she didn't recognise, standing beneath a tree, over another young man on his arse. Puffer jacket. Fortnite backpack on his stomach.

Gardner's adrenaline spiked.

'Caught at 10.15 p.m. on CCTV outside the Co-op on Borough-bridge Road,' O'Brien said. 'This is a still I took from the footage. The boy on the ground is Stephen Best.'

Fallen heads around the room started to rise.

'I've watched the footage repeatedly,' O'Brien said. 'Stephen comes here alone. He stops by the tree, while the other two lads are on the bench. I don't think they're meeting up. Eventually, they start to communicate. Stephen seems erratic. He's moving awkwardly, and he seems in some kind of panic. The boys on the bench eventually rise. You'd hope they'd be going to help, but it doesn't play out that way. There's an argument between the boy on the right and Stephen. Eventually he grabs Stephen's backpack.'

Was he trying to steal the bag? Did he know what was in it?

'Stephen manages to keep hold of the backpack, but he stumbles. And that's the still of him on his backside. He starts to scurry away. Our aggressor here *could've* got to him, retrieved the bag, potentially assaulted him, but doesn't. Because the other lad blocks him. Gets in between the both of them. Buys Stephen enough time to get up and run off down Boroughbridge Road towards Bond End.' She paused to let her findings sink in.

'To the Waterside,' Rice said. 'A clear route to St Robert's Cave. Would fit with the timeline if he was murdered around 11 p.m.'

Gardner nodded. 'Do these boys follow, Lucy?'

'No. They head in the opposite direction on Boroughbridge Road about a minute or so later.'

'We need to find out who these two boys are. *Desperately.*'

'Already have done,' O'Brien said and smiled.

Atta girl, Gardner thought. *You can be late anytime you want.*

She looked at her notes. 'Our scrapper is Pete Wilson, fifteen. The one who prevents an assault is Milo Hardy, who is also fifteen. I have their addresses and have prepared some background notes on them both. Pete is a troublemaker. Truants regularly. His father also has a record and has spent time inside for assault. Milo is the opposite. Squeaky clean. Head down at school. Bit of a loner by all accounts. Lives alone with his mother who is terminally ill.'

Gardner nodded. 'Outstanding work, Lucy. So, we need to know what that bust up was all about. Phil and I will handle this immediately. Everyone not already on overtime, head home now please and rest for tomorrow. Those with overtime tasks – they're pinned to the front.'

O'Brien approached Gardner as everyone was leaving. 'Boss?'

'Yes, Lucy?'

'I was wondering if I could help with the interviews... I feel kind of invested now.'

Gardner looked at Rice, hovering close by, and then back at Lucy. 'I think you've earned that.' She looked back at Rice. 'Thoughts?'

Rice nodded. 'I've met Sam Wilson, Pete's dad, before. He's a piece of work, but I could handle him. You and Lucy could talk to Milo and his mother.'

Gardner thought for a moment. Rice was doing much better

than she feared, but something still niggled at her. 'Lucy and Phil, you go and speak to Pete, and I'll go to Milo's.'

Barnett was lingering by the door, looking at them.

'Ray?' Gardner said with her eyebrow raised.

'Boss, I don't mind tagging along with you?'

Gardner smiled. 'Nothing like a keen team.'

24

The snow was coming down hard on Riddick's windscreen, and his wipers were having a torrid time batting it away. So, despite riding a wave of adrenaline, Riddick kept his speed down on the journey to HQ. He wasn't about to put himself back in hospital.

Especially not after his discovery. He was close to something. He was positive.

The Rt Hon Cassandra Jacoby MP had been formerly known as Cassandra Rice. DCI Derek Rice had been her elder brother.

So, Cassandra, you were the minister of crime, and your brother, DCI Derek Rice, an SIO investigating a child's murder. What happened when you found out that Anders was sniffing around your son, Cassandra?

Was it you who had Anders' suspicions shut down by top brass?

Or was it Derek? Desperate to protect his own nephew?

Riddick sighed, hoping that the truth wasn't dead and buried with Cassandra and Derek.

He thought of the two remaining people left in the Rice clan.

One was, according to the medics, immobile and unable to communicate.

The other, well, the other was a detective inspector, and also the assistant SIO on this current bloody case.

He narrowed his eyes. Did Phil Rice know anything about this?

He wouldn't put it past the sanctimonious prick.

His phone rang. The caller was unknown. Riddick answered using the hands-free.

Silence. A quick burst of static. Then more silence.

'Hello?' Riddick said again, readying his finger to kill the call.

'Paul Riddick?' It was a male voice, and not one he recognised.

'Who is this?' Riddick asked.

'The past, I'm afraid—'

'Think you got the wrong number, mate,' Riddick said and killed the call.

The world was full of nut jobs. He'd received a fair share of crank calls over the years, especially during the time he'd investigated the mother of a suicide victim. He'd had the patience sucked out of him then – hanging up on the nutters was the best option.

The unknown caller rang back.

'Bloody idiot,' Riddick said.

Against his better judgement, he answered, his current build-up of adrenaline needing an outlet. '*Listen*, I'm a police officer, so—'

'I know Detective Inspector, I know.'

'Well, if you know, what's with this daft bloody phone call?'

'I'm trying to *help* you, Detective Inspector ... keep you alive.'

'Who is this?'

Silence.

Riddick pulled up. He wasn't overly concerned about this crank, but he didn't want to be distracted from the heavy snow. 'Was that a threat?'

Silence.

'Well, buddy, if it is, best we meet up and *hash* it out – what do you say?'

'Good idea.'

'Do you fancy being arrested then?'

'You wouldn't arrest me.'

He sounded different from most crank callers he'd experienced in the past. Less emotional. Cold and straight to the point.

Riddick snorted. 'You sure about that?'

'Yes.'

'Do you know what? This is a waste of time.' Riddick went for the button on the dashboard to kill the call—

'I know all about Ronnie Haller, Paul.'

Riddick's finger froze mid-air.

The man continued, 'It took them hours to clean that prison shower block. You had him emptied out good and proper, didn't you?'

Riddick could taste bile. 'Who is this?'

The man laughed. 'Who *are* you? Aren't you supposed to be a copper?'

Riddick narrowed his eyes. 'I don't know what you're talking about, dickhead—'

'But then, since when was every copper a do-gooder?'

'Who the hell are you?'

'Do you still want to meet and *hash* this out?'

'Do I have a choice?'

'Not if you want to stay *free*. Not if you want to stay *alive*. I'll send you a location. A quiet little spot. No cameras. I'll give you forty-five minutes. No longer.'

'How do I know I won't be found face down in the river?'

'You don't. But if I don't see you in forty-five minutes, you can be certain of one thing. Your superiors will know about Ronnie Haller.'

The phone went dead.

Riddick took a deep breath, killed the windscreen wipers and then the engine.

He stared at the window as it disappeared under snow, trying to think but too stunned to do so. He slumped back in the seat and rubbed at his face.

The adrenaline over his recent discovery had been replaced by cold dread.

His phone pinged. He clicked on the Google Map pin sent to him, and then punched the coordinates into the Sat Nav.

He started his engine and moved back out into the road.

It wasn't the first time he'd felt the walls of his fragile world coming down around him, but he couldn't recall a time in which he'd ever felt so frozen and clueless.

25

Cherie Hardy was thirty-six years old and had one of the kindest smiles Gardner had ever seen, beautiful dimples in her cheeks and the gentlest set of eyes. She was also dying. A travesty that was far too common in this world.

'Get yoursens in here. It's freezing out there,' Cherie said.

'You're telling me,' Barnett said, shivering. He stooped as he entered. The door frame more than compensated for him, but the tall black man no doubt had a history of clocking his forehead on less forgiving entrances, and so had developed this habit as a result.

'Again,' Gardner said, when they were in the lounge. 'We're so sorry to disturb you.'

She waved them away with a smile. 'Don't be. If it's about Milo, you can't possibly disturb me. And you said he wasn't in any trouble?' Cherie adjusted the head scarf on her head. 'Would you like a drink?'

Gardner had spent the best part of her life fighting for justice, but here, in front of her, was one of the greatest injustices she'd ever seen. Yet, Cherie was completely stoic in the face of it.

'No thanks, Cherie. We just need to ask him a few questions regarding another boy he was seen talking too, and another friend he was with.'

She smiled. 'Are you sure? One friend would be a stretch, but two? Milo likes to spend time alone. He's never been one for friends.'

Gardner nodded, struggling to buy into the idea of any child being completely friendless. 'Does the name Pete Wilson mean anything to you, Cherie?'

Cherie shook her head. 'No, is that one of the boys he was with?'

Gardner nodded.

'How about Stephen Best?'

'No, sorry... You know, Milo's head is permanently in a comic. He never socialises... not to my knowledge, but you're welcome to talk to him.'

'Thanks Cherie.'

'I'll bring him out,' Cherie said, rising slowly and heading out of the room.

'Poor woman,' Barnett said.

Gardner went over to the mantlepiece and looked at a school photograph of Milo Hardy. He was smartly dressed and smiling. 'Poor kid. He's already lost his dad, and he's about to lose his mum.'

'Look at this.'

Gardner turned. Barnett was standing over the coffee table, holding up a Batman comic. 'I used to love these!' He started thumbing through it. 'Would be happy to have another go with them too.'

Gardner smiled. First, Rice's secret Warhammer figure and then Barnett's comic addiction. She was learning more and more about her team with every passing day and none of it, she was glad to say, predictable—

Cherie screamed loudly.

'*Upstairs,*' Gardner said, and they both started to run.

26

Rice knocked at the door a second time and blew on his cold, exposed hands. The temperature was dramatically falling.

He glanced left at O'Brien, who was bouncing from foot to foot, hands thrust deep into her pockets, wearing an oversized coat that looked ridiculous, but that he was envious of.

'He's a shitbag, you know,' Rice said. 'If you want to wait in a warm car, I can deal—'

'I can handle the cold, sir,' O'Brien said, without looking at him. 'And I can handle shitbags.'

'A shitbag out of the *very* top drawer this one though,' Rice said, under his breath.

The door opened. The air that billowed out was both warm and stank of marijuana.

Shitbag Sam Wilson had a can of Strongbow in one hand, and his eyes were like two piss-holes in the snow.

Sam leered at O'Brien as he drank.

Did warn you, Rice thought, looking at O'Brien. Although, to be fair, she didn't look fazed. The lasses he worked with were made of stronger stuff these days. Rice turned his attention back to the odious stain on humanity.

'What do you want?' Sam asked, eyeing Rice up and down.

'Well, I'm not here for a go on your bong.'

He sensed O'Brien's eyes boring into him – probably shocked by his sarcasm and antagonistic attitude. Best rein it in; she'd clearly feed back to the boss. Last thing he wanted was to end up behind a desk again.

'Joker, eh?' Sam asked.

'You don't recognise me?' Rice asked.

'Should I?'

I did arrest you a few years back... 'I guess you've met a lot of us.'

O'Brien pulled out her badge and introduced them both.

Fair play, Rice thought, *do it by the book, lassie. Won't get you far with this shitbag though.*

Sam grunted. 'Explains it... yer kind all look same to me.'

Rice made a point of sniffing at the air. 'So... the bong... is that for medicinal purposes?'

'Don't know what you're talking about. No bloody bongs 'ere. What yer want?'

'Your son, Mr Wilson. Pete. Do you know where he is?' O'Brien said.

'Pissing in a river more than likely. Spends his time out wandering. Why you ask me? He's old enough to take care of himself.'

'Actually, he's fifteen,' Rice said. 'So, it's still your job.'

Sam took a mouthful of Strongbow and smirked. 'Guess you need to fire me then.'

Rice looked at the dishevelled man. *Can't fire you for a job you never did.*

'Is he home?' O'Brien asked.

'Nah. He's never in. Apart from maybe this morning.'

He drank from the can again, and Rice noticed Sam's bruised knuckles. 'What happened to your hand?'

'Eh?' Sam looked at it. 'That! Trapped it in the door.'

'Is your son safe?' Rice asked.

Sam waved his can in front of Rice. 'Ey up! Here he comes. Bent Bob. I know where this is going! Gonna force yer way in, are you Bobs? *Listen*. He's *not* 'ere.' He looked at his watch. 'It's not even eight. Maybe you should try in the early hours?'

'Can you check his room please?' O'Brien said.

He leered and smiled at O'Brien again and offered his can. 'Okay... I'll look. Can you hold this for me, darling?'

'No.'

Sam winked. 'Don't make policewomen like they used to, do they? Used to be more pleasant.'

'It's police officer, and I find it hard to believe that anyone was ever pleasant with you, Mr Wilson – not with this attitude.'

Rice forced back a smile.

Sam grunted, put his can down on the floor and turned back into his home to take a look, although looking seemed to consist of minimal movement and lots of shouting at the top of his lungs. 'Oi, gobshite, you 'ere?'

'Father of the year,' O'Brien said in a low voice.

'The grunts are 'ere for you!' Sam shouted.

'Brazen, isn't he?' O'Brien said.

'Aye,' Rice said, nodding. 'That's certainly someone who doesn't give a shit.'

'The place smells like a drug den, sir; should we not bust him?'

'We could but should probably keep focused on the task at hand. I'll get it on someone's radar, though.'

'Busting him would give me a rush of endorphins.'

'A rush of what?'

O'Brien looked at him. 'Feel-good chemicals.'

'Drugs? Never touched them, and neither should you...' He looked back through the door. 'No judge is going to waste cell space on this plonker.'

'Even though he hits his son?'

'Won't be long before his son is hitting him back, I imagine.'

Sam returned to the door. 'Not 'ere.' He picked up the can from the floor.

Rice said, 'Can we come in, check for ourselves?'

'Rather you didn't.'

'Because of the drugs?' Rice said. 'We're only concerned about Pete's safety.'

'If you're worried about his safety, you need to look elsewhere.'

Rice and O'Brien exchanged a glance. Didn't seem worth forcing entry. They'd heard him storming around the house, shouting for Pete. There had been no response.

'Does Pete have a mobile phone?' Riddick asked.

Sam shrugged. 'I've seen him with one... yeah. Don't have his number, like.'

'You said he likes to wander... piss in a river,' Rice said. 'Any clues as to where?'

'Pick yourself any country lane!'

'This is Knaresborough – a lot to choose from,' Rice said.

Sam shrugged.

'Who does he tend to hang about with?' O'Brien asked.

He guffawed. 'Other knobheads?'

Rice inwardly sighed. This was going nowhere. The man was a prick, and even if he knew anything about his son, he wasn't going to share.

O'Brien tried a few more questions, but Rice decided to wrap it up and handed over a card. 'Please call me when he comes home.'

Sam took the card. 'What's he done anyway?'

'We'll chat more when he's back.'

'Be middle of night... Can't promise I'll be up.'

'Try your best,' Rice said.

The front door slammed.

O'Brien looked ready to kick it down.

'Warned you,' Rice said.

'Yeah, still, it's his son for Christ's sake. He doesn't sound like he cares whether he lives or dies.'

'He's too stoned to care about anything,' Rice said.

'Let's hope he doesn't live to regret it.'

'The only thing that man is going to regret is his heating bill,' Rice said, pointing up at the open windows on the top floor.

* * *

Back in his car, Rice answered a call from Gardner.

'Not good news on my end, Phil. Milo isn't home, and Cherie, his mother, is in a right state. The ambulance has had to take her to hospital.'

'It's not too late. Why's she so shocked?'

'Apparently, this is a lad who's never out past eight unless he's heading to the shop for her.'

'Doesn't appear that way from that CCTV footage! How late was that? Ten?'

'I know... but Cherie was *genuinely* stunned, so I suspect he must've started sneaking out while she's been resting. The cancer and the treatment to try and prolong her life are exhausting her. Also, she picked up a voicemail from Milo's school telling her he'd not come in today. At that point, she just kind of folded. What'd you find out from Pete?'

'He's not here, either. And his dad is the opposite of shocked, but just as little help.'

'At least they're probably together. I've contacted Marsh. She's speaking to the relevant people and putting some resources into searching for them. Go home, Phil, get some rest. If they show up, you'll be the first to know.'

27

Whoever had decided to set this small patch of land up behind a ruined building as a car park had been chancing it, and the fact that it was now abandoned was unsurprising. Most of the corrugated iron fences bordering it had fallen, and the ground was riddled with potholes that had filled with water and frozen over. Ironically, the signs promising all-day secure parking for only five pounds were still in place, but the cameras providing the security were in pieces.

The place was firmly off the grid. It was a suitable location to kill someone, Riddick thought. Was his life in danger? Probably. Although the dickhead he was meeting had given him little option.

A man in a beige suit and a three-quarter length grey coat stood beside the snow-covered old pay booth.

Looks like a dickhead too, Riddick thought, driving past him, and finding a space as far from the man as possible, before parking and killing his lights. He watched, with some satisfaction, the suited man negotiating the treacherous ground, carefully avoiding the ice puddles, but almost going over once or twice.

Don't break your neck...

The man peeled off his grey coat and climbed into the passenger side. He laid his coat over his lap. Riddick looked him up and down in his beige suit. No wonder he'd almost slipped over, he was wearing polished black brogues – hardly the footwear for the dead of winter. His hair was neatly styled into a quiff, and there wasn't a hint of facial hair. His top two buttons were undone, exposing a gold chain.

Riddick nodded. 'Good spot. No cameras. No witnesses. Good place to make someone disappear.'

'I told you. I'm not here for that. I'm here to *save* you.'

Riddick looked at him. 'And how do you know I was referring to the reason *you* were here?'

He nodded and smoothed out the coat on his knee. 'I think you must know that I've put contingency plans in place should something happen to me, but we'll get to that in due course, Paul.'

'You know my name. I think it's fair to tell me yours.'

'Of course.' The man looked at him. 'KG.'

'What the bloody hell kind of name is that?'

'The only one I have. Or, at least, the only one I have when it concerns you.'

'Well, KG, do you mind getting to the point?'

'Ronnie Haller.'

Riddick sighed. 'Yes... we've been over this.'

'I want to say that Ronnie had it coming.'

'Many people have it coming,' Riddick said, keeping his eyes firmly on the sharp dresser. 'Unfortunately, people like Ronnie aren't a rarity.'

'I disagree, Paul,' KG said. 'People like Ronnie are rarer than you think. Most people in Ronnie's world only do what they have to do; there're very few that actually take pleasure from it.'

Riddick snorted. 'And I suppose, KG, you're one of those poor,

poor folks forced into a life of malevolence? What do you want? An applause for not getting a buzz over your shitty behaviour?'

KG regarded him. 'You seem angry, Paul.'

'Are you serious?' Riddick asked, shaking his head. 'You've just pulled me away from an investigation to sit in a deserted car park in the arsehole of nowhere to what? Blackmail me, I assume. Forgive me for not being all smiles.'

'I regret this—'

'No, you don't. I know you. I know you very well. I've a career built on losers like you. You're a predator, KG. Just like Ronnie. Just like all the others. And, before we take this conversation further, you may want to think twice about who you're preying on this evening.'

'I'm preying on a man whose hands are far from clean. Maybe you should ask yourself if you, too, are a predator for what you did to Ronnie.'

'That bastard killed my family.' Riddick gritted his teeth.

'Does justification excuse you then?'

'I'm not giving you justification. I'm just stating a fact.'

KG reached into the inside pocket of his beige suit jacket and pulled out his mobile phone. He ran his finger over the screen for several moments before a recording crackled from the speakers.

Riddick closed his eyes as he listened to himself negotiating the hit on Haller. He sounded different, somehow. Yes, he'd been pissed. Very pissed. But there was something else.

Despair.

'Turn it off.' Riddick grunted. 'I get it.'

KG stopped it.

'Is that you I'm talking to?' Riddick said. 'What do your superiors think about you making recordings and blackmailing their customers? Do they know?'

'I've worked my way up. These decisions are mine to make.'

Riddick leaned over and gripped the steering wheel, focusing his frustration into his knuckles. He closed his eyes and shook his head.

Why now?

His life wasn't perfect by any means, but there had been green shoots of late.

'You're here to burn me down.'

'No. It needn't go the wrong way. You still have a choice.'

Riddick opened his eyes and focused on his white knuckles again.

He turned his eyes slowly onto the greasy pillock beside him. 'Oh, I have a choice all right.' Riddick switched his hands from the steering wheel to his blackmailer's throat.

KG's eyes widened, and his hands flew up to clutch Riddick's wrists.

'Didn't expect this, did you?'

Riddick lifted himself slightly in his chair, and leaned in so he could tighten his squeeze. He watched KG's face starting to glow red. 'Yet... here we are... and you've made it so bloody easy.'

Riddick could feel the man's nails digging into his wrist, but the pain was irrelevant. 'You *had* a choice too.'

Did KG believe him capable? The fear in the bastard's eyes suggested that he did.

Riddick pulled back. KG rubbed at his throat, gasping for air.

Riddick looked forward, took a deep breath and then pointed at a corrugated iron fence that was blowing back and forth in the wind like a tooth hanging by the final thread of a ligament. 'That scratches my bonnet, you're paying.'

The man had caught his breath beside him. 'That was stupid. Do you *really* think I work alone?'

Riddick watched the swaying fence. 'You seem self-obsessed

enough. Barmpots like you think they can take on the world all by themselves.'

'If anything happens to me, the recording is scheduled, by email, to be delivered to your superiors.'

'Bollocks.'

'You should trust me.'

'Trust? Jesus, you're deluded. I'm not going to kill you, KG, but what do you think will happen when you eventually burn me? You really believe I won't take you with me?'

'At that point, KG will cease to exist.'

'You think a false name is going to protect you. Your voice is on that recording.' He grinned. 'Your DNA is probably in my car.' He looked down at the scratch marks on his wrists. 'And probably in my bloody skin now.'

KG didn't respond.

'So, together we fall,' Riddick said, looking at him for the first time in a while.

'Why?' KG said, looking back at him, raising an eyebrow, while rubbing his neck. 'You don't even know what I want. The alternative being offered is simpler.'

Riddick grunted. 'Money may be simple for you, but I don't have a great deal to offer.'

'Not money,' KG said. 'I don't need your money.'

'Unusual. Go on, then, what?'

'The smallest of favours and we're done, Paul. It pales into insignificance when compared to what you've done already.' KG reached into his suit pocket. 'You know, Paul, there's not many people on God's green earth that would've done what you just did to me, and lived to fight another day, but if you get this done within the next twenty-four hours.' He pulled out a folded piece of paper. 'I'll forget about your hands around my throat, and I'll forget about Ronnie Haller.'

Riddick nodded at the paper. 'What's that?'

'A list of five of my employees. All grown men, don't worry. I'm asking you to cross another line, but I feel it's one you can live with.'

'Get to the point.'

'One of them is a rat, I'm convinced.'

'A criminal informant?'

'Either that or he's an undercover copper.'

He shook his head. '*No.*'

'Think about this.' KG proffered the note. 'I need to know which one. The things that your people know, the information that you people have, can only have come from one of those on that list.'

'You're deluded if you think I'm sending a man to his death.'

'Sorry,' the bastard said with a raised eyebrow, 'haven't you done that already?'

'Ronnie wasn't innocent.'

'No one is innocent.'

'What if this is an undercover officer with a family?'

'Unlikely. Would he have signed up for it if he had?'

'So, if he has no family, then he's fair game? Jesus wept. I'm not giving you one of our own. Can't believe you'd think that can happen.'

'Might be an informant... might be a right nasty piece of work... might be cathartic to give him up. Why not at least *see* first?' He proffered it again.

Shit! 'What the hell game you into, KG?'

'You'll know soon enough when you run those names, but it's standard enough fare round these parts.'

'County lines?'

KG gave him a barely detectable nod.

'So, I identify your informant, and as a result, you get to

destroy more children's lives? At what point does my conscience not collapse, you shit stain?'

'Listen carefully, Paul, and I'll make this even easier for you. If you don't do this, and I give you to your superiors, then I'll rid myself of all five of those employees anyway. Additionally, if, like you said, I go down with you, then whoever steps into my shoes will also clean shop. All I'm doing here's reducing the waste. If I know which employee is the issue, then the other four can continue none the wiser. So, for you, Paul, the outcome is the same. If anything, you're doing a good thing here, sparing those who are truly innocent of betrayal.'

Riddick shook his head. 'Well, when you put it like that...'

Realising that Riddick was not going to take the folded paper, the man opened the glove compartment and slipped it in.

'What makes you think I can even find out?'

The man shrugged. 'You have proven very resourceful in your life to date. I had a good look at you, Paul. Yes, you've pissed a lot of people off, but you're still in the job. Why do you think that is?'

No idea. Nine lives?

'Because you get results. Find out who is causing me problems, or all five men die, and me and you rot in prison together. Do you know what they do to coppers in jail?'

'I know what happens to people who exploit children,' Riddick said with narrowed eyes. 'We can compare notes?'

'One man... or five men? Another shot at life... or years of torment?' He opened the door and stepped out. He put on his coat and leaned in again. 'I know you'll make the right choice, Paul. If I doubted it, I wouldn't be here.'

'Even if I did it,' Riddick hissed. 'How'd I know that this would be it? That you wouldn't keep coming back?'

'You don't, but I imagine if I did come back again, you'd definitely kill me.'

'Now there's a nice thought.'

KG slammed the door.

Heart thrashing in his chest, Riddick watched the beige-suited idiot skip around the ice puddles with more skill than he'd done earlier.

Did he have a spring in his sodding step?

Have I given him any indication that I'd comply?

Riddick's stomach turned. He looked at the glove compartment.

Is this what I am now? Is this what I've become? The go-to bent cop for a local gangster.

He felt Anders' hands on his shoulders as a young man.

Maybe you did see yourself in me, Anders. Maybe, after all this time, we really are exactly the same.

He looked in the mirror again and saw that KG was gone.

Riddick opened the door and stepped from the car. Wind and snow buffeted him. He walked over to the panel of corrugated iron fence swinging loose from the other panel. He grabbed it and tore it free, swearing at the top of his lungs as he did so.

28

After a tough day, Gardner was gutted that no one, other than Barry, was awake when she arrived home. A hug from Rose and Anabelle would really hit the mark right now.

Gardner was reaching up to the wine rack when she heard Barry enter the kitchen behind her. 'You never used to drink this much.'

'Yes, and my husband never used to cheat on me.' She opened the utensil drawer and rustled around for the corkscrew. 'At least not that I know of.'

'There's only ever been Sandra, and that was after you left.'

'After I *left*?' She worked the corkscrew in. 'I was seconded, Barry – I didn't have a great deal of choice.'

'You were happier then – back in Salisbury.'

'Was I?' She pulled the cork. 'I certainly wasn't when I was stabbed in the chest or killed someone in the line of duty. When I quit my job for a bit? Yes, maybe. Although, I went back and lost two of my closest colleagues over the next couple of years... Do you know anything about me, Barry? Do you know anything about what I've been through?'

'I know your job has ruined this marriage.'

She poured herself a large glass of red wine and turned to look at him. She leaned back on the counter. 'Really? Nothing to do with you shagging someone else?' Gardner took a large mouthful.

'As I said, that came later after you left, after you stopped being attentive.'

It was a good job she'd swallowed her wine before he'd finished that sentence. 'Attentive, Barry? Do you even know what attentive means?'

'Yes... but how can anyone be attentive to someone who is never there?'

'I was there, Barry, you just never noticed. You had opportunities to make me feel special.'

'That's bollocks, Emma. Just before you left, I spent ages researching that trip to New York!'

'Yes... the trip to New York... loved it... oh wait, never happened—'

'You *left*.'

'I love the way that you consider it a choice.'

'There's always a choice. And what was I supposed to do about the damned trip? I had to cancel it; we were on separate sides of the country...'

'Was that the real reason?'

'What's that mean?'

'You hated going away with me. You aren't interested in exploring, seeing new things – you just want to lounge by a pool. I bet you were relieved to cancel. Did you research another break?'

'How could I? You were always busy.'

'So, you gave up? And shagged someone else?'

'Stop making it sound so crass.'

'Like it isn't! You're married, you idiot.'

She drank another large mouthful of her wine and then grabbed the bottle.

'And you're unreasonable,' Barry said as she walked past.

'We're getting a divorce. Let's stop re-treading old ground.'

'You're going to look back on all this and realise you could've done more to save this marriage.'

'Ha! You'll be too busy with Sandra and your new family to give your old one a passing thought.' She turned on to the stairs.

'Listen...' He came after her, red-faced.

She didn't often see Barry lose his temper and took some pride in the fact that she'd managed it.

'You're supposed to be a mother. There're two children up there that need you and' – he looked at his watch – 'you're back at this time.'

She paused on the fourth step up and glared at him. 'I have a dead fifteen-year-old boy, and two other boys unaccounted for – can you even comprehend that responsibility?'

'And what about your responsibility to Ana and Rose?'

'They're always safe and cared for.'

'Because I'm here!' Barry said, thrusting his thumb into his chest.

He had a point, but this just made her feel even more wound up.

'Not for long,' Gardner said.

'Okay... Emma... then what?'

'I'll make arrangements.'

'Arrangements?'

She continued up the stairs. 'Yes.'

'Get the neighbour to look after the kids? Or, worse still, one of your colleagues? How did that work out last time? Oh yes, the colleague was almost killed by your psychopathic brother!'

Gardner flinched. That was brutal. He knew how plagued she

was by the guilt over that incident. 'Piss off. We'll manage. You're not even that useful.'

'I'll take Ana.'

'No, you won't. Not after a good lawyer hangs your dirty linen out! Shagging a colleague while he was supposed to be looking after his daughter and supporting his long-suffering wife.'

'Believe me, when they see your work schedule, they'll give her to me. I've already spoken to a solicitor.'

Gardner felt a wave of nausea. It was an unthinkable scenario. 'Well, if that's the case, I'll quit,' Gardner said, taking a large mouthful of wine and making her way to the top of the stairs. 'Done it before.'

'You're impossible. Do you even know what's going on with Rose? Do you even know how she's feeling?'

Gardner paused on the top step. That stung. She gripped the banister.

'She's missing her father,' Barry said. 'She asks about him all the time. Your bloody brother. She *wants* to see him, you know?'

She can't.

'You need to talk to her. I'm not going to be the bad guy stopping her from seeing her father. Why should I be?'

You'd be anything but bad stopping her from seeing that sociopath, Barry.

She turned onto the landing.

'You have responsibilities,' Barry called up from the bottom of the stairs.

'Keep your voice down, Barry, the children are in bed.'

'Yes, I know, I put them in there.'

She went into the bedroom, closed the door, locked it, sat on the edge of her bed, drank more wine and then burst into tears.

* * *

The wine helped relax her, but it didn't knock her out, unfortunately. Another bottle would've done the trick, but tomorrow would then be a living hell, and she'd have no time to run it off in the morning.

There was so much rattling around her brain, yet, oddly, every time she closed her eyes, she only saw Ron Best standing at his living room window, staring out at her as she knocked on his front door.

Wide eyes... mouth hanging open... knowing his already fragile life was going to collapse completely.

All I ever wanted for Stephen was to avoid the mistakes I made.

But Lynda saved me. If I hadn't have met her I'd never have pulled my socks up.

And every time I think about how lucky I am to have got my son into a safe life, I come down hard on him.

Right now, the guilt would be tearing Ron to pieces.

She'd seen it many times.

Those bad boys coming good, pushing their children, relentlessly, into a life that would bear no resemblance to their own.

She sat up, trying her best to focus on the other events of the day, but in her relatively drunken state, many of the experiences fused together in a rather irritating collage of aggravating images and sounds: Kyle Alexander's coughing; Hugo Sands picking a Big Mac from his teeth; the deliveryman at Warhammer rolling a coin over the tops of his fingers; Rice's incessant knocking as Ron stood at the window...

There she was again, back at Ron.

'And who is the mysterious friend?' she asked out loud. 'Who used Warhammer as a hook, and reeled you in, Stephen?'

Eugene Scarrow?

Unlikely. His non-binary partner, Alexia, had already served themself up as an alibi.

She looked down at her mobile and thought about Riddick. Her eyes closed, and she was suddenly lost in that moment when he had been asleep on the sofa next to her.

Then she felt his hand on her shoulder, the previous evening, when she'd visited him to reprimand him about the Morgan Lark cock up...

Her skin flushed again as it'd done in that moment.

You've always got my back.

She opened her eyes and stared at her mobile, considering whether or not to call him – just to touch base. She opted against it. He'd been irritated this morning about being sidelined, and until she'd a better handle on this case, she doubted he'd be too receptive.

She looked at her watch and saw that it was past ten now.

And still no phone call from Marsh or any of her people, which meant that Milo Hardy and Pete Wilson, two more *vulnerable children*, were still out there.

She longed for the phone to ring. Longed for the words: We've found them together.

Knocking around together down by the river.

Sitting near the rugby field.

Vaping on a park bench.

Anything.

She thought of Stephen Best's pale face.

Anything but that.

She thought of her brother, the bastard who'd not only scarred her head, but had scarred her entire life with his sociopathic ways.

And she recalled, in detail, their final words together.

'You've left me burning that same torch for that little girl as you have.'

'I've done the right thing. Her mother isn't long for this world anyway, and even if she does survive, Rose will end up in care. I couldn't

just ask you all those months ago to be a mother to my daughter, Emma.
But now, I can. And now, you'll say yes.'

Not asking.

Telling.

And now she misses you, you bastard.

Her phone rang. It was Marsh. 'Yes.'

'Emma.' There was a short pause. 'I have some bad news...'

29

'Shit!' Riddick looked at the glove compartment.

Inside, five names. KG, the beige-suited arsehole, had presented him with clear choices.

One man or five men?

Another shot at his own life or a life in prison?

Yet even these decisions, some of the heaviest he'd ever had to make, just felt like a distraction.

He shook his head and thought of the dead boy lying next to him at St Robert's Cave, and George Jacoby, a potential child killer hiding behind a wall of nurses.

KG wanted his rat in twenty-four hours.

Sod you, KG – I'm a busy man. I'll attend to you when I've sorted this.

He parked his car, jumped from it and moved quickly, head down, through the falling snow. He'd forgotten to grab his jacket from the back seat, but the fire of adrenaline in his stomach kept him warm.

He banged heavily on the front door of a moderately-sized new-build, then he stood back, pacing in the snowfall.

To a passing observer, he may have looked like a man possessed. A man needing to slow down, take a breath, potentially sleep and then revisit any unresolved issues refreshed.

But that passing observer would be wrong.

If Riddick slowed down, then he'd place himself at the mercy of his demons. Letting them out to play was unthinkable.

Rice opened the door dressed in a small silk dressing gown adorned with Japanese symbols. So jarring was this sight that Riddick was speechless, despite knowing exactly what he wanted to say.

'Eh?' Rice said. 'You can't be serious?'

'Let me in.'

'Piss off. I'm not alone.'

'Watch your tone.'

'Why should I? You're intimidating and reckless, and *not* coming in my house. Do one before I lodge a complaint.'

He looked Rice up and down in the dressing gown again and felt a surge of revulsion. 'Who's in there with you? And what's with that kimono?'

'None of your business on both questions.'

Riddick narrowed his eyes and slowed his breathing. Feeling like a wild animal was one thing but behaving like one was a recipe for disaster.

Rice smirked. 'Do you think it's the boss? Is that why you're here? Rumours were true then—'

'Shut it. Come out and close the door behind you, Phil.'

'Sod off. It's freezing. No.'

'You don't want me to announce this to whoever you're entertaining...'

Rice went to shut the door on Riddick. 'You're a ridiculous man.'

'When was the last time you saw George Jacoby, Phil?'

Rice stepped out and closed the door behind him. 'Are you serious? Are you investigating me now? You really can't help yourself, can you man? You leave shit up the walls everywhere you—'

'Ain't got the time for your pathetic attempts at posturing, Phil. Tell me about your cousin.'

'Lay low... weren't your instructions clear?' He crossed his arms. It didn't work. His teeth chattered.

'My instructions are nowt to do with you. Your cousin?'

'Not until you tell me why you're looking into me. To say you're unhinged is an understatement; this is a whole new level.' He widened his eyes. 'Jesus... you can't possibly think I had anything to with Stephen Best!'

'Thanks... I didn't know his name.'

'Shit,' Rice said, shaking his head. 'Ah well, it's being released to press in the morning anyway. And just so you know, you're barking up the tree outside of a sodding mental asylum with this one! You think I was the one in that car you can't remember?' He laughed. He pointed at his red Volvo. 'Does that ring any bells? Does it shake your amnesia?' He crossed his arms again. 'Thought not.'

'I'm here about George—'

'Man's a corpse – wake up!'

'Talk to me about him,' Riddick said again, determined not to lose his temper. To keep himself focused. To drive forward for the truth.

It was all that mattered.

'George is my cousin,' Rice said. 'He has locked-in syndrome. But I guess you know all this already? Do you think I have anything to do with him? Because, if you do your research properly, you'd know that I don't. In fact, I have nothing to do with any of my family. Why would I trouble myself with someone who is bedridden? And if that sounds heartless, I don't care. You see, you don't know me, and even if you did, I wouldn't give two shits about what you thought.'

'I think George Jacoby, *your cousin*, may have killed Graham Lock in 2003,' Riddick said. He stopped himself short of saying, 'And maybe even Stephen Best last night,' because then the conversation would probably be over, and Rice would be inside phoning HQ to suggest a mental hospital.

Rice shook his head. 'I'd laugh if this wasn't *beyond* ridiculous. You don't look drunk, Paul, but surely... are you drinking again? You know what, don't answer that. I don't care. I'll file a report about being dragged out into the cold by an unhinged colleague, and having accusations fired at me, and let top brass decide whether you're fit for duty.'

'Your father was the DCI on the Lock case, Phil. There's no way you don't know more than you're letting on.'

Rice uncrossed his arms and struck an aggressive pose. 'Stop right there. I think that amnesia you picked up is worse than you thought. When we were both wet behind the ears, who was it that got the all-important push? Was it me?' Rice said, touching his chest. 'Son of a successful DCI, or was it' – he pointed at Riddick – 'you, son of... well... son of nobody?'

'Ah, I see,' Riddick said. 'This explains a lot. I always wondered why you were such a gobshite around me. It's bitterness. All along.'

'The fact that your career flew over a bloody teddy bear, when my own father kept overlooking me... yeah, it did leave a bitter taste, but it wasn't the only reason I was a gobshite. I was a gobshite because, guess what, no surprises here, you're the biggest gobshite of them all!'

'Well, save your jealously. You're a DI now, anyway. Not like I've overtaken you.'

'You would've done if you'd not spent the last couple of years flushing your career down the pan.'

Riddick struggled with a surge of anger. 'After what happened to me, you've the balls to say that?'

'I was referring to your professional conduct, not your personal issues, so don't play that card. You know what the others call you behind your back, Paul? Captain Chaos. I'd have made better use of those early bumps up the ladder if they'd come my way.'

'Okay,' Riddick said, shaking his head. 'Back on point. Your father was DCI on the Lock case, so you know stuff—'

'You're not bloody listening! Read my lips. My father didn't let me anywhere near the case. Anders gave you more exposure to the sorry affair than I ever got! I really don't know what you're on about regarding George.'

'Even in the years following, he never talked to you about the Lock case?'

'My father was a prick. You *must* know that having met him yourself. I barely ever spoke to him. And I have no idea what George has to do with this.' He paused, shivering, while regarding Riddick with a thoughtful look. 'Where the hell is all this coming from anyway?'

Riddick shrugged. 'The case notes. I re-read the case notes.'

'So, what'd you see in these case notes that suddenly convinced you that Russell Lock – God rest his kid-beating soul – was the wrong man? And my cousin, who's spent most of his pitiable life incapacitated, is the real monster?'

Riddick told him about the eyewitnesses who saw George talking to Graham. He told him about Donna Morfett sighting two people out on a boat. And, most importantly, he told him how, despite Anders' suspicions, it was pushed to one side and never looked into.

Rice shivered as he considered. 'Wait... if it was never looked into... then, how'd you read about it?'

Riddick bit his lip.

'Christ on a bike. You went to see Anders?'

Riddick looked away.

'And he got you all het up... Typical.' Rice shook his head and grunted. 'I'm staying away from this shite storm. Anders! For God's sake, man. What's up with you?'

Riddick narrowed his eyes. 'What's relevant here is that Anders told me that Jacoby was overlooked. It's always plagued him.'

'Plagued him enough to do nothing about it! Do you really think Anders has a moral bone in his body? Shit the bed! And you're the *great* detective who weeded him out too.'

Riddick flinched. 'Phil, listen to me. There's something in this, and—'

'No, you listen to me. Anders is leading you up the garden path. My father was a complete and utter bastard. I hated him, and he hated me back. In spades. Everything I have achieved is down to me. And not as a result of some sugar daddy, like you. Still, when all that is said and done, I'll say one thing for the bastard. He was dedicated. More moral than the *bloody* lot of us put together. I can assure you, from the bottom of my heart, although you don't think I have one, that DCI Derek Rice got the right man.'

Riddick inwardly sighed. *You don't know anything, do you?* 'Okay... just hear me out on one more thing.'

Rice shivered and looked away.

'Please?' Riddick said, the word causing him serious discomfort on its way out.

'I'm done freezing my bollocks off. You've one more minute, Paul, before I slam the door in your face.'

'Your aunt, Cassandra Jacoby, was an MP. The minister for

crime and policing no less. Your father, her brother, was a DCI. George could've blown their worlds apart.'

Rice's eyes moved back and forth, indicating that he was at least giving it some thought. Eventually, he shook his head. 'But I can't see them burying this. Are you also going to suggest that that they induced George's stroke?'

Riddick shrugged.

'I mean, is that even possible?'

'I don't know. But there's something else bothering me. People can recover from locked-in syndrome. It's not unheard of.'

Rice shook his head. 'I know people who've seen him. Down by the river. Being pushed. He's frail.'

'When was the last time *you* saw him?'

Rice rolled his eyes. Riddick was losing him again. 'This is bollocks... God, I don't know. Obviously, I saw him working by the Waterside, but when did I last interact with him? Let me think. Well, when I was a child, I guess – and that was down to my mother. My father never got on with anyone, and that included Aunt Cassandra. When my mother died when I was ten, we didn't really stay in touch with anyone in my extended family.'

'How'd George strike you when you did see him?'

'When I was ten? Are you for real?'

He nodded. *Better than nothing.*

Rice shook his head. 'Bloody hell. I remember going fishing with him. Seemed to really enjoy it from what I remember. Might explain his choice of profession, boats on the river.' He paused and rolled his eyes. 'This is ridiculous. We're done.'

'Do you know anything about his later years?'

Rice shook his head. 'Nada. Now, if you let me get back to the warmth and... you know...' He fiddled with the belt on his kimono. 'Other more interesting things.'

Riddick turned around, and a horrible thought struck him that filled him with nausea. Was he being played? Had Anders sensed his vulnerability? Sought out a way to play some sick joke on him?

Was Anders now chuckling away over his act of revenge?

'Go home, Paul, get some rest. For crying out loud...'

Worried he might suddenly vomit, and not wanting to look pathetic in front of Rice, he stumbled away down the path.

Riddick heard Rice's door slam.

When Riddick reached his car, he placed his hands on the roof and took a deep breath.

Maybe Rice was right. Maybe he was barking up a tree outside a mental asylum.

He looked up and let the snow pepper his face.

Maybe it was time for him to shut up shop.

Go to jail and die in a cell. Spare everyone the Paul Riddick drama which seemed to just go on and on and on...

He climbed into his vehicle and looked at the glove compartment.

Inside, five names.

He closed his eyes and visualised Anders, smirking behind the table in the visiting room earlier.

I wish I'd never met you that night at the cave.

I wish I'd never taken that promotion that eventually led me to the Ronnie Haller investigation.

And I wish, more than anything, that my family were still alive.

30

Milo sat on the edge of the bed toying with the belt on the thick, blue dressing gown that the nice lady who wore a lot of make-up had given him with a wink. 'Terry towelling. Snuggle down in that chickie; just don't be tellin' Tommy.'

Apart from the peeling blue wallpaper, the room wasn't too uncomfortable; it was clean, tidy and most importantly, warm. Beside the bed was a small desk covered in books. He recognised the titles of a couple of classics. Books had never really interested him – they just seemed to take too long to get to the point. Comics were rapid.

Also, how could he read when he was terrified? With only one thing on his mind. His mother.

He longed to take her hand, check she was okay and maybe cry with his head on her chest for a while. These longings led him down another disturbing train of thought. She'd want to know what was upsetting him. Where to begin telling her about Pete's horrible death, and the dreadful decisions her golden boy had made these past days?

He recalled KG's words earlier to convince him to come

without a fuss. 'It's that or lose your mother even earlier than anticipated.'

It was at that point he'd wet himself.

After he'd been brought to this house in Starbeck, the woman had taken his clothes to wash them for him.

'Hope I didn't worry you, chickie? Tommy's out till late, he won't even know. I'll have scrubbed them before he shows his face,' she said, and winked again, after he'd emerged from the downstairs toilet wearing the dark blue dressing gown.

KG had instructed the woman to lead Milo upstairs. She'd held his hand carefully, due to her long multi-coloured fingernails. It was a gentle grip. Much better than KG's which had left his shoulder sore after he'd been marched from his home.

'After KG's chewed my ear, I'll bring you some scran,' she'd said, smiling. He noticed she had red lipstick on her teeth. 'I'm Brenda by the way. Just call me Bren.'

He built some semblance of courage in the considerable time that passed before she returned, resolving to talk to her. He noticed her red lipstick was smudged, but at least it wasn't on her teeth any more. Her dress also looked dishevelled.

'Cookies and milk,' she said, handing a plate and a cup to Milo.

He opened his mouth to demand answers, but as per usual, his filter kicked in, and he closed it again.

She narrowed her eyes, possibly seeing the frustration on his face. 'Don't worry, chickie. You know, he isn't all bad. Not really. In some ways, he cares. He won't be long, and then he'll put every-thing right.'

She stroked his hand with those multi-coloured fingernails, smiled and left the room, locking it.

Put everything right.

How was that even possible?

Pete was dead, his mother was dying and now he'd some criminal threatening to cut short her life even further – if Milo even made it alive outside his house!

He looked at the glass of milk in his hand. *A weapon?*

Potentially. If his own life was in danger. He couldn't even imagine what his own death would do to his mother in her final few months.

He needed a way out of this.

After another short while, he heard the door unlock again, and KG, wearing his beige suit, stood there. He gave a swift nod. 'Milo, we need to talk.'

After walking in, he closed the door behind him. 'Shuffle up, please.'

Milo obliged and KG sat alongside him.

'Now you're calm, we can have a proper chat.' He looked at Milo, fiddling with the gold chain around his neck.

KG suddenly looked kinder than he'd ever looked before. Milo thought back to the woman's claim that he wasn't all bad.

An act.

He'd seen him on that computer screen in that industrial unit in York, barking orders to torture Pete to death. He'd also threatened his mother's life and imprisoned him in this room.

KG reached over and picked up a dusty old book that had seen better days. It didn't even have an image on the cover. It was just hard and red with *Robinson Crusoe* emblazoned in gold.

'It is never too late to be wise,' KG said.

Milo didn't respond.

KG put the book down. 'You read it?'

He shook his head.

'You should read it. Tommy reads. Tommy was like you once. Now, he's happy. Here, with Bren.'

I wonder how happy he'll be if he finds out that a boy who pissed himself is sweating in fear into his terry towelling dressing gown?

KG sighed and fiddled with his chain some more. 'I could put the fear of God in you, but I'll just be honest with you, pal. Pete's death was a shitty mistake. Unfortunate. Between you and these four walls, no one feels worse about it than I do.'

Liar.

'In some ways, he was like a son to me.'

Sounded like it when you were slagging off his mother and forcing that junk into him.

'The mistakes he made...' He rubbed his face with his hands. 'They were significant. When they start to bite the hand that feeds them, then it's only a matter of time before they move onto the rest of you. I had to make a point. I didn't expect that... I really didn't.'

You tortured my friend.

He shook his head, wearing a sombre expression before sighing. Then, a smile broke out on his face and he looked at Milo and wagged a finger at him. 'I saw something in you, Milo, that night at the park. I already knew about Pete, but I gave him another chance, because of you – because of the potential I saw in you.'

I hardly spoke! Stop pretending. Stop acting. You can't manipulate me like you manipulated all the others. My mother taught me better than that.

KG pointed at *Robinson Crusoe* on the table. 'It's now your time to be wise. Just like Robinson. It is never too late. Please consider the situation you're in, Milo. Consider what's best for you. Pete's gone. It pains me to say it, but...' He rubbed his face as if he might suddenly burst into tears. *Liar.* 'And don't consider his father either, because he's a disgrace, and the real reason behind Pete's woeful decisions. And please Milo, don't take this the wrong way... but you need to take your mother out of the picture too. You'll be there for her, no question, what good son wouldn't? But please, Milo – this is all about you now.'

This display of kindness, of *compassion*, made Milo burn

inside. He wasn't sure if he wanted to shout and scream, or simply burst into tears, but he knew neither was the best option.

He needed to step up now. *Initiate control.*

'Do you want to hear what I think?' KG asked.

Tell me then. Let me consent... for now. Let me get home so I can come up with a plan. He nodded.

'When're you sixteen?'

'March.'

'Okay.' KG nodded and thought. 'When she finally passes, Milo – and I know it's horrible to think about, but she will and you must think about it – then you'll be sixteen. What'll you have? I know that you rent your house, and your mother, bless her, has little in savings, but it doesn't have to be a desperate situation. You know, Tommy is seventeen. I have another lad here, Joseph, who is eighteen. You'd be in good company here. Good, solid lads. Good role models. What Pete should've been for you. And Bren, well, you met her... she knows how to take care of my lads.'

She knows how to take care of my lads.

He sounded as if he owned them.

'You'll have a family, Milo. Do you understand what I'm offering? It is never too late to be wise, remember?'

He nodded. *But I don't want to be anyone's property.*

'Bren has taken quite a shine to you,' KG said, and winked. 'Not a bad position to be in. She always orders pizza in on a Friday, and she's great at getting whatever you need. Saw those comics piled high at your home. She'll get you as many as you want.' He laughed. 'Leave *Robinson Crusoe* to the bookworms like me, and Tommy.' He took hold of Milo's shoulder. Fortunately, not as hard as he had earlier. 'So, what do you say, fella?'

He looked into KG's eyes. In a way, he wanted to believe him. Believe that the hellish clouds that had swamped him today had some kind of silver lining. But he knew, deep down inside, they didn't. KG would use him. He'd pay for his board by transporting drugs. There was no ray of light shining forth in this room.

He wondered how many young people had fallen into this man's trap. Not all would have this keen insight into who he really was. He guessed his manipulation tactics would be all the more powerful if you were oblivious to the fact that he was a murderer.

However, he knew there was no thinking about it. Not really. If he refused, his mother would be rubbed out, and he'd shortly follow.

He nodded.

'In the meantime.' He reached into his inside pocket. He proffered a bundle of notes.

Milo stared at it, stunned. He'd never seen so much money in his life.

'Take it,' KG said, waving it at Milo, insistently. 'It'll keep you going over the next few months – while it gets tough. Then, after that, we'll be ready for you.'

Milo took the money.

There was a knock at the door.

'Come in,' KG said.

Brenda came in holding Milo's clothes. 'Fresh and pressed.'

Milo felt some shame over soiling the clothes and looked down.

She put them on the bed behind KG. 'I'll leave them there.' As she was walking out, she smiled back at him. 'I hope you come and stay here, Milo. I'll get a room ready for you.'

'Batman posters everywhere, Bren,' KG said with a smile.

She gave them both a multi-coloured finger wave at the door.

'You get dressed now, and I'll run you home,' KG said, squeezing Milo's shoulder and standing up again. 'Use that money to make your mother's last few months comfortable. Whatever she needs. She deserves it. If you need more, just let me know. She's given the world a right gem in you.'

When he got to the door, he turned. 'Ah, just one more thing. Before I forget. You need to know. Be wrong not to tell you. It's unpalatable, I know, but you're complicit in what happened to Pete. I know it's not your fault, Milo, you're young, but they'll still make an example of you, somehow. I couldn't bear it. Your mother couldn't bear it.' He bobbed his head from side to side. 'I know you won't do anything to jeopardise these opportunities, but I thought I'd make it clear how important it is to keep silent on everything. Is that okay?'

Milo nodded.

He smiled, turned, paused and then turned back again. 'I'll get someone to keep an eye on you. Just to make sure you're safe. You're important to me now, Milo, and you're going through a rough patch. I'll sleep easier knowing that you're okay. Get yourself dressed and I'll see you downstairs.'

After he left, he didn't lock the door.

He must have been confident that he had him trapped now.

Milo rubbed at his tears.

The monster had every right to be confident.

31

The phone call from Marsh stirred her into action, but Gardner had drunk far too much wine to get behind the wheel of a car. Frustrating as this was, it was probably a good thing. Throwing herself onto the streets would've felt more purposeful than pacing around her bedroom, but at quarter past ten at night, it would probably have been a complete waste of time, and a faster track to burnout.

Eventually, out of breath from pacing, she sat on the edge of her bed and rubbed at her temples.

Sleeping was the best option here – some attempt at a recharge for the long day ahead. However, was that even possible with the conversation with Marsh rattling around her mind?

'Emma, you still there?'

'Yes, sorry ma'am. Just shocked. I just can't believe this is happening. Kyle Alexander too? I can't... I just can't get my head around it.'

'It's strange, I know—'

'Strange, ma'am? A dead fifteen-year-old and three boys out

there doing God knows what! *Three* missing boys. What if... what if—'

'Not yet, Emma. You need to take a deep breath. It's not been that long. We don't know that any of them are really missing. Ten at night isn't *exactly* life or death for a lot of teenagers.'

'Apart from Pete Wilson, these're teenagers with no history of late nights, and they're certainly not teenagers who wouldn't keep their parents informed of where they were.'

'I know, and I'm not ignoring this, Emma. Relevant departments are in the loop.'

'Collette Alexander must be beside herself! Maybe I should go and—'

'Hang back, Emma. Her husband is there, and we have decent officers with them. Everyone descending on them is the last thing they need in this moment. It's in hand.'

Now, perched on the edge of the bed, she looked down at the notes she'd made during the call from Marsh.

Mobile phone left at home... no suspicious activity on logs...
Collette checked his room at nine thirty and he wasn't there...
must've left house while parents were watching television.

Gardner realised something that made her cold inside.

She couldn't remember ever feeling this clueless.

She lay back on her bed with a fractured mind. Where to turn her thoughts? To the missing children, to Rose and her sociopathic father, to her closest friend, Riddick, to her failing marriage?

Not only was she clueless, but she was completely overwhelmed...

Her phone rang again.

'Yes?'

'One down.' Marsh grunted. 'Milo is home.'

Gardner breathed a sigh of relief. 'Thank Christ. Where's he been?'

'He told his mother he was out walking.'

'Until almost eleven? Was he with Pete Wilson?'

'Apparently not.'

'So why was he even out then? Pre-Pete Wilson, he was never out past seven.'

'I don't know, Emma.'

'We need to speak to Milo right away. It's important—'

'It has been suggested to the mother, but she knocked it back abruptly.'

'Shit... so, we force the issue?'

'He's a minor, and the mother is very sick. Do you suspect him of anything, Emma?'

'No... I don't know... there's a lot to process—'

'In that case, we tread lightly. Give them the night.'

Gardner stood, sighed and began pacing the room again. 'Understood. I'll take a gentle approach first thing.'

'Thanks, Emma.'

'Any other news?'

'No. Like I said, one down, two to go. We'll get there. Now, try and sleep. I'll promise to ring you when number two shows.'

Gardner climbed into bed, fully clothed, clinging desperately onto the only piece of good news she'd heard in a while. Milo Hardy was safe. She let it soothe her. It wouldn't necessarily guarantee her sleep, but it was all she had.

32

Riddick was at his computer, head in his hands, the sense of doom introduced by KG's blackmail fuelling his urge to drink.

He was fighting with every ounce of his being. If this was indeed his swansong, he *must* negotiate it with dignity and control. He owed it to them all.

Rachel... Molly... Lucy... Emma.

Riddick dropped his hands, looked down at the sealed envelope on his desk and traced his name and address with his fingers – his mentor's scrawl.

What could you possibly have left to say, Anders?

Alongside the envelope was the list of five men given to him by KG.

He looked at his computer screen. His work database was prompting his password.

Would he have the clearance to find out which of these men was an informant, or God forbid, an undercover agent? Probably not. But it was a starting point. And, like the beige-suited predator had said, he was resourceful. If this fell through, there were other ways.

He typed in his password – a combination of his daughters' names – and hit enter.

After working his way through several menus, he brought up a search bar. He looked at the first name on the list and typed it out: Stewart Waller.

His shaking fingers hung over the enter button.

And now what?

If he discovered, as if by some miracle, that Stewart was the man, what came next?

Stewart's death?

Someone's son? Brother? Father?

What gave him the right to inflict that damage on anyone?

Also, when Stewart disappeared, then what? This search would be linked directly to Riddick's login. It was as good as a confession.

He took his fingers away from the button and looked down at the envelope, tracing Anders' writing again.

What would you have done, Anders?

You seem to think you made me! Maybe you did.

So, what would you have done?

He thought of the off-licence down the road.

How easy it would be to lose his mind... just once more.

Just tonight...

He looked up at the name. Stewart Waller.

He pressed enter.

The screen glazed over as the database searched.

No result.

'We both live to fight on, Stewart... for now...' He looked at the next name: Nathan Parkinson.

He typed it in. His finger hovered over the enter button.

What the hell are you doing?

He thought about his empty kitchen cupboard.

Wouldn't drinking himself to death be a better option than this?

He ran his hands through his hair. He needed a distraction... anything. To stop himself from spiralling further down this dark path. He glanced anxiously around, and his eyes fell onto Anders' letter again.

What the hell.

He tore open the envelope and pulled out three pages of notepaper.

He skimmed the first two.

I've heard it all before.

You love me... I'm the son you never had... you couldn't control the drinking...

He moved onto the third page.

Regret... longing... Same old, Anders, same old.

He stopped dead.

He re-read the sentence... once... twice... he couldn't move on from it.

It was as if a claw had reached into his chest and clutched tightly onto his heart.

He needed a drink.

Needed.

It was consuming him.

'No!' He slammed his fist on the table and then pushed enter.

The database whirred.

Riddick threw Anders' letter on the floor.

No result.

'Is this what you want, Anders? To take us all down? One final swoop?'

Third name. Enter. No result.

'We're playing Russian roulette,' Riddick said, entering the fourth name.

No result.

He typed in the final name and hit enter, hoping for the bullet.

* * *

With a trembling hand, Riddick held the phone to his ear. 'Hi Claire... sorry... it's Paul Riddick from the grief counselling.'

'I know. Are you okay, Paul?'

'Yes, kind of... Do you want to get that coffee?'

'At eleven at night?'

'Shit, I didn't wake you, did I?'

'To be honest, I don't sleep that much.'

'Ah,' Riddick said, suddenly feeling guilty and self-centred. Claire had been bereaved too. 'I shouldn't have called this late; I should've waited until tomorrow.'

She chuckled. 'Pack it in. I'm glad you phoned. And coffee sounds good... but there's a condition attached, remember?'

Riddick smiled. 'To keep attending your sessions?'

'Uh-huh.'

'I'll be there,' he said, knowing it was a lie. He'd be banged up before the next session. It was a near certainty.

'And you have to promise to stay awake this time?'

'Of course.'

'Okay. Coffee it is then.'

Riddick sighed and rubbed his forehead – he could feel a right headache coming on. 'I'm sorry, Claire, I'm not being totally honest. There's another reason I'm phoning.' He broke off.

'Go on then, spit it out.'

'Yeah. Look, I know you're a grief counsellor, and it's not your thing, but... I'm feeling the urge to drink...' He felt his face redden and was so glad that she couldn't see him.

'Nonsense... not my thing! I've been there. Where you are. Talk to me, Paul.'

Her accepting tone of voice helped bring his blood pressure back down.

'Does it still get you?' Riddick asked.

'It tries. I still get the urges like the next person, but I don't let it win, because I've learned it's a choice. But I think you've learned that too?'

'Yes. Doesn't seem to make it any easier though. Some nights it's agony. Like tonight. It's practically burning. Do you ever feel like that?'

'Sometimes, yes. You know what I do?'

'Go on,' Riddick said, desperate for her to prescribe something. Like a heavy dose of Vitamin C, or a ten-mile run.

'I pick up the phone and talk to someone – just like you have done.'

Riddick nodded and smiled. He was already starting to feel less overwhelmed by his cravings.

'Because then you realise it's okay to be vulnerable, Paul, like you are right now. If you've got your people around you, you can always make the right choice. You told me, before, about one of your people?'

He took a deep breath. 'Yes... Emma. She's bailed me out an unbelievable number of times.'

'I take it she's out tonight?'

'Not exactly.' His heart sank again. *She's been forced to push me to one side.* 'She has her own issues...'

'I see. I imagine she'd still want you to call her.'

'Yes, she would, but she needs a break from me. God knows, she's the patience of a saint, but I'm bloody high maintenance.'

'Stop being hard on yourself. She wouldn't do it unless she

really wanted to. It's not just sympathy, Paul, it's friendship. And I'm sure you'd be there for her if she picked up the phone.'

Of course. Because I... because... because she's special. He shook his head. He didn't want to go there. Confront his potential feelings for her. They might not be real. They could be a side effect of his vulnerability. She deserved better than to end up on a roller-coaster with him. 'Still, I prefer to give her a break. I know how that sounds though – like I'm using you! It's not the case. It really isn't.'

'I never thought that for a second. Do you want to talk to me about whatever has made you worried?'

Where to start?

Waking up next to a dead boy?

Realising that Russell Lock was probably innocent, and a child killer walked free?

The fact that he'd had someone killed, and was now being blackmailed for it?

Anders' letter?

'I can't talk about it. It's work related. I'm sorry for throwing up a dead end.'

'There're other directions,' Claire said. 'Tell me about yourself, Paul. Who are you and what do you like doing?'

He went out of the kitchen and up the stairs, telling her about himself. He realised when he got to his bedroom that there was very little to say. 'Sorry... I'm rather dull.'

'I'd say you were anything but dull. I've got an idea of something we could talk about.'

Anything. Anything to take my mind off everything. He went and sat on his bed. 'Go on.'

'This might sound strange, but would you like to talk about your family, Paul?'

The question should have taken him by surprise and should

have led to a rather awkward moment. But it did neither of these things. He looked over to Rachel's side of the bed and imagined her there reading one of her cheesy romances. He glanced down at the floor where they used to lay a mattress should one of their girls wander in late at night, having had a bad dream.

He suddenly felt very warm inside. 'Yes. I'd like that. I'd like that very much.'

33

Ron Best had spent most of the day in Stephen's room.

The family liaison officer, Lyndsey, had brought him hot drinks and food and suggested, on many occasions, that it was good for him to maybe get a change of scenery and maybe even a nap.

He'd remained polite, and always acknowledged her words, but he was unable to reply coherently – his mind was too cluttered.

Even now, close to midnight, he was unable to leave.

Perched on the end of Stephen's bed, he looked around his son's room. Wanting to understand.

All I ever did, Stephen, was try. To spare you the life that I had before your mother. She was everything to me. Without her, I'd be dead in a prison cell. I vowed to spare you that. I vowed to protect you.

Ron stood, paced, turned and stared down at the bed, recalling, not for the first time today, and certainly not the last, what had happened last week.

The whole event, the whole *ordeal*, just felt like a spear through his heart right now.

He'd been changing his son's bedsheets when his hands had touched the magazines beneath the mattress. At first, Ron had smiled. A fifteen-year-old boy with a couple of saucy magazines. No biggie. If anything, he liked the fact his son was going retro. Most people sought it out on their phones now. He was sick of seeing kids staring at their screens like zombies.

Yet, when he had pulled out these magazines, Ron's whole world collapsed.

Not because he was disgusted by the images. Naked men. Erections. He'd always been quietly curious about these things himself.

But curiosity was one thing – acting on it was another.

Gay people led chaotic lives. Sleeping around, fighting the system, becoming victims of those who were *truly* homophobic and spiteful.

Not a calm life like Ron had found with Stephen's mother.

Dangerous lives – like Ron's used to be back when he was outside of the law.

Calm and safety. That was my promise to you Stephen. This had the potential to change that...

Ron had been no stranger to an argument with his son, but this had been on a new level. Objects had been thrown and smashed. But it hadn't been just material things broken. Something had divided them. He'd seen it in Stephen's eyes. That act of severance.

I'm a man and I'll make my choices now.

And then he was gone.

Not physically, but emotionally.

For the next seven days, they hadn't talked.

There hadn't been an eighth.

* * *

Ron took Lyndsey's advice and left Stephen's room.

Without really thinking about what to do with himself next, he grabbed a jacket, and left. Lyndsey attempted to stop him by reminding him that it was almost twelve.

If he wasn't so sad, he may have just laughed. *What meaning did time really have any more?*

The snow was coming down heavily again, and he realised that the thin jacket he'd opted for wasn't fit for purpose.

Not that it mattered. Marching head down, he picked up enough speed that he was soon sweating rather than shivering.

He didn't pay much attention to the world around him, but it was quiet, and he couldn't see anyone else about.

All the time, his mind kept replaying the argument with his son.

And then it dawned on Ron as to why his son's sexuality had been so unsettling for him.

They'd been the same, hadn't they? Him and his son. The same wants and desires.

Ron's own chaotic life. His youthful fight against the system. His descent into crime. All of it'd been born from anger and bitterness over who he was. *Repressing* who he was.

He'd have died if not for Lynda. She'd found him. Accepted him despite his true desires.

But he'd been born in a different time. Repressing his nature had seemed sensible.

'What have I done?' he said out loud.

How gross his error had been – expecting his son to do the same, just because he'd done it.

'Stephen, I'm sorry.'

Stephen *could've* had a good life doing exactly what he wanted to do. Ron's hot argument about it being dangerous for homosexuals now – was just that. Hot. And full of bloody air.

He came out of his reverie and noticed that he was marching along the Waterside on Abbey Road. He stopped close to St Robert's Cave – where his only son, his *everything*, had left this world.

He was hot, sweaty and exhausted, but he wouldn't stop. He kept going, desperate to reach the place where his boy had—

It can't be!

He shook his head.

It just can't.

He squinted, but still couldn't be sure, so he shielded his eyes from the falling snow too.

A figure in a red puffer jacket remained, leaning against the gate that led to the steps down to the cave.

'Stephen?'

Ron began to sprint.

'Stephen?'

It was dark, and there was still some distance, but it could be his boy. The closer he got, the more it felt like a certainty. 'Stephen?'

The young man stiffened, and shook his head, and Ron recognised him. 'Kyle?' The disappointment immediately tore through him. He stopped.

'Ron?' Kyle said.

Those seconds, that brief flicker of hope, had transported him elsewhere, and now, he was back there. In hell. He opened his mouth to speak but could think of nothing to say.

'Are you all right, Ron?'

What kind of question was that? He'd never been worse, but here was a boy who needed an adult right now. And, whether he liked it or not, he was the adult. He steeled himself. 'I'm fine. What're you doing here, Kyle?'

Kyle shook his head. 'I don't know.'

Ron put his hands on Kyle's shoulders and sighed. 'Makes two of us.' He leaned in slightly, so he could look the young man in the face. 'We're a pair.'

Kyle avoided Ron's eyes, but this was standard for Kyle, who avoided eye contact at the best of times. What wasn't standard was how pale the boy was.

'I'm sorry, Kyle, I really am,' Ron said.

Kyle flinched. He looked down at the floor. 'He was your son. You—'

'But he loved you, Kyle. He really did.'

Kyle started to cough.

'You don't look well... You need to get home to rest,' Ron said, tightening his grip on Kyle's shoulders. 'Why are you out anyway? Your mum and dad. I can only imagine...'

'I came to meet someone.'

'Who?'

Kyle didn't respond.

'A girl?' Ron asked.

'No.'

'A boy?'

'I'd like to go now.'

Ron nodded. *Good idea. But who were you meeting, Kyle? Who's the mysterious boy?*

Was Kyle gay too?

'Did you know my son was gay, Kyle?'

Kyle looked off to his side, trying to move his eyes as far from Ron's gaze as possible.

'Kyle... talk to me. Did you know?'

Kyle nodded.

'I only just found out,' Ron continued.

Kyle had no response to this.

Ron took a deep breath and blew it out. It lifted up in a giant icy plume above Kyle's head. 'Are you gay, Kyle?'

Kyle became agitated. He moved his head further away but remained in Ron's grip. 'I want to go—'

'I'm sorry, Kyle, I'm not trying to upset you. None of this means much now anyway, does it?'

Kyle didn't respond, but he remained agitated.

'Just tell me one thing, please. Were you and him... you know?'

Kyle began to shake his head vigorously.

'Ah, it's okay, son.' He hushed Kyle, trying to soothe him. 'It's okay.'

It seemed to work. Kyle stopped shaking his head. Ron reached up and touched Kyle's cheek. His skin was smooth. 'You're a handsome boy.'

Ron took a deep breath. *Had he just said that?*

It was the truth though, wasn't it?

He *was* handsome. Very.

Ron couldn't gauge Kyle's response to the compliment. He always looked awkward anyway. But he hadn't pulled away. Would he have pulled away if he'd been offended?

Ron could feel the stirrings within himself.

He closed his eyes, searching out Lynda. *Help me, Lynda. Please, just help me.*

But, today, following the loss of his son, she hadn't been there any more, and the worst thing was, he'd no idea where she'd gone, and if she'd come back.

It was only when he opened his eyes that he realised he was leaning further in, and his hands were slipping from Kyle's shoulders to his back. 'We will get through this, Kyle... I promise... we will.'

Ron embraced him. He expected Kyle's hands to move around

his back to complete the embrace. When they didn't, he wasn't stunned, because Kyle still hadn't pulled away, making it feel right, *natural* somehow.

Without really intending it to happen, Ron felt the side of his cheek pressing against Kyle's.

He thought of his son's anger last week, and the fire in his eyes as he had admonished his father for being homophobic.

He hated you, Ron. At the last, he hated you.

'I've been wrong, Kyle. I've been wrong for as long as I can remember.' He closed his eyes and turned his face inward to kiss Kyle.

* * *

Why did you have to fight me, little bear?

We were the same, you and me... peas in a pod and all that.

I told you, but you didn't listen, my beautiful freak of nature. Those around us. They lie. They can't fix us. They certainly couldn't fix you.

You should have let me do it properly.

Fix you, that is.

Solidify you... freeze you...

You were the most fluid one I'd ever seen. Like a gas escaping into a room, and filling every crack in the wall, or rushing water loading every crevice in the ground.

You needed this more than anyone I ever met.

Your eyes pleaded with me to halt the change. To stop the movement. To be frozen... to be solidified...

Oh, my dear bear.

No one truly cries like I cry tonight.

I was so close to fixing you, so close.

I could swear now, but it's not befitting my memory of you. The purity you sought, that I know you needed, cannot be sullied.

We were almost in the warm embrace of Mother Shipton. The Petrifying Well spilling its magic...

We could see it!

You had to just hold on for a moment longer.

What made you panic? What made you concerned?

You seemed so calm, collected in my presence... you could be yourself... you didn't have to be like escaping gas, or rushing water... I gave you clarity.

Was it me? Did I betray you somehow? As we drew closer to the cave, did you see what was to happen next?

A wonderful end to pain and fluidity?

You hit me so hard with that rock. Where did you get it from? How did you manage to keep it hidden from me?

My wound continues to bleed, and the scar on my forehead will be a torturous reminder of the soul I didn't save.

I had to squeeze the life from you, dear bear.

It hurt me to do it. Destroyed me to do it. But if I didn't, then what? Nobody else could be fixed. It was for the greater good.

I will never forget the moment you vanished beneath the surface of the water.

My poor, broken, sunken bear.

I never gave you what you wanted, but I wanted a memory, just the same.

So, I took another bear. Smaller, this time, but still disfigured. Both eyes were lost beneath the stone. Strangely enough, it has split on the stomach. And it looks like a long scar.

It looked unfinished.

Like you.

So, in you go. Into my fireproof haven. Don't worry, you'll have company.

Fingers will never brush against you again – not even mine.

It's dark. It's cold. But remember, my beautiful bear.

When all is said and done, when your life was so tortured, there can be no harm in being locked away forever.

34

As soon as Gardner opened her eyes, she patted the bed around her until she found her phone.

No missed calls or messages.

Shit.

That meant that Pete Wilson and Kyle Alexander were yet to return home.

Five forty-five. Fifteen minutes to her alarm. She was up, dressed and fed before it went off.

She chanced a call to Marsh despite it being exceptionally early.

Marsh sounded out of breath. 'Emma... morning.'

'You okay, ma'am?'

'Rowing machine... helps with the menopause. Give me a second... Okay, that's better. Do you have any news, Emma?'

'No... I was hoping you'd an update on the lads—'

'Despite my promises to do so as soon as anything occurred?'

'Sorry, ma'am.'

'Anyone would think I'm not sincere enough.'

'Just anxious, ma'am. Okay, I'm off to see Milo Hardy and his mother before the briefing.'

'At six?'

'Is seven better?'

'Marginally.' Marsh sighed. 'Look... this is important. Just do us a favour... maybe leave Phil. Keep this sensitive and low-key. The mother's dying, and has been through hell; let's not end up in one of Marianne Perse's trashy news articles.'

Marianne Perse. Freelance journalist. She'd tried her best in the past to tear Riddick to pieces, and almost succeeded. She'd have no second thoughts about turning her malevolent attention towards Gardner.

Gardner went and stood in Anabelle's room for five minutes. She stood above her daughter, wondering how a world with such beautiful things in it, could so often be a turbulent hellhole.

She then changed rooms and spent five minutes looking at Rose's sleeping face and recalled Barry's words the previous evening. '*She wants to see him.*'

Sorry Rose, but it can't happen. It just can't happen.

Glad that Barry hadn't yet emerged for the sequel to last night's blazing row, Gardner sat over a coffee in the kitchen, contemplating Ron Best; Warhammer manager, Eugene; unfortunately, but needs must, first on the scene, Riddick; and the now-missing best friend, Kyle.

Hoping that Milo Hardy would unlock something on Operation Lost Light, Gardner's mind returned to Marsh's plea to keep it sensitive with Milo. This reminded her of Collette Willows – her old colleague and friend, who'd died less than twelve months ago during an investigation. Willows was always good at that. *The sensitive.*

She forced back tears as she often did when she thought about Willows. She missed her friend. She also fought the feelings of guilt, because although no one had considered her responsible, Gardner refused to believe she wasn't.

She finished her coffee and stood.

Letting loose emotion like that was a one-way ticket to derailment – and completely detrimental to solving this puzzle.

* * *

Gardner rang ahead so as not to spring an early surprise on Cherie and Milo Hardy.

Cherie said she was already up, eating breakfast with Milo, who was readying himself to go to school. She was happy for Gardner to come in and ask some questions.

Cherie opened the door. Last night, following the discovery of her son's absence, she'd been beside herself. For Gardner, it'd been a harrowing sight. Her terminal illness had manifested itself on her pale, desperate face, and she'd looked more withered and closer to the end than she may have done otherwise.

Fortunately, the relief over Milo's return had had the opposite effect. And it was remarkable. There was a sudden glow to her skin, and a strength in which she held up her thin body. Right now, she looked like she could take on anything.

Milo was eating at the kitchen table. He was wearing a school blazer, shirt and tie.

'How many Weetabix?' Gardner asked, nodding down to his bowl.

He looked up at her, then back down at his bowl.

At first, he didn't answer, so Gardner prepared to move on, not wanting the awkward situation to linger, but he then said, 'Four.'

'I got that beat.'

He looked up and raised an eyebrow. 'Oh?'

'Five.'

'Really?'

She nodded, although she was cheating slightly. When she had five, it was usually for her dinner, and she didn't really want to disclose that. It revealed far too much about her lifestyle – and not in a good way. 'I've quite a busy job, calorie intake goes through the roof. Is it okay if we talk for a few minutes, Milo?'

Milo nodded.

'Please eat though.'

Gardner sat down on one side of the table, and Cherie sat down on the other.

'You like school?' Gardner asked.

Milo shook his head.

'He likes comics,' Cherie said and smiled. 'Obsessed with them.'

Milo looked up at his mum, nodded and eventually smiled.

'The police officer I was here with yesterday likes comics,' Gardner said.

Milo regarded her with an interested expression. 'Which?'

'Batman, I think.'

He nodded again, but didn't say anything.

She could already tell that he was a kid of very few words.

'I'll take some recommendations from you to pass along...' Gardner took a deep breath. 'Okay... where'd you disappear to last night, Milo?'

Milo chewed his food. Gardner looked at Cherie, who looked a little concerned, but a swift nod showed she was okay with this.

They waited. Milo was taking his time.

'Honey?' Cherie asked.

He swallowed. 'I went for a walk. I was up at the castle for a while.'

'We like the view of the viaduct,' Cherie said, winking at her son and then looking at Gardner.

'Did you have anything on your mind when you went for that walk?' Gardner asked.

Milo looked a little frustrated. He stirred his Weetabix to mush.

'Honey, it's okay... Tell her about Pete. Exactly what you told me.'

'That would be helpful,' Gardner said, looking at Milo. She tried to read his expression, but his face was like stone. She thought it would never move. When it did, it almost made her jump.

'I had a friend called Pete. *Had.* I was wrong.' He looked back at his mother. 'I made a mistake. It's over.'

'What was the mistake, Milo?' Gardner asked.

Milo shrugged. 'Being his friend.' He looked down at his mush. 'I'm just better off on my own. Last night, I needed to think, by the castle. I promise that everything is okay now.'

'Okay,' Gardner said, smiling. 'I'd like to ask you about the night before if that's okay?'

Milo looked up at Cherie. The colour seemed to drain from his face.

Cherie looked at Gardner. 'He doesn't know you have that camera footage you told me about yesterday.'

Milo's eyes flicked between them. 'What camera footage?'

Gardner talked through the CCTV footage taken outside the Co-op on Boroughbridge Road. Throughout, Milo looked down at his half-eaten cereal.

Sensing his distress over having these events relayed back to him, Gardner was happy when Cherie reached over and held the back of his hand. *Poor kid.*

'Don't worry, honey,' Cherie reassured him. 'You *tried* to stop Pete hurting that boy. Another reason why you've had a change of heart regarding your friendship.'

'What're the other reasons?' Gardner asked Milo.

It was Cherie that answered. 'Pete was trying to get him to smoke and shoplift, would you believe? Convincing him to skip school. Milo told me everything. Thank God. He's realised in time that this isn't the right path for him. Someone trying to turn you into something you aren't is never worth bothering with.' She looked back at her son. 'Isn't that right, honey?'

Milo looked up at her, stared for a moment and nodded.

Why does he look so guilty then?

Gardner considered bringing up the fact that Pete was still to be located, but it felt incendiary, so she decided against it. Instead, she went for a softer approach. 'When'd you last see Pete?'

Milo thought about it. 'Early afternoon. We argued and I said I didn't want anything more to do with him.'

'What caused your argument?'

Milo shrugged. 'I just saw sense. I felt awful about truanting. I knew how it would make Mum feel.'

Gardner looked at Cherie, who had tears in her eyes. She glanced down at Cherie's hand which was squeezing her son's harder now, the tops of her knuckles glowing white.

'I'm going to make a few notes,' Gardner said, taking her notebook from her pocket and readying her pen. 'What happened while you were truanting?'

Cherie snorted. 'Being badgered into God knows what.'

Gardner smiled at Cherie. 'Is it okay if Milo answers this one? It may help.'

Milo referenced a few misdeeds he was influenced into doing before concluding with: 'When he dared me to steal something from a charity shop... well, I just had enough.' He was an awkward, nervous boy, that was for certain, so she may be wrong, but Gardner couldn't help but feel that he was trying to convince himself that this was true by nodding as he spoke.

She also noticed Cherie nodding along, and wondered if she too was desperate to buy into this narrative.

Marsh had called it right. Situations like this were very sensitive.

'It sounds like you made a good decision,' Gardner said. She smiled at Milo and then smiled at Cherie. Cherie seemed to glow a little more.

'And he's straight back in school again, today,' Cherie said. 'No moping. Just straight back at it.' She looked at her son, eyes wide with pride.

'Is it okay if I just go back to that camera footage?' Gardner asked. She didn't wait for anyone to voice a concern. 'Good on you for defending that boy from Pete. Did you know the lad?'

Milo nodded.

'Yes... you knew him?' Gardner prompted.

'He's in my year at school. We'd never spoken before, but I know who he is. Stephen Best.'

Gardner nodded and looked at Cherie. 'That's the boy who was found? By the cave?' She put her hand to her mouth.

'I'm afraid so,' Gardner said.

'What?' Milo asked, sharp to the sudden change in atmosphere.

Milo's eyes darted back and forth between his mother and Gardner. This was the most emotional he'd been since she'd come into the room. 'What happened to the boy by the cave? What happened to Stephen?'

'You mean you haven't heard?' Gardner asked.

'Comics,' Cherie said. 'That's it. He doesn't watch the news. And he didn't go to school yesterday, where he probably would've found out.'

Gardner offered Milo a sympathetic expression. 'Stephen Best lost his life by St Robert's Cave the night before last...

not long after you saw him. After you *helped* him by the Co-op.'

Milo was shaking his head from side to side.

'I'm sorry, Milo.'

'How'd he die?'

'It's still under investigation.'

'Was he *killed*?'

'I can't answer that.'

Milo looked at his mother and then back at Gardner. 'Something isn't right here... this isn't right...'

You can say that again! 'What do you mean by that, Milo?'

'I mean... I mean... I don't know. You don't think it was Pete, do you? He stayed with me. That night. It was only the next day, in the afternoon, that we, you know, called time on it.'

'Neither of you are under suspicion.' *Currently.* 'However, the time of this recording is so close to the time he may have died,' Gardner said. 'You and Pete could've been two of the last people to see Stephen alive. That makes you so important in all of this.'

Milo's eyes were narrow now, rather than wide, and he was shaking his head. He looked like he was having some kind of internal meltdown. Gardner tried not to read too much into it. A child learning of the death of a peer was always shocking and disorientating. His reaction didn't imply guilt, although she couldn't help but feel there was something significant here. Something odd about this triangle of Milo, Pete and Stephen.

'I... I... I...' Milo began but stopped. He just couldn't get there.

This inflamed his mother. 'Do you need a break, honey?'

Gardner inwardly sighed. *I'd prefer to just get to it.*

'I want to explain,' Milo finally got there.

Gardner nodded. 'Please.'

Milo gave his version of events. It began with Stephen coming along. 'He looked... I dunno... out of it?'

'How so?'

'His eyes were all over the place like he was on something. He seemed... agitated about something. He wasn't making much sense... at one point, he looked terrified.'

He described Pete attempting to get him to open his bag, and then the fall. He referenced the moment he intervened to stop it getting out of hand. 'And then he was... like... just gone! Up and running. Down Boroughbridge Road.'

Gardner regarded Milo. She knew from the footage that they didn't give chase but asked anyway, curious to see how he'd react. 'Did you go after him?'

'No! I swear... honestly!'

'It's okay, Milo... and did you see Stephen again that evening?'

'No.'

'Do you recall what time it was?'

'About ten or so?'

Gardner nodded. 'More or less. It was quarter past ten. What'd Pete have to say about the whole thing? Was he angry with Stephen?'

'No, not really. He calmed *right* down. I mean right down. He was like that. Up and down in a heartbeat! He didn't want to go after him or anything.'

'*Was* like that?' Gardner asked.

'Sorry, I don't—'

'You said "was like that". Strange to use the past tense when talking about someone that is still with us.' *At least, I hope he's still with us.*

'I dunno,' Milo said, growing pale. He looked down. 'It's in the past. We're not friends any more.'

Could explain it. Maybe.

'So, you recognised Stephen from school. Did Pete?'

'I don't know. If he did, he never said.'

Cherie jumped in. 'My son was only friends with this Pete character for a short time. And Milo often just keeps himself to himself. He knew very little about Pete. Didn't you Milo?'

He looked at his mum a moment before nodding his head.

'Did Pete keep himself to himself too?' Gardner asked Milo.

'He was rarely at school,' Milo said. 'But when he was there, he had confidence, although no friends to speak of. I think most people were scared of him.'

Not surprising judging by the Stephen Best incident. This Pete Wilson seems unpredictable.

Gardner asked a few more questions to pull apart the encounter between the three boys, staying within the boundaries set by Cherie's reactions. She certainly didn't want the mother calling time on this.

'What'd you do after seeing Stephen? Where'd you and Pete go?'

'We walked... we *just* walked...'

'It was quarter past ten. It was late and quiet. You must have some specifics,' Gardner said. She smiled. 'It's better to have a complete picture. We need to do it with everyone.'

'We headed down Stockwell Road.'

No, you didn't. Gardner nodded. *What're you hiding?*

'One moment... sorry,' Gardner said, looking back through her notes. She pretended to read some of them. 'The camera footage shows you sticking to Boroughbridge Road. You didn't head down Stockwell Road.'

Milo paled.

'What's happening here, DCI Gardner?' Cherie asked, widening her eyes.

'Nothing. I just need to establish exactly what happened in order to help us decide—'

'Do you suspect Milo of anything? You know how ridiculous that'd be, don't you?'

'I'm just trying to jog his memory,' Gardner said. 'We need to think of Stephen's family too – establish whatever truths we can.'

Cherie thought about this and nodded.

'I remember,' Milo said. 'We continued up Boroughbridge Road, in the *opposite* direction from where Stephen ran. The other way from the caves.'

Gardner tapped her notebook. 'Yes, that's what I have here.'

'See,' Cherie said, breathing a sigh of relief. 'They didn't go after Stephen.'

No they didn't, but he did lie. Why's that, Milo?

'So, now the memory is jogged, Milo, can you tell me what happened next?'

'Nothing much. We went down Boroughbridge Road, and then we turned off onto Halfpenny Lane, past my primary. We knocked around in Stockwell Park for a bit before cutting through onto Stockwell Road again... yes, sorry, that's where I made the mistake... we were there the other night, just walking in the other direction.'

'Did you go back up to the Co-op?' Gardner asked, realising she could check the footage on that one.

He shook his head. 'No, we turned off before then onto the path that cuts through to town by the doctor's.'

Gardner nodded and made a note.

'I think this is enough now, DCI Gardner,' Cherie said. 'We really want to help, but my son has been through a lot. This boy, Pete, has done a right number on him.'

'Okay, I understand. Almost there. A few more questions, please?'

Cherie nodded, but the glow on her face was fading fast.

'What'd you do then?'

'Not much. Headed home. That was it... I promise.'

'And you never saw or heard from Stephen again that night?'

'No,' Milo said.

'Okay... thank you, Milo,' Gardner said, not willing to try any more of Cherie's patience right now. 'I'll let you get off to school.'

He looked up and nodded. She took the opportunity to look into his eyes. She caught his gaze and held it. At first, he found it difficult to pull away, and in that small moment, before he managed to finally break it, she noticed something.

Milo Hardy was terrified.

She'd seen it before countless times.

The boy needed help.

'Sorry... I almost forgot. Milo, do you know where I could find Pete?'

Milo shook his head. It was quick and sharp. He looked around as if suddenly concerned someone might overhear.

What's happened, Milo? Are you in danger from Pete? Are you in danger because of Pete? She opened her mouth to ask another question.

'Enough... *please*,' Cherie said.

Gardner closed her mouth. *Keep the situation as calm as you can.* 'Okay, thank you so much for helping.' She reached into her suit pocket and took a card out. She placed it on the dinner table, keeping her fingers on it. 'Can I tell you what I think though, Milo? I think it'll put your mind at ease.' Milo looked at her. She saw the fear again. He nodded. Gardner looked at Cherie for her approval which she gave.

She still had her fingers on the card. 'I don't suspect you've done anything wrong, Milo. At least not regarding Stephen. So, if either of you are thinking those things, please don't. Please, please don't.'

As anticipated, the fear did not drain from his eyes.

'But I'm concerned about you, Milo... concerned about how you're currently feeling. Is there anything else you want to tell me? Anything I can help you with? You know it's my job to help... and on occasion, some have said I'm rather okay at—'

'I don't understand?' Cherie said.

Gardner turned her head slowly to look at Cherie, who was staring right at her. She offered a reassuring smile. 'I just want to make sure everyone is okay.'

Cherie nodded.

Gardner looked back at Milo who still had his head raised, and his eyes on her. She saw tears grow in the corners of them. 'Yes, I... I...'

Good... go on...

'I'm—'

A car backfired.

Gardner nearly jumped out of her skin. *Bloody hell!*

She looked at Cherie, who had a hand to her chest, and was shaking her head. 'Sorry. It happens all the time. It's the pillock opposite.'

She looked back at Milo, who had lowered his head.

Shit. Don't retreat. Not now. 'Milo?' she prompted. 'You were about to say something?'

Eventually, he looked up. She took a deep breath. *Go on.*

'I want to go to school,' he said.

'Of course, honey,' Cherie said.

Frustrated, Gardner lifted her fingers from her card and then prodded it. 'If you need anything, either of you, phone me. Not just about Stephen Best. Whatever you need. Do you understand? Do you have a phone, Milo?'

Milo shook his head.

She looked at Cherie. 'I suggest today, when he goes to school, he borrows yours with my number on it. Maybe just for the time being.'

'Why?' Cherie said, hand still to her chest. She looked ready to vomit. 'Is he in danger?'

I don't know... but something is going on here...

The anxiety... the terror... This isn't simply a child that has fallen out with another and so is off to school in a bad mood...

'It's just a precaution.'

'You promise?' Cherie asked.

'Just let him borrow your phone, Cherie, please?'

At least until I get more of an idea of what's going on.

Cherie nodded.

35

From his car, Andy Marshall was keeping an eye on Milo Hardy's home.

Keeping an eye on things wasn't Andy's favourite job. He leaned more towards interaction. He liked communicating persuasively and, when all else failed, he enjoyed getting his point across in a physical manner.

But Andy had a remarkable memory. That, coupled with the fact that he was born and bred in Knaresborough, made him the go-to for identifying people. If Andy needed to *find* you, he most certainly would.

But unusually, today's target had his mind in a whir.

Because even though he recognised the black-suited woman that went into the Hardy household, he couldn't recall her name; and right now his mind was a blank over where he'd seen her before.

Not like him at all.

Yet, despite his unease, he remained confident that when he caught a glimpse of her walking the other way, out of the Hardy house, his memory would deliver as it always did.

He checked his face in his mirror. His eyes were still red from the late night. One of the curses of a mind that stored so much information. It worked overtime, and insomnia was a side effect. He rubbed sleep out of them. When he looked back out of the window, Cherie Hardy was showing the familiar woman out.

Here we go. Where'd I see you?

She walked up the path, head lowered, long hair hiding her features. Deep in thought, or watching the ice? Neither option helped him.

Lift your head, girl. Spark my memory...

She reached the end of the path and approached her car, head still down. She leaned against her roof, and was looking down at her mobile, punching out a message.

Just bloody lift it. He took a deep breath, trying to resist becoming too frustrated. If he forced it, it wouldn't come. It was rare but this had happened before.

Anyway, he had her licence plate. He could always follow her. All wouldn't be lost.

Still...

Lift your bloody head, lass.

She did.

Andy looked at her face, drank in her features. It didn't take long for it to filter into his memory banks.

I see you.

You work with Paul Riddick.

After the black-suited copper drove away, he phoned KG to tell him, thinking, *Oh Milo. Not sensible you tyke. Not sensible at all. Rejecting his offer and betraying him? You think he can cope with that?*

But that wouldn't be Andy's job. Those above, in the shadows, they knew how he felt about kids. They'd given him the job based on it.

So, if you want it done, KG – you're going to have to do it yourself.

36

The snow had stopped overnight, but the temperature was still low, and the ice-cold wind, bracing.

Riddick would be inclined to blame the climate for his throbbing temples; after all, his sinuses had never been the best. But any doctor worth their salt would look at the bandage on his head and laugh him and his sinus concern out of the room!

Hopefully, the two paracetamol he'd taken thirty minutes ago would be due to kick in. He'd another two on hand if necessary. He met Dr Yasmin Dharni outside George Jacoby's home. Like Gardner, she dressed smartly in a tailored black suit. As she shook his hand firmly and introduced herself, she gave off a confident, astute air of someone deep into middle-age, despite possessing a youthful look you'd see on someone in their mid-twenties. Her dark skin was unblemished, and her black hair was glossy and full of vitality.

It soon became apparent that her appearance was not an indicator of mood.

She marched towards the house ahead of him, explaining that

she was short on time, and this was an unexpected addition to her diary.

Riddick knew he shouldn't underestimate the success of Sylvia, his contact at HQ, in getting him time with the bedbound George Jacoby, but he was already starting to rue the fact that Sylvia had bowed down to this condition of medical supervision. Yasmin looked like she was all set to be a hindrance rather than a help.

At the door, Yasmin continued to test his patience.

'You do know he can't move, DI Riddick?' Yasmin asked and knocked.

'Yes, I did my research.'

'Why're we here then?'

Her attitude was intensifying his headache. He preferred someone to just come right out and call him a daft apeth – there was nothing worse than having it implied so smugly. 'Sorry, I thought that may have been explained to you.'

'You think things are explained to me? You think people have the time for conveniences like that? And even if they did, do you think I have time to listen?'

She was hostile, but he kept himself in check. He was too close now. So, he let his headache rage without letting out some of the emotional pressure. 'I thought he may be able to shed some light on a case from 2003 – involving the murder of a child. It happened prior to the stroke. There were witnesses, too. He was *seen* with the child more than once.'

Let her chew on that.

'You know he can't communicate?' she said, still smug.

Good lord, I just told you about a dead child! 'He is able to communicate with his eyes, I believe.'

'He used to be able to, DI Riddick. He hasn't done for many, *many* years.' She glowered at the door which was still to open. She knocked again, more fiercely this time.

With such high stress levels, he wondered how she maintained such a youthful complexion.

He opened his mouth to hit back again but then closed it. It was pointless. She was gunning for him.

Just dodge the bullets, Paul, and get what you need.

Not that he quite knew what that was...

The door opened. The nurse from the previous day stood there. She greeted the doctor with a smile, but it so obviously started to fade when she glanced at Riddick.

'How are you, Ms Hartley?' Riddick asked, meeting her fading smile with a large one of his own.

'Yeah, okay. Sorry it took a while to answer the door... I was just upstairs with George.'

'Is he okay?' Yasmin asked.

'At the moment, yes.'

'As long as you're sure, Ms Hartley,' Yasmin said. 'If the patient has been distressed or is showing signs of being unwell, it's important to reschedule.'

'No,' she said. 'Everything is as it should be. And please call me Julie. Follow me.'

Inside, they kicked off their shoes, and were led upstairs to George's room.

Yasmin placed a hand on Julie's shoulder. Her demeanour with the nurse was courteous, and more in keeping with that warm appearance.

It was a demeanour Paul didn't expect to see being used on him any time soon!

'Can you come in with us, please, Julie? If you see any changes – signs of discomfort or distress, perhaps – that I don't notice, can you let me know please?'

'Of course,' Julie said and opened George's door.

Riddick felt his heart rate increase and his temples throbbed more than ever.

The stench of disinfectant was almost eye-watering, but par for the course, Riddick reasoned, if you'd been bedridden for the best part of twenty years. Better than the alternative – the smell of festering.

Julie walked in first, glancing in the direction of where George would probably be lying. She paused for a while.

Riddick felt a cold sweat starting up on his back.

Would she turn? Tell them it wasn't a good time? Usher them back downstairs?

'Dr Dharni,' Julie said, beckoning her in.

'Wait here,' Yasmin said to Riddick and then moved in next.

Riddick fought against the pain in his head. He should have been concerned about it worsening into a migraine, but right now, he was more bothered about having this avenue closed off from him.

Yasmin and Julie disappeared from view.

Come on!

He rubbed his head and felt for the extra paracetamol in his jacket pocket, wishing he'd some water with him.

'Can I come in?' he asked.

There was another long pause. *Jesus...*

'Yes, come in,' Yasmin said.

Riddick's stomach turned over as he made to enter, and he had to steady himself against the open door. Did he have this one badly wrong?

Everyone seemed to think so.

Everyone.

Had he let Anders' ridiculous suggestion root itself within him, and grow to an unmanageable size?

Beyond the growing pain in his head, he sought out that image of George Jacoby, the showman, beckoning people towards his boats, waving at Graham Lock by the wishing well.

Then, he saw the wide, dead eyes of Stephen Best, before looking at the bear in his bag...

It galvanised him.

Hold on to these images, Paul. This isn't the first time you've been written off. It wouldn't be the first time you've proven them all wrong...

Hold on to them.

And end this one way or another.

He crossed the threshold and turned to look at the showman, George Jacoby.

37

After Gardner phoned Rice and stunned him with the instruction to lead this morning's briefing, she headed to Kyle Alexander's house.

He'd been missing all night now, and she steeled herself for an emotional encounter.

Luke Alexander, who sold chutneys for a living, immediately started to showcase his belief – a belief that too many shared these days – that their public sector servants rarely put in the hard yards when called upon.

Gardner assured him that they were, and then some, as politely as you could when under attack, and when he settled somewhat, he took her upstairs to see Collette.

Collette was sitting on Kyle's bed, staring off into space.

Gardner looked around the messy room, and at the Warhammer figures scattered all over.

Collette was bouncing her left knee up and down, while resting a clenched hand, holding a tissue, on top of it.

'I wanted to see you, Collette,' Gardner said, sitting beside her, but stopping herself from reaching out and taking her hand. Not because of the soggy tissue, but because she wanted to keep it professional. 'Just to let you know we're trying our best, but we still don't have any news.'

Collette didn't respond. Instead, she dabbed at her eyes with the tissue she was clenching.

Gardner nodded. 'I know you've both answered a lot of questions already, but I was wondering if I could ask one or two more, just to make 100 per cent sure that none of my colleagues have missed anything?'

Collette dabbed at her eyes again and then nodded.

'Do you think the trauma of Kyle's best friend's passing has caused this?'

'He wouldn't run away. It's out of character.'

'You mentioned his diagnosis with ADHD yesterday. Is he currently taking his medication?'

'No,' Luke interjected. 'I found a packet in the bin the other day!'

Collette glared at Luke. 'You didn't tell me.'

Luke looked away. 'He made me promise not too – said he wouldn't do it again.'

'With that in mind,' Gardner continued, 'is he likely to behave erratically? Impulsively?'

'It's possible,' Collette said, turning her head for the first time; her eyes were red and swollen. 'But running away is a leap.'

'Ultimately, he's a bright boy,' Luke said. 'Even if he did something impulsively, emotionally, he's able to reflect afterwards. He *would* have returned home by now.'

'And he's got flu!' Collette said. 'You saw him. He was in no fit state to be wandering around' – she waved her hand at the window – 'in this weather.'

'You said he left his phone behind,' Gardner said. 'Sounds like he was in a rush. Maybe something in particular happened to cause him to behave irrationally? Do you have a tracker on his phone so you can keep tabs on him?'

Collette nodded.

'He may have left his phone here because he doesn't want you to know where he's gone?'

Collette was shaking her head. She didn't want to buy into her son's deception.

Gardner thought about the phone. It had already been scrutinised for messages. There'd been nothing of note.

'No chance he'd another phone?' Gardner asked. 'One he kept secret from you?'

'This isn't who my son is. Impulsive, yes. Awkward, yes.' Collette stood and wandered over to the Warhammer figures on the chest of drawers. She lifted one and twirled it around as if admiring it. 'Messy, yes. But he's not deceitful. He doesn't lead a double life... I'd know. I know my boy.'

'What about the mysterious friend of Stephen's? Kyle knew about him. Could he—'

'No,' Collette said. 'He isn't that confident. Something like that – meeting someone he didn't know – he *would* tell me.'

Gardner nodded, saddened by her naivety. She'd heard similar comments from many parents over the years and had witnessed first-hand how blindly trusting children often carried consequences.

Collette picked something up and came over to sit down again. 'Do you think he's dead?'

Gardner flinched. 'It—'

'Too soon,' Luke said, the colour draining from his face. 'Please... just don't go there.'

'I agree,' Gardner said, nodding. 'It's too early to suggest anything like that.' She looked back at Collette. 'Can you think of anything else that stands out over the past couple of weeks? I'm aware he wasn't spending as much time with Stephen... but was there anything else off apart from this mystery friend? Did he mention any other friends – from the Warhammer club, perhaps – or go out anywhere different?'

Luke shook his head. 'Whenever he has free time, he's in here, painting. That's it.'

'Okay, thank you.' She inwardly sighed. 'I'll—'

She broke off when she turned her head and saw what Collette was doing beside her. She then shook her head, her eyes fixated on Collette's hand, unable to finish her sentence.

'Are you okay?' Luke said.

No, I'm not.

'DCI Gardner?' Luke sounded insistent. 'You look like you've seen a ghost.'

Gardner forced herself out of the daze. 'Sorry, lack of sleep catching up with me.'

She asked Collette a couple more questions about what she'd just witnessed before checking her watch. 'I really need to get back to work.' She stood up and smiled.

She didn't want to rattle the Alexanders just yet.

So, as she was shown out, she fought to keep her demeanour as calm as possible.

A real battle, now that she knew who the mysterious friend was.

38

The bastard headache behind Riddick's eyes was relentless.

Unsurprising.

He'd been a prize dickhead.

He looked up into the eyes of Yasmin and Julie who were both faced away from the bed, staring at him. He expected them to shake their heads. Expected one of them to say, 'See... pillock... there's nothing here for you. Didn't we tell you that?'

Why, Anders? Why'd you start this?

He approached the bed.

He'd read somewhere that surviving twenty or more years with locked-in syndrome was highly unlikely. Gazing at a man so withered, to the point that he'd shrunk to the size of a child, he could understand why.

An actor. A show pony.

Really?

Grow up Paul.

There's no actor here.

No show pony.

He circled around to the other side of the bed, so he was away from Yasmin and Julie, and looked down. The fact that George was even still alive was a miracle in itself. In fact, if not for the whistling noise he made as he breathed, he'd have called that into doubt. The man had made a fair journey into the process of decay.

He looked up and saw that Yasmin and Julie had turned again so they could see him over the bed.

'So?' Yasmin crossed her arms. 'Do you have what you need?'

Don't be smug... just don't... I won't be able to cope.

'I need to wake him up.' He sounded desperate. He was.

'I can't allow that,' Yasmin said. 'Besides, he *can't* be woken, DI Riddick. Even if you somehow manage to, he'd fall unconscious again almost immediately.'

Enough, Paul. Put yourself out of this misery. 'Does he ever wake?'

'He used to open his eyes for a minute or so,' Julie said. 'But it's rare now.'

Riddick looked around the room.

It was sparse, and the furniture he did have was old-fashioned. It was polished oak though, and probably carried some value. He looked at the wardrobe and then over at the chest of drawers.

He wished he could tear the room to pieces – and then the house – for evidence that George had murdered Graham Lock.

But that would take a warrant.

And, he could safely say, that no warrant would be forth-coming – not with the impending destruction of Riddick's complete reputation.

'So, was there anything else?' Yasmin looked at her watch.

No. It'd all been for nothing.

He clutched his head.

'Are you okay, DI Riddick?' Yasmin asked.

He didn't answer. His mind was turning over – as was his stom-ach. His temples throbbed beyond belief.

He fought an urge to reach down and shake George. Did he

have anything to lose? This was almost certainly his last day of freedom.

But if he shook him, and caused a dying man damage – an *innocent* dying man in the eyes of the law – then what? He would disappear from the world as a true monster, rather than just a drunken fool who'd taken revenge against the rodent Ronnie Haller.

So walk away?

Could he do that? Was that his style?

He leaned in nearer to George's shrivelled, ashen face. '*Graham Lock.*'

He looked for a flicker on the withered face. *Nothing.*

'That's enough,' Yasmin said. 'DI —'

'Graham Lock.' Louder this time.

Still nothing.

'DI Riddick. *You must stop—*'

'Did you *kill* Graham Lock?'

'Enough!' Yasmin said, raising her voice now.

And then George's eyes opened.

39

Heart thrashing in her chest, Gardner contacted Rice and told him to wrap up the briefing.

'It's only just started!' he hissed.

'I'll ignore that, Phil. This *bloody* second.'

Rice sighed. 'Why?' he asked.

She told him.

'Shit the bed.'

'Precisely. Wrap it up and meet me here.' She gave him the address she'd acquired from HQ before calling him.

Throughout the entire journey, she couldn't shake the sight of Collette Alexander moving that Warhammer coin back and forth over the top of her hand, between the cracks in her fingers...

'Neat trick. Where'd you learn it?' she'd asked Collette, desperate not to reveal how rocked she was.

'Kyle taught it me.'

'Looks difficult – who taught *him*?'

'Stephen, of course. Everything came from Stephen... Everything was always about Stephen.'

She recalled Eugene examining the boxes for missing

Warhammer figures, while the deliveryman rolled the coin over his fingers.

The deliveryman she now knew to be Eric Oakes. Thirty-three.

She parked up several doors down from his home and waited for Rice.

Eyes closed, she recalled Eric brushing snow from his blue beanie hat that sat over long black hair, thanking Eugene. '*The kid loved Hedonites of Slaanesh.*'

Except, there's no kid, is there Eric?

You're single and childless.

Then, she remembered Eugene's complaint. The missing box of Lumineth Realm-lords...

You've been stealing from those deliveries, haven't you, Eric? Grooming Stephen with them?

But the Lumineth Realm-lords were stolen *after* Stephen's death...

Her blood ran cold.

Did you use them to lure out Kyle?

Come on Rice!

She looked up at the terrace three houses down.

Eric's shifts went from midday until eight at night. Chances were he was home.

Was Kyle with him?

That was enough to prompt her from her vehicle.

Rice was just pulling up.

She nodded at him but continued her march towards the home.

'Bloody hell,' he called after her.

She turned into Eric's driveway, slid past a red Kia and went for the door.

Rice caught her up, huffing and puffing. 'Boss, my knees...'

Sod your knees. She knocked hard on the door and pulled out her identification.

The door opened as far as a security chain would allow. She recognised the deliveryman's eyes peering out and then widening.

'DCI Emma Gardner and—'

The door was slammed closed.

'Guilty as charged,' Rice said, sprinting for the side gate. 'I'll go around the back.'

'Eric Oakes... you need to open this door right now...' She bent down and pushed open the letterbox. 'Backup is on the way. Don't let this get out of hand. I cannot guarantee your safety if the door has to be broken down—'

'Boss!'

Shit. Rice!

She legged it and turned sharply. Fortunately, Rice had left the side gate ajar for her, or she would surely have smashed into it.

'Help!'

Her heart thrashed in her chest as she sprinted down the path alongside the house, forcing back the memory of chasing that lad with a knife on a twelve-storey high-rise estate, while her colleague, and friend, DS Willows, was being thrown to her death from the eighth floor.

Not again.

'Boss!'

Not again.

Her phone buzzed in her pocket. *Not now.*

When she reached the end of the path, she was presented with a dishevelled garden. Rice was lying on the floor by an overturned wheelbarrow, clutching his eye. Eric, dressing gown open and flapping behind him like a cape, was sprinting towards a large wooden fence which separated the garden from the property behind his.

When she reached Rice, she slowed slightly, 'Rice. Are—'

'I'm fine! Just bloody get him!'

Still moving at speed, she weaved around Rice and watched Eric throw himself at the fence. The bastard managed to grip the top of it.

'Police! Stop, Eric!'

He was pulling himself up, trying to work his left foot over the summit, his dressing gown hanging down behind him.

Despairing, she put as much into the last metres as she could, her hand already outstretched to clutch the dressing gown which was suddenly inches from her...

He got his left foot over, and the dressing gown moved further from her reach.

Bollocks! No.

'Eric—'

He wailed.

She sensed he was going to fall and sidestepped before he did.

The idiot landed back on the frozen earth, his dressing gown fanned out around him, his nakedness exposed. He then yanked his left knee up to his chest, clutching his ankle, which was bleeding considerably.

He was moaning and rocking from side to side. 'A bloody nail. It's pissing blood.'

Gardner looked down, ensuring that she kept her eyes on his bloody ankle rather than his manhood. 'Just a bit.'

Rice came up alongside her. 'You clocked me, dickhead.' He looked down at the naked man and grimaced. 'That's my lunch ruined.'

Gardner knelt behind the writhing man. 'Is there anyone in the house, Eric?'

'Can't you see I need the hospital?'

'Your son in there?' Rice said with a sneer.

Eric narrowed his eyes.

'The one that loves Warhammer, remember?'

Gardner looked up at Rice. No wonder he was pissed off – his shiner was already starting to flourish. 'Call it in. We need a team for the house.'

Gardner looked back down at Eric. 'Where's Kyle Alexander?'

Eric groaned. 'I don't know what you're talking about.'

'Why did you run then?'

He winced. 'I need the hospital... I—'

'Why'd you run?'

'I'm going to bleed to death.'

She looked at his wound. It wasn't pretty but it clearly wasn't life threatening. Still, she'd let him think what he wanted. 'Your choice. Tell me about Stephen Best and Kyle Alexander and I'll get you medical attention.'

'Are you going to arrest me?'

'Depends on what you tell me.'

He looked down at his wound and gritted his teeth. His eyes watered. 'You've got it all wrong.' He squeezed them shut. 'I didn't kill Stephen. I *loved* him. And he *loved* me.'

'Yet, he's dead,' Rice hissed. He'd returned from his phone call.

Gardner glared up at him, but he didn't acknowledge her for once.

He looked *furious*. 'Fifteen. You disgust me. You had sex with a child and then killed—'

'Detective Inspector!' Gardner interrupted.

Rice continued to glare at Eric. He bared his teeth.

'You go and wait for backup. That's an order.'

Rice narrowed his eyes, turned his head, spat on the floor and stomped off.

'I didn't kill Stephen,' Eric shouted after Rice. 'It's been the worst few days of my life.'

'Look at me,' Gardner said. 'I'm the one arranging the medical attention.'

Eric looked at her.

'What happened with Stephen?'

'He ended it with me earlier on the day that he died by that cave... he *ended* it. We were together, *here*, late afternoon.' He nodded at his house. 'And out of the blue, he just called time on everything.'

The semen.

Gardner couldn't be any more certain that it belonged to Eric now. From that final afternoon.

'Why?'

'He couldn't cope with his sodding father any more. The man's a shit stain. A bully! Watching Stephen's every move.'

'Did he find out about you?'

'No... just that Stephen was gay, but that was enough! That old bastard tortured my Stephen. He *loved* me and yet he bloody well ended it because of that old prick. But kill him. Why would I do that?' There were tears in his eyes. 'I've never loved anyone like that... never will again.'

Gardner was disappointed by her sudden doubt. Before, she'd felt so certain that this was it. The end.

Fair enough, anybody could sound convincing when needs be.

But it'd take some skill to do so, naked in the cold, believing that you were bleeding to death.

'Do you know who might've killed him?'

'If I did, I'd get them.' A coldness came over his eyes. 'You can be sure of that.'

'Kyle. You know where he is, don't you? You stole those Hedonites of Slaanesh to draw him out.'

'I swear I don't know where he is... but yes, I did meet with him. But you make me sound horrible. I gave him those Hedonites to make him feel better, not to bribe him! We met near the cricket ground.'

'So, you simply met up to make him feel better – nothing else intended? No bribery for his silence?' *No attempt to groom a second boy?* She reserved this question for now – she didn't want to inflame him too much.

'No, I gave Stephen a phone so we could keep in touch. He told me he was going to destroy his phone after he finished with me. After I found out about...' He shook his head. '*After* that horrendous moment, I called the phone, desperate to hear his voice, despite knowing it wouldn't happen, and then Kyle answered. Stephen hadn't destroyed it after all, he'd left it at Kyle's for safekeeping. So, I asked Kyle to bring me the phone in exchange for the Hedonites...' He scrunched up his eyes and moaned.

'His silence seems rather cheap.'

'Kyle wouldn't say anything because of how Stephen felt about me. There's honour between them two.'

'Shame there's no honour with you, Eric.'

Eric's eyes flew open.

'You abused Stephen.'

'No... no... Are you not listening?'

'I am listening. Protest undying love all you want, Eric.' Gardner raised an eyebrow. 'Stephen was fifteen.'

'He was old enough to know what he was doing... what he wanted.'

'If you're so innocent, why run?'

'For this reason, the fact that you wouldn't understand that we were in love.'

'Maybe we should see how a jury feels about this love story?'

He winced and looked away. There were tears falling down his face now. 'I knew from the moment I saw him. The way that he looked at me. You can't question what feels so right.'

'You can and you should.' Gardner shook her head. 'He was a child. We're adults. We have a responsibility.'

'Should we not have any responsibility to ourselves? For our own needs?'

'It doesn't work like that.'

'I was close to... you know... ending it before Stephen came along,' Eric continued. 'He saved me.'

Did he? Or is that just more justification? She felt the anger surging through her. How dare he put his needs before those of a child.

'Were there others?'

Eric scrunched his eyes up and moaned.

'Were there others?' she repeated.

He didn't respond. Her stomach turned.

She felt a hand on her shoulder. It was Rice. 'All arranged.'

Gardner stood up and walked him a metre away. 'He abused Stephen, and others too, I suspect.'

'Did he admit to killing him?'

'He says he didn't,' Gardner said. 'He's a bloody good liar if he did.'

'We've met liars before.'

'We have. Let's get him booked in and take another run at him.'

Her phone rang. It was Marsh. She put some distance between her and Rice.

'Ma'am?'

'Emma, you need to get yourself into HQ... get this all wrapped up pre-press conference.'

'I would, but I'm not 100 per cent on Eric. In fact —'

'Really? You mean you haven't heard? I thought Ray was calling you?'

She recalled the phone buzzing in her pocket while she was running. 'No... Heard what?'

'Ron Best has confessed to murdering his son.'

* * *

'Graham Lock.'

Who said that?

'That's enough... DI—'

'Graham Lock.'

Again... that name... that sweet, sweet name.

'DI Riddick. You must stop—'

'Did you kill Graham Lock?'

Who's asking?

Where am I? Who am I?

Christ above... the light is too bright! Turn it down. Whoever you are, turn it down. It burns. You want to blind me?

Oh God... I remember. They're all I have left. My eyes.

Please don't blind me!

I beg you – they're all I have left!

I've so many moments that I live inside... so many beautiful, beautiful moments and you bring me back to this hell?

I could scream.

Except I can't.

Okay... okay... that's it. Good. The pain is settling, but still, I'm here. Who brought me back?

Who dared to do that?

There's the window. The one I cannot walk to. The one I cannot look through...

The one I cannot jump through...

Because I would.

Sweet Jesus above, I would!

'You killed Graham Lock, didn't you?'

Ridiculous question!

Your face is worn, your eyes hang heavy. A face I don't know. A face I've seen a thousand times.

Broken.

'*Can you talk, George?*'

Silly man... look at me! If I could laugh in your face, I would do.

Mind you, my strange guest, there're places where I can talk. Far from here though. But, alas, there're moments that you cannot reach.

Moments in which I danced.

Still, here you are. What can I do for you? If talking is not an option, take yourself and that beautiful name on your lips far from here...

'*If you can hear me... If you can hear me, George. Just let me know.*'

Persistent bugger, aren't you?

How about this?

Blink. Blink. Blink.

'*You can hear me George, can't you? You really can. Blink three more times.*'

Haha. Whatever floats your boat, strange man. Blink. Blink.

Hold your breath...

I can feel your tension...

Wait for it...

Blink.

40

'He can hear me,' Riddick said, heart racing. 'He understands. Did you see that?'

'Julie, you said this didn't happen any more,' Yasmin said, turning her wide eyes onto the nurse.

'I've never seen it happen,' Julie said, shaking her head.

Yasmin glanced back at Riddick, her eyes narrowing again. 'Be careful, DI Riddick. He's frail, and we don't know if he's actually communicating.'

What the hell do you think he's doing? 'George, blink three times if you can hear me.'

George obliged.

Riddick looked at Yasmin with a raised eyebrow. Her expression was stony. *But don't deny you aren't fascinated, Yasmin... don't you dare deny it.*

He didn't want to waste a moment; he'd not get a second chance. He needed to go straight for the truth. 'Blink once for no, and twice for yes. Do you understand?'

Blink. Blink.

Riddick thought his heart might suddenly burst from his chest.
'Did you kill Graham Lock in 2003?'

Blink.

He waited. No second blink. *Shit.*

'Did you *know* Graham Lock?'

Blink. Blink.

Riddick felt every nerve in his body tingle.

'Is there anything you can tell me about what happened to Graham Lock?'

Blink. Blink.

The answers to everything...

Adrenaline made him feel light on his feet.

The truth in a frozen man...

He fumbled around in his suit pocket for his notebook. It rarely made an appearance, and usually came at the behest of Gardner, but Christ, did he need it now!

'Can you blink when I get to specific letters?'

Blink. Blink.

Okay... okay... He reached up to wipe sweat from his brow and his hand brushed over his bandaged injury. His headache reminded him that it was still there.

'A... B... C... D... E... F...'

Blink.

He wrote *F* down with a trembling hand.

'A... B... C... D... E... F... G... H... I...'

Blink.

F. I.

He went again and again and again, until he spelled the word FIXED.

'Fixed? Fixed what?'

He looked up at Yasmin, who shrugged.

'Fixed what?' Riddick looked down and asked.

He started to read the letters out again.

George gave a blink on F and then I.

You're spelling the same bloody word!

He finished it anyway, and stared down, disheartened. *FIXED.*

When he looked up, Yasmin was looking at her watch. *Don't you go there. Don't you sodding well go there.*

Riddick leaned down, so his eyes were less than a metre away from George's. He felt the man's weak, broken breath on his cheek.

'Tell me what you did! What'd you fix? Did you fix Graham Lock, is that it? For the sake of your soul, George, tell me. Did you fix Graham Lock?'

No blinks.

'Damn you!'

George closed his eyes.

Riddick's breath caught in his throat.

His eyes stayed closed.

'No... no... George, I'm sorry, open your eyes.'

Nothing.

Riddick reached out and put his hand to the paralysed man's withered cheek. '*Wake* George!'

'That's quite enough, DI Riddick,' Yasmin said. 'I think you should be satisfied. You got much further than anyone anticipated.'

Riddick looked up at Yasmin. 'Satisfied? This man killed a fifteen-year-old boy. Satisfied?' He thrust a finger in her direction. 'If it was your son, would you be satisfied?'

He heard her draw breath. Her eyes narrowed. She meant business, this one. She'd already placed him way beneath her and nothing he said would elevate him now.

He shook his head and looked at George again.

His eyes remained closed.

'I'm sorry, Doctor.' He nodded. 'You're right. We're done.'

'Good,' Yasmin said.

Riddick looked up and watched Julie turn and exit the room first. Riddick came around the bed, shaking his head.

Fixed.

Fixed what?

Graham?

As he followed Yasmin to the door of the room, he said, 'You do understand why I had to try, don't you, Dr Dharni. If we don't get to the truth, what's the point of any of this? That boy innocent.'

Yasmin walked back out into the hall and turned so she was staring at Riddick through the door frame. 'I read about the case. The truth was there. It was the father. Why pull up trees around this dying man? Does his own tragedy not count?'

'I'll get back to you on that one,' Riddick said, taking a step back and slamming the door closed. He turned the key in the lock, and then slid the bolts top and bottom for good measure.

He listened to the muffled pounding of Yasmin's fists, and her muted voice. 'Open the door. This is unacceptable...'

A solid old-fashioned door should hold the obnoxious doctor out. Of course, it wouldn't keep out those she'd contact.

Best be quick then, eh, Paul?

He returned to George and looked down at him. 'You *fixed* Graham? I need to hear it from you. *Now.* If anything, do it for the sake of your soul!'

He waited.

Nothing.

Just the pounding on the door.

He leaned in and hissed in his ear. 'A predator... reduced to nothing. *Pathetic.* How does it feel to have your wings clipped? Good on nature. Intervening. Shutting you down.'

Nothing.

Frustrated, Riddick closed his own eyes as he leaned over George. The pounding on the door had stopped now. Yasmin would be on the phone.

'I should've left Ronnie Haller to nature too,' he whispered. 'I should've left him to the inevitable.' He shook his head. 'But I didn't, did I? I killed him. I've nothing left to lose. Do you understand, George? Nothing at all.'

He opened his eyes.

George Jacoby was looking up at him.

41

Gardner recalled Ron Best at the window. Wide eyed... open mouthed... gaunt and pale... transfixed by Gardner and Rice on his doorstep, *knowing* the dire reason that they were there.

At the time, Gardner had put it down to the fear that existed within every parent's mind over such a late-night house visit.

But had she been wrong? Had Ron known the reason behind the visit because, in actual fact, he'd killed his own son?

Gardner shook her head. She'd been a fool to rely on her gut. After all, Ron had never provided a decent alibi.

What would be the cost of her mistake?

Kyle? Another fifteen-year-old?

As Gardner's brain rattled with the revelation of Ron's reported confession, she was at least glad of a break from Rice. He was accompanying Eric Oakes to the hospital. She was trusting that Rice's anger over the black eye had subsided, and he was going to approach the situation professionally; this case needed to be dressed up nicely for the Crown Prosecution Service. The recovered semen would be Eric's, but she wanted it locked down tight. Anybody that preyed on a fifteen-year-old boy wasn't walking free.

Gardner ran through the details of the revelation in her head again as she neared Ron's home. FLO Lyndsey had taken Ron breakfast into his room earlier and had noticed a head wound. At first, he'd dismissed it as a slip on the ice during his late-night ramble, but when Lyndsey had pushed further, Ron had lost his composure. Apparently, he'd confessed to killing his son several times, before sliding to the floor and curling up.

Ray Barnett had been called in to support, but Ron was yet to break from his stupor. Gardner had insisted that there would be no arrest, and no heavy-handed behaviour from anyone, until she'd seen and spoken to him.

Gardner drove up to Ron Best's home.

'Shit!' It seemed like her orders had fallen on deaf ears.

Two officers were leading Ron Best up his driveway by his arms.

She jumped from the car and glanced angrily at each officer.

Ron's head looked in dire need of medical attention. Was there any need to manhandle him? Ron didn't look as though he'd be able to fight his way out of a paper bag! 'Go easy, officers.'

'We're just keeping him upright, ma'am,' one of the officers said.

Gardner took another look at Ron. They were right. Ron clearly wasn't looking where he was going, and his legs appeared as if they could buckle at any moment.

Barnett emerged from Ron's front door. His eyes widened when he saw Gardner, and he jogged up the driveway towards her. He moved quickly around the suspect and the two officers. It didn't take too many strides. Barnett was as big as a basketball player.

'Boss... sorry... I had no choice. He started to hit his head against the wall. I thought it best to just get him up and out.'

'Stay here, please,' Gardner said to the officers. She moved

Barnett to one side. 'Relax Ray, the right call, I'm sure. Did you ask him about Kyle at all?'

'I asked him about many things, boss. He's not communicating.'

'Shit.' Gardner sighed. 'Okay... let me try.'

Gardner tried to make eye contact with Ron, but he just seemed to be staring at something off in the distance behind her.

Riddick, Eric and soon, Ron... this investigation was keeping the NHS busy.

'Ron, if we let go of your arms, can you please hold yourself upright?' Gardner asked.

She waited. Eventually, Ron gave a brief nod.

'Is that a good idea, boss?' Barnett said quietly behind her.

'Now, please,' she said, shaking off the irritation she felt over Barnett's request – he was only trying to do what he thought best. No doubt she'd have responded in a similar way.

The two officers let go and watched with creased brows – they looked as if they expected the bereaved father to just topple over. He didn't.

'Ron,' she said, still trying to catch his eyes with her own. 'It's me. DCI Emma Gardner.'

Nothing.

'The night before last, you showed me photographs. Beautiful photographs of Lynda and Stephen.'

She thought she saw something stirring in his eyes, but when he said nothing, she concluded it was blind hope.

Barnett leaned in. 'Exactly how we found him – until he just started to lose it. Honestly, I've tried everything.'

Everything you had at your disposal, Ray. But I have more.

She took a deep breath. Her next move felt callous, almost brutal, but it could be the spark that would bring him out of himself. 'Ron, we have a man in custody. We have reason to believe that this man abused Stephen.'

The stirring in Ron's eyes was certainly more evident now.

She felt Barnett's hand on her shoulder. He was panicking. 'Boss, I think you should move—'

'Who?' Ron said.

Gardner shrugged off Barnett's hand. 'We'll get to that, Ron, but first, I need to know if you're okay, and I need you to elaborate on what you meant before when you said that you killed Stephen.'

'I never wanted anything but the best for him. I told you that, didn't I? The other night?'

'You did, Ron,' Gardner said, looking at him with compassion. 'And I could see then, as I can see now, that you mean it.'

'But I killed him. What more is there to say? Doesn't matter my intentions, I killed my own boy.'

'How, Ron? How'd you kill Stephen?'

Ron sighed. He brushed tears away. 'He was just like his mother, you know. Quiet, but so bloody sincere – straight as a die. He is... *was*... one of the best. He'd have done anything for anyone. Not like me. I'm an old bastard that still has no idea where he is from one day to the next...'

This was too ambiguous. Too frustrating. If he literally killed Stephen, which she was doubting more and more, she needed to hear it. Have it confirmed. Assess it as truth or fabrication. Right now, this really did just sound like a lament. A sense of guilt, not an admission of actual murder. 'What happened at the cave, Ron?'

'The cave?'

'Yes. St Robert's Cave? What happened there?'

'Nothing happened.' He looked flustered. 'Why? Who told you something happened? *Nothing* happened at the cave.'

'Your son, Ron. Your son, Stephen, died at the cave.' She eyed up his head wound. Maybe he'd done some serious damage.

'Sorry, yes, I thought you were talking about last night.' He looked away. It was clear he was frustrated at himself for mentioning this piece of information.

'Is that where you banged your head? At the cave last night?'

He shook his head, slowly. 'I don't feel so great.'

'Did you go back to the cave? Why?'

He flinched.

'Why?' She raised her voice.

'Because... because... that's where it happened. I didn't mean to scare him. It's not his fault... he pushed me, but he was scared...'

Kyle.

She looked at Ron. 'Did you see Kyle at the cave?'

Ron looked down. She could see the tears running down his face.

She turned to Barnett. 'Get officers to the cave now!'

Then she turned and ran for the car.

* * *

'If anything, do it for the sake of your soul!'

My soul!

Are you blind? Do you not see what I've been reduced to?

I live in hell already. Even if my soul is torn to pieces and fed to demons, at least I might be able to feel something again...

Besides, my soul is safe. Is yours? You talk about killing, but what I did was different.

I fixed.

And nothing is more admirable than that.

Graham Lock was tortured. You don't know the half of what his father did to him. You couldn't even begin to understand the chaos in that dear bear's mind. Chased back and forth by demons, he was. He showed me the scars where he cut himself. He told me about his night-mares and pain... He showed me his vulnerability.

All of it.

He couldn't handle the volatility any longer. He needed what I offered. He needed to be solid.

Just like I needed it too. As a child, I prayed for it every night, and twice after he came to my room. My uncle, my two-faced uncle, Archie... a pillar of the community... a rat...

What did she call you?

DI Riddick. Yes. That's it.

Well, DI Riddick, you talk about saving my soul, but where do you think that soul is?

In hell, DI Riddick. Whether that be as a trembling boy in my bedroom, or as this husk in a bed...

But at least I did some good in my pitiful life.

At least I gave others the solidity they craved.

That pounding on the door... you really have locked the others out.

Now you interest me, DI Riddick. You're a driven man, indeed. What is locked inside of you? What is causing your instability? Your volatility?

'A predator reduced to nothing. Pathetic. How does it feel to have your wings clipped? Good on nature. Intervening. Shutting you down.'

No, I am not a predator, DI Riddick. You don't know me. Can never know me.

I gave Graham what no one else was willing to give him. And I offered the same to Julian Greaves. He, too, was broken. Abused until he had no home. He was like running water on the ground waiting for heat to vaporise him. But he panicked. And this is my cross to bear. He changed his mind, and I lost my bear in the worst possible way. Seeing him sink below the surface of the Nidd instead of finding solidity under Mother Shipton's waters was my greatest tragedy. Not nature clipping my wings as you so colourfully claim!

'I should've left Ronnie Haller to nature too. I should've left him to

the inevitable. But I didn't, did I? I killed him. I've nothing left to lose. Do you understand, George? Nothing at all.'

Who are you, DI Riddick? Who are you really?

I must admit you really do have my interest now!

Let me look at you.

Worn face, eyes closed as if in silent, desperate prayer. A murderer, you say?

Broken.

Like Graham, like Julian, like I was before I found my calling...

That's it! Open your eyes, DI Riddick!

Let's talk.

42

Gritting his teeth over the agony in his temples, Riddick stared hard into George's small, yellowing eyes. He took a deep breath. 'Why'd you fix him? *A... B...*'

Blink. Blink.

The rush of adrenaline made the burning in his temples intensify, but he managed to scribble B down onto his notebook.

He continued until George had spelled out *Broken* with his eyes.

'You fixed him because he was broken?'

Blink. Blink.

Riddick stood up straight, his mind whirring, his heart thrashing, his forehead throbbing...

The sudden pounding on the door following a short break made him jump out of his skin. 'I've contacted the police,' Yasmin shouted.

Riddick put his hands to his head. *Shut up! Let me think!*

He'd so many questions... *so many*. Where to bloody well start?

'What're you doing to him?' Yasmin asked. 'Are you hurting him?'

Shut up!

He wanted to know why this living corpse in front of him had killed Graham, but motive at a snail's pace would be a challenge. The priority was evidence. He needed proof that he was a killer. That Riddick had not gone mad with paranoia.

Undeniable truth.

Would it give purpose to the life he'd led from the moment he'd stood at Mother Shipton's Cave staring over the Nidd at Knaresborough twenty years ago?

Riddick shook his head, frustrated that his worn-out brain was delaying him. 'How'd you fix Graham?'

George blinked twice on S. Then, O. Eventually:

Solidified.

Broken – fixed – solidified.

Riddles.

Riddick hated riddles. Always had. He wanted facts. *Wait...* Something stirred in his banging head.

2003. Graham Lock, sitting upright beneath the steady drips from the Petrifying Well.

Petrification.

Calcification.

'You wanted to solidify him in the cave, didn't you? You led him willingly to the Petrifying Well, promising him an end to the instability of his life?'

Blink. Blink.

'And you gave him the sleeping pills?'

Blink. Blink.

'It makes no sense. You must've known the body would be removed, taken away. You'd know that? Calcification takes years.'

Blink. Blink.

'But that's not the point, is it? With a mind like yours, George, you saw the Petrifying Well merely as a performance, a display, a recreation of the true process of solidifying Graham – taking his life.'

No response.

Riddick expected relief over having the truth finally confirmed. What he found instead was fury. 'You're a monster.'

Blink.

'You took a child's life.'

No response.

Riddick thumped his own chest. 'I lost both my children.' He couldn't remember his heart ever beating so fast. 'Senseless.' He leaned in, considering the pillow beneath the old man's head. Thought about it pressed firmly over his face.

It would be so easy.

The idea felt so right... so tempting.

But then what?

A confession from a dying man through blinking. Delivered by a detective that was crossing lines left, right and centre?

The truth would be lost all over again.

'If what you did is so right, George; if fixing Graham really was the right thing to do. Why hide it? Especially now. Look at you. Give me something.' It made him feel sick to say the next bit, but how'd you get into a serial killer's mind? Ego, perhaps? 'Cement your legacy.'

He waited... George's eyes didn't move.

Shit.

'Let the world see what you did. For Graham. For others like Graham that need this... fixing. Show what you did for George. Show them the solidity on offer.' He realised he was sounding like a madman, but where were the choices? Really? There were none left.

George's eyes moved. A reaction.

But no damn blinking.

Riddick turned, fists clenched, listening to the continued pounding on the door, and reeling over the constant pain in his head.

He wanted to scream at the top of his lungs. He could feel the despair rising from his gut. He forced it down. So close... he'd come so close... and now everything was about to end.

Riddick turned. 'You want to fix, George? Is that what you want? Is that *all* you've ever wanted?'

Blink. Blink.

'Then fix me, George. Look at me, look at my desperation, my pain. *Fix me.*'

Nothing.

Yasmin shouted again. 'They're less than five minutes away; do yourself a favour, DI Riddick. Come out now.'

'Precisely, George,' Riddick continued, ignoring Yasmin. 'You're a fake. A fraud. If you weren't, you'd do this.'

Blink. Blink.

Feeling like his heart was going to burst from his chest, Riddick readied his pen. 'Go on then, George. Fix me. We've got minutes. A... B...' He cycled through the letters.

Blink. Blink.

N.

Eventually he spelled *number*.

'You want to give me a number?'

Blink. Blink.

'Zero... One... Two...'

Blink. Blink.

'Two. Is there more?'

Blink. Blink.

'Zero...'

Blink. Blink.

'Zero...'

Blink. Blink.

'Zero... One... Two... Three...'

Blink. Blink.

2003.

He didn't need to ask if there was any more. It was the year that Graham died.

But now what?

'They're here!' Yasmin called.

Game over.

'There must be more,' Riddick shouted. 'Give me more. A... B... C...'

George started to blink erratically. He wasn't playing any more.

Riddick turned in a circle, fists clenched. 2003? The year Graham was murdered. 'I know that, George. Goddamnit, I was there!'

He looked back at George. His eyes were looking left. Riddick followed his line of vision to a wardrobe door.

He charged and threw open the wardrobe door, reached in and tore clothes from their hangers. He cast them to the floor. Pressed shirts and trousers; jumpers; stale jackets. He cleared the entire rack, and then his breath caught in his throat, he fell to his knees and leaned forward.

He pressed the palms of his hands to the top of an electronic safe.

His breath was fast and shallow, his heart threatening to burst from his chest. What was this? What was *in* this?

And how did he get in?

Of course!

He reached a trembling finger out to the keypad.

Two.

He felt Anders' hand on his shoulder.

Zero.

He needs people like me. People like you. People who see things.

Zero.

Something about a bear?

Three.

2003 glowed on the LED screen.

He pressed the button. *Clunk.*

There was a knock at the door. 'DI Riddick? This is DS Steve Hamill. What's happening in this room?'

Riddick looked at the closed door. He could barely breathe, wondering what was in the safe. 'Police business,' Riddick called. 'I'll be there in a moment.'

'Dr Yasmin Dharni has reason to believe that her patient is in danger.'

'She's wrong,' he said, turning his attention back to the safe. He turned the handle.

The door to the room rattled. 'Why's this door locked then?'

Riddick could see a familiar shape in the darkness inside the safe. He took a deep breath, feeling every single nerve ending tingle.

'This is your final chance, DI Riddick.'

Riddick reached into the safe and closed his hand around the stone object. He pulled it out and forced back a gasp.

Riddick stared down at the misshapen face. He traced his finger over the sockets where the eyes should have been and then set the bear down gently on the floor.

Riddick glimpsed something else in the safe. *Jesus... no...* He reached in again and his hand closed on a second stone object.

He pulled out another stone bear; smaller, but weirdly, heavier.

He stood and turned, thrusting the bear in George's direction. 'You did it again? Who?'

'Sorry?' Hamill said through the door. 'Are you talking to us?'

'No,' Riddick hissed. 'And you're interfering with a murder

investigation, Detective Sergeant. Know that before you break the door down. I'm in the room with Graham Lock's killer.'

'Then open it.'

Riddick charged over to the bed, so he was back in George's line of sight, and held the second stone bear in front of him. 'Two souvenirs. Was there someone else?'

Blink. Blink.

He noticed that it'd grown momentarily quiet outside the room. Hamill was probably having a slight panic over his comments about interfering and was possibly seeking out the advice of a superior before breaking the door down with whoever was with him.

'A... B...' He got to N before George blinked twice.

'DI Riddick,' Hamill shouted, louder now. 'I've checked. You don't have permission to speak to the patient without medical assistance available. Additionally, there's no active murder investigation involving Graham Lock.'

'A... B... C...' This time, George double blinked on I.

NI.

'Make sure you're not in the way of the door, DI Riddick,' Hamill said.

Ignoring Hamill, Riddick went through the process with George again.

NID.

There was a tightening in Riddick's chest. He knew where this might be going.

Thud.

The door shook on its hinges. It wouldn't take many more blows.

'Are you spelling the River Nidd?' Riddick asked.

Blink. Blink.

Thud.

'Wait, Hamill stop! I'm in front of the door – you'll hurt me.'

'Then, open it or get out the bloody way.'

Riddick ran over and turned the key. It wouldn't budge – the lock had started to break through the door frame, so it was jamming.

'Shit... wait...' He pushed his weight against the door and turned the key. This time it unlocked. The top and bottom bolts had already broken loose.

He opened the door and stepped back.

A younger officer looked up at him over his battering ram, and then moved to one side, sheepishly, revealing the gruff-looking DS behind him.

Riddick stepped back, and Hamill eyed him suspiciously.

'Check your patient,' Hamill said and nodded through the door.

Yasmin glared at Riddick, and approached George. She took his pulse and observed him for a moment. 'He seems okay.'

'Why wouldn't he be? I was interviewing him,' Riddick said.

'How? He's non-communicative,' Hamill said, stepping into the room and looking over at Yasmin for confirmation that he was right.

She nodded.

'Really?' Riddick said, raising an eyebrow. 'Then how'd I get the code for his safe?' He pointed at the open wardrobe. 'And how'd I get the location of the second victim?' He stared hard at Hamill, desperate to intimidate him. And avoid an arrest.

Hamill kept looking at Yasmin for reassurance. But even she was starting to look dubious.

Riddick pointed down to the bear on the floor by the wardrobe, and then held up the one in his hand. 'Both are from Mother Shipton's Cave.'

'Stone bears?' Hamill creased his brow. 'How're they relevant?'

'Well, that one on the floor has always been relevant. This one was a surprise, mind. I need you to write this down, Detective Sergeant.'

Hamill looked confused.

Riddick didn't want to allow him the time to work out if he was being played by a rogue superior. 'Now!'

Hamill fumbled around for a pen and pulled out a notebook.

'There's another child in the Nidd. I suspect they're near to the Petrifying Well. I need you to call it in, get the river searched.'

'Me?' Hamill said, putting his hand to his chest.

'Yes. Do you have an issue with that?'

'Well... I... no... but what're *you* doing, sir?'

'I need to alert the rest of the team.' Riddick approached Hamill, who was blocking the door.

Riddick stared hard at him.

The expression on Hamill's face suggested he was giving this serious thought. But Riddick was confident. Arresting someone who'd solved an extremely cold case in incredible circumstances might not endear him to the press or his superiors.

'Could you move out of my way, Detective Sergeant?'

Hamill moved.

Riddick threw one last look over at George, who had his eyes closed again.

'Thank you, Dr Dharni.'

He went into the kitchen to swallow his other two paracetamol.

As he left the house, a solitary thought ran through his mind again and again.

That's it. I'm done.

43

Cursing, Gardner slowed as she approached St Robert's Cave. Abbey Road was no place for acceleration in summer. Throw in ice and snow, and it was a death trap.

Yet Ron had been with Kyle last night. In the place where Stephen had died. He may not have admitted it, but it'd been as clear as day in his eyes.

When she saw the entrance to St Robert's, she hit the brakes sharply. The car skidded slightly, turning towards the gate, but fortunately ground to a halt before doing any damage.

Outside the car, the wind was coming in strong over the Nidd. This was one ruthless winter. It knew how to get deep into your bones and set down icy roots. She did the sensible thing and grabbed her parka from the boot.

As she unbolted the gate, an image flashed through her mind.

Stephen Best lying beside the cave. Frozen and pale. His young life knocked out of him.

Trying to ignore the most obvious question racing through her mind – *did more of the same await her?* – she went through and started to descend.

The steps were icy, and she couldn't go as quickly as she would've liked, but she still opted for a risky pace.

She thought of Riddick, two days previous. Was this heading the same way? She gulped over the possibility of finding Kyle lifeless at the bottom.

Near the bottom, she looked over the trees and the Nidd.

She sucked in a deep breath, and took the final few steps, warding off the images of dead children.

She heard a hacking cough.

She'd never expected to take such delight in such an unhealthy sound.

'Kyle?'

'Yes,' he said, quietly.

Thank God.

And then she saw him. Sitting against the cave wall, beside the entrance, his knees drawn up to his chest and his arms locked around his legs.

He gave her a swift look, confirming who she was, and then switched his gaze back to the Nidd.

As she approached, he coughed some more. He was wearing a jacket, but the idea of him sitting out here all night and most of the morning – which she suspected he'd done – made her want to cry and throw her arms around him. Neither option was appropriate, so she peeled off her parka.

'Lean forward, Kyle.'

He did, without looking at her, coughing again as he did so.

She knelt and placed the parka around him, seizing the inappropriate words, *you'll catch your death out here*, before she'd managed to release them. 'Pull it around yourself.'

Gardner still had some body heat from her descent of the steps, so she didn't feel too much discomfort just yet. It would come, though. Quickly. She sat beside him. 'Have you been here since last night?'

He nodded.

'Why?'

He shrugged. 'It's quiet. It's the only place that is. Everything is so loud these days.'

Gardner nodded. 'Everyone likes the quiet from time to time.'

'Especially Stephen... Neither of us ever liked the noise.'

Gardner reached over and squeezed his arm. She kept her hand there.

'Mum and Dad?' he asked, staring at her. He looked guilty.

'They're worried, obviously. But they'll be over the moon when they find out you're safe.'

He turned away, nodded and coughed. 'I can't stop thinking – could I have done something? And if I had, would he still be alive?'

'You cannot feel responsible, Kyle.' She squeezed his arm again.

'When we played Warhammer together, we never got tired. It was like the whole world around us didn't matter any more. I'm never going to have that again, am I?' He looked at Gardner.

Gardner inwardly sighed. *Not with Stephen, no.* 'You'll heal. In your own way. Everyone does, eventually...' She paused. 'Why didn't you tell me who the new friend was?'

Kyle shook his head and coughed. He slipped free of Gardner's hand and pulled the coat tight around himself. 'Because I promised. He asked me never to tell anyone who it was – even if they begged. I knew I should've said something *after*... but I just kept thinking Stephen would never have broken a promise to me, *never*, so, I just couldn't do it.'

'Did you meet Eric Oakes last night, Kyle?'

Kyle nodded at a rucksack by his feet. 'He gave me that.'

'May I?' Gardner asked.

Kyle nodded.

Gardner opened the rucksack and looked at the box inside. Hedonites of Slaanesh.

'He's not bribed me or anything. I gave him the phone back because it's what Stephen would've wanted.'

'I see,' Gardner said. 'But aren't you worried that Eric was the one that hurt Stephen?'

Kyle shook his head. 'Stephen never stopped talking about him. He loved him. It made me sad, but now, I'm glad he was happy for a time. Stephen would never be in love with someone who would hurt him.'

Gardner did not share Kyle's sentiment. Even if Eric was innocent of the murder, he was *still* in the wrong. And he'd be punished for it.

Gardner shivered and crossed her arms. 'Kyle, sorry if this is personal, but are you gay?'

Kyle shook his head. 'There's also a girl in my year I quite like. I've liked her for years actually. She has a nice smile.'

Gardner nodded and smiled. 'What's her name?'

'Emma.'

'Great name.'

'I've never actually spoken to her.'

Gardner nodded again. 'It'll come... It always comes.'

Gardner could hear people coming quickly down the steps.

'My colleagues are coming to help. There will also be an ambulance up there, Kyle. Nothing to worry about, but it would be good to get you quickly checked over.'

'Okay. What'll happen to Eric?' Kyle asked.

'You don't need to worry about that, Kyle... you really don't. But tell me, who do you think hurt Stephen?'

Kyle shrugged. 'That's why I came *here*. I thought if I stayed here, then, somehow, at some point, he'd tell me. Give me a sign. It hasn't happened yet. I'm starting to think it won't.'

No, unfortunately it won't, Gardner thought. *It doesn't work like that.*

'Did you see Ron, Stephen's father, here last night?'

Kyle nodded.

'What happened?'

'I'm sorry.' He sighed. 'I didn't mean to hurt him. But... he... you know...'

'It's okay, Kyle, take your time.'

Two officers she recognised were now metres away; she held up her hand to gesture at them to stop. They nodded and complied.

Eventually, Kyle looked at Gardner. 'He tried to kiss me.'

Keeping the shock inside was difficult, but she managed, and she gave him an understanding nod. 'And what happened?'

'It felt wrong... so... I panicked...' He broke off and looked away.

'Understandable,' Gardner reassured him.

He sighed. 'I pushed him away and he slipped on the ice. He fell over and banged his head.' There were tears in his eyes.

She was holding his arm again. 'And?'

'Nothing. He just got up and ran. He's not really hurt, is he?'

Gardner shook his head. 'Not that I know of.' She didn't want to reveal Ron's confession to Kyle, but she did have one question. 'What was Ron's relationship with Stephen like?'

'Ron took us to Warhammer club sometimes. He was always nice. He stopped coming when we were old enough, but he always seemed to get on with Stephen okay. Recently though, Stephen told me his dad couldn't accept he was gay. Stephen got angry while he was talking about it and started crying too. But, you know, I was seeing him less and less because of Eric, so I didn't have any chance to help.'

Gardner smiled at Kyle. 'We're going to get you warm now, and I'm going to contact your mum and dad. Is that okay?'

Kyle looked up at her with tearful eyes. 'I'm so sorry for this.'

'You don't have to be sorry, Kyle.'

As she watched Kyle being led away, she pulled her phone out and contacted the Alexanders.

The stunned silence... the tears of relief... the heartfelt apologies for not trusting the police...

After ringing off, Gardner realised that her day-to-day life was consistently filled with people at their most vulnerable.

An emotional maelstrom.

She turned her mind back to the fractured father. Ron.

I killed him.

Did you Ron? Did you really?

I'm finding it bloody hard to believe.

44

Riddick hoped his second dose of paracetamol would make light work of the headache still raging behind his eyes.

As he walked along the Waterside to where he'd parked his car, he sighted Mother Shipton's Cave on the other side of the Nidd, where a young policeman, a real fish out of water in that busy crime scene, had craved truth one dark night in 2003.

Now, twenty years later, that fish out of water had found the truth.

And yet, there was no comfort in that.

It was just confirmation that the last twenty years of his life had been a lie.

He stopped by the wishing well and fished a pound coin from his pocket. He slipped it in the slot at the top of the well, and watched it roll down the flat, concave metal sheet that had been fitted within it.

After the coin had disappeared down the hole with a clunk, he looked up at the boat stand, which was currently closed due to the snow and ice.

He imagined George Jacoby standing there, waving in this direction at Graham Lock.

His head throbbed and his stomach turned.

The preying child killer that lived in the house by the Waterside.

That *still* lived in that same house.

Soon, the police would be dragging the Nidd, looking for George's second victim. Riddick had already made a call to Mother Shipton's Cave on the doorstep of Jacoby's house. They'd checked their records and discovered that another bear had gone missing from the Petrifying Well, two months after the first. A month before the stroke that would incapacitate George.

The police had never been notified of the bear. At that point, Russell Lock was under lock and key. The owners of the cave had not wanted to subject themselves to any more unnecessary attention.

His contacts in HQ were now trying to link this date to any reports of missing children in North Yorkshire.

Missing children who were never found again.

Ironically, Riddick thought with a wry grin, Morgan Lark could have lent a hand here. His dossier on missing children had been rather extensive.

For a moment, he dared to believe that his headache might just be improving.

He continued his walk to the car, his mind turning to Claire and their conversation last night.

They'd been up late talking about his family. Having avoided such conversations like the plague in the past, it was a new experience for him. In fact, he'd actually laughed with Claire over some of the memories. Many of those moments with his children, and his wife, hadn't lost their humour. Their poignance. Like old photographs, they demanded attention and reflection.

Better late than never, it had made him realise something important too. He didn't need to see them any more. Rachel, Lucy and Molly. He didn't need to conjure them up at a dinner table, chat to them, live his pathetic life around holograms.

They were there... in his memories, his experiences, his conversations with others.

Claire had made him realise that there weren't just two extremes to opt for in his tragedy. Ghosts walking your floors or complete shut out.

There was a third, less extreme, option. Reminiscence. Keeping them alive inside you.

He was so grateful to her for this because he'd need that for what lay ahead.

For his incarceration.

Yes, KG. You lose.

Last night, in his agitated state, all five of those names had drawn up a blank on the database.

Good. It'd been a mistake. That wasn't *him*.

Because regardless of his drunken decision to request the death of Ronnie Haller, he was still that young man in 2003, staring out over Knaresborough, demanding truth.

Last night, his mind had been scrambled, but his conversation with Claire, and the discovery of the truth today, had made him remember who he was.

He was not the man to send an informant, or undercover officer, to his death. Never had been. Never would be.

Just before he reached the crossing over Bond's End that took him to the car park, he contacted Gardner.

'Paul... Hi...'

'Boss, is it a good time?'

'Yes. Are you okay?'

'Graham Lock and Stephen Best were never connected,'

Riddick said, hitting the button on the crossing. 'You were right. All of you.'

'So? It's not something for anyone to be proud of. I'm just glad your mind is at ease.'

It's never at ease!

'What've you been doing Paul?'

The green man appeared. As he crossed, he began to tell her everything. He finished his story by his car in the car park behind The Ugly Duckling café. 'Shame he'll never see a courtroom.'

'But the truth will be there. And people will remember. People never forget. Paul... I can't believe you found all this out.'

'I've had time on my hands. Now, please tell me about Stephen, boss.'

'We're almost there.'

He knew that was all he was getting. It was frustrating, but he trusted her.

'As soon as it's finished, you'll be the first to know, Paul.'

He sighed. 'There's another reason for my call, Emma...' His retreating headache suddenly flared again. He leaned against his vehicle, concerned he might just go over.

'Sounds heavy.'

There was another bolt of pain. He retched, holding the phone away from himself.

'Paul?'

He forced the phone back to his face. 'Yes... sorry... I... shit!' He clenched his teeth and squeezed his eyes closed.

'You don't sound all right!'

'A headache.' He groaned.

'A headache doesn't reduce you to your knees... Where are you?'

'I'm fine... give me a second.'

'No! Where are you?'

'Please. I *must* tell you something...' He broke off again and hit the palm of his hand against the roof.

'You're not making any sense. I'm calling an ambulance.'

'Emma, I—' He groaned; the pain was excruciating.

'Tell me where you are!'

'Water... side.'

'Be more specific.'

'By the...' And then a funny thing happened. The headache started to lift again. He stood up straight. He was still disorientated and nauseous, but the pain was literally pouring out of him. 'Wait... it's going... and I... shit, Emma... I can't believe it.'

'What?'

'I remember everything. I remember the car and I remember the reg.'

45

The door to the mortuary opened and Dr Hugo Sands stepped out into the cleaning area, snapping off his gloves before reaching up, unhooking his face mask and sighing.

'Something wrong, Doc?' Riddick asked.

Hugo looked up at Riddick. The colour drained from his face, and he touched his chest as if his heart had skipped a beat.

Riddick was only just getting his breath back after his frantic journey here, and so was leaning against the far wall. He took a step away from it now, standing tall, wanting to portray himself as unruffled – even though he clearly was.

'DI Riddick?' Sands said, edging over to the bin.

Too late, prick. I saw your face. Saw the colour bleed away.

Sands pressed the foot pedal on his bin and disposed of his gloves and mask.

'Everything okay, Doc? You seem tense.'

Sands shrugged and smiled. 'Fine, I just wasn't expecting you. You're not on the case, are you?'

'No, I'm not,' Riddick said, taking a step towards him.

Sands creased his brow, doing his level best to look confused, but his panic shone through brightly. He shook his head. 'Why you here, then?'

Riddick took another step forward now, so he was within three metres of the pathologist. 'Professional curiosity? How'd Stephen die?'

'You'll have to ask DCI Gardner.' Sands looked over at the door that led to a stairwell back up to the ground floor of the hospital – it was several metres to his right. Riddick used Sands' glance to close the gap by another metre.

When Sands looked back and saw how close Riddick was, his skin paled further. 'Kate, my assistant, is on the way down – she has the toxicology report on Stephen's death. In the interests of the case, it might be best if you leave. I'm sure DCI Gardner will pick this up with you.'

'She's on her way anyway. I called her.'

Sands looked as if he was going to throw up.

'Anyway, Doc, I had a right bastard behind the eyes this morning. Do you think it's down to the head wound?'

'You should probably go upstairs and get that looked at, DI Riddick. I could make a quick call?'

'Maybe. The strangest thing happened though, Doc. The headache suddenly went.'

'That's good.'

'Yes... and it took some of the cobwebs with it.'

'Cobwebs... I don't follow.'

'I remembered, Doc. I remembered everything.'

Sands gulped.

The door to the left opened. A young lady in scrubs stood there looking between the two men. She held a brown folder. 'Sorry, Doctor, I didn't realise that you were—'

'It's okay, Kate, DI Riddick was just leaving.'

Riddick smiled at Kate. She returned his smile, nervously.

'Do you know what car Dr Sands drives, Kate?' Riddick asked.

Kate's brow creased. She looked at Sands, then back at Riddick. 'I... I...'

'It's okay, Kate,' Sands said, stepping forward and reaching out for the folder. 'I'll just finish up in here with DI Riddick, and then I'll read this. We can talk it through shortly.'

She nodded, looking over at Riddick again.

'Thanks, Kate,' Riddick said, opening the door for her.

Kate looked up at Sands, but couldn't resist another glance back at Riddick.

'It's fine, Kate,' Sands insisted.

Kate left the room.

Sands closed the door, shook his head, wandered to the front of the room and leaned back against the stainless-steel sinks.

'You're confused,' Sands said. 'I expect you're still experiencing concussion.'

Riddick took a step. 'Maybe. Unless I've remembered something that you've forgotten?' He then moved even closer. Sands drew back, pressing himself firmly against the sink. 'I wonder if you need something to jog your memory.' Riddick cracked his knuckles. 'A headache can work wonders.'

Sands, realising his time was up, scowled. 'And if I walk out covered in bruises, where does that leave your career?'

'Pretty much where it already is!' He snorted. 'What happened that night at St Robert's Cave? I've already confirmed the reg was yours.'

'You may remember seeing me. But it isn't what you think. I had nothing to do with what happened.'

Riddick narrowed his eyes. 'If you were there, dickhead, you have *everything* to do with it. Try again.'

'There's nothing to tell you.'

'I'm going to ask you some questions now. I know how you like to hesitate before you answer. Every time you hesitate, I'm going to push you further and further into that sink. Do you understand?'

'Yes.' Sands spat the word out. 'It seems you're everything you're rumoured to be.'

'There's a lot of rumours. Only the worst ones are true.' Riddick took a deep breath. 'Did you kill Stephen Best?'

'Don't be ridiculous!'

'I'm finding a lot of answers in the box labelled ridiculous, these days. Was it you?'

Sands shook his head, wearing a horrified expression.

'Answer!'

'No... No, I didn't even know Stephen Best for pity's sake! Are you seriously thinking I've anything to do with *that*? Your anger is misplaced – as it often is!'

'I'll ignore that,' Riddick said. 'He was fifteen, Sands. A child.' He moved his face closer to Sands'. 'A child.'

''This is nonsense!'

Riddick grabbed the doctor by his scrubs and drew his fist back. 'And then you tried to kill me, you little shite...'

'What? I didn't. I swear I didn't.' He lowered his head and cowered. He dropped the brown folder on the floor and white papers spilled out. He then held his palms up as if in surrender, keeping his eyes closed, preparing to be hit. 'I tried to save him for pity's sake... I tried so bloody hard... but it wasn't possible.'

'You're not making any sense, man,' Riddick said, shaking him by his scrubs. 'What're you talking about? Tried to save him, how? You smashed him over the head with a frigging rock. Then you hit me, and I woke up next to that poor boy.'

'No, you have it all wrong. The whole thing just so random. It was all chance. I put myself in the wrong place at the wrong time. I was so stupid... I wish... I wish...' He didn't finish.

Frustrated, Riddick opened his hand and slapped Sands on the face. 'Speak. Wish what?'

Sands had tears in his eyes now. 'It'll ruin my career... It'll ruin me.'

Riddick thrust Sands back hard against the stainless-steel sink. He slid partway up onto it, his spine jammed against the taps. 'I know a thing or two about being ruined... but I'll give you a simple choice... your back or your career?'

'I wish...' He broke off again.

Riddick pushed him again. Sands howled in pain as the taps poked into his back.

'Wish what?'

'I wish I hadn't been so stupid. I wish I'd never bloody met her!'

The door to the room burst open again; Riddick didn't look – his adrenaline kept his eyes firmly fixated on Sands. 'Met who?'

'Her!' Sands said.

Riddick did look now. He saw Gardner at the door, her eyes wide.

'Paul, what the hell are you doing?'

'Struggling to find out what his fascination with you has caused,' Riddick said.

'Let go of him,' Gardner said.

Riddick held on a moment longer, but then sighed, and released him.

Gardner came up alongside Riddick and spoke to Sands. 'Why were you at St Robert's Cave the night Stephen was killed?'

'I was following him.' Sands nodded at Riddick, while rubbing his back.

What?

Riddick shook his head.

Following me?

'Why?' Riddick asked.

Sands sighed. 'Why do you think?'

Riddick shook his head. 'I've no *bloody* idea.'

Sands looked between Riddick's and Gardner's faces. 'Because... you two...'

'Because you two what?' Gardner said, sounding as frustrated as Riddick felt now. 'Spit it out before I pick up where Paul left off!'

Sands wiped his eyes. 'Because I've fallen for you... and you only have eyes for him.' He screwed up his face and gestured to Riddick with another nod of his head.

Riddick looked at Gardner. Her face reddened.

Sands stared at Gardner, more tears in his eyes. 'He's dangerous... can't you see that? Did you not just see what he was doing when you walked in? I wanted to protect you.'

'Protect me?' Gardner shook her head. 'From him?' She nodded at Riddick.

Riddick shrugged, not really sure how to interpret that comment.

'I don't know what you think you know about me or about Paul, but you have it all wrong. We're *just* work colleagues. Please tell me, and be crystal clear, Hugo, what did you think following Riddick would achieve?'

He scowled at Riddick. 'The man is a criminal, a thug. I knew I'd catch him up to something sooner or later.'

'Jesus, what'd I do?' Riddick said. 'Run over your dog?'

Sands glared at him.

'How long were you following me?'

'A while.'

'Morgan Lark's place too?'

Sands nodded. 'But you messed that up all on your own. My photos would be surplus to requirements. I also saw you at the grief meeting at the Methodist church. All for show.'

'You've really got to know me quite well, haven't you?' Riddick asked. 'It's not going to make pretty reading during your investigation. Anyway, what did you think would happen after you'd ruined me and had me locked up?' Riddick waved his finger between Gardner and him. 'That Emma would fall into your arms? That you'd be her knight in shining armour?'

'Please, Paul,' Gardner said. 'I'm feeling sick.'

Sands reddened. 'You misunderstand. My intention was to protect her from you, that's all.'

Gardner shook her head. 'Any more references to me as a damsel in distress are going to end with a spate of career-ending violence... so let's just all park it, okay?'

'This is going to ruin me,' Sands said.

Like anyone cares right now, Riddick thought.

'So, what happened, Hugo?' Gardner said. 'What happened after you saw Paul that night?'

'I watched him chase a young boy down those steps, so—'

'Hang on,' Riddick said. 'Less of the chase. I was trying to help him. Didn't see you lending a hand. Unless... did you follow us down, Hugo?'

'Let him speak, Paul,' Gardner said. 'Carry on, Hugo... *now*.'

He looked flustered. 'Well, obviously, I wondered what was going on. I mean, I know DI Riddick is many things, but children? No, I never thought that. But this may have been relevant – it may have been what I was looking for. Besides, the kid may have been in trouble and, you know, whether you two believe it or not, I'm a good person.'

Riddick couldn't help but laugh out loud.

'And when I got down there—'

'You went down!' Riddick said. 'You *were* there. You told me you had nothing to do with it!'

'Please, Paul,' Gardner said.

'I wasn't. At least not in the way you're thinking. God, I'm sorry... I really am. I should've come forward with this, but how could I? The truth of why I was there would've destroyed me. But I'm finished anyway. I'll go to jail for this – obstructing—'

'What happened?' Riddick said. 'For goodness' sake, get to the bloody point.'

'Stephen was agitated. He came out from where he'd been hiding from you. I stopped near the bottom of the steps and watched. He was pacing about while you were shining a light in the cave. He was rubbing his face, his head... there was something very wrong with him. Very wrong. Then, he picked a rock up off the floor.'

Riddick took a deep breath. *No. This wasn't what happened. It doesn't sound right.*

'I never thought for a second you were in danger until he was right behind you. Then, when I did realise, you were already turning. I shouted to warn you, I really did, but it was too late. He'd hit you already.'

'No. Why would he do that? Why would he hit me?'

Riddick felt his heart racing. He gritted his teeth and shook his head. No...

But wasn't the reason obvious?

A young boy hiding in a cave while a middle-aged man he'd never seen before hunted him in the darkness.

Yes, he'd told him he was a police officer, but he'd never shown a badge. Why should Stephen have believed him?

Why wouldn't he be scared?

Why wouldn't he defend himself?

'You're covering,' Riddick said. 'Even if he hit me, so? That doesn't explain what happened to him. You came down and you—'

'No!' Sands shouted and flecks of spit flew from his mouth. 'No, I didn't.'

His eyes widened and he stood up tall. For a moment, he looked as if he might just go for Riddick.

Riddick clenched his fists.

'I watched him die, okay? I *watched* him die. You may think that it wouldn't bother me – that I'm using to seeing corpses on my table, but it did. I've never seen someone die before, and he was a child. Just a child!'

Riddick saw the anguish in Sands' face. So believable. He took a step back, but still kept his fists ready.

'He heard me when I shouted to you. He turned to look at me. He *wasn't* right. I was some distance away, but it looked like his face was contorted and his eyes were rolling all over the place. He started to pace back and forth, mumbling incomprehensibly and then... and then...' Sands looked down. 'He fell to the ground and started to convulse.'

Sands wiped at his eyes. 'When I got to him, he'd already stopped breathing. I saw that he'd banged his head, and there was blood. He had no pulse. I *tried*. I tried for so long to resuscitate him. But I couldn't.' Sands was crying now. 'I watched him die...'

Sands leaned back, covering his eyes.

Riddick and Gardner exchanged a glance.

Really? That simple? A natural death? After all this?

'You've obstructed justice. There's been a major investigation. Do you realise what you've done, Hugo?' Gardner asked angrily.

He shook his head, crying freely now. 'I was in shock! I'm still in bloody shock!'

'You knew he wasn't murdered, Hugo. You knew. And the world needed to know, too.'

'But can you see why I didn't say anything? What it would've done to me?'

Riddick turned and pointed a finger in his direction. 'Did you think I'd take the fall for it? Is that why you did it?'

'No,' Sands said, stuttering. 'No... not at all. The reason for his death will be in this folder at my feet. I'd never do that. You don't deserve your career, and you don't deserve Emma, but I'd never frame you for the killing of a child. He had a heart attack. I was clear about that early on.'

'Yes, but you suggested it could've been caused by the blow to the head,' Gardner said.

Sands nodded, still wiping tears away. 'And yes, it could've been, but I don't think it was. I think he killed himself.'

'How?' Riddick said, marching forward again. 'You're not making any sense.'

'I told Emma about the inflammation in his stomach.' He pointed down at the folder. 'May I?'

Gardner nodded. Sands picked it up and scoured through the papers, trembling and nodding.

He looked up. 'Dexamfetamine. A stimulant used to treat ADHD. The dosage in his blood would be enough to trigger a heart attack. He overdosed.'

'Jesus,' Gardner said.

'The only thing is, he wasn't diagnosed with ADHD – so where'd he get the controlled substance?' Sands asked.

'His best friend, Kyle. He has ADHD.' Gardner was shaking her head.

'Why on earth would he give his—'

'He didn't,' Gardner said. Kyle didn't want to take them and so was disposing of them. Stephen must've observed Kyle throwing them away and taken them back out of the bin.'

Sands looked down at his notes. 'This was a large dose. I don't think this was an accident, and that's a lot of tablets to force down someone. I'd suspect suicide.'

Riddick lowered his head sadly.

'Meaning we were both too late,' Sands said, nodding at Riddick. 'No one is to blame.'

Riddick looked back up and offered a wry smile. 'So, after attempting to destroy my life, you now want to make me feel better?'

Sands sighed. 'Like I said, I'm not a bad person. Neither of us should feel guilty about what happened to Stephen Best.'

'I don't.' He pointed at Sands. 'I feel guilty that I didn't spot you coming a mile off before you turned everything on its bloody head.'

Sands looked at Gardner. 'I'm sorry. I did it because I... I...'

'Please,' Gardner said. 'Don't even say it.'

'Do you think I could ever make it up to you?'

'Can I answer that question for you, boss?' Riddick said.

'No,' Gardner said. 'It doesn't warrant an answer.'

46

After Gardner had arranged for some officers to take Sands away for further questioning, she sat with Riddick in her car. 'Poor kid... Between his overprotective father and that shitbag, Eric Oakes, Stephen Best stood no chance. A fifteen-year-old, dealing with all these massive changes in his identity, being pulled every which way, and look what happens? It's a tragedy. And now who picks up the pieces of this awful mess?'

Riddick sighed. 'At least there's some closure, I guess.'

Gardner glared at him. 'Closure?'

Riddick shrugged. 'I said some.'

'I think even that's generous! All we ever do is move from one mess to another. Every time. Sands? Dragging the Nidd for another missing child? An inquiry into a corrupt investigation led by Rice's father and Anders? Let's not forget the fact that I have to tell Ron that his son took his own life, and that he was probably the reason for Stephen's awful decision...'

'I know. It never ends.'

'Well, at least I'll get you back to lend a hand.'

Riddick looked away.

'What?'

'I'm sorry, boss.'

'Sorry for what?'

'I'm meeting with Marsh at five.'

'About?'

Riddick looked down and sighed.

'About?'

'About calling time on me.'

'Calling time on you? Bloody hell. Did you excel in drama at school, Paul? No, strike that. I bet you were crap at it. You're far too melodramatic. You probably had the teacher's eyes rolling, like mine are now. Resigning? Pack it in. I'm in no mood...'

'Wow,' Riddick said. 'You really aren't.'

'So, you get on the blower and cancel that meeting.'

Riddick looked up, smiled and took a deep breath. 'No.'

'No?'

'For the first time ever, I'm not doing what you tell me. Plus, you know how Marsh will respond to being messed around.'

'She won't be as pissed off as me... and you never do a single thing I tell you to do.'

'True, but I'm sorry, Emma, I know this is going to drive you nuts. And I hate disappointing you after everything you've done for me. I no longer think of you as a southern dipstick. Although, I still struggle to shake that image of you in the bright yellow raincoat that night by the castle keep when it wasn't even raining. You're the best I've ever worked with. I've known that for a while, believe it or not! For once, I know I'm right about something.'

'Have we not had enough self-pity from Dr Dickhead down in his tomb?'

'I'm not self-pitying! But come on! How often do I get it right? You asked me the other day how many lives I've got.'

'You weren't wrong about George Jacoby.'

'Well, even a fool can be right sometimes.'

'A fool doesn't get to that kind of truth. Imagine the parents of that second missing child if they find that body? Do you not comprehend what you've done?'

'I guess...'

'Good. So, shall I phone Marsh, or will you?'

'This isn't just about doom and gloom, Emma. This is bigger than that. This is a natural consequence of something else...'

'All you're doing is fuelling my curiosity and getting me very frustrated in the process.'

'I'm sorry, Emma. But I can't bear to tell you. Not now. Not after I've missed you so much over the last couple of days. I just don't have enough left in me to break you with the truth. You deserve more. And I'm exhausted.'

'Break me? Don't flatter yourself. You been up to no good; you're fair game like the rest of them.'

Riddick shook his head. 'I know that you care about me.'

Her face reddened slightly, just as it had done in the mortuary.

'Like I care about you,' Riddick said.

Gardner opened her mouth, but no words came out. She thought about him asleep next to her on the sofa, his hand on her shoulder. She'd be lying if she said she hadn't missed him these past couple of days too.

'Because you've helped me Emma... more than you'll ever know.'

Gratitude. Was that all it was? Maybe Sands' suspicions, and now her own, had been misplaced.

Gardner stared at him. 'You need to talk to me, Paul. There's nothing we can't solve together. You won't be able to walk away anyway... I tried before... it pulls you back.'

'This can't be solved.'

She narrowed her eyes and raised her voice. 'Listen, dickhead.

You *owe* me. I've put up with your bullshit long enough. Spit it out, before... before...' She'd the urge to slap him across the face.

'Let it fly, Emma. It's the least I deserve,' Riddick said.

She took a deep breath and chanced a look back at him. Her heart sank.

'You'll know the truth soon enough,' he said, opening the passenger door.

She reached out and grabbed his arm. 'Please.'

He shook his head. 'I can't handle the look in your eyes when you find out. I could tell anybody but you. You're the best of us, Emma. You won't forgive this... and I'm glad of that really. Because it speaks volumes about who you are.'

'Bollocks!' *I'd forgive you anything... anything... don't you realise that?*

He turned back to her, reached over and took her face in his hands. She closed her eyes as he leaned in, and she felt his lips on her forehead.

'Please... Paul. Please.'

He let go of her face and stepped from the car.

'Paul!'

He leaned back in. 'There's someone else I need to say goodbye to first and I'm low on time.' He slammed the door and started to jog towards his own car.

She exited her vehicle. 'Paul!'

He didn't look back.

She considered giving chase, but he'd be gone before she caught him up.

* * *

On the way to the station, she contacted Rice and gave him the full update on the tragedy of Stephen Best.

'That bastard, Oakes,' Rice said. 'It's his abuse that's killed Stephen. It'll help convict him, but he'll never do the time he deserves.'

Gardner then gave him an update on George Jacoby, his cousin. She tried to be sensitive, because the inevitable inquiry would undoubtably throw his father's legacy under the spotlight. It was unusual to hear him so silent. She'd never known him lost for words before.

Her instincts were to probe him. The questions were on the tip of her tongue. *Did you know about this? Did you suspect your father of anything?*

She controlled herself. Rice had conducted himself well in this investigation; he didn't deserve to be torn to pieces.

She was just about to call time on their chat, when his dam burst. 'My father was a bastard, boss... he truly was. Treated me like the scum of the earth.'

'I'm sorry, Phil.'

'Don't be. Those days are long gone. But I'm disappointed, boss. I always thought he had integrity. That he believed in what he was doing. I always thought that if I could take one thing from him... one thing... it would be that. Integrity.'

'Recently, Phil, I've watched you handle yourself with integrity.'

There was a long silence. She wondered if she'd caused him to choke up. 'You mean there's hope for me yet?'

'One day at a time, Phil.' She laughed.

He laughed too.

After Rice, she contacted Marsh, who praised her, as she always did, on getting closure. To be praised on George Jacoby was peculiar. 'That was down to Paul. His drive, his passion not to stop. And even the outcome of Operation Lost Light was down to a headache that sparked his memory.'

'He's a tenacious bastard, Emma. I did tell you that on day one. But still, take your credit too, he's on your team.'

Well, technically, he wasn't. I haven't seen him for days!

'He's in with me at five, anyway. I'll be sure to give him his due. After bollocking him for not going home like he was asked to.'

In at five.

Gardner's blood ran cold as she considered that meeting again.

It wasn't just a resignation, was it? His voice had been laden with doom.

I can't handle the look in your eyes when you find out. I could tell anybody but you.

What was it?

She phoned ahead to Barnett to debrief him. 'Don't go in and talk to Ron. I'll do it.'

'Are you sure?'

'Yeah... I'm sure,' Gardner said.

* * *

Ron was slumped in a chair behind a table in Interview Room 2 at the police station in Knaresborough. He'd refused counsel, and so sat alone, looking as broken as he'd done since the outset. He had a plaster on his forehead from his fall last night when he'd encountered Kyle.

Gardner sat opposite him. 'Ron. I know you didn't kill your son.'

He scrunched his brow. 'I've given a full confession.'

'Still, I know you didn't do it.'

'No. I—'

Ron looked down at the table; his eyes darted back and forth, his face reddening. She could see his bottom lip tremble. He looked on the edge of breaking down into incoherence again.

Gardner leaned forward. She was trying to sound sympathetic, but she was losing patience, and she didn't want to call him out by just announcing Stephen's suicide. It would be cruel and devastating. 'I *know* you blame yourself, Ron, but I also *know* you didn't kill Stephen.'

Ron looked up. His eyes widened and his nostrils flared. 'I have no one left.' He sat back and glared. 'No one. Don't you get that? Put me out of my misery – I beg you. I don't want to be here any more. Put me away and let me die.'

'This isn't Texas, Ron – there's no death penalty. What're you hoping life imprisonment will do?'

'I deserve it. Every last second of it. I killed him. I'm telling you now. And I'll tell the judge and jury, too. It's my choice.'

Gardner sighed. She was running out of options. 'Okay... Ron, if it was really you, then you'll know that someone else was down there with you both.'

He looked confused. He shook his head.

She took a deep breath and steeled herself. 'I'm sorry, Ron. I'm so sorry for what I'm about to tell you. We now know that your son wasn't murdered. He overdosed.'

'What? You're lying. Overdosed on what?'

'Dexamfetamine. An ADHD medication.'

'He doesn't have ADHD. This is nonsense. Where would he get it from?'

Gardner told him about Kyle throwing it in the bin, and Stephen slyly retrieving it.

'No... you're wrong. I *gave* it him. It was me,' Ron said, tears in his eyes. 'I forced it into him.'

Gardner held her emotions in check. It was devastating to watch this.

'It was suicide. Ron, I can't tell you how sorry I am. I know that it won't give you much peace. Moving forward, I'll ensure you get all the support we can give you. But ultimately, you need to know that you're free to go.'

'Free?' He looked down at the table in silence. Time moved slowly. Agonisingly slow. Eventually, he said 'free' again before the cycle of agonising silence was repeated.

Gardner stood. 'I'll send someone in to you. They can talk you through next steps. There's counselling available and—'

'You think I'll ever be free? Really?' Ron asked, looking up at her.

'I'm sorry, Ron,' Gardner said.

Then, as if the air had gone out from a balloon, his entire face seemed to fall in on itself. He kept glancing both ways as if suddenly disorientated, and unaware of his surroundings. Then, he tumbled from his chair and curled up on the floor.

Gardner circled the table, went down to her knees and lifted Ron's head onto her lap.

She stroked his hair, listening to him cry, harder than she'd ever heard anybody cry, wondering if Riddick, too, had folded this same way when Ronnie Haller had delivered his horrendous news.

* * *

After composing herself in the bathroom, Gardner met Barnett outside. He was vaping. She opted for a mouthful of tic tacs.

'He'll never stop blaming himself,' Gardner said.

'Hopefully he'll find some peace one day.'

'I suspect it'll only get worse,' Gardner said and sighed. 'It'll come out in the wash that Stephen had deep feelings for Eric. That Ron's reaction to his homosexuality would've made his boy feel trapped and scared. This will cement itself as the reason for his suicide. The press won't help with that.'

'Ron was only trying to protect his son. Others will help him realise this, help him hold onto it.'

'And the fact that Ron is also homosexual?' Gardner said with a raised eyebrow.

'I didn't know that.'

'He just admitted it to me on the floor in there. I think it makes the narrative worse for him. He came down hard on his son's sexuality because he was repressing his own. Oh, Christ.' She rubbed her temples. 'What a mess.'

'Yes,' Barnett said and looked at Gardner. 'But we encounter many of them. And there has to be a time to let it go and move on to the next one.'

Gardner sighed and thought, *okay, onto the next.*

Who'd want this bloody job?

47

Riddick told Anders everything and then fixed him with a stare. 'Because you didn't stop him when you had a chance, he killed a second child.'

Anders sighed. 'What chance, Paul? Didn't I make it clear to you last time you were here? There was no chance!'

'Typical. At the time, you didn't want to get your hands dirty – ruin your own precious career. Now, years later, guilty, you thought you'd have one last chance at playing the puppeteer. God almighty, I feel like you've been stringing me along my whole bloody life.'

Anders shook his head this time. 'You're wrong. Who was the second child?'

'The body is still to be recovered, but there's suspicion that it may be fifteen-year-old Julian Greaves. A runaway from York. There was a reported sighting of him in Knaresborough around that time. Sleeping rough. He'd have made a suitable target for George, I guess. Broken... in need of fixing... whatever all that means.'

'I'm glad you got to the truth, Paul. *Really*. I hope Julian is found.'

Riddick looked at his watch. 'I have an important meeting coming up, so—'

'You read my letter, didn't you?'

Riddick flinched. He looked down, shaking his head. Was Anders right? Had the contents of that letter dragged him back here?

'I came to give you closure, that's all.'

'Precisely. Closure is what every dying man needs.'

Riddick stood and turned from the table. The emotion was overwhelming, and he didn't quite know exactly what it was he was feeling.

'You know, Paul, there's a lot of guilt – you're right about that. But there're also things I don't regret. If I'd have gone after George Jacoby, I'd have ended my career, and then I'd never have helped you to build yours. And, ironically, the fact that I never caught him brought you right back here to me.'

Riddick turned. 'Helped to build my career? That's why it feels like it's on quicksand. All those lies... all that manipulation. The bear this... the bear that... You play everyone around you.'

'You'll never lose your flair for the dramatic, will you? Quicksand? Lies? Your career was, and still is, a good one. You're a natural. As you've just demonstrated once again.'

'What hypocrisy! No one could ever put on a performance like you, Anders. You've a career's worth!'

'Maybe so, and you'll always know, Paul, that you learned from the best.'

'Bollocks, Anders. I'm nothing like you. You manipulate people. You've spent your whole life doing it, and no good comes from it. Do you remember putting your hand on my shoulder that first day at the cave? Defending me to Rice? Singing my praises? You manipulated me from the off.'

'Yet, here you are, again, at the end of it all, smelling of roses. You exposed me, you exposed Jacoby... you exposed Dr Hugo Sands! You're on a roll. They claim you're a maverick, a liability, that your days are numbered. It's lies. *All lies.* They need us to get things done that no one else can. You're the best Yorkshire has; you're bloody invincible.'

Riddick looked at his watch again and smiled. 'That important meeting is soon. With Marsh. Want to know what it's about?' As dire as the subject matter was, he felt a tingle of excitement over delivering this reality check to Anders.

'Promotion?'

'Disgrace, Anders... *disgrace.* I'm finished. What's the food like in here?'

Anders shook his head. 'I don't follow.'

Riddick put his hands on the table and leaned in. 'Follow this: Ronnie Haller... dead in the show—'

'Quiet, son. Keep your voice down.'

'Keep my voice down? After I meet Marsh, there'll be fireworks. Can't keep them quiet.'

'Paul... *listen* to me—'

'No! Never again,' Riddick said. 'It was me, your honour. Not my knife of course, but my money. You can give me old Anders Smith's cell, because he won't be needing it any more...'

Anders' face dropped over this last comment, and Riddick immediately regretted saying it.

'Anyway, I'm not walking away from this one, Anders. You got what you wanted; you effectively turned me into you.'

Anders stared down at the table for a while, shaking his head. Eventually, he looked back up and stood. Then, he started to work his way around the table, limping and clutching his lower back. He paused mid-way to catch his breath.

He'd done a good job of masking the condition of his health on his last visit, but on this occasion, the deterioration was more evident.

'Sit, Anders. Save your energy. There's nothing that can be done.'

Anders was still catching his breath.

Riddick went around the table and helped him back to his seat while the words from the letter flashed over and over in his mind.

Brain tumour.

After Riddick had seated him, he hovered there so he could keep an eye on him.

For one horrible moment, he wondered if Anders had just played him to draw him closer. But then he dismissed it. The man looked a complete mess.

Anders stared at Riddick, his face etched with sadness.

Riddick swallowed. 'Is this just another lie?'

Anders' top lip twitched. 'I wish it was.' He looked down. 'To think I'd lie about my own demise. Is that how far I've fallen in your eyes?'

Further, Riddick thought, but the overwhelming sympathy he now felt – something he inwardly cursed himself for – held his tongue.

'I haven't seen my daughters since it happened, you know?' Anders said. 'Since you arrested me.'

Riddick shook his head. Was he blaming him? Again, sympathy made him steady his tongue.

'But at least I've seen you. Twice, now. I'm a lucky old sod.'

Not sure I am, Riddick thought. *You almost drove me to the bottle again.*

'You were always like a son to me, you know?'

Riddick sighed.

'We did good things together, Paul. We had real successes. That can't be taken away. Hopefully, this thing in my head will kill me *before* it destroys those memories.'

Riddick shook his head. *I need to get out of here.*

'They reckon another month at the most.'

Riddick flinched.

'What's happening at five, Paul? What problem cannot be solved?'

'You need to rest, Anders. And I need to go—'

'No! Damn you, son. And I'll call you son whether you damn well like it or not. You tell me what's happening even if it's the last thing you bloody say to me. You don't owe me anything, Paul, but goddamn it, listen to a dying man's last request.'

'The showman again, eh?' *Whatever.* Riddick told him about KG. About the blackmail. At Anders' request, he described KG in more detail.

'Kieran Greene,' Anders said and sighed. 'Ambitious little shite. I knew about him – he was on my radar...' He shook his head. 'It didn't take him long, did it? Less than a year outside the loop and look how the prick rises to the top. He's anything but cream though, that one... anything but. *Shit.*' Anders shook his head again. 'He'd never have got that high if—'

'Don't you dare,' Riddick said. 'Don't you dare make this about me taking you off the street.'

'But it's that equilibrium I told you about, Paul – that day when you arrested me. Someone has to keep it, manage it, before it gets out of control.'

'You were bent Anders. You *killed* someone.'

Anders shrugged, sighed. 'Let me think, son, let me think.'

Riddick had seen enough. He circled around the table and threw one last glance at Anders who looked like he was half asleep. 'Save your energy, Anders. You know there's only one option, and if you even suggest that I hang someone out for that prick, then I'll swing for you – no matter your condition.'

'Calm,' Anders said, holding up his hand. He closed his eyes and rubbed his temples. 'Calm. Let me think. Let me think...'

Think about what? Riddick eyed up the door. *This is it now, Paul. This is your chance. Just walk away...*

'Just don't confess. Give me time.'

'Why would I do that? I feel good about it. In fact, I'm even excited. All the peace and quiet...' Riddick approached the door, determined to leave. 'Goodbye Anders.' He raised his fist to knock, and gave one last look back at his old colleague.

Anders was now leaning back in his chair, eyes closed, hands by his side.

'Anders?'

He ran quickly around the other side of the table and pressed his fingers to Anders' neck.

Riddick's own heart started to beat furiously which made it hard to find a pulse.

But, with relief, he eventually did.

He went back around the table and knocked on the door. The guard answered.

'He's fallen asleep.'

'Yup. He does that now. Part of the condition and the painkillers too.'

Riddick looked back. *Is this the last time I'm going to see you, old man?*

It probably wouldn't be such a bad thing.

Goodbye Anders.

He looked at his watch. Nearly time.

As he exited the room, he couldn't resist one last glance at the man he'd looked up to for most of his career.

48

Anders felt someone shaking him and opened his eyes.

He looked up at the worried face of Ethan Towers. A prison guard teetering on the edge of retirement. A friend of Anders in a previous life.

'You still with us, Anders?'

'Aye. Unfortunately,' Anders said, rubbing his eyes. He stretched out. 'These new painkillers have a habit of knocking me out when I least expect it. Where's Paul?'

'He left.'

Anders nodded. He looked up at Ethan again.

He got on with most of the guards here. They knew that he still had influence beyond the bars. They tended to either leave him be, or cosied up to him, knowing that he could come in useful should the need ever arise.

Ethan did neither, just treated him with respect and dignity. Once upon a time, many years back, in *that* other life, Anders had come to his aid.

A bunch of local youths had been terrorising his youngest boy, Tony.

Anders had put a stop to that immediately. How he'd done so had never been important to Ethan. But the fact that it'd happened had meant everything.

'Let's get you back, old man.'

'No... I need to do something first. I need a favour.' He looked up at Ethan. 'Okay?'

Ethan nodded, but he paled slightly. 'I'll do what I can.'

'It's no biggie,' Anders said. He groaned as he stood – fighting gravity with his size was becoming more and more difficult these days. 'I just need to use the telephone.'

'My mobile?'

He shook his head. 'No. That wouldn't be good... for you. A landline. One that isn't monitored.'

'There's one in an office on the way back, but you have to log the call, so...'

'So we don't log the call.'

Ethan took a deep breath and nodded. 'Okay, but I can't guarantee the office will be empty.'

'Let's take a look,' Anders said. 'I'm sure we can work it out.'

49

Now she finally had a chance to breathe again, Gardner realised that she'd not eaten anything but tic tacs today. She was starving. So before taking the journey to HQ to debrief the rest of her team, she opted for a bite to eat. She also chose her home over a service station because when your days were filled with so much tragedy, getting your eyes on your own children whenever possible was a must.

She parked on her drive, hopped out and approached her home, taking care on the ice and snow—

Her breath caught in her throat.

The front door was ajar.

Not in any frame of mind to consider sensible explanations, she thrust the door open wide and marched in. 'Hello?'

Nothing.

She burst into the lounge and saw the snoring pig on the sofa. 'Barry!'

His eyes snapped open. 'Yes... what... Emma?'

'The front door?'

'What?'

'It's *bloody* open!'

He rubbed at his face, jumped to his feet and crossed his arms. 'That's why it's so cold!'

'The children?'

'Upstairs, playing together... last I looked.'

Gardner turned and sprinted upstairs. She tried Rose's room first. No sign of her. Then, she was in Anabelle's room. Anabelle was colouring a picture at her desk.

Thank God.

'Hello Mummy.'

'Where's Rose?'

Anabelle continued to colour. 'I don't know. We were playing, but then she said she was going.'

'When? When was this?'

'I don't know. Back when I started this.' She pointed at her picture.

Gardner bolted forward and looked down at the scene from a Disney movie she was colouring. It was only partly done. She couldn't have been at it for more than a couple of minutes.

She flew out of Anabelle's room.

'Rose?' she called.

She checked the bathroom and the other bedroom on the floor. 'Rose?' she called again, louder this time.

'Is she there?' Barry shouted from the bottom of the stairs.

Gardner charged down the stairs, barging past him. 'Check the top floor.' Then, she was out the front door and on her drive. She turned onto the access road on her housing estate. Her blood ran cold. Ahead was York Road and all its fast cars.

Her feet didn't have a good grip on the pavement due to the ice, so she moved onto the gritted street. 'Rose... Rose!'

Up ahead a multitude of cars.

But no little girl.

50

Milo stayed for chess club.

It'd been a while since he'd played. He'd got bored of it at roughly the same time his preoccupation with violent comics had grown.

But he was good at it, and it did wonders for keeping his mind focused on something other than real life.

And real life sucked right now!

When he emerged at four twenty, twenty minutes before the club was due to finish, the sky was already starting to darken, but it was still bright enough to see.

Fortunately.

He froze as he approached the school gates.

Ahead was KG's Tesla.

Milo took a deep breath. Why was he here? Outside his school?

He'd promised to check in on him, and have someone keep an eye on him, but a sudden appearance at the school gates less than twenty-four hours later?

His stomach turned over. Had they seen DCI Gardner come to his home this morning?

He stared at the stationary Tesla. His entire body was screaming at him to turn and run back into the school.

But if he ran, then there'd be no doubt in KG's mind.

Betrayal.

And KG had made no bones about what he'd do if he was betrayed.

It would start with his mother, and it would end with him.

Just tell him the truth. You told DCI Gardner nothing. Nothing.

Milo moved forward as his head continued to scream at him, *He's going to kill you.*

He bit his bottom lip. *He's going to kill you. He's going to kill you.*

Tears sprang up his eyes.

He looked behind himself. Still time to run...

He thought of KG holding a pillow over his mother's face.

And then an idea settled on him.

A dangerous one. But one with potential.

And, anyway, what choice did he have?

He fell to his knees, pretending to do his laces.

Time to put the plan into action.

51

Riddick was glad there was no one else in the chapel garden.

He wouldn't have had enough time to come back before his meeting with Marsh, and he so wanted these last five minutes alone with them.

When he came, he usually sat on the benches that looked out over the trees, which were in all stages of their growth, but today, he opted to go up close to the patch on the right-hand side.

He looked down at the three saplings.

'I don't know how long it'll be before I can come again,' he said.

And if I'll ever come again, he thought, but didn't wish to give such a possibility airtime.

He knelt, pulled a clean tissue from his pocket and wiped the three plaques.

Rachel.

Lucy.

Molly.

The three most special gifts he'd ever had.

'It's not goodbye. Don't worry.' He touched his chest. 'It'll never be goodbye. I remember everything. And that's all I need.'

52

Gardner couldn't run any faster. Her calves and hips burned, and it was nothing short of a miracle that she hadn't yet slipped.

'Rose?'

Up ahead, she saw two people, off to the right, by the salesroom for her housing estate. The salesroom was still in operation because there were many homes still to shift, but the lights were off, suggesting it was closed.

From this distance, it looked like a man and child standing outside of it, so she raced towards them, praying that the child was Rose.

It was.

If she wasn't already out of breath, she may have just cried out in relief.

Rose and the man with her began moving in her direction. Gardner bent over, clutching her knees, sucking in air, and when Rose was close enough, she embraced her.

'Good job I stopped to enquire after their homes,' the man said – he'd a West Country accent like her own. 'You don't want her running anywhere near that road behind me.'

An irritating comment, but he was right, and she'd have said the same.

She looked up at him. He appeared to be in his late fifties and was smartly dressed in a suit. 'Thanks.'

'No problem.'

'I just want to see Daddy,' Rose whispered in her ear.

'I know,' Gardner said, recalling Barry's warning to her the previous evening.

'Please, can I?'

Gardner's instinct was to refuse outright, but fortunately, she caught her reply in time. Now was not the moment to be answering questions like this. 'Let's go home and discuss it after a hot chocolate.'

She stood and felt Rose's small hand close around hers.

Gardner looked at the smartly dressed man who came from her neck of the woods. He had white facial hair, and long white hair tied back in a ponytail.

'Thanks again,' Gardner said.

'You're welcome,' the man said, kneeling and shaking Rose's available hand. He winked. 'You go home and give Ronald a big hug from me.'

Ronald was Rose's stuffed elephant. Gardner had bought it for her on the day that she'd first started to live with her.

The man stood.

'You know about Ronald then?' Gardner said.

'She was getting quite upset about leaving Ronald, but I explained that he'd be pleased to see her when she got back.'

'You're not from around here, are you?'

'Neither are you by the sounds of it. Where in Wiltshire are you from?'

She could feel her work phone buzzing in her inside suit pocket. She pulled it out.

'I'm pretty sure I asked you first,' Gardner said, looking at the screen on her phone. The caller was unknown.

'Amesbury...'

'Salisbury, myself...' Despite being intrigued by this meeting, she was more bothered about answering this call.

'Yes. I have friends in Yorkshire,' the man said. 'Looking to relocate... You look like you need to take that, Emma.'

'I do... really... thanks.'

Gardner answered the phone and nodded her goodbye to the man. 'Hello?'

He smiled, turned and wandered towards his vehicle, holding his hand up behind him to say goodbye.

'Hello?' she repeated into the phone.

Nothing. The phone call was a dud; all she could hear was static.

Wait a minute...

'Stay here,' Gardner told Rose, who nodded.

She moved forward towards the vehicle the man was climbing into.

The man had used her first name.

And if he hadn't have known who she was – why would he have let her walk off with a child?

Stupid, Emma, stupid, stupid...

The mysterious man's sporty black Audi burst into life.

'Wait!' she called out, holding her hand up.

He didn't.

She squinted, preparing to read his number plate—

She was interrupted by something on the phone that made her blood freeze over.

53

KG stepped from the car before Milo reached it, and opened his arms.

The idea of an embrace repulsed Milo, yet... *obedience was the best play*, he reasoned.

When Milo was close enough, KG patted him down, and checked his pockets. 'Just a precaution, Milo.'

An embrace! How naïve was he?

KG checked his school bag and then smiled. 'Jump in, Milo. Sorry for the caution. Just checking you don't have your phone.'

Milo nodded.

KG gestured to the passenger side. 'Jump in then, buddy.'

Obedience was the best play.

Try telling that to his stomach!

KG opened his car door, and then looked back at Milo who was still standing where he'd been searched.

'Are you coming then?'

Milo gulped. 'I need to get home and check on Mum.'

'This'll take five minutes and then I'll drop you back. I'll probably still get you back quicker than you would do on foot.'

Milo needed to move, but his brain wouldn't let him.

It was obvious what was happening here. If he got into that car, he was done for.

KG shrugged. 'Listen. I got someone near your house. I'll get them to check on your mum.'

You bastard.

'It would panic her.'

KG smirked. 'My men are discreet, Milo. They'll be in and out without making a sound.'

He thought of his mum in bed again with one of KG's men on each side of her, looking down at her.

'You don't need to,' Milo said, walking around the car to the passenger side. 'I'm sure she can wait a few more minutes.'

KG winked at him over the roof of the car and they both climbed in. Milo heard the clunk of the automatic locks.

54

Riddick looked up at HQ from the car park.

The imposing building was cold and unwelcoming.

He checked his watch. He was early.

Early to his own funeral.

A cat with nine lives, indeed. A cat was cool, measured and operated on its own agenda come what may. It would probably be late to its own funeral if he even bothered to attend.

Riddick stepped from his vehicle.

Early or late; did it make any odds?

'When you're dead, you're dead,' he muttered to himself. 'And I have no lives left.'

55

They drove up the high street.

'How was school?' KG asked.

Milo felt as if his mouth was glued shut.

'Cat got your tongue, Milo?'

Milo forced it out. 'Dull.'

'Remember it well. Went to the same one as you, in fact. All rules. No fun. By the time we get you all set up at Bren's, you'll be old enough to knock it all on the head anyway.' He smiled. All teeth. Always the charmer.

Milo thought of KG smiling on that computer screen as Pete was forced to overdose.

Charming you until he ended you.

Milo felt like he needed to be sick, but knew he had to stay in control. As they approached the roundabout on Bond Lane, he said the first thing that came into his head. 'If you fail English or maths, then you have to retake in sixth form.'

KG indicated right and moved onto the roundabout. 'You're not going to fail them though, are you? Bright lad like you.'

Milo didn't know. Right now, he didn't care. 'Teachers like to keep you on edge. Mr Lawrence likes to say, "It's never in the bag, until it's in the bag."'

'Still flogging that one, eh?' KG laughed. He put on a silly teacher's voice. 'Don't count your chickens before they hatch, eh?'

Milo forced out a laugh. He sighted the Co-op on Borough-bridge Road.

'You look like you've seen a ghost, Milo.'

Milo pointed. 'That Co-op there... me and Pete saw that lad that died night before last.'

KG nodded. 'Yeah, read about it.' He creased his brow and looked at Milo again. 'You and Pete had nothing to do with that, did you?'

Milo shook his head. 'Are we going to Jacob Smith Park?'

'No. Why'd you ask?'

'Because this is the way.'

'The ice is melting. It'll be muddy as shit.' He winked at Milo. 'Got somewhere better in mind. A little treat for you. Something to show you how grateful I am for your support.'

Milo felt his insides turn over again.

How grateful I am for your support.

He knew he was toying with him.

He thought of his mother, forced to die with no knowledge of where he was. Leaving the world with no clue as to whether the person she loved most was alive or dead.

He thought of his plan.

It now seemed flimsy... pathetic.

They passed the bright lights of the Kia showroom. 'That's where we got our Kia from.'

KG regarded him. 'Get you a better motor than that in a few years, Milo. If things carry on as well as they have been doing.'

Talk of the future?

Dare he hope?

Or was it just more bullshit, leading him into a false sense of security?

His stomach groaned.

'All right there? Hungry?'

No... anything but. I should've run back into the school.

God, he hoped his plan worked. Otherwise...

He looked down at his hands.

He'd have to fight.

Something he'd never done in his life.

KG indicated right onto the road. Milo now knew where they were going. 'I've never been to Calmwater Bay before.'

'Haven't you? You're in for a treat.'

'But the gates are closed.'

KG parked and hit the door control. The doors unlocked with a clunk.

'Get out, Milo. We're going over that fence.'

Milo stumbled from the vehicle, swallowing as he did so, desperately forcing the vomit back down into his stomach.

He looked at KG, who was beckoning him on with his finger. 'Come on, Milo, nothing to be worried about.'

'I don't feel well. I want to go home.'

He looked behind him. He watched a multitude of cars streaming past on Boroughbridge Road. No one would notice them parked down here. KG had killed his lights and there was no streetlamp.

'Come on now, Milo. Don't spoil the fun. I promise it's worth your while.'

He could run to Boroughbridge Road, wave his arms above his head, scream for help. If he avoided being mown down, then he'd certainly have the attention he needed.

'Tempting, isn't it… Except… will you get home before my men check on your mother?'

Milo felt tears in his eyes. He looked back at KG.

'Coming?' KG asked, pointing at the gate. There was a sign on it that indicated the deadly dangers of cold-water swimming.

56

Riddick sat down outside Harsh Marsh's glass-fronted office.

She was at her desk, hammering at her keyboard.

He was fifteen minutes early so he didn't try for her attention, but after he took a seat on the chair outside her room, she noticed. She stared at him over the top of her glasses.

He couldn't recall ever seeing her in glasses. Were they new, or did she only wear them at her desk?

Whatever the reason, she looked even more severe – which was an achievement for someone who already lived and breathed that look.

His insides felt like they were on fire. Not because of the severity of her stare, although that would've brought many other adults to their knees, but because he was fifteen minutes away from confessing murder.

She waved him into the room.

Shit. Fifteen minutes just became *now*. His stomach suddenly turning over, he stood up and opened the door. 'Ma'am.'

'Is it a quick one? I'm expecting a call?'

Quick in that it'll take me seconds to confess, Riddick thought. *Not sure how long it'll then take for you to dismantle me.* 'It's rather sensitive, ma'am.'

'Sensitive from you, Paul? You're as sensitive as a brick to the head. No reference to the state of your head intended.' She pulled off her glasses. 'Shit. Please tell me you're not chelping about being pushed off the case again?'

'No, it's more sensitive than that.'

She sighed. 'There're more twists and turns in your life than a bloody novel, Paul. Sit down then.'

He sat.

'Go on.'

His heart started to race. 'Okay, on the 29th of—'

The phone started ringing.

She answered. 'Yes?' She nodded. 'One second.' She covered the mouthpiece. 'You weren't quick enough.'

Ridiculous woman, he thought, climbing to his feet and taking a deep breath.

She waved Riddick back out of her office as if she was sweeping dust off the floor.

57

While KG made a phone call, Milo looked back at the large gate he'd just scaled. He now felt completely sealed off from the outside world.

KG tried to keep his voice down, so Milo didn't hear what he was saying but he caught some of it. 'Where are you? I'm here. Good.'

Milo gulped. Who else was coming?

KG finished on the phone and turned to Milo. 'Your mother is fine.'

For now, he thought. *Until she finds out that I'm gone. Then what?*

Would she die knowing what he'd done? What he'd become in these last few weeks?

He'd have to fight. His plan hadn't worked. He looked at his hands.

As soon as he gives you the chance... as soon as his back is turned...
Play ball until then.

'Follow me.' KG started to walk.

Milo stayed rooted to the spot. He wanted to give the impression he was complying, but his brain, and therefore his muscles, seemed to have made their own decision.

Milo swallowed. 'Okay.' He kicked into action and followed.

KG led him to the trees. He stopped and pointed. 'There's a nice spot through these trees.'

'Who's coming? Who were you speaking to on the phone?'

KG looked at Milo. 'You really don't trust me, do you?'

'I do. Honestly, I do—'

'I told you the truth at Bren's. I really did. I offered you a life you wouldn't otherwise have had.'

Milo nodded. *Manipulation. That was all it was.*

'Without trust, we have nothing, so walk with me through the trees. I want to show you something.'

Milo shook his head, forcing back tears.

KG sighed. He clutched Milo forcibly by the shoulder. 'I like you, Milo. You're growing in confidence every second. Your potential excites me. But I'll ask you one last time: do you trust me?'

Milo nodded.

'Then come.'

As they walked, KG talked some more about the life that was on offer to Milo. He wanted to believe him, he really did, but it was clear that KG currently had more sinister plans. He looked down on the ground for a rock, or something else he could potentially use as a weapon. But KG had his arm completely around his shoulders now and had control of him.

'With me, I'll give you the world, Milo. It was the same offer I gave Pete, but he decided against it. What'll you decide? Will you be sensible?'

'Yes.'

'Good. Up ahead...' He pointed. 'Where the trees end. We take a right and then we can go and see the water. There's nothing like it. The peace and quiet. The tranquillity.'

'The sign on the gate said it was dangerous.'

KG laughed. 'You planning to go cold-water swimming?' He took his arm from around Milo's shoulders and patted him on the centre of the back.

They broke through the trees onto a large muddy field. Far ahead were more trees; in the dark, the branches looked like the spiny claws of birds of prey.

'As I said, right here,' KG said.

They turned in the direction of another line of trees, but Milo could see the glitter of the lake just beyond them.

Some light from the tall streetlamps back on Boroughbridge Road, as well as the clear sky and a three-quarter moon, allowed them to navigate the field.

Milo continued to keep his eyes on the ground for debris he could use to defend himself, but KG was smart. The bastard kept himself close enough to stop Milo if he attempted to swoop for anything.

And then, as they drew closer to the line of trees and the lake beyond it, KG slid his arm around his shoulder once more and Milo realised that his window of opportunity was almost closed.

'Who came to your house this morning, Milo?'

Milo was under no illusion that KG already knew, but to hear the words out loud, so close to the water, carried the same impact as if it was unexpected.

He tasted bile.

Milo opened his mouth, expecting nothing to come out, but surprised himself by stuttering, 'DCI Gardner... I told her nothing... I promise, KG... I kept my word.'

KG nodded as they walked through the trees. 'I believe you, Milo.' He sounded sincere.

Milo rubbed away a tear. God, he hoped he was sincere, and it wasn't just more of his charming bullshit.

KG led him to the lake and then stopped. 'Beautiful, isn't it?' KG's arm was tight around him now.

This was it, Milo realised. If KG wasn't sincere, this was the end of him. If necessary, one last final fight, but what would he hope to achieve with that? The man was so much bigger and stronger than he was.

'See the ice on the surface, Milo? As a kid, I came out here and walked on it with some mates. Did you ever do anything like that with Pete?'

Milo shook his head.

'What'd you get up to with Pete?' KG asked, looking down at him.

'Not much... read comics... I didn't know Pete that long.'

'Ah,' KG said. 'You two seemed thick as thieves.'

We were, I guess. For a short time. Until you.

KG looked back up. 'Of course, we could walk on the ice now, but I doubt it would hold. In fact, I know it won't. Temperatures have shot up today; this will be thawing. Milo, what happened this morning cannot happen again.'

'I know! It wasn't my fault. DCI Gardner came round to ask me questions about something that happened the other night outside the Co-op on Boroughbridge Road. We saw that lad, Stephen Best, that turned up dead at the cave. I swear that's all that happened.'

'The night that you met me?'

'Yes. Just before...'

'Okay... so I guess she was interested in where you went next?'

'Yes, but I lied, and she thinks we went into town.'

KG nodded, staring out over the icy lake. 'So, she knows nothing about our meeting in Jacob Smith Park?'

'Nothing.'

'Smart boy, although they've a knack for not leaving things alone. I reckon she'll be back.'

'I don't think so. She seemed happy.'

'The police? Nah. They're never happy. The pigs will be looking into it as we speak.'

'I won't say anything to them. I didn't today and I won't again.'

KG shook his head. 'I'm sorry, Milo. I can't take the risk. I thought I could swing it, yesterday, when I sat with you. I genuinely wanted to make it happen. But I was stupid. The police are like a dog with a bone, and they've forced my hand.'

Now. Kick him now.

But just like before, at the entrance to the trees, he couldn't get his body to obey. 'Please. I wouldn't say a word. I wouldn't.'

'This hurts me, but it always comes down to the same thing, Milo. Better safe than—'

Milo kicked him.

KG cried out in pain.

Milo went for another. This one also hit home too, but it didn't illicit the same response, and KG had already used his tight grip around his shoulders to start propelling him forwards.

He felt air beneath him as he was launched from the bank. Then, he landed with a thud. He gulped at the air. He expected to feel cold water rushing up around him. He steeled himself.

The water didn't come.

'Luck of the bloody devil, Milo,' KG said, kneeling and rubbing his ankle.

Milo felt the cold on his back. He tried to move, but just slipped about on the ice. He felt something slip loose from his sock, and he recalled the moment back at the school gates when he'd knelt and pretended to do his laces.

'What's that?' KG said.

'My mother's mobile.'

'You little shit,' KG said and smiled. 'Why don't you reach for it, call for help?'

'Don't have to.'

'Really, looks to me like that ice is going to break. Go on, Milo, sit up, wriggle over, grab it and make a call.'

'I said I don't have to because I already did.'

KG's face fell. 'When? Bollocks. I had my eyes on you the whole time.'

'Yes... and during that whole time, you've been speaking to DCI Gardner too.'

The colour drained from KG's face.

Despite his precarious position, Milo felt adrenaline surging through him. He hadn't stood up to KG before. In fact, he hadn't really stood up to anyone.

'You're going to rot in hell for what you did to Pete,' Milo said, smiling.

He'd never felt more alive.

But then the ice began to crack.

58

It was only when Gardner touched down on the other side of the gate that she realised she'd cut her hand. The wound wasn't deep, but her palm was bloody. She reached into her pocket for her work mobile with her uninjured hand and placed it to her ear.

A mixture of static and wind. KG and Milo were still walking.

She gazed back through the gate and saw only KG's Tesla. *Shit!* She cursed and turned, remembering KG's instructions to Milo to break through the patch of trees just ahead of her before heading right towards the lake.

Alone and without a weapon, Gardner would do well to wait for backup, which would come in the form of armed response. After all, irresponsibility was something she'd vowed to avoid after the loss of Collette Willows less than a year ago, and something she was forever trying to drum out of Riddick.

Practise what you preach, Emma...

Except Milo was fifteen and he'd trusted her with a sneaky phone call to come to his aid.

If we don't show a little bit of irresponsibility every now and again, then what'd that make us? Robots? Well, certainly not human at any rate.

She sprinted through the patch of trees, out onto the muddy field and swivelled right. After taking an icy blast of wind which stung her hot, sweaty face, she continued onwards to the lake.

Ahead, she could see two figures making their way between two trees. Knowing she wouldn't need the phone any longer, she thrust it into her pocket. She was relying on the whistle of the wind to mask the sounds of her approach, so she didn't slow her pace until she reached the line of trees.

Her breath caught in her throat.

She could see the man she assumed to be KG, but where was Milo?

She broke through the line of trees. 'Police!'

KG swung around to face her. She flinched, expecting him to be holding a weapon. She was relieved to see he wasn't.

At first, he looked concerned, but then a smile broke out on his face. 'DCI Gardner? Alone?'

'Backup on the way. Where's Milo?'

'I'm here. On the ice. It's cracking! Help me!'

KG gestured backwards with his thumb. 'He took the words right out of my mouth.'

Gardner's stomach was suddenly in knots. She looked at KG's position at the edge of the bank. He wasn't wielding a weapon. If she charged, pushed him backwards onto the ice, then she could gain the upper hand. It was a risk; she wasn't 100 per cent sure where Milo was exactly, and KG could end up smashing through the ice and taking the boy with him... but what choice did she have?

She prepared herself to charge.

Then she felt something against the back of her head and her blood ran cold.

A man's voice. 'Down on your knees and hands behind your head.'

'The water is coming up around me!' Milo cried.

'Down. On. Your. Knees.'

'Best do as he says,' KG said and smiled. 'I know him well. He doesn't bluff.'

She started to lower herself to her knees and linked her hands behind her head, every ounce of her being screaming at her not to do so – that submission was unlikely to keep her, and Milo, alive. Still, if she could just hold on a little longer, there was one hope.

Come on armed response, she prayed. *Get your goddamned finger out.*

'You don't want to do this,' Gardner told the gunman. Her fear forced the words out louder than she'd intended.

'Oh, I do,' the gunman said, also raising his voice. 'I really do.'

'He's one of my keenest,' KG said and laughed. He turned. 'Ice *still* bloody holding. You might have to come over here and help him along...'

Milo was struggling to speak. His words were coming out in gasps. 'It's freezing... DCI... Gardner... help... if I move... I'll go under...'

KG turned back to Gardner and his gunman. 'Okay, we need to get the hell out of here. What's with the balaclava anyway?'

'You're sloppy; you brought the police with you.'

'Watch your tongue!' KG said, the smile dropping from his face. 'The little shit tricked me.'

'Sloppy.'

'Say that again.'

'Help!' Milo shouted.

'You don't move, okay?' the gunman hissed down at Gardner.

'You can't let this child die,' she said as she saw the gunman step alongside her. The urge to throw her arms around his legs was intense, but she resisted the sudden spike of adrenaline. Something else was at play here. A distraction of some kind.

'Her dogs will be here soon; why're we delaying?' KG hissed at his approaching gunman.

'Sloppy.'

KG shook his head. 'How dare you—'

The gunman raised his weapon and pointed it at KG's head.

KG snorted. 'You think you'll get away with this?'

'Yes. They contacted me before. They want it done.'

'Nonsense...' He shook his head, confusion creasing his brow. Why...?'

'You broke the rules. Haller's death was clean. Paid for. You tried to blackmail the client. There's honour, KG. Honour. You don't have any. And those above us, they want to keep it. So you're the cost.'

Gardner put a hand to her mouth. *Haller. Ronnie Haller!* The murdered killer of Riddick's family. Paid for? The client blackmailed? Something was unravelling inside her head. Something horrible.

Milo was screaming.

'A pig!' KG snorted. 'We don't lose honour by hanging out a pig for God's sake.'

A pig...

They were talking about Riddick. The world swam around Gardner. It was all coming together. Rather than be blackmailed, Riddick was turning himself in... She may just have passed out cold if Milo's cries for help hadn't dragged her focus back.

'I didn't debate it. I was happy enough to take this particular gig,' the gunman said.

'Do as you're told and put that down. You're my dog,' KG said, pointing at him.

'Not any more. What'd I say to you about kids, eh? Anyone but kids. You never did listen, you prick.'

The gun shot echoed. A small cloud of liquid, colourless in the limited light, erupted from the back of KG's head. He was thrown backwards over the bank, his hands clutching at the air uselessly. At first, there was a thud, as he hit the same sheet of ice that was keeping Milo from drowning, but then came a loud crunching noise, alongside a horrifying realisation that the ice was broken.

Following that were horrendous gasping sounds as the child who'd called Gardner for help started to drown.

'Milo!' She started to raise to her feet.

'Stay put,' the gunman hissed.

'He'll die.'

The gunman waved his gun again. 'You've been warned.' And then, to Gardner's surprise, he turned, and marched to the edge of the bank.

Gardner was about to disobey him and spring up when she saw him lay the gun by his side and lean out. *He was helping Milo.*

'That's it, son... that's it,' the gunman said.

Gardner rose to her feet, anyway, but she didn't move forward. Instead, she breathed a sigh of relief when she saw the gunman pulling Milo up the bank.

Glancing back and seeing Gardner on her feet, the gunman was quick in laying Milo, shivering, on the ground, and recovering his weapon.

His tiny eyes poked out through the slits in his balaclava as he aimed the gun at Gardner. 'I told you to stay on your knees. You should've listened. You're no child.'

Milo was moaning and shivering on the ground between them.

The sound of sirens broke the relative quiet of Calmwater Bay.

Gardner looked down at Milo. 'He's going into shock. Someone needs to get him warm and fast. That can only be you if I'm not here.'

The sirens grew louder.

The gunman nodded, turned and sprinted off into the trees.

Gardner fell to the ground beside Milo and wrapped her arms around him. He was like a block of ice. She held him as tightly as she could. 'Hold on, Milo, hold on. Hold on for your mother.'

As Milo shivered against her, Gardner's mind turned to Riddick.

How could you? Yes, Haller was a monster... but still, why put your head into the guillotine? Things have been on the up, haven't they?

Or have they?

What'd I miss?

'I'm cold...' Milo said.

At least he was talking again.

She thought of KG, floating among the broken chunks of ice.

He was gone.

And with it his threat to blackmail Riddick.

She managed a look at her watch.

Too late.

The blade in the guillotine would have already fallen.

59

The paramedics didn't want Gardner to leave without checking her over and getting her bleeding hand attended to.

However, once they'd confirmed that Milo would be fine, she ignored their pleas and drove off.

En route, she punched the hands-free repeatedly. She didn't leave Riddick a single message. She just hung up and tried again. Over and over.

In her mind's eye, she saw him sitting in Marsh's office, spilling his guts.

The narrative in her head developed further. His phone was confiscated, and he was led away, disgraced and cuffed, to begin his new era of incarceration.

After parking at HQ, she entered the building at speed, taking the stairs two at a time rather than wait for the lift. Then, as she ran down the corridor packed with the offices of top brass, she took in the strange looks from colleagues she recognised, and some she didn't.

A woman possessed.

And all this because of a man who'd broken every rule in the book. A man that had become the very thing they were supposed to despise.

'I can't handle the look in your eyes when you find out.'

You knew exactly how I'd feel about this, you bastard... exactly...

But still, she ran.

Why was she so intent on saving him?

And even if she got there in time, then what?

Scream at the top of her lungs at him?

He's dead! The man called KG is dead! You aren't being blackmailed any more.

Close your mouth, damn it, Paul!

She took the corner sharply, almost knocked over Celia from human resources, who was transporting a tray of hot drinks to her colleagues.

She burst into Marsh's office without knocking.

Marsh looked up at her from above the rim of her glasses.

The chair opposite her was empty.

Too late.

'What're you doing, Emma?' Marsh said. She looked bemused rather than angry.

Gardner leaned against the wall. She felt like bursting into tears but didn't feel as if she'd the energy left to even do that.

'Emma? What's wrong?'

Gardner sucked in deep breaths and held up her hand, requesting a second.

'Sit down, DCI. You've had a hell of a day.'

Gardner shook her head. 'Paul,' she managed. 'Paul.' She looked up at Marsh. 'Where is he?'

'You're too late, Emma.' A sombre expression fell over Marsh's face.

'Shit... shit...' She squeezed her eyes with her finger and thumb. 'Shit.'

She suddenly didn't care how this looked. She'd every right to be sad about the loss of her colleague, no matter the circumstances. 'I didn't know...'

'Don't think any of us saw this one coming, Emma. Your hand, you need to get it looked at. You're bleeding everywhere.'

Gardner stumbled forward and leaned over Marsh's desk. There, staring up at her, was Riddick's badge.

'It's over, Emma,' Marsh said. 'It breaks my heart as much as it breaks yours. But we must prepare for life after Riddick.'

Gardner put her bloody hand over Riddick's badge.

EPILOGUE

Milo closed an issue of one of Pete's favourite comics, *Watchmen*, and set it down by his sun lounger, sighing.

A smile spread over his face as he remembered Pete's reaction to the first couple of pages. *'Chew me up and shit me out... is this for real?'*

Up ahead, Milo saw his mother waving to him from the shallow end of the pool. It felt as though she'd spent most of her holiday in the pool. She was far too weak to swim, but she'd developed a real fondness for the feel of the water on her skin.

He waved back and she smiled, looking happier than he'd seen her in a long time. She was here making memories with her son, *for* her son, and this was everything to her right now.

As it was to him.

He thought of the money that KG had given him that night in Bren's house. The police were none the wiser, so the prospect of handing it over to them had never crossed his mind. Not when it could be put to such wonderful use. And it was. It really was.

He recalled the moment he'd pushed a wad of notes through Pete's father's door, and smiled when he thought about how Pete would've reacted. 'Nah, kid, keep it for you and your ma. He's a prick and a half.'

Pete would have been pleasantly surprised. Sam Wilson had used it for a half-decent funeral for his son with a good spread at the wake and had invited Milo and his mother along. Sam had tried his best that day to stay sober and be hospitable.

'You forget, you know, that people aren't forever,' he'd said at the service. 'I should've been better. But I only realised that now – when forever is no more.'

Pete's body was still to be found despite Milo's statement, and Giraffe-neck and Knuckle-cracker were still missing. He wondered if the gunman who'd saved his life had cleaned up KG's mess.

His mother smiled and waved again. She was doing it every five minutes on the dot. She was doing it on purpose.

He laughed.

She was so bloody good at making memories.

* * *

Ron Best sat alone with his photo albums. They'd multiplied this past month. An old friend, Reggie, had requested access to the Apple iCloud used by Ron and Stephen, and had printed a good few off.

Like every day, he took his time over the photos, tracing his wife's and son's faces with his fingers. They'd always looked so *bloody* happy!

And he'd *lived* for their happiness.

In their memory, he vowed to hang onto his own life, and do something one day soon that would make them both proud.

He rose from his chair, walked to the window and looked outside. A cat was skipping along his fence. It turned its attention to Ron.

'No worries, fella. Enjoy yoursen.'

One day, soon, he'd tell the world that he was just like his son.

That he too was gay.

He nodded, still smiling, a tear running down his face.

'I'm proud of you, son,' he said. 'So very proud of who you became.'

* * *

George Jacoby had been alone for a great many years now – lost inside his own world.

But now the truth of *who* he really was, and what he'd done, was out.

It'd been impossible to find someone to care for him, alone, at his home. Especially since the recovery of his second victim – Julian Greaves – from the River Nidd. The fact that these murders were twenty years ago, and that he couldn't move, didn't sway anyone, so, eventually, his house was put onto the market, and he was put into a local care home.

Relatives of those already in the local care home were outraged and threatened to go elsewhere. But, when they discovered the cost and effort of moving their loved ones at such a ripe old age, they feared for their inheritance, and quickly relented. Still, the care home tried its best to keep George isolated from the other residents.

George wasn't neglected. He was fed, watered and his health cared for. But he wasn't spoken to, not really. Everything was very functional around him. People earned their money to care for him, but there was no compassion, no sweet words. They allowed him to see out his days on a full stomach, but never once did someone move the hair from over his eyelids and tell him that he had probably been a handsome fella in his youth.

Only one thing of note happened in what remained of George Jacoby's life, several days before he died.

A family member came to see him.

Due to his health, a nurse was required to be in attendance.

The family member, who introduced himself as DI Phil Rice and George's cousin, didn't mind a chaperone.

He claimed he was only here to deliver a brief goodbye.

But he never did say goodbye, according to the nurse who stood in there with him.

In fact, he said nothing at all.

He did, however, do two things worthy of comment.

First, he stood and stared long and hard at his dying relative.

'There was no compassion in those eyes. It was the stoniest look I ever saw,' the nurse later reported.

The second action was only noticed on the day of his death, after they'd removed George's body and were changing the sheets.

There were two photographs under the pillow that must have been left by the detective, as no one else had come into the room.

The nurse on duty did not recognise the boys in the photographs, but one of her colleagues did, because she'd read a recent news article concerning George Jacoby.

One of the photographs was of Julian Greaves.

And the other was of Graham Lock.

* * *

Gardner felt ready to reach out to Riddick.

It'd been a couple of months now, and the pain and disappointment she felt, although still there, were less debilitating.

Probably because the circumstances around her own life had started to improve.

Barry had left to be with his new 'squeeze' in Salisbury. Fortunately, Sandra already had two children, and didn't fancy taking on another one. Gardner knew Barry wouldn't be content with this arrangement for too much longer, and would be chipping away at Sandra. He would believe, as did Gardner, that Sandra would fold sooner or later. When that day came, Gardner would be ready, but for now, at least, she appreciated the space to think. Things had a habit of suddenly changing, and Gardner had to be on guard, but still, she enjoyed the relief that this gave her.

As a result of having two children to nurture, she'd had to cut back on her hours. The costs of childcare were extortionate, and she didn't get a great deal of financial support with Rose. But money paled into insignificance when she considered how much better she felt. To feel at ease was priceless.

Last week, she'd finally taken Rose to see Jack. The meeting had been cordial. Gardner had not aired any of her past grievances with Jack, nor had she allowed it to bleed into the atmosphere in the visiting room. Jack, who originally tried to distance himself from Rose, due to his unsavoury past, had accepted that Rose wanted a father figure in her life.

Gardner would remain vigilant, scrutinising both the meetings and any written correspondence between them. She knew Jack well. She knew that he was missing something inside. Fatherhood was an imaginative leap, and she'd police it at all junctures.

Less frequently these days, her mind wandered to the man who'd stopped Rose in her charge to the main road. He'd been from her neck of the woods and had known her first name. Added to that, he'd not challenged Gardner for ID to check she wasn't holding Rose prisoner or something.

This all added up to one simple fact. He'd been there to see Gardner. To unsettle her. And would surely return. She racked her brains over why. Was he connected to Jack? Had he left some unfinished business?

Two months was a reasonable length of time though, and just as it was softening the blow over Riddick's transgression, it was also softening the dread she felt whenever her mind drifted back to the smart man with the white ponytail.

Hugo Sands was also gone and had been replaced by his assistant, Kate. He'd avoided jail time, but he hadn't avoided the collapse of his career. The last Gardner had heard, he was moving away. Every now and again, she checked her rear-view mirror, or stopped dead on a walk to look behind her, but she never saw him peering out from any bushes.

She often shuddered when she considered the fact that she'd almost been on a date to see Ed Sheeran with him!

So, now things were settling, she found herself toying with the idea of seeing Riddick again. This had been happening for almost a week. While considering it, she often found herself in Marsh's office again two months earlier, pressing her bloody hand over Riddick's badge, despairing over the fact that he'd confessed to murder, and that she was about to lose him forever, yet, knowing, deep down, it'd been the right thing to do. The honourable thing.

They were in the business of truth and justice after all, and no one was above the law.

She'd never felt so conflicted about anything before that day.

Her morality tore her one way, while her feelings for Riddick yanked her the other. Feelings. Where the bloody hell had they come from?

* * *

'He's resigned,' Marsh said.

Gardner was confused. 'Sorry?'

'He just resigned. Isn't that why you barged in? To stop him?'

Gardner backed away from the table, adrenaline whipping her.

'Emma, are you okay?'

'Yes,' Gardner said. 'Of course.'

'Bloody hell,' Marsh said. 'What a friend he has in you! How'd he manage that? Emma, go and get some rest – you've earned it. Milo and Kyle are safe because of you – top drawer that. It makes me happy that you're here. With us. Rather than with all those pompous pricks in the south.'

It was nice to get a compliment from Marsh, even if it came at the expense of all her beloved colleagues down in Wiltshire.

Gardner returned to her own office, dazed and confused. When she opened the door, she saw Riddick standing there.

She turned, closed the door and placed her head against it.

'You know, don't you?' Riddick said.

'It was obvious, really. KG was gunned down for blackmailing someone over the murder of Ronnie Haller – the person who ruined your life. Put that together with your grand march into Marsh's office to confess something... well, it doesn't take a genius.'

'Sorry, I—'

'Just give me a minute, Paul. Let me process it.'

After a minute, she'd still not managed to turn her head.

'I'm ready now,' he said.

'Ready for what?'

'To handle that look in your eyes.'

'Shut up. I thought you'd confessed. I thought you'd... you'd... never mind. Were you ever going to confess?'

'Yes... but then you saved me again.'

'What? How?'

'Marsh kept putting the meeting off; her phone never bloody stops! By the time I got more than two seconds of airtime with her – guess what? The pissing phone goes again. She heard about you saving the day and, over the moon, she decided to share every-thing with me – including the fact, that a man called KG had kidnapped a child, and then been gunned down. And, you know, I froze. With KG out of the picture, there didn't seem a need to blurt everything out. Because of you I've been thrown another bloody life.'

Gardner guffawed. 'You think you deserve another one?'

'No. Still, did I ever deserve any of them? But, you know, I just didn't feel like spoiling anyone's day at that point. Take the lime-light off you. What you did, for those boys, that's what everyone should be focusing on... not me... not a piece of shit—'

'Don't.'

'You're special—'

'I said, *don't*. I can't think right now. I'm struggling to under-stand. Why? No, forget that. I know why. Bloody hell, no one had a better reason to do that to Haller. But how? How could you have done that? It isn't you...'

'Isn't me? Are you sure? I'm not sure any more.'

Gardner still had her forehead against the door. She was still unable to turn and show him that look in her eyes he was fearful of. 'Then, you need to go back to her office and tell her, Paul. Because if that was you... if that really was you that had Haller... you know... then, you have to... *you* have to...' She broke off.

'Be punished?'

She didn't respond.

'I almost told you, you know? That night when I was drunk and I fell asleep on your couch. If you hadn't have told me to shut up, right there and then, I would've told you. When I woke up the next day, I just bottled it. I'm glad I never did that to you. Made you make that choice.'

'You're still making me choose!' She finally turned and jammed her finger in his direction. 'You dickhead! You... you...' She couldn't bring herself to say the words. *Killed him.*

'What I did was inexcusable. I know that. I'll go and see Marsh. I'll put this right. I'm not scared.'

'You should be – a copper in jail.'

'If that's what you want—'

'Piss off. Take this ball out of my goddamned court.'

He held up his hands in mock surrender. 'You're right. I'll call this.'

'No... no you won't!' Gardner said, moving closer to Riddick. 'When I figured out from that bastard what you did, I was disgusted. I still am. Yet after he died, and we were safe, I felt relief...'

'You survived hell; it's understandable.'

'No, you pillock! I felt relief that I wouldn't lose you.'

He looked away from her. He appeared to be fighting off tears.

Eventually, Riddick stepped forward, closer to her. She could tell that he was desperate to take hold of her, embrace her perhaps, offer a thousand apologies.

In a way, her desire to let that happen was all-consuming. She needed to end this meeting before she succumbed and forgave him. She needed to think about this and decide if that's what she truly wanted.

Riddick continued. 'I told a lie before.'

'Just one?' Gardner spat.

'No... about not telling Marsh because it would take attention from you. I didn't tell her because I realised something. Something that terrified me.'

'Go on.'

'I realised that you wouldn't abandon me, that you'd live through the whole bloody mess with me.'

She shook her head. There were now tears in her eyes. 'Are you really so sure?'

'Yes.' He reached out to touch her; she pulled away.

Riddick nodded, and headed past her. He stopped. 'I'm sorry, Emma. Once I'm gone, it'll be better for you. I promise. I know it will be...'

At that point, her despair flared into anger and she turned as he reached for the door. 'No, you don't get to walk away, indulge yourself in chaos and alcohol again. You can damn well make up for what you've done. You can dedicate however many lives remain... to doing it right. And that doesn't involve resignation.'

He shook his head. 'I considered it, but I can't do it. For you. I don't want you to live my disgrace. Having to see it beside you every day.'

She pointed at him. 'Then transfer. Get out of my hair. But you don't get to quit. You have a debt to pay, Paul; you can bloody well pay it.'

He nodded and she saw the acceptance in his eyes.

And then he was gone.

* * *

In the two days that Riddick had been at Anders' bedside, the old man had woken frequently, but only for very short periods.

Each time, Riddick pressed a straw to his old mentor's dry lips and was thanked with a hoarse whisper. 'You're a good 'un, son.'

Anders' deterioration had been quick, and Riddick had taken some leave from his new posting in South Yorkshire to come and bid him farewell. His request had been met with more than one raised eyebrow; after all, it'd been Riddick who'd brought Anders down – why would he feel sentimental over the old fool? But he didn't feel inclined to explain himself.

It wasn't too difficult for Riddick to obtain permission to sit with Anders. His family, including the daughters he'd adored, had completely turned their backs on him. The fact that someone wanted to sit with him during his final moments was welcomed by the doctors.

Riddick understood why Anders' family was aggrieved, and if he'd been them, he probably would've done the same. But Riddick knew that he couldn't really take the holier-than-thou approach. Riddick was more like Anders. Flawed. And for that reason, he offered this one final service.

He didn't speak during these final two days. Not because Anders was pumped with painkillers and was only semi-lucid when awake, but because he really had nothing to say. Try as he might, he struggled to dig out any words. So, he simply gave his old boss water, read a paperback in the chair beside him, and, sometimes, if the mood took him, reflected on better times.

Anders had never had the chance to tell Riddick that he'd acted on his behalf and made a phone call that had led to KG's untimely death, but it couldn't be any more obvious. His old mentor had been truthful in his claim that he'd loved Riddick like the son he'd never had. His final act had been his way of proving that. His years on the streets, controlling and managing the chaos and the crime, had built him enough contacts, and gathered him enough favours.

It seemed that at one time, Anders hadn't been above the law, he'd *been* the law, and such an influence never completely waned.

Anders' breath had grown shallower. The doctors were surprised he was still ticking over. Riddick almost remarked on how strong the man had been in his day but opted to remain silent instead. One of the nurses said it was Riddick's presence here that had kept him hanging on.

Riddick was just reaching the end of his paperback, when Anders stopped breathing.

Having become so attuned to the shallow rasp, the sudden silence startled him.

He stood and looked down on the ashen face of the man that had strengthened him and empowered him in his search for truth and justice, at least for a time, and then he proceeded to pack his belongings into his rucksack.

He pressed the buzzer behind Anders' bed to alert the nurse.

While he waited for the nurse to arrive, Riddick reached down and gripped his friend's shoulder.

And held it for a time.

* * *

Riddick didn't go straight home. He hadn't shed a tear in a good while and wasn't expecting to shed one now. He felt composed enough to drink a coffee in the hospital café. A few times, he paused to watch the energy of the people around him.

Life did go on. Yes, it was a cliché. But was it a cliché to wonder where he fitted into it all? Who was he? *What* was he? Did he deserve the chances that kept falling his way?

He wondered, briefly, what Claire was up to, and then he thought, for a time, about Gardner.

He looked up as a woman in her late fifties sat down opposite him.

She was smiling and didn't say anything.

Riddick returned her smile, gave a brief nod and then finished his coffee. He reached down to check his backpack was fastened.

When he looked back up, he saw that she was still regarding him.

He smiled at her again as he rose from his seat. 'The coffee isn't bad—'

She reached out and took his hand. 'Stay a while.'

'Okay,' Riddick said, sitting back down. On another day, his instinct would've been to decline. But not today, for some reason. 'I could get you a drink?'

'No, thank you, dear. I'm happy just to see you.' She smiled again.

As peculiar as the encounter was, Riddick felt no need to flee the situation. She seemed kind and calm. 'Thank you,' Riddick said. 'It's a rarity to hear that.'

She didn't catch his self-deprecating sarcasm, or at least, she didn't display any signs of catching it. She continued to stare at him, smiling.

When no words were forthcoming for a while, Riddick felt the urge to break the silence. 'I just lost someone.'

'Oh dear, I'm sorry to hear that. Were you close?'

'No—' Riddick broke off. He took a deep breath and thought about the last two days at his friend's bedside, holding a straw to his mouth. 'Sorry, yes. Very.'

'I'm sorry... I really am.'

'Thanks.'

She smiled. He suddenly caught sight of years of pain in this woman's features. 'I lost someone very close to me once, too. A child.'

Riddick's breath caught in his throat. Without any thought, he reached out and took her hand instead this time. He opened his mouth to tell her about Molly and Lucy but caught the words. This was her moment. She was sharing *her* grief. 'I'm sorry about that. I truly am.'

'I know you are, DI Riddick.' She nodded and smiled. 'I know you are.'

So, she knew him. It wasn't unusual. People often recognised him from his time in the newspapers. It was highly likely she knew about his own profound loss. He nodded.

'I have a confession to make,' she said, tightening her own grip on his hand. 'I've been following you for a time now. I hope you don't mind.'

This reminded him of Dr Hugo Sands and, yes, he did mind being followed, but he could never be annoyed or feel threatened by the lady sitting in front of him. Still, he was curious. 'I see. Why exactly?'

She pulled her hand away and unclipped the bag on her lap. She rustled inside and pulled out a photograph. She looked at it herself and smiled. The bags beneath her eyes trembled again. 'Thank you, DI Riddick. Thank you so very, very much.'

She slid the picture over the table to Riddick.

He looked down at a younger woman cradling a baby.

'That's me.'

'Beautiful... both of you. Boy or girl?'

'Boy. His name was Julian.'

The breath caught in Riddick's throat. He stared at the woman. 'Mrs Greaves?'

'Hannah, please.'

Riddick took a deep breath in through his nose and closed his eyes. He felt her hand on his again. Squeezing.

'Thank you for bringing him back to me,' Hannah said. 'Thank you.'

Riddick opened his eyes to see the happiness on a face that had been scarred by pain, and he couldn't hold back any longer.

The tears came.

* * *

Having decided earlier that she was ready, Gardner drove to Riddick's.

This was the first time she'd been here since he'd taken up the position in South Yorkshire.

She parked on the other side of the street and killed her lights. She needed a few minutes to compose herself, to decide *exactly* what she was going to say.

She couldn't trust herself off the cuff – who knew where that might lead?

After a couple of minutes of preparation, she reached for the door handle.

She drew her hand back when she saw the headlights of a vehicle on the road behind her.

Riddick's car.

As he drew nearer, she caught a glimpse of him behind the windscreen.

She took a deep breath.

He'd changed. His hair was longer. He'd put some weight on. Not too much, but enough to give him a healthier appearance.

She clicked the door handle, and her car lights went on.

He was unlocking his front door as she stepped from the vehicle. She stopped herself short of calling out to him.

How would that have looked? *Have some decorum, Emma!*

She closed her car door behind her.

Stay cool and collected, Emma. A check-in. This is all it is. You've already run through what you'll say.

She started to cross the road, keeping her eyes on Riddick.

His front door opened. A woman Gardner didn't recognise stood there.

Shit!

Gardner froze in the centre of the road.

The woman put her arms around Riddick, and they started to kiss.

God, what a fool you are, Emma!

Face flushing, Gardner wanted to curl up in a ball on the road and die.

Instead, she took the sensible option. She turned to go back to the car before someone saw her—

She was suddenly illuminated by headlights.

Shit!

She held her hand up, apologising to the approaching driver, and jogged back to her car.

The driver gave her a honk for good measure.

No!

She turned and looked back up at Riddick's home. Two pairs of eyes in her direction.

Now she really did want to curl up and die.

She spun again, opened the door and dived back in the car.

Sensible as always, she checked her mirrors before she pulled out, but there was no way she was looking back at the house.

* * *

1990

The boy was tired.

His nightmares had been keeping him up till late. Nightmares about everything breaking around him. The ground, the walls, even the faces of those looking at him.

All of it splintering, crumbling, falling to pieces before his very eyes.

But tired as he was, nothing could take away from the magnificence of what was in front of him.

Hanging from the lip of the Petrifying Well. The china teapot, the cricket bat and his favourite, the—

'My dad said it looks like a giant's skull from the side.'

He turned and looked at the boy beside him. He didn't recognise him, but they were a similar age.

He switched his attention back to the lip of the cave, the dripping water, the petrified objects.

'Those things were scared to death, my dad said.' The boy laughed. 'By the giant's head.'

'That's not how it works.'

'I know... he's just funny sometimes. It's to do with minerals.'

'No, I don't mean that. What I mean is, why fear? Why say they were scared? Everything is frozen solid. Fixed. Still. Why call it the Petrifying Well when everything looks so peaceful?'

'Paul,' a man said from behind them. 'Paul, let's move on.'

'Okay.'

He was glad when the boy beside him departed.

He didn't get what he was saying.

No one ever seemed to get what he was saying.

When he told his schoolfriends about his nightmares, they laughed. When he told grown-ups, they shrugged.

No one understood.

All the time, in the dream world, or out of it, everything seemed to be breaking.

Everything.

But here, it was different.

His eyes moved between the stone bears.

So very different.

ACKNOWLEDGMENTS

Taking Riddick into Mother Shipton's Cave, the heart of Knaresborough, was my most ambitious challenge yet. I am glad to report that the events portrayed here are entirely fictional, and that it is a wonderful place to visit, especially on a summer's day.

Boldwood, again, went above and beyond, in providing me with the expertise and unwavering support I needed. Emily Ruston, Candida Bradford and Susan Sugden are a formidable team!

Thank you again to my wonderful wife and two children. How they put up with my long retreats into this alternate universe I have no idea! Great patience, I expect.

Special mention to Kath Middleton for her last-minute proof-reads too. She's always there in times of overwhelming work pressures!

I am forever grateful to all the many bloggers, Donna and Sharon, as well as my readers. With you all championing my books, and being forever supportive, I am an extremely lucky author.

MORE FROM WES MARKIN

We hope you enjoyed reading *The Crying Cave Killings*. If you did, please leave a review.

If you'd like to gift a copy, this book is also available as an ebook, large print, hardback, digital audio download and audiobook CD.

Sign up to Wes Markin's mailing list for news, competitions and updates on future books.

https://bit.ly/WesMarkinNews

Explore the rest of the Yorkshire Murders series...

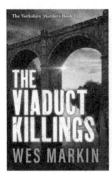

ABOUT THE AUTHOR

Wes Markin is the bestselling author of the DCI Yorke crime novels, set in Salisbury. His new series for Boldwood stars the pragmatic detective DCI Emma Gardner who will be tackling the criminals of North Yorkshire. Wes lives in Harrogate and the first book in The Yorkshire Murders series was published in November 2022.

Visit Wes Markin's website: <u>wesmarkinauthor.com</u>

Follow Wes on social media:

twitter.com/MarkinWes
facebook.com/WesMarkinAuthor

THE

Murder

LIST

THE MURDER LIST IS A NEWSLETTER DEDICATED TO ALL THINGS CRIME AND THRILLER FICTION!

SIGN UP TO MAKE SURE YOU'RE ON OUR HIT LIST FOR GRIPPING PAGE-TURNERS AND HEARTSTOPPING READS.

SIGN UP TO OUR NEWSLETTER

BIT.LY/THEMURDERLISTNEWS

Boldw⊙⊙d

Boldwood Books is an award-winning fiction publishing company seeking out the best stories from around the world.

Find out more at www.boldwoodbooks.com

Join our reader community for brilliant books, competitions and offers!

Follow us
@BoldwoodBooks
@BookandTonic

Sign up to our weekly deals newsletter

https://bit.ly/BoldwoodBNewsletter

Printed in Great Britain
by Amazon